THEIR PAST WAS LEG
IN TEN YE

Kathy was standing in
wearing nothing but lace pantes,
her chest, while the guys ignored her and paid homage to her
ex-husband.

She cleared her throat. "If you all wouldn't mind?" she said,
stressing the last word.

Ridiculous. The cops didn't even notice her irritation—or
her state of undress.

"You're Jordan Treveryan! Wow!" the young cop breathed.
"Is *Blue Heron* getting back together?"

"Want to set those guns back in their holsters?" Jordan suggested, his tone level and calm, his smile casual. I think you're
distressing Kathy."

"You're Kathy Treveryan? Ow, wow, what a night!"

Now the cops were all staring at her. She felt like a lobster—
only lobsters had shells and all she had was a handful of cotton.
"Will you all please get out of my bedroom?"

"Ooops." It was now the young cop's turn to become beet
red. "I think we—oh, no—I think we interrupted . . ." His voice
trailed away awkwardly. It was quite clear what he thought he'd
interrupted.

"You didn't interrupt anything. I was just changing for
dinner. I appreciate the fact that everyone here was concerned
for my safety. I'll be very much better if you'll all leave me
alone so that I can get dressed."

The cops nearly tripped over themselves in the effort to leave
her room.

Jordan was in no hurry. He grinned broadly at her, his
hands resting on his hips. "You do provide excitement."

"You took it in stride," she said.

"So did you." A glow of amusement lit his eyes. "It's good to
know the police could move that fast."

"Oh, yeah?"

"They weren't pointing their guns at you," he reminded her.

"They didn't find you half-dressed!"

"I'd rather be naked than shot," he said dryly.

"I wasn't naked," she said defensively.

"Then why the outrage?" he demanded softly.

"Do you want to go out for dinner or not?" She walked past
him, then paused, waiting for his answer.

It was a new beginning.

Also by Heather Graham

Lie Down in Roses

Blue Heaven, Black Night

Princess of Fire

The King's Pleasure

Come the Morning

Conquer the Night

Knight Triumphant

Seize the Dawn

The Lion in Glory

When We Touch

Ondine

An Angel's Touch

UP IN FLAMES

HEATHER GRAHAM

ZEBRA BOOKS
KENSINGTON PUBLISHING CORP.
http://www.kensingtonbooks.com

To Diana Violette and Rita Astrella,
who will always be lovely, charming,
intelligent women—ageless!

ZEBRA BOOKS are published by

Kensington Publishing Corp.
119 West 40th Street
New York, NY 10018

All Kensington titles, imprints, and distributed lines are available
at special quantity discounts for bulk purchases for sales promo-
tion, premiums, fund-raising, educational, or institutional use.

Special book excerpts or customized printings can also be created
to fit specific needs. For details, write or phone the office of the
Kensington Sales Manager: Attn.: Sales Department. Kensington
Publishing Corp., 119 West 40th Street, New York, NY 10018.
Phone: 1-800-221-2647.

Zebra and the Z logo Reg. U.S. Pat. & TM Off.

First Printing: May 1995
ISBN-13: 978-1-4201-4314-0
ISBN-10: 1-4201-4314-X

10 9 8 7 6 5 4 3

Printed in the United States of America

Prologue

He stood in the darkness, staring out the window, wondering at the tension that seemed to riddle him. A soft breeze slightly lifted the sheer white underdrapes that framed the sliding glass windows to the balcony of his second-floor bedroom. He could see out over the pool, on to the water, and to his far left, the guest house. All lay beneath a strange, tropical moon. Blood red tonight, perhaps a portent for rain. The breeze, as well, seemed to promise a storm. It was late summer when the weather could be hotter than hell, when the humidity seemed to weigh down upon the earth's surface like a wet blanket. Maybe that was why he felt so restless.

Where was she?

Broodingly, he kept his eyes trained on the night. Nothing stirred beyond the window. A far different scene from that which had taken place earlier. Just hours ago, the pool and patio had been alive with music, laughter, voices. Chinese lanterns had cast a colorful glow over the assortment of guests: press agents with their nasal accents, Californians with easy drawls,

Midwesterners twanging away. Here and there something Southern had slipped into the conversation, and many sentences had been pieced together with Spanish words or phrases inserted here or there.

The laughter and gaiety had all been on the surface. Tension had lurked beneath. It had been building. Layer upon layer. Maybe it had been there a very long time, a slow growth at first, heightened by the trouble in France last August, smoothed over, yet the roots remaining. To him, that tension had seethed beneath the surface of the party tonight like a palpable, living, breathing creature.

Was it just him? Had the others simply enjoyed the party, with no feeling that they were headed for disaster? Was he too self-righteous, too demanding a taskmaster?

It brought him back to the same question he had asked himself already.

Where was she?

He started to move, restless still, ready to pace the room. But something kept him where he stood, staring out at the silent night, now bathed in the eerily red glow of the strangely tinted moon.

For all outer appearances, he should have been a happy man, secure, content. He had achieved professional success, acquired an admirable income, wed a beautiful woman, fathered two beautiful daughters. Things hadn't come easily; he had worked hard, they had worked hard. But he'd loved the work, loved it still.

Loved the music, the words, the sound of a perfectly tuned piano, the melody of a flute, the warmth of a guitar— his favorite instrument, one that could perform gently, passionately, tenderly . . . or grind out a refrain, screech into heavy metal. He loved it all still. Music, at its best and at its worst, was somehow honest. Unlike people, unlike appearances.

When had the doubt settled in?

Appearances were what others saw. Fabric knit together upon the top. Yet beneath, too often, the threads were coming unfrayed. Sometimes, he wanted the picture. What might be seen in a black and white glossy. Before people became three dimensional. With thoughts they couldn't always voice, with secrets they were too ashamed to share.

Move away from the window, he told himself. Forget the night, forget the fears. Live with the black and white glossy, and don't question what lies beneath.

No good. He wasn't a man who could ever live with lies.

So what was going on?

A cloud swept in with the breeze. Not a heavy cloud, not one that completely darkened the sky. But it added to the strange and surreal glow that was cast down upon the earth by the reddened moon. Everything seemed bathed in dark and secretive, deep crimson shadow.

Then he saw her.

How strange. She was as much a part of his life as if she were actually a limb, a skein of yarn

8

knit into his creation. They'd known one another almost forever. They'd dreamed together, seen dreams come true, fantasies turn to reality. He'd fallen in love with a girl, when they'd both been in the sometimes painful and confusing— but exquisite— bloom of youth. They'd grown, they'd aged. A beautiful girl had become an elegant woman. Confusion for them both had often become conviction. They'd changed; sometimes together, sometimes apart. He knew her face, her half-smiles, her full smiles. Her frowns, worried and anxious. He knew the nuances of her face, each and every one of them, the sound of her laughter, the glistening in her eyes when she'd refuse to shed tears. He knew her better than anyone on earth.

But did one human being ever really know another? Know everything that played within the heart and soul?

Did he know her now?

He couldn't see the face he knew so well. She was as surreal as the night, a figure clad in flowing white, long dark hair made redder, touched by the blood on the moon. She seemed incredibly graceful, moving with the flow of the breeze, part of it, feet barely seeming to touch the ground.

She came from the back patio below. She was swiftly gliding toward the guest house.

She ran through the blood red shadows, around the night-tinted crystal of the pool. Finally, she disappeared down the tiled path to the guest house, and into the shadows of the croton and hibiscus surrounding it.

What the hell was she doing? He'd kill her when he got his hands on her. He braced himself, leaning against the wall for a moment, feeling the tension in his limbs, anger knotting the muscles in his arms and fists. He stayed there as seconds ticked into minutes, fighting for control, knowing damned well that he would confront them both. The tension had been building, growing. He had seethed tonight, even if it had only seethed within him. She'd claimed innocence before, and he swore now that he wouldn't blindly believe evil in those he loved, but by God, he would have the truth.

Yet even as he turned back to the window, still furious but with the steel grip of reason upon his anger, the night shifted. As he stared toward the guest house, he became aware of a startling new streak of red in the night. Combined with gold, it silently leapt and flared into the night sky.

The guest house was on fire, he realized incredulously. As swiftly as the knowledge entered his mind, there came a sudden explosion as if something highly combustible within the small dwelling, caught by the flames, burst within them and above them in a shower of sparks.

He shouted hoarsely, not certain of his words or to whom he spoke. Horror and fear tightened around his throat, nearly paralyzed him. He'd just been thinking about killing her. He'd die if anything happened to her.

Yet he had seen her go into the building that was now a wall of flames.

The night itself seemed to be burning.

He raced from his room, shouting now articulately, demanding that someone dial 911. He tore down the stairs, out of the house, and across the back patio, racing for the guest house which was fully ablaze. Flames shot out before him, no longer just red and gold, tinged with the strange cool blue of excruciating heat. That heat scorched his skin, his brows, his hair, yet he came closer to it. He had to get into the guest house. Had to reach her.

Hands fell upon him, shaking him, dragging at him. He heard his name shouted. He turned. Frightened, anxious amber eyes met his. The heat all but engulfed them both as he looked down into those eyes.

"Jordan!"

She was tugging at his arm. Tears streaked down her face. *"Jordan!"*

There was another explosion from within. Instinctively, he clutched her shoulders and propelled them both as far from the fire as possible, helped by the force of the blast. They landed hard, buffered only somewhat by the fact that they hit dirt and grass rather than the concrete and tile of the patio.

Sirens pierced the air. Shouts began to break the night, now completely dyed in shades of blood red flame. Shaking, he stared down into those amber eyes.

He'd wanted to kill her. He'd been so angry, so damned ready for a confrontation.

Yet now, he could only be excruciatingly grateful that she was alive. That the smell of burning flesh that swept around them did not come from her mortal remains . . .

She cried out his name again, her eyes glazed with tears and confusion, the word tremulous on her lips. Because they were both alive, and there was tragedy within the guest house. He wrapped his arms around her, once again, just so very grateful. He didn't realize then that special bonds had been burned to cinders along with the guest house, or that trust had died along with the friend inside. He didn't think about the others who then peopled his house, he just took those few sweet moments to revel in life.

The doubts would come later . . .

One

Nearly Ten Years Later . . .

It was strange, the way life could move along according to a set of coincidental circumstances. She hadn't been thinking about the past at all, just thrusting an old volume back into the bookcase when the album suddenly seemed to fall as if pushed out by some unseen force. The bookcase was just too jammed, that was all, but all the same it seemed strange when that album fell.

She didn't want to open it at first. It had been nearly ten years since she had seen him, since she had changed her own life so radically, and yet the pain remained. Something nostalgic, something so strong, it hurt all over again. *It had been right, the breakup had been right. They hadn't been good for one another anymore.* It didn't matter. Being right just didn't ease that awful, annoying, creeping pain that could still sweep over her, just upon occasion, just when she was taken off guard. Like now. When the stinking album had jumped from the shelves, and into her hands.

The damned pages flew open on their own—
she was quite certain she hadn't touched them.
Nor did she remember sitting on purpose, going
through them. First page, there he was. They
must have been fourteen, building sandcastles
on the beach. He was already acquiring that
long, lean, yet well-muscled, build which was to
become part of the legendary man. The photograph was black and white; somehow, she could
still see the cool lime green color of his eyes,
the sun-streaked sandy shade of his hair. And
that face. Firm chin, high cheekbones, strong as
the chin, handsomely configured. His face
hadn't changed. Well, she didn't think it had.
Oh, hell, she knew it hadn't, no matter how she
lied. She had seen him often enough in magazine pages and the occasional "live" appearance
when he was caught by a television camera going
in or out of a restaurant, a theater, or the like.

She flipped a page. There she was with Jordan, at the junior prom on one side, at the senior
prom on the other. She ran a finger along the
side of the picture, almost as if she could touch
the past by doing so, go back a bit. They had
been beautiful then, both of them. Jordan so tall!
and handsome, she with her deep auburn hair
swept up, her amber eyes aglow like fire with excitement. She flipped another page. There they
were with the group. She and Jordan and the
others. Larry Haley, with his mile-long blond
hair, good-looking hair at that; Shelley
Thompson, already a petite but elegant beauty
with wide eyes and golden hair; Keith Duncan,

dark, handsome, brooding; Miles Reeves, freck-led and red-headed; and Derrick Flanaghan, tall, broad-shouldered, becoming a big man. And Derrick's wife, Judy, was there. Judy had never played an instrument or sung a single note, but she'd been with them all forever. Their hardest and best critic. Tall, slim, no-nonsense Judy. She lacked any kind of musical talent but she recognized someone with potential in a flash and she kept them looking at the *realistic* picture at all times, reminding them that bills had to be paid no matter what.

The picture must have been taken maybe five or six years after their college graduation, Kathy thought. They were all still together, they were sprawled out on a lawn somewhere, there were glasses of wine or champagne in their hands, raised to the photographer, and everyone was still young enough to be smiling with a great deal of hope, confidence, and enthusiasm. Jordan's hair was longish again, so it had to have been a while after he had come home from the service.

And everyone was still alive.

Her fingers trembled suddenly. It must have been another five years after that photo had been taken that Keith had died. And even if she and Jordan had gone on a few months after that, it had never been the same. For Jordan had changed. Something had bothered him terribly, and he had closed off. Jealousies, suspicions. Shadows unspoken. Maybe they had all closed off to one another. But Kathy had lost whatever it was that had kept her and Jordan together—

believing, trusting, no matter what chaos came from the outside world. She hadn't actually realized it at the time. They'd all been in agony. Numbed, stunned, pained by the loss. But the thread that bound them had been lost with Keith.

She flipped the page.

Yes.

The funeral. They were all there again, except for Keith. Actually, Keith was there. He was the one in the box. The photographer had managed to get in a shot in which the coffin was to the left, nearly ready to be lowered to its final resting place. Keith's family was immediately behind it, their heads lowered. Judy Flanaghan had an arm slipped around Keith's mother's shoulders. And then they— *Blue Heron*, the group, and his very best friends, co-workers, and associates— were all lined up as well.

This photo, taken with color film, was a study in black.

Jordan was in a black suit; Kathy in a black dress. He had his hands on her shoulders. She was fairly tall for a woman, an even five-eight, but he rose high behind her. His steady gaze upon the coffin was not just sad, but wary, pensive. Even in the photo, she could see the tension in his knuckles, and was aware of the protective way he had been holding her. That had been nice. That was something she had missed very badly; it had been part of the feeling she had never found again, anywhere, with anyone. It had always given her an incredibly secure feeling. Perhaps because among his very good qualities were a certain integrity and courage. Had she ever been in danger, she knew he would have risked his own life for hers.

But she hadn't been in danger. He had. Threatened by the slings and arrows of the press and media. Maybe she still wasn't seeing it entirely clearly. Perhaps they had all been threatened. Because things had begun to change then.

She started to close the album, but just as it had seemed to fly from the bookshelf, it suddenly seemed to jump from her fingers and land on the floor. When she picked it up, it had opened again. She started; she had never seen the picture of him that now rested upon one of the later pages. It was a recent photograph, a good one. Alexandria had probably taken the shot, she was becoming a very good photographer, capable of capturing the special essence that made a person unique.

She had certainly captured her father well.

At forty-six, Jordan was exactly five days younger than Kathy was herself. When they'd been very young, friends had loved to tease them about her being the "older" woman. Hmmm. At times now she did feel darned old. Forty-six was treating Jordan well. He wasn't the perfect young thing he'd once been; he was . . . better. The years had added a very special fascination to his face—character, she thought—and his daughter had illuminated it well. Silver threads streaked through his once-sandy hair, and yes, she thought—not without just a twinge of malicious pleasure—it was thinning. But whether he had a headful of blond hair, a half-headful of graying tresses, or a shining pate, Jordan was and would be a handsome man. His face, masculine, strong, classic, hinted at intriguing traits. Like a Sean Connery or Yul Brynner, each year he seemed to become more attractive.

He was seated at the piano. He had seldom played keyboard when performing; he liked to move on stage and so preferred the guitar. He could play almost any musical instrument. He had been born with a gift, and in return for that he loved music passionately and with his whole heart— to listen to, to play. He treated every instrument with reverence. His fingers were long and agile, made to stroke strings and keys . . .

And a woman.

Or women, she corrected herself, clenching her teeth together. He was currently seeing a young model-sometimes-actress, she had heard. More power to him. He meant nothing to her.

Bull. It hurt like hell.

But he wasn't part of her life anymore. She had a good life now. She liked it.

Still . . . It was so strange seeing this photograph. One taken by his daughter, who loved him very much. Alex had captured a strikingly handsome, mature man with incredible character. Nothing detracted. He hadn't actually changed so very much in the ten years since she had seen him. Strange. He'd changed more when they'd been young, after the first photographs. Between college . . . and Keith's funeral. But again, maybe they had all lost some of their youth when they had lost Keith. Naivete, innocence. The belief that they had been immortal, indomitable. That love could last forever. She didn't really know.

And she was growing morose. She wasn't going to allow that. The past was over. Gone. Determinedly, Kathy rose and thrust the album back onto the bookshelf. Even while she was trying to cram it into a space without injuring any of the other volumes the phone began to ring. She swore softly, finished with the album, and hurried toward the white pseudoantique model on her desk, then decided to let the machine take the call. She heard her own voice give the message, then Jeremy's voice.

"Pick up, Kathryn. I know you're there, and I don't care how busy you are— come over here and pick up the receiver and talk to me. Okay, okay, I can just go on and on. I'll just call back. I know you're there, because you're supposed to be *here!* You missed our session. And I'm dying to talk to you. I have to find out if what they're saying in the newspapers is true— "

She'd been grinning. She would have picked up the receiver in a minute anyway, but this last intrigued her. She plucked it up instantly.

"If what is true?"

"I shouldn't tell you," Jeremy said. "You let me sit here chatting away to myself as minute after minute ticked by."

"That wasn't even a full sixty seconds!"

"A very long time when you're aimlessly talking to an answering machine."

"If what's true?"

"Why aren't you here?"

She sighed. She hadn't realized she'd been asking for a third parent when she'd signed up with Jeremy. She loved going to the gym. She really did. Though it had seemed a dreaded necessity at the time, she'd been amazed to discover that she really had more energy for the rest of the day after a good workout, but she'd never imagined what a friendship she might form with Jeremy when she'd decided to go with a "personal trainer." He could be a cruel taskmaster. She almost felt as if she needed a note for the teacher when she missed a session with him, even though he was paid whether she showed up or not. Which was good. He did care about her.

"I'm sorry. Really sorry. I forgot. I was on deadline with a project. So busy—"

"Listen to those excuses!" he moaned theatrically. "A busy life is all the more reason to look after yourself," he scolded.

"Ummm. You're right, of course. But—"

"You couldn't care less about your health or my lectures at the moment, right? You just want to know about what they're saying in the newspapers, right?"

"Jeremy, what are they saying?"

"That you're getting back together."

Her heart didn't just skip a beat; it stopped. She was certain of it.

"What?"

"That you're getting back together. You heard me correctly. Your hearing isn't going yet."

"Jeremy, I'm forty-six. A person's hearing doesn't necessarily go bad in his or her forties."

"It's just the eyesight, right?"

"Jeremy," she said sweetly. "You are crawling higher and higher in the thirties, aren't you?"

"Well, not that high . . ."

"The eyesight will go any day," she promised.

"Ouch. Better be nice to me. Want me to tell you what you haven't read or not?"

"Yes, I want you to tell me. Who's getting back together?"

"Your group."

"Group?" she echoed with a whisper. "I never had a group."

He sighed with a great deal of exasperation. "Kathy honey, I know you stayed in the background, that you tried to avoid the press, that you've become a very respected editor of fine literature— well, some of it is fine, anyway— and that you've been living the life of a dignified schoolmarm, but you were part of one of the most legendary bands of this century. And you were married to Jordan Treveryan— you're the only one with who he's ever had children—"

"Whom," she corrected automatically.

"Whom!" Jeremy agreed impatiently. "You are the mother of his—"

"Great. I feel like the dowager queen."

He ignored that. "And since they're doing the movie—"

"The movie?"

"Yes, Kathy, get your nose out of your books and *read* something, will you, please?"

"Wait, wait—"

"Oh, Kathy! Jordan Treveryan announced that he's having a get-together at his Star Island estate because of all this. He wants to give the band members a chance to meet the scriptwriters and vice versa. He'd been approached by MoonGlow productions— they can do this with or without anyone's approval, you know, if they choose. But anyway, according to what I read, it seems Jordan decided he liked the group determined to make this movie and felt he might have more control over what went into the film if he cooperated. The papers are saying the *real* group will get together again for a benefit performance, the proceeds to go to local hospitals and drug-awareness groups. You mean you didn't know any of this?"

She sat suddenly on the chair behind her desk.

"No."

"Well, at least you weren't holding out on me."

"No, I wasn't. When does he plan to do all this?"

"At the end of the month."

"The end of the month!"

"Yeah. You are going, aren't you?"

"No."

"No?"

"I hadn't heard a word about this until you called. I'm not sure I'm even invited. And if I am—"

"You have to go! And you know you'll be invited."

"I don't have to be there," she said stubbornly. She couldn't believe this. It was shocking, numbing. All this in print, and she hadn't heard a damned thing. Although she hadn't talked to Jordan Treveryan directly in almost ten years, she was the mother of his children. Surely, if this was true, the girls would have said something to her.

"Oh!" She could hear the absolute frustration in Jeremy's voice. "You've got to go. It will be the best party of the year!"

"I've never been much of a party person."

"Your daughter is quoted as saying she'll be there, and she's looking forward to her parents speaking again."

"Which daughter?" Kathy demanded indignantly.

The girls did know something about this?

She stared blankly at the sheet-glass windows that encircled part of her condo and gave her a beautiful view of the Brooklyn Bridge from her dining room, bedroom, and office. It was a wonderful place to live. So very different from what she had known before. New York. Moving at a thousand-mile-an-hour pace. And her job at the publishing house had provided her with endless hours of work, into which she had plunged happily, grateful for many years not to have the time to think back.

"Alex!" Jeremy informed her. "Her twenty-first birthday falls during the same week. She says, I quote—I am reading directly from the paper right now— 'Spending the day with both of them—together—will be the best present in the world!' Unquote. How could you deny such a sweet child this wonderful present?"

"Ummm. Such a manipulative child, Jeremy. And just what rag are you reading, because—"

"The New York Times," he interrupted with a chuckle.

The *Times.* Damn Alex! She let her head crash lightly down upon the desk, and would have groaned if she hadn't been afraid Jeremy might read something into the sound. Alex, the older of her two daughters, the supposedly level-headed one who loved photography, knew what she wanted out of life, and exactly where she was going. The mature one who had understood the divorce. Now Bren might have said such a thing. She was an incurable romantic, always slipping Kathy some information about her father whether Kathy wanted it or not.

Amazing. Bren had somehow managed *not* to slip information this time!

She groaned inwardly, her emotions already in a turmoil. It should have been such a nice night. She had worked late at the office with members of the art department on some of her authors' newest book jackets, trying to tailor budgets with individual author's desires and needs and with what she thought was right for each book herself. Long, tiring, but satisfying. Then she had come home and actually gotten in the few solid hours of editing on an important project. With that done, she'd relaxed, had a hot, bubbling stint in the Jacuzzi. Then she'd slipped into a recent purchase from the Victoria's Secret catalogue— not something silky or lacy or sexy, but a cotton tailored shirtlike nightgown that was incredibly comfortable. She'd prepared herself hot chocolate and enjoyed it before a real fire. There she had taken her last glance over the edited manuscript that would now make it into production right on time. She'd been so damned pleased. Content, weary, comfortable, and proud of herself for time well spent and work well done. But then the picture album had fallen. Now this. And Alex had betrayed her, on top of everything else! What more could go wrong in a single night?

She took a deep breath.

"Jeremy, as I said, I haven't even been invited to this thing. I can hardly go— "

"It seems it's all been decided really quickly. Maybe so quickly that the newspapers were able to pick up on it before all the invitations went out. Obviously you're invited if your daughter is talking about how excited she is that you and your ex will both be with her."

"Jeremy— " She was going to hang up because she was in a state of shock and didn't trust herself to talk until she really understood just what was going on. Coincidences! First the album and now this.

"Kathy, don't you dare try to think up an excuse to get rid of me. I'm telling you— "

"Don't tell me! I—"

She suddenly didn't need an excuse. She was interrupted by a tapping on her hallway door.

It had to be Alex or Bren. Her conscientious doorman wouldn't have allowed anyone other than her daughters to come up in the elevator without calling her first on the intercom.

"Jeremy, there's someone at my door."

"I'll wait," he offered cheerfully.

"It has to be one of the girls—"

"Yes, but you'd best make sure, right? Life can be dangerous, my sweet!"

She started to set the receiver down, then paused, bemused despite all that had just assailed her. "Jeremy, if it is a killer-rapist-thief at the door, just how will you be able to help me over the phone?"

"I'll hear you screaming and get the police over there right away," he assured her. "Even if we lose you, we'll have a chance of catching him, right?"

"Jeremy— never mind!" She set the receiver down and hurried out of her office through the apartment's spacious living room to the "front" door. The other door— the kitchen door, opened just around the hallway, but in apartment living, that became the "back" door.

She didn't pause, but threw the door open, ready to lecture whichever errant daughter had forgotten to take her key.

She paused, her mouth open in mid yell, but there was no one there. She stepped out into the hall and walked down it a bit.

"Alex? Bren?"

There was no reply. She turned the corner to the elevators, saw nothing amiss, and gave a shake of her head. As she headed back down the hall, she saw that the front door remained open, but when she stepped through it, she thought she heard a rustling sound that moved through the kitchen to the dining room and out onto the terrace that looked out over the city. She held her breath, thinking maybe it was best that she had left Jeremy on the phone; someone just might be in her apartment. She started to silently slip through the living room, anxious to reach her office and pick up the receiver. Then she realized she was being an idiot, rushing into the apartment where she could be trapped. She started to turn back, hesitated as the rustling sound came from the kitchen. The place had seemed so innocuous just moments ago. Now it was dark and shadowy. And dear God, this was New York— not that all cities couldn't be dangerous, but by sheer force of numbers, there seemed to be more dangerous people here. She'd never been afraid before, though she'd been aware of dangers and how to avoid them. She didn't go into dark alleys, ride the subway through bad sections of town— or at midnight— or park in questionable areas on those few occasions when she did care to drive. And she had taught the girls to be careful. She had hammered into them that forewarned is forearmed. The apartment was in a nicely upscale area of the city with a true neighborhood feel about it, but . . .

Oh, God, there *was* someone in the kitchen.

Ice-cold fear swept around her. Paralyzed her for fleeting milliseconds. She tried to think. She'd read every article in the world on what to do under such circumstances. Don't fight an intruder. Do fight an intruder. Feign sleep. Don't see his face. Make sure he knows you don't see his face. Run. Scream like hell. Blow an alarm whistle. Spray him with pepper mist or mace or even bug spray. Shoot the sucker, and shoot to kill.

She didn't keep a gun; she didn't know how to shoot. She'd bought mace once, kept it in her purse for a while, taken it out and put it . . . where?

And the bug spray was in the kitchen.

With the intruder.

So much for forewarned and forearmed. So much for being careful.

So much for her upscale neighborhood.

And her conscientious doorman!

Everything she had ever heard swirled in her mind. Minutes seemed to have gone by; only seconds had passed. For all her thinking she'd realized only two things— she didn't want to die, and she wasn't going down without a fight.

The first thing she saw that she could curl her fingers round was a Lladro statuette. It was a stunning Deco piece of an elegantly slim woman in a swirling fur, an equally elegant wolfhound at her heels. It was one of Kathy's favorites, but she didn't even think about that, she picked it up, ready to wield it as a club.

Then . . . what to do?

Wait. Wait and see what came from the kitchen.

No, no, no, that wouldn't work. If he had a gun, he'd come from the kitchen. He'd see her there in the light spilling out from her office. He'd shoot her before she had a chance to wield her Lladro as a club.

Inch to the doorway from the living room to the kitchen. If possible, make a bolt for the hall-way door. If not, slide against the wall, at least have the element of surprise against him and make the first attack.

Oh, God, she was trembling from head to toe. Her heart was pounding so loudly it threatened to burst her ribs and leap from her chest. She was inhaling desperately for air. She warned herself to breathe normally. He would hear her panting, hear that frantic thunder of her heart . . .

She scampered across the room, flattened herself against the wall. An immense shadow started from the kitchen and she raised the statuette, bringing it down hard even as she heard her name called out in a puzzled fashion.

"Kathy?"

Crash.

The statuette shattered. The dark shadow swore and spun on her. She backed away, stunned. Shaking harder than ever. She'd hit him; hit her target.

She hadn't begun to stop him. But it didn't matter. She wasn't in any danger.

Not in any danger of death, at the least.

Because there, with little chips of painted porcelain dusting his shoulders, stood Jordan.

Oh, God. Speak of the devil. The devil had appeared.

Two

Different.

He was a little different, subtly changed with time. But it was him. He was there. After all this time, all the years of silence. He was standing just feet from her.

With her Lladro smashed over his head and shoulders.

"Jordan!" She'd gasped his name, too stunned at first to realize that she wanted to kill him for scaring her so damned badly.

He rubbed the top of his head with both hands, staring at her with narrowed eyes, his jaw taut, surprise and annoyance in his hard gaze. "Kathy, damn, I didn't think you'd exactly be pleased to see me, but this really wasn't necessary."

"Believe it or not Jordan, I am pleased to see you—I thought you were a thief! I didn't hit you on purpose!"

"Whoa, you must have quite a wallop when you do strike with intent!"

She crossed her arms over her chest, "Damn

you, Jordan, I thought you were some kind of dangerous—"

"Little has changed," he murmured.

"All right, I admit there were numerous times in my life when I did want to crack you over the head with something, but this wasn't one of them. I thought you were a robber—a murderer, rapist, or worse."

"No, my life hasn't gone that down far downhill yet. Your door was wide open after I knocked, I thought you were hurt, or something was wrong. I was calling out to you. Both your doors were open, and you wouldn't answer me!" He winced, touching a sore spot on his head. "Dammit!" he murmured again, gritting his teeth and turning away from her, pacing to get a grip on his temper.

His footsteps took him back out into the hall, and he spun again, jaw set hard, eyes glittering. "Fine, we start over! Kathy, damned nice to see you. May I come in?"

May he come in! She was still shaking, just beginning to accept the fact that she was going to live. He'd been out of her life for years, and she wasn't ready to have him slip back into it tonight, scaring her half to death in the bargain.

"No!" she snapped, and slammed the door in his face, still completely unnerved. She hadn't meant to slam it. It was just that . . .

Imagine! She had thought nothing more could go wrong in a single night.

Jordan Treveryan was here, in New York, at her home. She had left him nearly ten years ago, had closed the door to the past. She had been civil. She'd left with dignity, but she had nearly died, it seemed, to create a new life. She'd been right to do so. She loved her new life. But when she had struggled so hard to forget him, it hadn't seemed to help that she had been so damned *right*.

And it didn't help now. Because he was back. With the door closed, she could still see him clearly in her mind's eye. As tall and straight as ever. A few more lines in his face— "character"— but darned handsome. His silvering hair was longish, curling around his neck, he'd grown a mustache and a beard. His lime green eyes were as sharp and bright as ever, and he seemed, if anything, a little slimmer than he had been when she had seen him last. He wore dark jeans, a blue silk shirt, and a soft leather, tan jacket with a casual ease. He was wearing an aftershave that was mild and subtle, yet irritatingly alluring.

It was a nightmare, an absolute nightmare. She had to be dreaming.

No. Jordan was here, and she had clouted him on the head before slamming the door in his face.

Wrong! she told herself. So wrong. They had fought too many times like children. She had accused him of doing it. Now she was not being terribly mature herself.

But she wasn't ready for this, any of it, and certainly not for facing Jordan!

She drew the door back open. He hadn't moved. He stared at her, a sandy brow arched.

"Sorry. Instinct," she told him.

"Like the crack on the head?" he asked politely.

"Jordan, honest to God, I was terrified. I thought someone had broken in here while I was out in the hallway."

"What were you doing in the hallway?"

"Looking for the person who had knocked."

"I knocked."

"Then where were you?"

"Trying the other door, then getting worried when I saw the first one wide open with no sign of you. Kathy, you've got to be more careful— "

"I am very careful! This is life. I do manage alone, and you've no business— "

"My daughters live here," he reminded her.

"I am usually very careful."

"You left that door open."

"I won't let it happen again."

He sighed. Obviously, his head didn't hurt quite so much anymore. He was trying very hard for patience again. "Okay. Can we try to start over?"

"We can."

"I'm the one with the bump on the head."

She nodded, grinning slightly. "That was one of my very favorite Lladro pieces."

"It's the only head I've got."

"It was a gift."

"From someone special?"

"It was a gift from you," she said wryly.

"I am sorry," he said.

"Fine. I'm sorry about your head."

"But Kathy, you wouldn't have stopped a burglar that way, you'd have just made him mad."

"I'll hit harder next time."

"You'd need a better weapon, and there shouldn't be a next time!"

"Jordan, I apologize for hitting you on the head."

He inhaled and exhaled. "It's all right."

"Maybe you should see a doctor."

"It's all right."

"Want me to take a look?" She stepped toward him in the hallway.

"No. I do not want you looking at my head!" he snapped, scowling, "especially out here in the hallway."

"There's no one around," she assured him.

"Kathy, may I come in?" he asked, swallowing down his impatience, speaking very politely.

She inhaled, taking a good look at him.

Oh, God. He was nicely dressed. He had the ability to look both elegant and rugged all in one. She was without makeup, in a cotton nightgown that was not one of the sexy choices she might have made. And she was *older* than him, for God's sake!

"Kathy, please, may I come in? I need to speak with you."

"I have a telephone."

"Please . . . Allow me to speak with you now."

She'd hit him on the head, slammed the door in his face, and now she was being childish. "Of course, of course . . ." she said and moved aside, sweeping out an arm. "It's nearly midnight, I wasn't expecting you, I haven't seen you in a decade, and you just scared me half to death, but please, Jordan, do come in."

He arched a brow at her sarcasm, but stepped past her, not responding to it. He didn't touch her, but she could almost feel him as he moved by. She breathed in and recognized that scent, that subtle aftershave that somehow still managed to tantalize. He hadn't changed it. Why should he? Certain things about him were set. She had known him most of her life, they had only been strangers for the past ten years and certain things didn't change. He drank his coffee with one teaspoon of sugar. He wasn't a heavy drinker—and never had been—but he liked good red wine with an Italian dinner and he loved beer—Budweiser—when he was playing poker or spending a hot day at the beach or fishing or boating. Since they'd been really young, he'd loved a good volleyball game, chicken on the barbecue, and though he loved music more than anything in the world, his favorite evenings were spent in quiet, before a low-burning fire, no lights except for the soft streaks of red and yellow that illuminated from the flames.

All of that might have changed.

But it hadn't, she was sure. Just seeing him, she knew. He hadn't changed much at all.

Right. He was still pigheaded and stubborn. Dominating. Their arguments had nearly raised the roof upon occasion.

But had that really been why she had left? The

question taunted her suddenly. *She* had left, but he had been the one who had filed the divorce papers. Almost before the door had closed behind her, she remembered bitterly.

But it had ended!

And now, just like that, he was back. In her home. The same man who had set his hands so protectively upon her shoulders. Ten years and she could still remember way too much— way too clearly. It hurt to see him. It was also good.

She closed her eyes and gritted her teeth as he walked by. He wasn't just stepping past her.

He was walking back into her life.

And God help her, she didn't know if she could bear it.

The bad . . .

. . . or the good.

But that didn't seem to matter— to Jordan, at least. He walked in, glanced around the living room, his green gaze giving away nothing of his inner thoughts. He turned by the large, beige, soft leather sofa and lifted a brow to her.

"Please, sit down," she invited dryly.

He did so, near the edge of the sofa, watching her, elbows on his knees, hands folded idly between them. He waited for her to seat herself, and she gingerly sat before him in the recliner. As she felt his gaze sweep over her she wondered if he was giving her the same assessment she had just given him— seeing what damage the last decade had brought upon her. She waited for him to make a comment. Perhaps, You look great, Kath. The years haven't changed you at all. But he didn't. He just watched her. Damn him. She didn't like surprises. If she'd known she was going to see him, she'd have had on makeup, her hair would have been brushed and styled, and she would have been wearing real clothing. Something black probably, black was such a dignified, *slimming* color.

She wanted to appear dignified, not slim, she assured herself. This had been over long ago. She didn't need to prove anything to Jordan.

She wondered why it mattered what he thought of her. It shouldn't. It did.

Still, he didn't comment, but his eyes remained upon her, intent as he studied her. Unnerved, she determined she was going to be casual. Calm. At ease. She would ignore the Lladro pieces on the floor and the little specks of porcelain dust on his shoulders and in his hair.

"Since you're here," she said, "may I offer you anything?"

"Yeah, sure. I'll have a— " he began, then paused and shook his head. "Let's go somewhere. Let me take you to dinner."

"Jordan, it's nearly midnight."

"And this is New York. The theater crowd will be out in numbers."

"What are you doing in New York?" she inquired carefully, without responding to his invitation.

"I came to talk to you."

"As I said before, I have a telephone. You could have called."

He nodded. "Yeah. And you just bashed me on the head before you closed the door in my face."

"I didn't mean to hit you."

"Did you mean to close the door?"

"Jordan—"

"Instinct, right?" he taunted softly. "Kathy, you'd have hung up on me if I'd called you here, and your assistant would have had you in continual meetings if I'd tried to get you at work."

"You could have warned me you were coming."

"You'd have left town."

"We have written upon occasion."

"This is important."

"To you."

He shrugged. "Yeah, to me. And our daughters."

She hesitated a minute, watching him. "Are you here in New York alone?"

A slow smile crept onto his lips. "Why? Have you room on the sofa?"

"Not on your life," she said sweetly. "I was just concerned about that sweet young thing with whom you're involved at the moment."

"Tara Hughes?"

"Is that her name?"

"Yes."

She shrugged. "Is she with you? She may be expecting you back for a late-nite supper."

"She's not here. I'm alone."

Hmmm, all right. So his little playmate wasn't

even concerned about his taking a trip to see his ex-wife. Not exactly flattering, Kathy decided. "She must miss you," she told him.

"My life is my own." He shrugged. "Kathy, will you have dinner with me? It really doesn't seem that much to ask." He hesitated just a second. "You did leave me, remember?" he asked softly.

"You filed for divorce."

"Somehow, I didn't get the impression that you were just on a vacation."

"You didn't—"

"Kathy, didn't we do our fighting long ago?" Ouch. Maybe he was right.

"It was why I left."

"Was it?"

"What do you mean?"

"Sometimes I think you left because you were afraid."

"Of what?"

"I don't know exactly. You tell me."

She started to rise. "Jordan—"

"Sorry, I'm not trying to wage war again. It's just that I sometimes wonder if you didn't just throw everything away because you weren't willing to fight."

"I didn't want to have to fight. I wanted marriage to be an equal, trusting relationship."

"Why didn't you trust me?" he demanded tensely.

"Why didn't you trust me?" she countered.

"And just what wasn't equal?" he responded. "Didn't you just say we'd already done our fighting?" Kathy asked. It was absolutely incredible that after so much time had passed, they came up with these questions— with so much passion still, and so much anger. It didn't matter anymore. It was over.

Yet it was frightening to see how much emotion remained, how much anger would not go away.

"Yeah," Jordan breathed softly. "We've done the fighting. It's all in the past, isn't it?"

"Definitely," she lied.

"Then surely, by now we can be civil. Kath, can we go to dinner?"

Dinner. Out with him. He just didn't understand— even if he was close in a strange way she would never admit. He didn't realize why she had left. She was okay when she didn't see him. When he wasn't a part of her life. But being with him again . . .

She could manage, and she was going to do so. Maybe they could never actually be friends— their time together had been far too intense for that, as they had proven to one another in a matter of seconds after nearly ten years— but it might help her to get on with things if she could exorcise the ghosts of their marriage and at least have a decent speaking relationship with him again.

"All right. Just give me a few minutes. There are sodas and beers in the refrigerator if you want to help yourself to anything."

"Thanks."

"Sure."

She rose and started toward her bedroom.

"Kathy!"

She paused and turned back. He was standing, tall, straight, arresting, his green eyes sharp, intelligent, and curiously soft as they lit upon her. "This is a nice home you've created here."

"Thanks."

"And you look great."

Was that what he really thought? Or was it polite conversation because she'd agreed to go out for dinner?

"Really great!" he said.

It sounded sincere. As if the words had resulted from the intent scrutiny he had given her before.

"Thanks, again," she murmured. Keep the tone casual, she reminded herself.

She started back to her bedroom again, wondering what she was doing. This was a mistake. She had been better off when she'd closed the door on him. She should have told him to go away. Then he would have been only a minor interruption. She would have been tortured by his face in her dreams for a month or so, but then the memories would fade.

This was just dinner. They'd been apart ten years. She loved what she did for a living. She had good friends. She did date upon occasion. It was just . . .

She'd never found what she had once had. Long before the divorce, of course. But somehow she'd wanted it just right, she'd wanted it all— the love, the laughter, the devotion, the passion. And if she couldn't have it, she hadn't wanted a commitment that offered anything less. Jordan, on the other hand, did have something going. He hadn't remarried yet, but she was convinced it was just a matter of time before he did.

She threw open her closet door and stared at the rows of clothing. Hmmm. What was just the right outfit for a late dinner out with an ex-husband she couldn't help but want to impress?

Back to basic black?

She almost managed to grin to herself. Summer in the city was hot, and she did have the perfect black dress, a cotton knit halter-type with a not-too-long and not-too-short skirt. Not too dressed up and not jeans and a T-shirt either. She drew it from the closet, tossed it on the bed, and warned herself sternly that her ex-husband was a man she had left for a reason, that she wasn't up to a good time in the least, that he was involved with a girl not much older than their daughters.

It wasn't that. She wasn't looking to recapture the past. She just wanted the dignity of Jordan knowing that she hadn't fallen apart, that she was still a person. One who counted in her own right, perhaps. She sighed. Who was she kidding? He'd always respected her intelligence. She'd found that to be one of the most endearing of his traits when they were young. He'd loved to listen to her, sometimes argue a point— be it about the house, their lives, or world issues— and sometimes concede.

Certain that he considered her a person still, and respected her intelligence, she wanted more. Pride, perhaps. Vanity. She wanted him to still consider her desirable. Because she found him attractive.

"No, no, no!" she chastised herself firmly. Jordan was no longer a part of her life.

But what had gone wrong between them had never been physical. She didn't want to let herself remember just how good sex had been, not now. Maybe she'd been alone too long. Maybe she'd taken "responsible" relationships too far, and maybe that was why intimate details were now springing unbidden into her mind. Yet more than those came to her. Memories of closeness . . . *after* intimate details. Waking together, being held—

"Quit this! Or else you can't go to dinner with him!" she hissed to herself. *She had left him because she had already lost him, somehow. Because the trust had been gone. Because of the way he had looked at her.*

Maybe she had thought he would come for her, she told herself wryly. That he'd follow, determined to break the barrier that had risen.

After Keith's death . . .

She wasn't going to dwell on it now. She was going to go to dinner and establish a civil relationship between them. Dignified and civil.

All right, so she still hoped she could be dignified and sexy.

She pulled her tailored nightshirt over her

head, ready to slip into a dignified and— hope-fully— desirable black dress.

And that was when all hell broke loose.

She heard the shuddering of the condo's front door; the slam as it was thrown inward, striking the wall.

"Kathy, Kathy!"

Her name was shouted in a deep, male voice. Footsteps came tearing down the hallway to her room.

"Hey!" That was Jordan's voice. That incredible baritone, startled, outraged. Furious, defensive.

The door to her room burst inward, and all she saw at first was a blur. It had all happened so quickly! She let out a shriek, startled and alarmed.

Caught naked except for the lace panties she'd worn beneath the nightshirt.

Her fear quickly faded as the blur cleared as two men hit the floor, Jordan having tackled . . .

Jeremy.

Three

"Wait, wait!" she cried, making a mad dive for her discarded nightshirt, then grasping it to her chest and trying to break up the two men at the same time. They were well matched. Jeremy was honed to perfection—muscle-building was his job. But Jordan had always been tall and well built and he was the one who had tackled Jeremy.

"This guy just came bursting into the apartment!" Jordan grated as she caught his shoulder with her free hand, trying to drag him up and off Jeremy.

"Jordan, it's all right!" With a great deal of effort, she managed to drag her ex-husband from Jeremy.

"What the hell is going on, Kathy? The doorman is right behind me; he's called the police!" Jeremy said indignantly. He scrambled to his feet, standing and straightening his shirt while watching Jordan with wary and accusing eyes.

"Jeremy, this is— "

"Whoa!" Jeremy exclaimed, his eyes growing very wide. He was staring at Jordan almost as if he had just met his Maker. He didn't need any introduction from Kathy. "My God— you're Jordan Treveryan!" He stared at Kathy as if she had betrayed him in the worst way, then offered a hand to Jordan. "Sorry. God, I'm so sorry. We were just on the phone, you see. Kathy and I. We were talking. When Kathy didn't get back on with me, I thought something awful had happened to her. I thought she'd been attacked. You know, big city."

Kathy winced. She'd forgotten that Jeremy had been on the line. So now both men were standing in her bedroom and she was undressed. Jordan had his hands on his hips, surveying Jeremy as if he were a rival on a high-school football team. Not that Jordan had any rights, but then, being Jordan, he would have defended her to his last breath whether they had any relationship left or not.

If she weren't in such a ridiculous and half-naked situation, that might even be nice.

"Kathy, who is this?" Jordan asked, looking to her at last.

Who was Jeremy? A lifesaver, at this particular moment, she decided.

She clutched Jeremy's arm, still trying to hold her nightgown to her breast and maintain a semblance of dignity. "Jordan, Jeremy Hunt, a . . . a very good friend." She looked to Jeremy. "I'm so sorry, darling, I was just so startled to see Jordan that I forgot the phone— "

"Ms Connoly!" The deep, masculine cry came from the doorway. Jordan arched a brow at her.

"Ms Connoly, are you in there, are you all right? Mr. Hunt? What's going on? Will someone please answer me?"

"James Tanner, the doorman!" Kathy said quickly to Jordan. "You must have met him on the way in."

He shook his head. "There was no one downstairs when I entered the building. A young man was outside helping an older woman into a car."

Jeremy gasped. "James said he'd been outside for a few minutes when I rushed in and saw him. He was going to call the police as I came on up here. Oh, Lord. I'm sure he did—"

"Did call the police!" Kathy said in dismay.

"I'll run out and explain the situation to James and maybe he can call them back and stop them before they get here," Jeremy said.

He pulled away from Kathy. She lost the nightshirt—it was caught in his arm—as he did so. Turning beet red, she made a dive to retrieve it.

Jeremy, flushed to a shade of crimson, returned it. He then walked out of the room as Kathy grasped the nightshirt to her chest. Jordan continued to stare at her, his lips curving into a smile of amusement . . . and something more. She wasn't quite sure what.

"Nothing I haven't seen before," he reminded her.

"And nothing you have seen in a long, long time," she reminded him.

He shrugged. His smile deepened. "Things don't seem to have changed much."

"Oh, but things have!" she assured him. "Jordan, will you please get out of here!"

She didn't need to issue the plea because at that moment they heard another voice. One she didn't recognize. "Hey, in there! What's going on?"

"The cops!" she moaned. What else could happen to humiliate her?

The police had not been stopped from coming. They were already here. Kathy was still clutching her nightshirt when two uniformed officers burst into her bedroom, guns drawn, James and Jeremy following behind them, both trying to explain, but so incoherently that nothing was made clear. The officers were convinced she was in danger. Once again, Kathy's blood raced to her cheeks as she tried to speak for herself, but the police were trained to move swiftly and she didn't have a chance to talk to them before they seized Jordan.

"Against the wall!" an officer roared, his hand upon Jordan's shoulder as he started to slam him against the bedroom wall.

"No, wait!" Jeremy cried in dismay.

"Sweet Jesus!" the doorman moaned upon reaching her room and falling back against the wall behind the second policeman who had burst in and now held his gun on the crowd of them, looking from one to the other. "Here goes my job!" James moaned.

"Please!" Kathy shouted, ignoring him and talking to the officers. "Wait, please! This is my home, and you don't understand the situation!"

"Is it an assault, a rape?" the older officer asked.

"It's just dinner," Jordan said wryly, staring across the room at Kathy.

The officer went still, both brows raised in confusion. "What?" he asked.

"Dinner. Ms Connoly was changing to go to dinner," Jordan said. He firmly caught the policeman's hand, easing it from his body. He wasn't angry or ruffled. "Officers," he said pleasantly, "thanks for coming, but there's really nothing wrong here."

"I thought someone was attacking Kathy," Jeremy murmured. "I told James to call the police when I came hurrying up."

"Mr. Hunt didn't realize that the man up here was Mrs. Connoly's husband," James tried explaining.

"Ex-husband," Kathy said. No one seemed to notice. James was still trying to explain.

"And I didn't know that Mr. Treveryan had come in because I was helping old Mrs. Lunstead from upstairs into a limo. It's really all my fault."

The officers—the younger one a twenty-something fellow with neatly cropped dark hair and large, soulful Latin eyes; the older one a grizzled-looking, blue-eyed Irishman— stared hard at Jordan. The older fellow was already grinning. "It is Jordan Treveryan, as I live and breathe!" he said.

"Wow!" said the younger fellow. He glanced quickly to his superior. "Really?"

"Oh, yeah!" the older man said on a breath of hero worship.

And Kathy realized that she was still standing in her own bedroom in nothing but lace panties and clutching a piece of cotton to her chest while these guys ignored her and paid homage to Jordan.

She cleared her throat. "If you all wouldn't mind?" she said, stressing the last word.

Ridiculous. The cops didn't even notice her irritation— or her state of undress.

"So *is* Blue Heron getting back together?" the younger one asked.

"Want to set those guns back in their holsters?" Jordan suggested, his tone still level and calm, his smile casual. "I think you're distressing Kathy, but it sure is great to know New York's finest can make it here so promptly."

"Kathy!" the older one said with a gasp. He gave her his full attention at last. "Then you were with Blue Heron! Ex-wife, you were Kathy Treveryan, you were . . . Oh, wow, what a night!"

Now they were all staring at her. She felt like a lobster— only lobsters had shells and she just had a handful of cotton.

She tried to be pleasant, though she had to grit her teeth. "Will you all please get out of my bedroom!" she demanded with what patience she could muster.

"Oh, my God!" the young cop suddenly exclaimed. It was his turn to become beet red. "William," he said to the older officer. "Kathy and Jordan Treveryan. I think we— oh, no— I think we interrupted . . ." His voice trailed away awkwardly. It was quite clear just what he was afraid he had interrupted.

"You didn't interrupt anything," Kathy assured them all quickly. She wanted to hit them, but she wasn't about to give anyone a chance to say she had protested too much. She forced a smile. "As Jordan said, I was just changing for dinner. I do appreciate the fact that everyone here"— her gaze took in Jeremy and the doorman as well as the officers— "was concerned for my safety. I'm fine. And I'll be much better if you'll all leave me alone so that I can get dressed!"

"Of course, of course!" the older officer, Will, exclaimed. "Out!" he told the younger one. And Jeremy and James spun around as well, nearly tripping over themselves now to leave her room.

Jordan was in no hurry. He grinned broadly at her, his hands idly resting on his hips. "You do provide excitement."

"My life is usually nice and pleasant and dull as hell! You caused all this, sneaking up here behind my doorman's back!"

"I didn't sneak anywhere, I didn't see your doorman. And I knocked!"

"Jordan, just get out, will you?"

He shook his head and grinned, this time with pure amusement, then exited her bedroom.

"Damn them all!" she breathed out as she slipped quickly into her dress, spurred by the fear that someone else could further insult her dignity by bursting into her bedroom.

The two officers remained in the apartment. When she was dressed and had returned to the living room, they were still there, along with James, her usually competent doorman. Jordan was giving out autographs and musical advice.

Jeremy— her lifesaver— was watching Jordan with the same reverence as the others. She felt like kicking him. But at least, so far it seemed that nothing about her real relationship with Jeremy had been given away, and she intended to keep it that way.

As the officers apologized profusely for breaking in on her, Kathy prayed that they would just quit and go away— and that she wouldn't run into either of them at the neighborhood deli, market, or Chinese restaurant. She thanked them for coming so quickly when they'd thought she might in danger. Then James tried to explain all the confusion to them again, still dismayed at not having been able to see to the needs of two of the buildings tenants at the same time. Jeremy consoled James. They'd all been caught in a bit of confusion.

Right. But Kathy had been the only one caught nearly naked, she thought resentfully. Petty! she told herself. She should just be grateful to know that help would come so fast if she needed it! And she was remembering how frightened she'd been when she had thought a thief— or worse— was in her kitchen, she truly convinced herself that she was being ridiculous, and she thanked the officers sincerely.

The policemen finally left— with autographs. James had to be reminded that he needed to return to the door since he was the doorman.

And that left Kathy alone again with Jordan and Jeremy.

Jeremy was, bar none, the best-looking man Kathy had ever met. He had deep blue eyes, so dark they were cobalt. His hair was thick and nearly jet black. He stood at an even six foot two and since he spent most of his life working out, he had the body of an Adonis. His face matched his godlike body, and he was one of the nicest human beings Kathy had ever met. She loved him dearly— as a friend. She could only pray that he would go along with her now.

"Jeremy, Jordan and I were about to go to dinner. Would you like to join us? Jordan, you wouldn't mind, would you?"

"I . . . no," Jordan said, though it was evident that he did.

"I . . ." Jeremy hesitated as well. He didn't want to step on Jordan's toes, but he did seem to understand that Kathy needed his support. "I think perhaps the two of you might want to talk." He took Kathy's hands and looked down at her with a warm smile. "I'll be home, if you need me." He released her hands and turned back to Jordan. "It's been a pleasure to meet you. I think I'll turn down the dinner invitation, but I hope to accept some other time."

Jordan nodded. Kathy couldn't help but wonder what was going on in his mind.

"I'm trying to talk Kathy into coming to Star Island for a week," Jordan said. "Naturally, you're welcome as well."

"Oh, but . . ." Jeremy began.

As subtly as possible, Kathy stomped on his foot.

"I really don't think he can convince me to come," Kathy said, smiling at Jeremy. "But I certainly wouldn't go alone." She hoped that Jeremy could see the plea in her eyes— and that Jordan could not.

"Well, let me know what you decide," Jeremy said. He lifted her hand to his lips, then kissed it, and it seemed he felt he needed to go a step farther for her, for he pulled her close to him, brushed a kiss on her forehead. "Call me, Kathy. Mr. Treveryan, again, it's been a pleasure."

He left the apartment.

"Are you ready?" Jordan asked. "Or is the fire department coming as well?"

She shrugged. "You shouldn't have surprised me," she told him defensively.

"You should have remembered that your . . . er, friend was on the phone."

"I was startled."

"I didn't know I could still startle you that badly. Ten years is a very long time."

"You took it in stride."

"So did you," he commented, a glow of amusement in his eyes once again.

She swore beneath her breath. He heard her.

"Well, it was good to know the police could just about fly in like that, wasn't it?"

"Oh, yeah?"

"They didn't point their guns at you," he reminded her.

"They didn't find you half-dressed!"

"I'd rather be naked than shot," he said dryly.

"I wasn't naked," she said defensively.

"Then why the outrage?" he demanded softly.

"Do you want to go to dinner or not?" she asked.

He swept out a hand, indicating the front door. "I would very much like to go to dinner."

She walked on past him, then paused just as she had gone on by him. "Why?"

"Why what?"

"Why do you want to go to dinner with me so badly?"

"That's obvious, isn't it?"

"Is it?"

"I want you to come to Star Island."

"But I don't want to."

"You do."

"I don't."

"I'll convince you."

"You won't."

"I will."

"You won't— "

"Damnation, Kathryn!" he exclaimed suddenly. Then she was startled to feel his hands on her shoulders, startled by the tension and passion evoked by his touch— and by seeing the dead-set determination in his eyes. Her breathing and her heart seemed to stop, and yet she sensed the mad surging of her blood, the hot racing through her veins.

Let me go! she thought in sudden panic. He was really too close now, touching her. And he *felt* the same. His hands . . . she knew the feel of them; he had held her like this before. Time slipped away, so softly, as if it hadn't been. And the way he held her now, touched her, stared at her, it was as if the years had slipped away for him as well. As if they could almost pick up from where they had left off— without the gap of a decade in between.

Yes. *She knew Jordan.* Knew his touch, the feel of his hands . . . that look in his eyes. Something was haunting him, driving him. Yet despite his tension, his voice was deceptively soft when he spoke again.

"You've got to come. It's extremely important. So help me, Kathryn, unless I die trying, I will convince you to come!" he exclaimed. "By God, I will!"

Four

"Why?" she repeated stubbornly, after a minute. She pulled away from him nervously.

He lowered his eyes and his head briefly. She saw him knotting his fingers into fists at his sides, saw him release them with determination.

When he looked at her again, there was a smile on his lips, a casual light within his eyes once again.

He sighed with exasperation. "It's an honest, polite invitation. The girls want you to be there."

Ummm. He was taking a different route now. One that would surely get to her.

And she fell for it, despite being certain there was more behind this "honest, polite" invitation.

"The girls have known all about this for a while, I take it?" she asked.

He hesitated. "They've known. Not that long, really."

Traitors! The little darlings— ummm! the little *witches!*— lived with her most of the time.

Something sobering seemed to settle over her and she shook her head, still determined that there was far more to this than Jordan intended to admit. "Why a reunion? It isn't going to be the same. It can never be. Not with Keith dead."

He hesitated. Just a moment too long. Time might have passed, but she did still know Jordan Treveryan. Maybe better than anyone else. He was going to lie to her.

"I think we can create some excitement and make really big money for some really good charities."

"There's more to it than that."

He shrugged. "Music is in big at the moment."

"Music will always be 'in.'"

"Musicians who have kept their popularity are in. I've never suggested the group actually get back together; I wouldn't want that. But I've invited everyone who was involved to Star Island, I intend to put on a show and do good deeds with the proceeds. People are going to make movies whether I— or we— approve of them or not, and I do happen to like those making this picture. They approached me immediately; they were honest and direct. A lot of time has passed. Maybe it's the right time for all the tempest and trauma of Blue Heron to be put to rest."

Strange way to put it, Kathy thought. Though she was still certain he was keeping *something* back, she believed he was being sincere— to a point.

"Dinner?" he said.

She nodded. "But it's getting pretty late. The

girls should be home soon. I think I'll leave them a note."

"Are you going to tell them where you are?"

"Are you planning on seeing them?"

"Of course, I'd like to."

"Want to wait for them so we can all have dinner?" she asked.

She didn't know why, but she was glad when he shook his head. "No. Ten years is a long time. We should talk through some things first, before adding them to the brew, don't you think?"

"Your call," she said lightly, and preceded him out the door.

Jordan had never cared for many of the trappings that came with success. He liked to walk, on big city streets and country roads; liked to enjoy sunsets and study old buildings, but tonight, he had come to her home in a black stretch limo. It had been parked just down the street. The limo wouldn't particularly be noticed by the people living in her building— it was inhabited by Wall Street brokers, well-known actors and actresses, successful models, oil execs, and even an Arabian prince— a nice enough fellow except that Kathy was certain he was keeping a harem in his penthouse apartments. Though she wasn't exactly a bra-burning feminist, she couldn't help but feel indignant about the situation, no matter what the man's background. This was the U.S.A. She had risen in her chosen field, having become Executive Senior Editor and Associate Publisher, but in publishing, titles were often much weightier than paychecks. She'd only managed to get the apartment because Jordan had always been a smart businessman. Though she'd refused to take a settlement after their marriage, each band member still received royalties from the sales of records, albums, tapes, and compact discs. She'd bought the place from an associate who'd married a rich but weary stockbroker who wanted to leave the city behind and move to Jackson Hole, Wyoming, to raise sheep. The pair, happy as larks, were doing that now, and Kathy received Christmas cards each year showing the two of them smiling— along with their sheep. In the background was always beautiful white snow, and she promised herself every year that she would go out and see her old friend, her old friend's husband— and their sheep. She hadn't managed to do it yet.

Which left her with another dilemma. She probably could get time off, she was in a senior-enough position to throw a good pitch to the publishing company's president, Marty Rothchild, but at least a half-dozen books in various editorial stages required her close attention.

"Kathy?"

She hadn't realized that she had just stopped and was staring into the limo when the driver hopped out to open the door for them. She stepped in, Jordan followed her. The young driver quickly closed the door.

The limo— spacious and long— suddenly seemed too intimate. She found herself with a wild desire to run, and at the same time, looking across at Jordan, she felt an equally strong desire to burst into tears and ask him how so much could have gone so wrong. She wanted to fall into his arms, to experience his secure touch once again.

No. Oh, no. This was such a trap. This was why she had run. She had to admit it. Chicken.

But then, things had changed. He had changed. The rumors after Keith's death, the subtle, hurtful things that had been said had torn at them all. Relationships had been undermined. Jordan could have held the group together, Kathy had always thought. But he hadn't chosen to do so. He had wanted to be out of the limelight. He had continued to write, and had put out several solo albums, but he had never gone on tour alone, and Kathy was certain that he never would. He didn't like touring and, financially, didn't need to go out on tour.

"May I offer you something?" he asked. "The limo is fully stocked and neither of us is driving."

She shook her head. "No, thank you." She seemed to be very close to him. It was a big limo. Comfortable. Black interior, TV screen, video box, nice bar. Her knees were still brushing his. She pulled them back in.

"You know," she murmured, "maybe a—"

"Jack and ginger?" he suggested.

"If they have it."

He didn't reply. She suddenly realized that, of course, there would be Jack Daniels Black and ginger ale in this car because he would have ordered it. She might know him; he knew her.

He fixed two drinks, the same, while the car moved into traffic. Kathy heard street noises. The honking of horns, the shouts, the screeches when the zillion cars still on the roads no matter what the hour nearly bumped into one another.

She took the drink from him, meeting his eyes once again. She lifted her glass.

"Cheers," she murmured.

"To a good reunion."

"Jordan, I really don't want to come."

"Why not? If it's because of personal differences, I'll stay out of your way. I've done so very well over the last ten years, don't you think?"

Oh, damned well, she thought. Yes, he had done well. He had obliged her every wish. He had kept his distance. He had been a good father to the girls, while bowing to all her decisions. Not that they had ever quarreled over their children. The girls were beautiful and bright and warm, and loving to both of them; and they always had been. The divorce had hurt them badly, both parents knew, and so they had been very careful. If they had been noble at all, it had been in making sure that they had never spoken a negative word about one another to their children.

They hadn't communicated, though, in anything other than a few terse letters. He had probably thought her unreasonable at times. She hadn't thought it was possible to make him understand that, to survive, she'd needed an absolute severance from him.

"Jordan, honestly, I'm not trying to be mean or uncooperative. I'm busy," she said evasively. "Just because you've suddenly decided that we should all get back together doesn't necessarily make a reunion a good idea for the rest of us."

"Everyone else is coming."

She shrugged. "What are you trying to do?" she insisted.

"Kathy, besides everything else, we have two children who have weathered the past decade exceptionally well. Christmas Eve with me, a fast flight to New York with a million other holiday travelers for Christmas with you. Easter in Florida one year, Thanksgiving in New York the next. Let's give our daughter a decent twenty-first birthday."

"We can both have nice parties for her—"

"One good one instead."

She was quiet for a moment. "Where are we going now?" she asked him.

"The Oyster Bar?" he said, but there was a question in his voice. If she didn't like his suggestion of a place, he would be ready to change it.

"Fine."

"Will you come down?"

"For how long?"

"Say, a week at least?"

She shook her head, suddenly very curious as she watched him. "I just don't understand this. Does Miss April Pin-Up Queen know that you're in New York entreating your ex-wife to come to a party?"

A very slow smile curved his lips. "You are referring to Tara?"

"I am."

"She was never Miss April—or a pin-up of any kind."

"Sorry. Tacky thing for me to say. But does she know you're here."

"Yes."

"Jordan, this makes no sense."

He leaned forward suddenly. "You work too hard, you spend your life with your nose in manuscripts, you never take vacations—"

"And how would you know?"

"Your daughters tell me."

She lowered her head, flushing, frustrated. Great. Alex and Bren had led their father to believe that she had dived straight into books—given up on life completely. It was humiliating. Especially when he was dating a young woman who could easily have been Miss April or any other kind of pin-up.

"Jordan, I like my job. It's rewarding. I work with fantastic authors—"

"I'm aware of that. You've got quite a distinguished roster, from what I've heard." He looked slightly puzzled, shaking his head. "In fact, I was expecting . . ."

"What?"

He shrugged. "Never mind."

"No, what? Tell me what you were about to say."

He shook his head, lifting his hands in a typical Jordan gesture she knew very well. "I guess I had thought to find you with someone . . . more . . . dignified. A professor, a great literary talent, an older man maybe. You just never seemed to be the type for . . ."

"For?" she questioned curiously.

"Your young muscleman. All brawn, not much between the ears."

She stared at him, startled. He didn't sound insulting, just surprised and even a bit concerned.

She smiled around clenched teeth. Great. Just what she wanted. His concern. "You haven't had a chance to get to know Jeremy very well. He is one of the nicest human beings I've ever met. And you're mistaken. He has a lot between the ears. He's an avid opera buff, knows art backward and forward, loves the theater, and gives me wonderful opinions on all sorts of reading materials."

Shadows danced around the inside of the limo. She couldn't see his eyes, and she didn't have the least idea of what he was thinking.

"Well then, I do apologize," he told her. There was a slight strain in his voice as he added, "It's just that your muscleman is a bit young."

"And Miss April isn't?"

He didn't reply but leaned forward, suddenly taking both of her hands. "He's invited. And if you say he's a good guy, then he must be. You've . . . always been a good judge of people.

Well, almost always. And I didn't come here to try to destroy the life you've created for yourself. It's been a long time. Our fights should all be in the past. Will you please promise me to come down?"

"Jordan, I—"

The limo came to a halt.

"I don't know," Kathy finished.

"Damn," Jordan muttered.

The driver came around to let them out. Jordan thanked the young man, and helped Kathy out himself. He took her elbow as he led her through the Fifth Avenue entrance to the Plaza Hotel and along the stately corridors to the doorway of the Oyster Bar.

It was late, but a theater crowd had come in, and the place was busy, noisy, and somewhat smokey. Jordan procured them a table in the back, just a little bit away from the din.

Kathy opted for a shrimp cocktail and a second Jack and ginger— maybe not a good idea— and Jordan went with a Bud and oysters on the half-shell. Their conversation was idle as they waited to be served, Jordan commenting on the changes in New York since he'd been up last and Kathy telling him the girls loved to skate on the rink at Rockefeller Plaza every Christmas.

"Still skating yourself?" he asked her, watching as his oysters were delivered.

"Sometimes."

"Still diving?"

She hesitated. Diving had once been a family sport. South Florida had been a great place to indulge in it, and Jordan had kept a small apartment in the Keys to accommodate their love for it.

"I've . . . taken a few trips. I never liked diving in cold water, though I've checked out a few sunken ships."

"And gone on a few Caribbean vacations."

She arched a brow.

"The girls keep me informed," he reminded her.

"Ummm."

"You've still never acquired a taste for oysters?"

She wrinkled her nose. "Too slimy looking."

"They're delicious little buggers."

"Ugh." She watched him let one slide one down his throat and then shuddered.

"You don't know what you're missing," he assured her.

"Well, we all have to miss out on a few things in life." She hesitated. "Does Miss April like oysters?"

He grinned, arching a brow at her reference to "Miss April" again. "Actually," he informed her, "Tara doesn't like seafood at all."

"She looks too thin to be a lover of red meat."

"She's a vegetarian. How about muscleman?"

Kathy grinned now. "Moderation in everything," she said sweetly.

"Does he dive?"

She shrugged. "He doesn't swim," she admitted.

"Oh. Well, he does love the opera."

"And I'm sure Miss April does love . . . something!" she said even more sweetly.

He grunted, swallowing another oyster. "Well?" he asked when he had washed it down with a long draught of beer.

"Jordan—"

"The girls will think you very churlish if you don't come."

"Churlish?" she repeated.

"Churlish. It is a good word, right, madam editor?"

"It's a fine word. I suppose. But if they think I'm churlish, it will be your fault."

"It won't be, because you will be churlish if you don't come." He leaned across the table, strangely intent again. "Promise me that you will."

"Jordan, this isn't fair."

"Life never is."

"Yes, but we do have some control over our own destinies."

"Do we?"

"I'm sure of it."

"Please, come down."

"If I can get the time off," she said evasively.

He sat back, triumphant, pleased. "Then it's settled."

"It's not quite so simple—"

"Oh, come, come."

She smiled suddenly. "How about this, Jordan? I'll promise to come if you'll tell me what you're really up to!"

"What I'm really up to?" he repeated. "Is that grammatically correct?"

"Jordan, what is it you really want?"

"To see everyone back together again. And that's the truth."

There was more, but it was obvious she wasn't going to drag it out of him. Not now, at least. Maybe once she did to go Star Island . . .

But Miss April would be with him all the time. What would she learn then?

Ummm. Did it matter? Whatever she said to him now, she knew she was going to fly down for the week. Even if it did half destroy her, and ruin the fine cloak of independence and dignity it had taken her so very long to don. He was after something. Maybe she was, too. Maybe they— and the group— had parted too quickly after Keith had died, and maybe they needed to get back together again. Perhaps this was the only way any of them could really move on without being haunted by the past.

"It will really be nice. If you come down on Friday night, you'll have nine days and only miss five at the office. We can take the *Sand Shark* down to the reefs for a few days before the rest of the gang arrive."

"I thought Miss April wasn't fond of diving."

"Muscleman doesn't go in the water at all, from what you say, but I'm sure they'll both enjoy the sailing."

Muscleman. Somehow, she was going to have to convince Jeremy to come along. He was going to be in for a very big surprise.

"All right."

"All right?" Jordan repeated. He seemed to let out his breath. She was somewhat startled by the expression she caught in his eyes before he blinked, thick sandy lashes seeming to sweep away whatever she had thought she saw. He had really wanted her to come. This hadn't just been a polite and determined attempt on behalf of their daughters; it was important to him that she be there.

Why?

Their marriage was— had been— indisputably over. He hadn't been alone, though she had to admit he'd never lived the wild, reckless life she might have expected him to indulge in once he'd gained his freedom. Before Tara Hughes, there had been a voluptuous country-western singer. Not his type— Tara could have told him so. Before that, he had been seeing a very attractive television weatherwoman and, right after the divorce, the ballet dancer. He certainly hadn't been pining after her all these years. So what?

There was something very intense about him tonight. But then . . .

He had become tense after Keith's death. Sometimes then she had thought she didn't know him at all. She hadn't been able to reach him. She had felt . . .

As if she'd lost him. She had lost him. Lost all the trust, the belief.

She didn't want to think back. And her first

reaction had been the right one—she didn't want to go back.

But she was doing it.

She was setting herself up for a knife twisted in the heart. The Star Island house had been her home for nearly ten years before she had left it. She knew every nook and cranny of the place, knew the legends about the mobsters who had owned it during the thirties, could picture now the view from the backyard at night—stars in a dark sky and the lights from downtown Miami striking water blackened by into a rippling velvet sea.

Behind the pool where the guest house had been . . . Even when she had left, the earth had seemed parched and burned there, though the skeletal remnants of the cottage had been blasted and swept away.

Had he rebuilt the guest house?

She wondered as well if Miss April had done any redecorating.

"I'm not sure what good I'll be to you," she said suddenly. "I haven't done anything except sing in the shower in the past ten years. I never really was a musician, I—"

"You wrote the best lyrics," he told her.

Did he mean it? Or was it a polite way of agreeing that she had never been a musician?

"If you're really planning a performance—"

"I am."

"Then you won't be getting much help from me."

He shook his head. "I intend to on the second

Saturday night. By then, we'll have had five days of practice, and we'll do all the old songs we'd have to be dead not to remember. Most of the guys have kept working one way or another. And Shelley has been singing in Las Vegas. It's a benefit; you haven't anything to worry about."

She nodded, knowing he was lying through his teeth! He was worried about something himself.

But as she had realized, she did know Jordan. And she wasn't going to get anything more out of him tonight.

"All set?" he asked.

She had one shrimp left—his squiggly little oysters were all gone. Well, that was Jordan. He had what he wanted; he was ready to move on.

"Yeah, I'm all set."

He helped himself to her last shrimp, asked for the check, and paid it. He then politely pulled back her chair and just as politely set a hand at the small of her back to escort her out of the restaurant.

"Is this where you're staying?" she asked him.

He nodded.

"Well, you don't have to see me home. This is my city and I'm well over twenty-one—"

"Yeah, I know."

Great, she thought wryly. He knew her age.

"I can go home alone."

"Don't you think the girls will be waiting up to see me? You were the one who wanted to leave a note."

They would.

"Besides, I always like to take my 'date' home after an evening out."

"I'm not your date. I'm your ex-wife."

"Kath, quit being difficult, will you?"

"I'm merely truthful. To you it always seemed to be one and the same."

They were outside; their limo driver was waiting with the door open, smiling away. Obviously, he was pleased to be chauffering *the* Jordan Treveryan for the evening.

Kathy slipped into the plush interior of the vehicle. Once again, Jordan sat across from her. She was suddenly exhausted, and acutely aware of a sense of danger. *She'd been okay— all this time— because she hadn't had to see him. Didn't he understand that?*

Apparently not. She felt his eyes on her in the shadows, saw his face in the sudden streaks and shafts of light that made their way into the vehicle despite the tinting of the windows. Something in her heart suddenly seemed to ache, and she wanted very badly to reach out and stroke his bearded cheek. God, she'd always loved his face! She wanted to ask him what was wrong, to tell him she knew something was haunting him.

She didn't have the right anymore. Miss April played with that bearded cheek, and Kathy was going to spend her week in Florida pretending that her every waking moment hinged around Jeremy— muscleman.

"When are you going back?" she asked Jordan, wishing once again that she didn't feel as if they were alone together in the blackness of a strange, vast—but confining—universe. She could still smell that damned aftershave. There was cruel irony in this. She'd spent ten years building up her own life, her own personality, her own world.

She'd been with him just a few hours, yet the protective wall of those ten years had seemed to crumble like dust. He was still Jordan; she still knew him. All the hurt seemed to be with her again, and still she was saying that she would set herself up for more of it.

She still didn't know exactly why.

Or did she?

Maybe she still loved him. Somewhere, deep inside her. And maybe she couldn't bear to see that tension still in him.

"Tomorrow. I fly back tomorrow," he said.

"No business in the city?"

He shook his head. "Just you."

"I'm flattered."

He grinned. "You should be." He leaned forward suddenly, taking her hands. "Kath, thank you," he said softly.

Oh, God. This was a Jordan she knew well, too. He could rant, he could rave, he could demand that things be done his way. But he'd always given credit to others, and he'd always been quick to apologize, quicker still to give thanks when he thought it was due.

She wanted to snatch her hands away, take them from that enveloping warmth she knew too well. In the shadows, she still knew exactly what his hands looked like. Very long, the palms large, fitting the man; his fingers slim and yet powerful. The fingers of a natural musician. His nails would be bluntly cut, clean, even. Once upon a time, he would have touched her cheek next, leaned closer to her, kissed her lips . . .

Damn! How could this seem so natural, so easy, when ten years had passed.

She managed to draw her hands from his, cursing the shadows yet thankful for them. She couldn't read his eyes, neither could he see what lay within her own.

The limo had stopped, she realized. They were back at her condo.

The driver opened the door. Jordan thanked him, helped Kathy out. They started for the street door, but before they reached it, there was a sudden flurry of blinding activity.

"Dad!" The shriek came in unison from the two young women emerging from the doorway.

Alex and Bren. Kathy stood back, watching her daughters, seeing the joy on their faces as they greeted their father. She realized with a pang that though they loved her dearly and were happy to have spent most of their growing-up time with her, they adored their father as well.

And time with him was something precious.

They are grown now, she thought. And still, they are their father's little 'girls.

Alex, Kathy's own height but absolutely her father's image. She had Jordan's sandy hair, his lime green eyes, his way of cocking his head. Her personality, as well, was more her father's. She was determined, and she was an artist. She meant to storm the world as a photographer, but more than that, she loved photography as an art, loved the play of light on a subject, the contrast of colors, the beauty of a sunset, the poignancy in the face of a lonely child.

People had liked to tease Kathy by saying there had been a dead-even splitting of genes when she and Jordan had decided to procreate. Bren, with her whiskey eyes and deep red-brown hair, was even taller than her sister and mother, nearly five-nine, and slim as a reed. Like Kathy, she loved books. Alex had to be coaxed into studying; she had made it through high school with mediocre grades, then scored miraculously high on the SATS. Bren, who would stay up all night with her books, had scored only moderately on the college boards, but her grades were among the highest in her class.

Kathy was incredibly proud of both of them.

Even if they were fawning over Jordan with such enthusiasm it was almost nauseating.

"Mom!" Alex said, at last seeming to realize that Kathy had emerged from the limo as well. She looked just a little bit uneasy, as well she should, since she was aware that her mother now had some idea of what she had been doing.

"Mom!" Bren echoed, still arm in arm with her father, but smiling broadly at Kathy. "You guys had dinner together? How great."

"Just dinner—" Kathy began.

"What a perfectly *civil* thing to do!" Bren exclaimed, grinning.

"Wonderfully civil," Kathy said dryly.

"We didn't throw a single piece of food at one another," Jordan said somberly.

"Dad!" Alex groaned, and elbowed him in the ribs.

"See, she did let you in," Bren murmured.

"Barely. She belted me on the head and slammed the door in my face."

"Oh, Dad!" Bren giggled.

"Then the police came."

Both girls giggled. "Oh, you two!" Alex sighed, not believing a word of what he had said.

Jordan shrugged, looking at Kathy.

Enough. He was going to fly back home tomorrow morning to Miss April. And Kathy— Kathy was going to remain *civil*. The events of this night had played havoc with her soul, and she was going to have to learn to be both very careful and very hard.

"I know you three will want to visit," she said lightly, "but I do have to go to work tomorrow. I'm going up."

"We'll all go up!" Alex said cheerfully.

They all followed her into the building's lobby, where they greeted James who, Kathy was glad to see, now had the good grace to appear very sheepish. Except that he was quick to grin when Bren tried to introduce him to her father, and he assured her he'd already had the "honor."

The light in the elevator seemed blinding. Kathy wondered if she might not look a hundred years old beneath it, and she could feel the three of them staring at her the whole way up. "Mom, have you agreed to come to Florida— ?" Bren began.

"Mom, you've got to, please? Twenty-one is a major event in a person's life. Please, you've got to come for me," Alex insisted, breaking in on her sister.

"Mother— " Bren began anew, ready with her own pitch.

"She's agreed," Jordan said.

"What?" the girls cried.

The elevator opened on Kathy's floor. She walked out, heading for her door, pulling out her key.

"Mother!" Alex insisted.

"Well?" Bren demanded.

With the door unlocked, Kathy spun around. "Will you all please hush up out here in the hall? Other people might be sleeping?"

The girls quieted quickly, and Kathy stepped on into her apartment, followed by them and then Jordan. She looked at him, reminding herself that she was going to be perfectly civil. And dignified. Dignity was in order now.

"Yes, I've agreed to come to Florida. But I really do have to work tomorrow."

"But, Mom, Dad's just come— " Bren began.

"And I think that's fine, and I want you to enjoy him. Jordan, please feel free to stay as late as you wish. The three of you talking out here won't disturb me in the least. Have a nice night, you've just got to excuse me."

"Of course!" Bren murmured, and came to

kiss her good night. Alex followed her sister. They both hugged her extra warmly.

Dignity had its own rewards.

But still she felt Jordan's eyes on her.

"Thanks, Kath," he called to her. That voice. That damned voice was his. Husky. Rich. Somehow sensual even with such simple words.

"Sure," she said. They stood a room apart. She wasn't going anywhere near him again. He had his own dignity. And she still had to admit, he looked damn good. Tall, straight. Handsome.

Why couldn't he be decently decayed? His face seemed all the more arresting. Hard to draw her gaze from him now.

"Good night," she said firmly.

The word echoed back to her from all three. She turned quickly to head for her room.

And she felt his eyes on her all the way. Felt a very strange warmth. Felt again, or sensed, his tension.

And something more . . .

What? Oh, dear God, just what was in that gaze? What was it she sensed but just couldn't touch?

Five

Jordan stood in the darkness, looking out the windows of his Plaza suite. The rooms were beautifully situated, offering a view of Central Park and of the avenue below. It was very late, but New York was never really in darkness, nor did the city bow to night and sleep. There were still horse-drawn carriages below. Their drivers, some of them garishly dressed, approached the tourist-types who embraced the mood of the city and still walked the streets, most of them now returning to posh parkside lodgings. Taxis still moved about, delivering their fares to various hotels. Occasionally a sleek limo swept along the street. Far across from him Jordan could see the large windows of FAO Schwarz, a delightful dazzle of color guaranteed to fascinate every child— and to entice adults as well. Tiffany was near, as were a multitude of high-priced and trendy stores. This was one of the best areas of the city, but not so far away some of the homeless were sleeping in doorways while junkies were making their buys. Gangs were busy stealing the streets from the innocents. Heat swept up from the subways to add to the summer haze caught between the walls of concrete and steel, despite the fact that it was night and the sun had fallen. New York. He'd loved the city. Loved to come here, go to the theater, hear good music, and enjoy the bustle and the unending flow of humanity as diverse as could be found anywhere in the world.

He'd avoided New York, though, for the past ten years. Because Kathy had run away from him and come here.

Staring out at the park, it was too easy to remember the first time they had come here together. She'd never been out of the far South, had never seen fall before. When they'd walked in the park, she'd worn her first pair of gloves, along with a friend's old lambskin jacket. "It's autumn, Jordan!" she'd told him, completely exuberant as she scooped up a pile of red and yellow leaves— along with some hardened carriage-horse droppings.

"Kathy, some of it is autumn. Some of it is horse manure!" He could still remember the face she had made at him, and the way they had laughed, and rolled in the leaves.

So long ago. Strange, he'd been the serious one then, the down-to-earth one. She'd been so quick to explore, to laugh: Blue Heron had already existed at a much smaller level— just Keith on drums, Derrick Flanaghan on bass, Kathy as backup, and himself on lead guitar. But he'd wanted to study music. He'd wanted all the background he could take in— not just to play and hope for a fleeting popularity, but to create with all his life. His father, who'd spent much of his young life playing bars on Miami Beach and cruise ships, had taught him, encouraged him— and warned him. "Get the education, too, my boy. Life plays funny games. Suppose you do get rich and famous, eh, son? You'll want to handle that money properly, you'll want to know where to travel. You'll want to know about the world, maybe— where you can give a hand, where you can't." So he had been serious in school, and Kathy— though she'd had an incredible flair for learning from the early cradle, he was certain— had taken the world much more lightly then. They'd been students, in their senior year at Florida State, but they'd married the year before and come up to stay with one of Kathy's aunts, an artist living a wonderfully Bohemian life in Soho.

The first snows had fallen while they had been in the city. They had both smoked in those days and Kathy had set the finger of her glove on fire when she had tried to light his Marlboro for him. They'd both ripped the glove off her hand, had crashed into one another while stomping on it and had laughed and rolled in the snow and made love in her aunt's little rooftop garret.

Sometimes it was surprising that she had run to New York to get away from him. But then, he had kept his main residence on Star Island, and there memories had never left him alone. She had remained in every room. She had decorated the place, and she had done so beautifully. Certain rooms had an Oriental flair, others were completely Early American. The patio area was done in Art Deco, with fascinating lamps, furniture, and ashtrays. The paintings on the walls reflected the period furnishings. She had made the home a showplace when they'd barely had the money to keep it, and later, when they'd hit it big, she'd been able to really indulge her taste for art.

But Kathy had left behind everything that had been hers, everything she had loved. He didn't know just what his feelings had been at first, but shock had been a part of them; his pride had been severely wounded, and he'd been bitter. So much so that he'd assured his lawyers he wanted no waiting time since reconciliation was out of the question, she could have had almost anything she wanted as long as they got it all settled as quickly as possible. She hadn't wanted anything. So fifteen years of marriage had ended in a matter of weeks. Amazing. He'd been even more shocked. And bitter. He'd always known he could be difficult, but she'd managed to cope with that before. He'd known there had been times when she hadn't felt secure anymore, but he hadn't been able to assure her.

He'd never gotten past the night of the fire . . .

Because he hadn't known what she had known. He hadn't known whether she had been with Keith the night he had died, whether she had kept silent because they'd been arguing so fiercely . . . and because Keith had actually been the subject of a few of those arguments. He just hadn't known if she had . . .

Killed Keith? He taunted himself. He didn't believe that, not for a second. In fact, he didn't know that anyone had killed Keith. Keith had taken barbiturates. They had rendered him unconscious. The doctor had said the smoke had killed him before he'd burned, that the drugs hadn't brought about his demise. Still, the scandal had rocked them all. Hurt, betrayed, they were anguished by the loss.

All of them. So it had appeared. Stunned. In pain. Even the figure Jordan had seen running to the guest house just moments before the fire had consumed it? The figure no one else believed existed.

Or admitted to being . . .

The figure he had thought at first to be his wife.

He closed his eyes in the darkness of the room, hoping to lock out a sudden onslaught of pain that should have died over ten years ago with his friend. Nothing had been clear; everyone had been fighting. At the inquest, he had stated that he was certain he had seen someone running to the guest house from the main house. No one had supported him; no one had believed him. Because the only people staying at the main house had been members of Blue Heron, their spouses and children, or employees Jordan would have trusted with his own life and the lives of his family members.

Everyone had talked of last seeing Keith alive. Then Jordan had to come out with what he'd seen. Because Keith had died that night. Because he had to know if Kathy had been running to Keith—and why. He'd asked her pointblank if it had been her, and she'd denied it, reminding him that she had been there when he'd been about to burst into the fire. He'd believed her. He'd claimed to believe her. But no one else had come forward. And so the doubts had haunted him, and to this day . . .

. . . He didn't know.

The attorneys had told him he was overwrought. He had doubted his own sanity. Indeed, he had backed Kathy into a wall, though she had never understood just quite what it was he meant to shake from her—he hadn't known himself. He'd been afraid to voice his worst suspicion—that his best friend had been murdered. Not that he wouldn't have made a prime suspect himself. He'd argued constantly with Keith. Theirs had been a truly strange friendship, because he had loved his talented friend like a brother, and because, most of the time, they had been almost as close as blood kin.

But Jordan had also been irritated by Keith at times. Jealous, maybe, because Keith and Kathy had also shared a special relationship. Sometimes, he'd been afraid it had been more. At the end, he hadn't known. His doubts were what had destroyed the friendship. But there had been more, of course. One of their major arguments had been over drugs. They'd nearly gone to jail in France because cocaine had been found in one of Keith's drums. Jordan had hit the roof, but Keith had adamantly denied that he'd tried to smuggle cocaine through customs. Hard to believe, when he didn't argue the fact that he found nothing wrong with a high now and then, but their lawyers had somehow managed to get the charges dropped. Shelley and Kathy had stood up for Keith, Judy had said flat-out that he should be thrown out of the group, Derrick hadn't been given much of a chance to express an opinion. Larry Haley had turned thumbs down on his friend, while Miles had been supportive. Miles always went along with Shelley. Strange, Jordan had always thought Miles was in love with Shelley, but in all the years the group had been together, and in all the years they had been apart, the two hadn't become a pair.

It had been amazing. Keith's death had first made them all incredibly close. Then they had split apart, as if unable to bear one another any longer.

Because something hadn't been right that night.

He'd quit trying to talk to the police because he hadn't known for sure if there had been anything to prove. All he knew now for certain was that he *thought* he'd seen a figure running to the guest house just a few minutes before flames had enveloped it. No remains other than Keith's had been found in the ashes. After the inquest, he'd kept his silence because he hadn't been certain— and because he hadn't been able to bring himself to believe that any of those present would have done anything to hurt Keith.

Much less kill him.

But now he knew. The first time talk of a screenplay being written on Blue Heron had appeared in print, he'd gotten a call at the Miami Beach studio, like something out of a thirties movie. A voice, muffled by some kind of thick material, coming through as neither male nor female, had given him warning. "Don't let a movie be made; don't let the group come back together."

"Who the hell is this?" he'd inquired, annoyed rather than frightened.

He'd been met by silence, then the voice had informed him, "Just do as I say!"

He'd never liked being threatened, and he was far more irritated than frightened by the call. He'd started to tell the caller just what to do with himself when a loud click in his ear let him know that whoever it was had gone.

Though he'd remained more annoyed than anything else, he'd been a little disturbed. That evening he'd called the phone company and arranged to have caller identification added to his home phones. It had been a hoax, he was sure, but it didn't hurt to know who was playing games.

He'd been at a local restaurant when the next call had come. It had been even stranger. "Let the dead stay buried."

"Who the hell is this?" he'd demanded.

"Let the dead stay buried. Do you know what happens when the dead come back to life? They take others with them."

This time Jordan did tell the caller what he could do; then he hung up angrily.

But the calls had gotten to him.

He'd stayed up nights on end, trying to go back, trying to think, trying to remember. He'd thought maybe he should just drop everything. But then he'd gotten even angrier, when he'd realized that he'd lost his marriage because there had been something more to Keith's death than they had known, and he'd decided not to let his friend lie in the earth unavenged.

The third call had come to the studio. And it had been different. The voice had been very soft, almost certainly feminine, but then again, it was so hard to tell. A different voice? Or just the same voice camouflaged? He didn't know.

The message was a different one, at the very least.

"The truth is what will set you free, right? The truth has to come out. Or someone else might be in danger. Remember the smell of the fire, of the burning . . . flesh? Jordan, you're the only one who *can* do something."

Again a click.

That night, he'd called Mickey Dean, a friend on the Metro-Dade police force. He and Mickey had sat in Jordan's poolroom that night, reflecting on the entire affair over a few too many Buds. "Jordan, there's not much anyone can do about phone threats like that. It might be a gag—"

"But, Mickey, something was wrong back then.

I did see a figure enter the guest house before it went up in flames."

"Anyone might have been with him. And whoever it was, was afraid to admit it after he died— obviously. Do you seriously think Keith was murdered? The coroner's report stated that he'd taken enough barbiturates to knock him out cold, that he died of smoke inhalation before the fire ever touched him. And the fire was very definitely caused by that stinking pipe he was smoking."

"Even if the pipe caused the fire, could it have made the flames grow so quickly?"

"There was no sign of arson. You and I went over all the reports at the time."

"I knew something was wrong."

"Jordan, Keith's death was probably a tragic accident, just what the hearing determined it to be. And these calls might be hoaxes. Whoever is calling you now might be the worst kind of publicity hound."

"And he— or she— might not be."

"But, Jordan, the point is, there's nothing anyone can do about a few phone calls. You know that. Christ! We get ex-husbands and boyfriends threatening ex-wives and lovers on a daily basis. Sometimes, when there has been a death threat, we can get a restraining order. Sometimes, there's nothing we can do. And even with a restraining, sometimes the ex blows away the wife or lover. We all know we should have been able to stop it somehow. But the best I can do for you is report these calls. There's no manpower to do anything about them. You're in a county with one of the highest crime rates in the country, and you know a lot about the workings of a police force because you've been listening to me talk for years."

Jordan was well aware that cops didn't have time to worry about a few threatening phone calls— or his *own* suspicion that a case closed nearly ten years ago was no accident but a murder. All the right procedures had been followed at the time. No one had shirked his or her duty.

But that didn't stop Jordan from wondering and worrying. *Someone else might be in danger.* Why? Ten years had passed, but now . . .

Now the past was haunting someone else. And others might be threatened. His wife— ex-wife— and daughters? Well, if things were going to happen, he was going to have some control over them. That was the reason for the reunion. Whatever had happened to Keith had come about because of someone associated with Blue Heron. Someone who had been there that night. Now things were going to explode again because the ashes of the past were being stirred. Jordan didn't intend to be helpless. He would make things happen in the way he wanted them to occur. On his turf, his terms. His children— and Kathy— would be where he could watch over them. Where he'd have Mickey to help him, a good friend, even if nothing could be officially done about the calls.

Kathy . . .

He let out a long breath in the night.

It had been so damned strange, seeing her again. The years had almost instantly evaporated. Maybe because they'd known one another so long. So well. They were familiar with each other's habits and tastes, expressions and moods. And none of these had changed. She hadn't changed. She looked like a million bucks. A little older, yes. But she defied time. He'd always loved her eyes. Warm, amber. Like a fire glowing in the night. She was still as slim as a reed, maybe even more so. Except that she'd maintained a few curves. Well, that was what happened when a woman was dating a muscleman. What the hell was she doing with that guy? She'd said Jeremy Muscleman was *nice*. Nice! He was so damned much younger than she was.

He reminded himself that he had just celebrated Tara's thirtieth birthday with her. She had lamented her age the entire night, and he'd had no patience with her. Already planning his trip to Star Island, he barely had paid heed to her plaintive words.

He inhaled sharply, suddenly praying that he was doing the right thing. Maybe he was *putting* Kathy into danger, all but forcing her to come down to Florida. And if not maybe he'd just be putting the two of them through a wretched stretch. Like tonight . . .

God, it still hurt. She didn't look one damned bit different. Her smile was still so quick, her eyes as warm as whiskey. Maybe she was more confident than he had remembered, but her voice was the same, with just a husky, sultry edge. A lot about her was the same—he knew since he had seen much more of her than either of them had intended.

But strangest of all had been his reaction when she had told him good night. *He could have followed her so easily.* Memories of earlier days had flooded back to him as he had watched her walk into the bedroom and close the door on him. It had been almost frightening to realize how strong the urge had been to go after her. As if ten years could be washed away like nothing. He could have held her so very easily. Made love to her. He remembered the way her lips parted when she was aroused, the smoky cast to her amber eyes, the way she moved. How she whispered in the darkness, cried out . . .

The phone rang, shattering the memories. He gave himself a rueful shake and turned in the darkness, picking up the receiver. He couldn't read the small print in a contract so perfectly anymore, but he still had great night vision, and tonight, in his brooding mood, he liked darkness.

"Darling?"

Tara. He wondered why he felt such irritation with her.

"Yeah."

"Well, what a greeting!" she murmured.

"Sorry. It's just late."

There was a second's silence from her, and he realized in that small beat of time that she had called to make sure he was in his hotel room. It probably shouldn't have bothered him, but it did.

"What's up?" he asked her.

"I just called to hear your voice," she said softly.

He felt a twinge of guilt—and still the impatience. They had a relationship, yes, but he'd never given his life over to her. They didn't live together; she maintained her own home on Key Biscayne, as well as her main residence in L.A. She'd suggested moving in several times, but he had vaguely mentioned that his daughters came down too often, and yes, he was old-fashioned. It was strange; though he'd probably engaged in more affairs than his ex-wife, he'd always feared that Kathy would be the one to remarry. He had no desire to do so himself. One try at marriage was enough. He was pretty sure Tara understood that he needed a certain independence. He made no demands; he gave no promises. He'd been restless and, like a cat in a strange jungle, on the prowl too long.

But he knew Tara cared about him, and though he would never again experience the desperate passion of his youth she meant something to him as well. She had often been a warm, giving body when he'd felt alone in the night. And she'd been a good friend upon many an occasion; she'd made him laugh sometimes when the world had seemed to weigh him down.

"I'm sorry," he murmured. "I'm tired, and it is just really late. It's . . . good to hear your voice," he lied.

"How's everything going?"

"Fine."

"Is she coming down?"

"Yes."

Another silence. Tara had been hoping Kathy would turn him down in no uncertain terms.

"The girls are very anxious for us all to be together."

Tara sniffed loudly.

"She's coming with a friend, I believe. A male friend." He hesitated. "A young, good-looking male friend."

"Oh?" Tara seemed much happier.

"Ummm."

"I just wish I understood this obsession of yours with bringing everyone back together. Half of your group is going to have changed for the worse. It's probably a big mistake. Some things are better left as they were, you know."

"People don't really change."

"Sometimes they do."

"You may be right."

"Well, I'll try to understand all this nonsense."

"Will you?" he inquired casually, though his spine stiffened. He wasn't going to be pressured, and her words sounded strangely like a threat. "If you're really unhappy with it, perhaps you should stay away while it's all going on."

"No . . . You might need me," she said hastily. "I have some photo shoots out on the islands for the next couple of days, but I'll come to your house just as soon as I can. I miss you."

He hesitated. "I miss you, too," he told her.

He was lying again, caught up in his own tumult and glad she was away. She was a natural platinum blonde, long, lanky and near perfect, with huge blue eyes, never-ending legs, and the ability to make love when necessary with the speed of a bunny. She had no inhibitions, closets were fine, any floor space provided her an ample bed. At the moment, he was damned glad to be alone.

"Was the gorgon decent to you?"

"Kathryn?"

"Yes, Kathryn!"

"She was fine."

"Did you recognize her easily? Has she gone squint-eyed reading all those manuscripts? Gained two tons at her desk job?"

"Wrinkled and dried up like a prune?" he suggested with a trace of humor.

"Something like that," Tara admitted.

"She hasn't changed much at all."

"Was she decent to you?"

"She was fine."

"Well, that's good. Of course, God knows, enough time has passed! Maybe her nastiness has just decayed away."

"She never was nasty."

"You said you fought like cats and dogs."

"We did. But I've always been fairly difficult. Demanding."

"Really?" Tara murmured dryly.

"Tara, you will probably like my ex-wife."

"Why? Do you?"

"Well, of course, I like her," he said impatiently. "I— " he broke off just in time. He'd been about to tell Tara that he had loved Kathy most of his life, naturally he liked her. "Never mind. Listen, I've got to get some sleep. You take care of yourself, and I'll see you soon."

"Jordan— " she began.

He hung up quickly, pretending he hadn't heard her try to stop him.

He walked from the suite's living room to the bedroom, stripping off clothing as he went until he reached his bed. Naked, he pulled down the sheets and crawled in, never having turned on a light. He folded his fingers beneath his head and stared up at the ceiling.

He could have been better to Tara. Hell, he could have been better to all of them.

He closed his eyes. He conjured Tara's face, her eyes. The sound of her voice echoed in his mind. He should have told her with feeling that he missed her.

But he didn't, not tonight. Oddly enough, he couldn't quite hold on to an image of Tara in his mind's eye.

Instead, his ex-wife was intruding. He kept seeing Kathy's amber eyes, hearing her voice. That sweet husky alto. She was a better singer than she had ever known, he thought. Tonight had been strange. When she'd walked into that bedroom, he could have just followed her so damned easily. He would have lifted her up, held her tenderly, made love hungrily to still the painful gnawings that were stirring restlessly within him tonight. Sex with them had always been good. Different, of course, over the length of time they'd been together. Comfortable, still exciting. Sometimes she'd been more in the mood, sometimes he'd been more in the mood. Sometimes, the patter of little feet had interrupted them. So much went on between a man and woman in a marriage of that length. Sometimes sex had been gentle, sometimes adventurous. Sometimes funny. There had been the night they'd first had the whirlpool and had half drowned one another in trying to find a workable position. Sometimes they had just looked at one another, felt the simmering sensations, and gone on from there. Without a word shedding their clothing, slipping into one another's arms. That was what it had felt like tonight. Meeting her eyes. He'd wanted to taste her lips, explore the sweet feminine silk of her flesh, run over the length of her with lazy wet caresses . . .

He gritted his teeth, slammed his pillow, and twisted around. His marriage was over.

Over.

He'd accepted that, he'd lived with it. He'd gone on. Kathy, out of sight, out of mind—or at the back of it. He hadn't lived the life of a monk; there was no sound reason for him to be lying here coveting his ex-wife.

Wanting sex, he taunted himself.

No, wanting *more*.

The feelings. Memories now. Shadow feelings. Feelings of closeness, of knowing one another, of sharing dreams, concerns, the love of children.

He stood up and strode back out to the living room of the suite, back to the windows overlooking the park.

Feelings. They haunted him, had never left him.

If his marriage was so damned over . . .

. . . why wouldn't the feelings go away?

Three thousand miles away, on the opposite coast, Larry Haley, musician turned documentary-film maker, remained awake as well into the wee hours of the night. He sat back in a leather armchair in his handsome study, staring out the window at the moon that rose high over his patio and garden. He held a brandy snifter in one hand, filled to the rim for the second time that evening, though he had learned moderation in drink— and all things!— in these later years of his. His hair, strikingly blond in his youth, and his pride and joy in those days, remained a source of pleasure for him— it had turned silvery white, but all of it— great thick strands of it!— remained on his head. "Thank you very much!" he said aloud at the thought, lifting his snifter to whatever divine entity ruled the universe. He still wore his locks long, queued back most of the time, and the style worked nicely with his California lifestyle. Of course, even in staid New England— where he'd recently gone to film whales off the coast of Maine— he'd seen more and more men in their prime wearing long hair queued back. Woodstock babies coming of age, he thought dryly, which brought him back to the reason for his imbibing so heavily.

Well, Jordan was doing it. At long last. A reunion. He wondered if the others had realized yet that Jordan had scheduled their benefit performance for the tenth anniversary of the night Keith had died.

Larry leaned back, swallowing down the full snifter of brandy, wheezing as the liquor burned into him. His eyes watered, he choked.

"Jordan, you bastard, you!" he said softly. "Why couldn't you have just left it all alone?"

He wanted more brandy; he didn't think he could stand up to get it. "Next time you're on a brandy drunk, old boy," he told himself, "make sure you leave the bottle where you can reach it."

He closed his eyes.

Jordan could have kept it all together all those years ago. He could have kept the group going, could have buried Keith and let them all go on with their lives!

But he hadn't chosen to. Not then. Now he was going to drag them all back.

And Larry meant to go. God help him, he meant to go. They would all go, he was pretty certain. Jordan had summoned them.

He picked up the telephone receiver at his side. Thought about dialing.

No. Not now. Not from his own home.

He hung up the receiver.

"Larry?"

He winced at the soft, hesitant sound of his wife's voice. Vicky Sue was an Alabama belle, a hopeful beauty who had discovered marriage with him rather than stardom during her quest in California. She was a sweet thing.

The fifth Mrs. Haley.

"You coming to bed, baby?" she asked him.

He grinned stupidly. The brandy. "Sure. Sure Vicky Sue, I'm coming. Come over here and give an old man a hand."

She helped him up. His vision blurred as he gazed at her. She looked an awful lot like wives two and three. He grinned. Didn't matter much.

"Honestly, Larry, I don't know what's gotten into you!" Vicky Sue drawled.

Well, she wouldn't. She had never been a part of Blue Heron. She hadn't been there the night Keith died. She didn't know what all of them had lost.

Or anything about what had gone on before that night.

He weaved a little, then determined to stand on his own. Her face came clear to him again. She really was a sweet young thing. "Vicky Sue, please. You go on up, honey. I'm on my way directly."

"Larry, you might hurt your—"

"I'm fine. I'll be up directly."

"Soon."

"I promise."

She believed him, and left.

He stared out at the moon one more time. He smiled suddenly. None of it would mean anything if Jordan didn't get Kathy to come back.

No, without Kathy, nothing would happen. She had been the one to weather all the creative storms between them, a friend to all of them. She'd been casual when tensions had mounted over someone being late, she'd known all their failings, their weaknesses . . .

Their secrets.

If Kathy did agree to come back . . .

Well, then . . .

Things just might be destined to happen. Oh, yeah. Hell, yeah.

Bang!

Laughing, and yet in pain somewhere deep within him, he made his way up the stairs to wife number five who looked just like wives number two and three.

Morning was dawning.

Six

Tuesday was a mess of a day.

Kathy arrived at work early, because of or despite her nearly sleepless night. She'd thought
to have some time to lay out her various projects
and see just what she had to take care of herself
and what she could delegate to her assistant. It
started out all right, but first thing, her coffee
maker blew, then an author called on her private
line, nearly hysterical because she had forgotten
to make a copy of the completed manuscript
with the revisions. She had sent the only one
she had by overnight mail last Thursday. Since
no one had received it on Friday, she was certain
it was lost. While Kathy was on the phone, calming the author and taking down the trace number, Jim Butler from the art department tossed
on her desk the cover designs for two mysteries
soon to be published. The first cover was perfect, an almost elegant layout of a candlestick,
a flashlight, and a poker along with a pristine
pair of white gloves. The colors were just right,
enticing, the weapons were just as they were de-
scribed in the book.

The second cover was awful. She had seen the sketches for it, and they had seemed fine. Now, with color and detail added, it was absolutely awful. The book was a fictionalized biography of a French countess who had fallen in love with the English lord helping her to slip French royalty out of France and away from the guillotine. The English lord was in his early fifties, his countess not much younger. The gorgeous couple depicted on the cover appeared to be nearly eighteen, tops. Their dress, supposed to reflect the period of the French Revolution, looked like something dragged out of a medieval morgue.

Jeannie Allison, the author who was sure her work was lost, was still talking.

"Jeannie, stop panicking, we'll check with the carrier and the mail room, I'll find out what happened and get back to you within two hours, promise."

Kathy hung up, stared at the misbegotten cover again, gritted her teeth, and laid her head wearily on her desk.

"Oh, my God, you're not crying, are you?"

She lifted her head, staring across her office to the doorway where Marty Rothchild, president of the small but prestigious Lightning Press, stood staring in at her.

"Crying? The art is wretched, but I've yet to cry over it!" she said, confused.

Marty, slim, graying, with the weary face of an aged bulldog and the heart and vigor of a lion, shook his head, laughed, and stepped on in, closing the door behind him and taking a seat in front of her desk.

"*I* read the papers," he announced to her. He pointed a finger her way. "And you did take back your maiden name, and you have certainly achieved a certain amount of anonymity, but despite the time passed— or perhaps because of it— Blue Heron is noteworthy. Jordan Treveryan was in town, and speculation has it, of course, that he was here to encourage his ex-wife to join in the reunion."

She arched a brow to Marty. "He was," she admitted.

"So are you going?"

"Can I take the time off?"

He mused over the question. "Are you going to give the art department a hard time over that cover?"

"You know damned well I am."

"We have budgets here, you know," he said, scowling.

"I will not tarnish my author's good work for a week off, which you are going to give me anyway," she informed him sweetly. She pushed the projected cover art over to him. "It sucks. Right?"

"Actually, they're very attractive— "

"It sucks."

"All right, it sucks. And I would have stopped it myself. We can only compete with the big boys these days because we can promise quality to our authors when the megapublishers are tied up with red tape on every level."

"I get new art?"

"You do."

"And a week off?"

"I wouldn't have you miss it."

"Why?"

"There's a book in there somewhere. A best-seller."

She groaned, letting her head crash back lightly to her desk. "Marty, I'm an editor, not a writer. I can pick out the weaknesses in a manuscript, I can come up with great suggestions to strengthen it, but I can't write. I— "

"You're a wonderful writer; you're afraid of the subject matter."

"Marty, you're right. I don't have a writing career, and I don't want to begin one with a book on my ex-husband."

He shook his head sadly. "Megamoney, the music world, sudden, tragic death, the dead heat of the Deco glitz of Miami Beach, and you as an insider! But she won't do a book!" He threw his hands up in dismay, shaking his head sadly.

"Marty— "

"Keith's death was on the front page of every major newspaper in the western world."

"Marty— "

"Sorry. You two were really close, huh?"

"He was a good friend. A sad person in a way. A genius moving a million miles an hour all the time."

"Rumor was rampant. He died with a mystery lover, he was murdered, he committed suicide— "

"No other body was found, Marty. And I can't believe anyone killed him. I'm even certain he didn't commit suicide. He'd just finished the music to a new song, he was very excited that day."

"What a book you're going to write, Kathy!"

"No book. Do I get to go anyway?"

"Let's see, on the norm, you work about a sixty-five hour week for a forty-hour paycheck. 'Course, it goes with the job, but . . . sure. You get to go."

"Thanks."

"But . . . think about a book, huh?"

"Sure."

"Liar."

"Marty— "

Her phone started ringing again. She picked up the receiver and Marty stood, giving her a thumbs-up sign as he exited her office.

As if things were not going well enough already, her mother was on the phone.

"Good morning, dear."

Sally Connoly was a cheerful person. She had been as long as Kathy could remember. Most of the time, she admired her mother very much for that characteristic; at the moment, though, it just seemed annoying.

"'Morning, Mom."

She inhaled, ready for whatever she was about to get hit with, sure that Sally— like everyone in the world other than herself— had read the papers. She had to be calling about Jordan, and the reunion.

"Are you going to Florida?" Sally asked, cutting straight to the chase.

"I . . . think I am," Kathy said evasively. She

had the time off; she'd agreed to go. She just didn't want to go alone, and she hadn't yet had time to try to talk Jeremy into continuing his charade.

"That's wonderful, dear." Her mother had always liked Jordan. So had her dad, who had passed away soon after Kathy's marriage. Jordan had never been easily swayed. When they had been young and drugs had been prevalent, he had kept clear of them. Despite his chosen profession and the customary parental disapproval of musicians, her folks had always liked him. But then, they'd watched him grow from a very young man.

"Mother, please don't go getting any ideas. I've agreed to go because we can benefit a good cause— and because it's Alex's twenty-first birthday."

"Yes, that's what I mean. It's wonderful that you two can now be friends. I've agreed to go because of Alex's birthday, myself."

"He invited you?"

"Don't sound so startled, dear, it's not exactly flattering!" Sally chided. Kathy grinned sheepishly, shaking her head. She shouldn't be surprised. She and Jordan had done a lot of their child-time exchanging through her mother when the girls had been younger, and Sally had been polite and sympathetic and fair through all of it. She had left her Miami home behind to follow her only daughter to New York after the divorce, but she'd always been as independent as a cat, choosing an apartment across town from

Kathy's and plunging into a social life of her own. She'd just been near in case Kathy needed help with the girls, and though her grandchildren were her first priority, Sally would cheerfully admit, she did maintain a busy life.

She dated more often than Kathy, but then she'd been a young mother, marrying right out of high school, having Kathy soon after. Now a tall, slim, very attractive sixty-five, she didn't look a day over fifty. In fact, Kathy thought just a shade resentfully, her mother reminded her of *The Picture of Dorian Gray*, Sally just looked better every year while Kathy sometimes felt she was catching up with her.

"Do you not want me to go? I wasn't planning on coming for long, just the weekend of Alex's party and the benefit performance. I'm anxious to see you all up on stage together again! Jordan says he'll have the girls doing some backup work. I think it's wonderfully exciting."

"Mom, I guess it will be great, and of course I want you to come."

"He'll have a full house," Sally said, and hesitated. "You'll be all right, going back, won't you, sweetheart?"

There was an anxious tone to her mother's voice.

"Sure."

"I wish he'd moved. I can't imagine you going back to that house . . . and not, and not, oh, dear, I don't know how to say this!"

"My old house— with Tara Hughes as hostess in it?" Kathy inquired dryly.

"I guess that's it," Sally admitted.

"Mom, I left that house, remember."

"And I'll never know why!"

"Mother—"

"Sorry! I don't meddle! But I do intend to be your moral support!"

"Mom, I'm going to bring a friend. I'll be all right."

"A friend. Who?"

"Just a friend. You'll see. And I'll be fine. I'm delighted you're going. I've got to get back to work, though, okay?"

Her mother was silent on the other end.

"Mother? I'm hanging up now," she said.

"Yes, of course, dear. I was just thinking that it might be a good idea if you were to go alone."

"Mom," Kathy said very gently. "Jordan is seeing a very beautiful young woman."

"Such a mistake."

"I don't think Jordan sees it that way."

"But it is a mistake. Women outlive men."

"Mom, Dad was quite a bit older than you."

"Yes, dear, I know that. I was the one married to him. And he was wonderful, wasn't he?" she queried, her voice both light and sincere. She didn't really want an answer—they had both loved Kathy's father deeply. "But the point of it is, sad but true, *men* usually are the ones dating younger women. And women outlive men, so the natural thing would be for more women to date younger men and more men to date older women."

"Interesting concept, Mom. It may or may not catch on," Kathy murmured ironically.

"And we all know that men are at their sexual peak when they're barely children, right around the age of eighteen. While women reach their prime in their late thirties, some even in their forties. Dear, just look at what you're doing with your prime."

Kathy held the phone receiver away from her ear and stared at it as if doing so might somehow help her make sense of her mother's very strange and taunting words.

"Mom, I'm leading a happy life."

"A content life. A safe life."

"Mother," she said sternly, "be that as it may, I am content, and Jordan is involved, so don't you and the girls go around thinking you can play 'Parent Trap' for the reunion."

"Kathy, I wouldn't dream of meddling. But it's a shame he's involved with that Miss Hughes. You two would be much better for one another now. You're *both* past your prime."

"Gee, thanks, Mom."

"Statistics and research, dear."

"I don't think Jordan considers himself past his prime, and, apparently, neither does his actress."

"Does that mean you consider yourself past yours?" Sally queried with sweet innocence.

"Mother, I am hanging up now. For real!"

" 'Bye, sweetheart," Sally said.

"See you soon, Mom."

Sally chuckled softly. "Tell Jeremy, that hot date of yours, hello for me, will you?"

"He hasn't agreed to go yet," Kathy admitted.

"Tell him I insisted."

"I'll try," Kathy said. "And don't you dare mention a word about the fact that Jeremy and I are only friends to Jordan!"

"I wouldn't dream of it!" Sally promised. "I'm hanging up now, dear!"

And she did.

The phone clicked in Kathy's ear. Shaking her head with a wry smile, she set the receiver back into its cradle and started from her desk. She'd have Angie, her assistant, start tracking the lost manuscript, and then go right on to the art department.

By six-thirty that evening they'd found the manuscript which had been delivered to the wrong department, and Kathy had had a satisfactory meeting with the art director, who'd decided she should talk directly to the artist, who had been charming and willing— for a price, of course— to start from the very beginning now that he clearly understood what was needed. One of Kathy's marketing meetings hadn't gone as well as she had hoped, but she had managed to scrape together something of a campaign for one of her new authors. She hadn't gotten any editing done nor had she read any proposals on books to be scheduled for publication, but despite her job title, she did do most of her editing at home.

Except that she wasn't going straight home. She left the office and headed for the gym, where Jeremy was at first all business, reminding her that she needed some warm-up time before working with the free weights, and that she'd been such a couch potato lately she deserved to start on the Stairmaster.

This was fine with Kathy. The most wicked machine in the place was alienated in its own little area, leaving her free to talk to Jeremy while she worked. She explained to him that she had decided to go to Star Island, but that she wasn't thrilled about doing it, that she was going to be very uncomfortable— and that she needed him.

He listened, intrigued. But when she finished, he shook his head uneasily. "You've got to come with me!" Kathy said firmly. She marched hard on the Stairmaster, heedless for once of the pain shooting through her legs. She didn't mind really working this evening because it was one way to get Jeremy's complete and undivided attention. "Please!" she begged.

"Kathy," he said firmly, standing at her side, arms crossed over his chest as he stared at her, "it was one thing to pretend last night that we're involved— that was a very sticky situation— but we're all grown-ups here, and you can't keep that kind of pretense up. Your daughters will know— "

"My daughters will not say anything."

"How can you be so sure?"

She stopped, breathing heavily, leaning over the stair machine rail. "Because they're daughters, Jeremy, girls. They understand pride and the like."

"I can't get the time."

"You're dying to see the Star Island estate, I know it."

She had him there. He shrugged, then snapped at her. "Don't you dare stop stepping, you've got another ten minutes to go here!"

"Jeremy—"

"Kathy, will you listen to this? You want me to come to Florida with you and pretend that we're having a hot and heavy affair so your ex-husband won't worry about you!"

"Ummm, something like that," she said evasively.

"Kathy—"

"My mother's coming, too," she said.

"You are in a sad situation!" he agreed.

"She said to insist that you accompany me. She wanted you to know she thinks you should definitely come."

"Is that a bribe? She'll start working out, too?"

"I think so."

"Kathy—"

"Jeremy, he's dating a little kid!"

"Ummm. Tara Hughes. Sexy little kid."

"My point exactly. She's very young."

"She's around thirty, I think."

"I'm at least fifteen years older."

"But very well preserved!" Jeremy said cheerfully. "No new decay today that I can see."

"You might not be looking closely enough," Kathy murmured. She sighed deeply. "Please try to understand. She'll be there. Hostess in what used to be my house."

"You left it," he reminded her stubbornly.

"Right. And I didn't mean to go back to it."

"But you agreed to do so."

She nodded, stepping harder on the exercise machine and still not noticing the pain of such determined effort. Were she only this worried on a daily basis, she'd have the best thighs in all New York.

"You told me I had to do it, remember?" she said to him. " 'The party of the century?' "

"When do you ever listen to me?"

"I feel I need to for some reason. Didn't you notice, last night, Jeremy? He was tense; this whole thing really means a lot to him."

"He didn't seem tense to me."

"That's because you don't know him."

"He was completely the gentleman. Not in the least tense. Even when the police had their guns in his face. I thought you said he had quite a temper."

"He does. On occasion. And we're getting off the subject."

"You mean about me going with you?"

"Right. Jeremy— "

"Kathy, we'd be living a lie," he reminded her very politely, as if explaining ethics to a stubborn child.

"It will not be a long trip— you just can't imagine how hard it would be to go back there alone!"

"Your daughters will be there," he reminded her stubbornly. "I consider them my friends as well. And they will know the truth about you and me."

"I know they won't say anything."

"He's their father."

"Right. And they're protective of both of us. Since he's the one really dating the gorgeous, sweet young thing—"

"Does that mean you're calling me a sweet young thing, too?"

She grinned. "Muscleman."

"What?"

"Never mind. I'm not sure you can really understand this, but I know Bren and Alex and they'll always hope their father and I will get back together. Naturally, they'll think Jordan will find me more appealing if I'm on the arm of a very handsome, younger man; so they'll encourage his belief that we're having a hot and heavy affair, but not one that embodies everlasting love!" she assured him.

"Kathy, you read too much."

"That's human nature," she assured him. "Don't we all tend to want something someone else has?"

"Does Tara have him?"

"Maybe no one really has Jordan," she murmured.

"I can't salvage your heart, Kathy."

"My heart doesn't need salvaging, but my ego can really use the booster. Jeremy, please, if I am going to go back, I need help."

"Help her," said a third voice, a rich, smooth, masculine voice.

Kathy missed a step. She and Jeremy both turned around, startled.

Tony Grant, another one of the instructors at the gym, had come over and stood grinning ear to ear behind them. He was about Jeremy's age, blond and tanned, and becoming a popular model in his spare time, though he loved being a personal trainer and had no intention of leaving the field even if he became an even more popular model. He liked people too much, working with them, helping them live their lives in a more healthful fashion.

"How loudly were we talking?" Kathy asked, feeling a mortified blush settling into her cheeks, and whispering now, though she was aware she was probably doing so just a little too late.

Tony shook his head. "I didn't really hear much. Don't look so panicked! Jeremy told me about your ex-husband's arrival and what that ex-husband assumed was going on between you and him last night."

"I probably should have been discussing this with you both," she said sheepishly. "Would you mind— ?"

"You've stopped stepping," Jeremy said.

"What?"

"You're on a stair machine, young woman! Start stepping!"

"I've been on this thing long enough to have climbed the damned Rockies!" She groaned, stepping off the machine completely and drying her face with the small towel she had cast around her shoulders.

"Kathy, this is not a proper workout," Jeremy said firmly.

"Jeremy, I will work my little butt off if you'll just help me."

"The object is to work your butt off anyway!" he announced sternly.

"Kathy, don't pay any attention to him. He'll do it. He'll be delighted to do it," Tony said.

"I will?" Jeremy asked.

Tony lifted his arms. "I'd do it! I'd do it in an instant. What's the matter with you? They're going to be making history down there! Besides, what are friends for if they don't help each other out?"

Kathy gave Tony an impulsive hug. "Whoops, sorry about the sweat!" she said.

"Job hazard," he said lightly.

"I'm the one going," Jeremy reminded her. "And he's already soaked up the sweat. You may show gratitude and appreciation to me, as well."

She laughed and hugged him, too, then looked at them both. "Thanks guys, really. I know it's childish, but I was married a long time. And he's got a gorgeous young thing at his side. Now I— "

"Will have one too," Tony teased.

She laughed. "That's the point. Jeremy is absolutely gorgeous and young. He's just not *my* gorgeous young thing. He's borrowed for the occasion."

"With my blessing," Tony told her.

"If you two have got this all settled now . . ." Jeremy began dryly.

"Hey, wait a minute. I want to be invited down for the big reunion concert," Tony said.

"You've got it," Kathy told him. "And Alex's birthday as well."

"Now it's all settled," Tony grinned again.

"I'll make it up to you both, I promise," Kathy said.

"I'm sure you will," Tony said. "But I think this means you'd better be getting to the whole roomful of machines, Kathy, my dear. Back to work now. We'll repair you before the big day so you don't have to worry about any decay. The plane isn't leaving yet! But do you know what?"

"What?" Kathy said.

He shrugged, and lifted her chin to meet her eyes. "Don't underestimate yourself. You're worth a dozen sweet young things. And I'm even willing to bet your ex realizes that!"

"Thanks!" she told him softly. "You guys are really good friends."

"Yeah. We try. And we really like a good party, too!" he teased.

As he walked away, leaving her and Jeremy to their work, a sudden surge of tremors swept through Kathy.

It was going to happen.

She was really going back.

Quite suddenly, the thought was almost paralyzing.

Because she was afraid of going home . . .

Seven

The house on Star Island was huge, with a
full ten thousand feet of living area plus a number of patios and the guest house.

It had been constructed along the lines of a
Mediterranean villa, in the style popular in
South Florida in the twenties when the place
had been built, when men such as Mizner, Fink,
and Paist had been creating homes— on small
and large scales— with unique architectural
overtones. In fact, Jordan's home had been built
in the very early twenties, before the hurricane
of the mid-decade had devastated nearly all of
the growing area, and it had stood up to the
winds and water, as it continued to do today.
Hurricane Andrew hadn't managed to do much
more than sweep away a few roof tiles.

The only real damage ever done to Star Island
occurred when the fire decimated the guest
house. Five years ago, Jordan had had it replaced. Since the home was on the historic reg-
ister, he'd been determined to restore it. It was
a two-story structure with arches and loggias, a
glassed-in porch on the first floor, a balcony on

the second. The single bedroom was upstairs, a small living area and kitchen were on the ground floor.

The main house was shaped like a horseshoe, the sides curving around the courtyard, patio, and pool; the guest house being to the left of the back of the house, almost directly on the water. The view was outstanding. Although the rear of the home was on a curve of the island, the yard afforded views of the bridge out to Miami Beach, nearby Hibiscus Island, and, at night, the dazzle of light from downtown Miami. From the small private dock, it was an easy sail or motor out to the open bay. From the first time he had seen the place, Jordan had thought it a paradise.

He'd just never imagined that he'd wind up living in paradise alone. And he wasn't sure why, at first, after the fire and the divorce, he had kept the house. Doggedness, maybe. Or perhaps the view. Maybe because it was a paradise, and he'd wanted it for his daughters and himself. No one could alter that, no circumstance change it.

He stood by the pool, leaned against one of the columns that was part of the trellised walkway on the bay side of the crystal water. From his vantage point, he had a view of the main patio and the guest house.

"Where are you going to put everyone?" Tara asked him.

He turned to her.

Blond hair straight down her back with an

unbelievable silky sheen, eyes shaded with dark glasses, skin honed to a perfect golden tan— and a great deal of it proudly displayed in a small yellow bikini— she was elegantly draped on a patio chair, a notebook and pen in her hands. She'd just come in from a shoot, and she was on her way back out to a shoot in the morning. He wondered if she would have flown back in if she hadn't been concerned about helping him with his guest list and the positioning. It somewhat amused him that she was so worried about where he'd put people for the reunion. Actually, he was quite certain she worried only about where he put Kathy.

The deep end of the pool might have suited Tara.

"Only the band members are staying at the house. And my father. My mother-in-law."

"You're divorced. You don't have a mother-in-law."

He shrugged. "I was only married once. And Sally is a great lady."

Tara wisely kept quiet on that one.

"The girls have their own rooms, so they're taken care of," Tara murmured. "For guests we need seven rooms, two for the parents, then there are your ex-wife, Larry Haley, Shelley Thompson, Miles Reeves, and Derrick Flanaghan. And they're all married or paired up, right?" She removed her glasses and stared at him. Her eyes were huge, a pure sky blue. She smiled. He felt guilty.

"We need eight," he said.

"Eight?"

"Shelley and Miles are coming alone. Larry has a new wife, and Derrick has been married forever. But I can't just presume that Kathy wants to be housed with this friend she's bringing."

"If she's bringing him, she probably wants to be 'housed' with him," Tara snapped.

"I doubt it. This fellow doesn't live with her in New York."

"How do you know?"

He sighed. "My daughters would have informed me of the situation."

"Then maybe she'd like to be housed with him for a change."

He shook his head. "I think she'd be uncomfortable. Her mother and her children will be here. I need two rooms for Kathy, so we need eight."

The house actually had fourteen bedrooms. The master was his, and the connecting bedroom he had turned into his office. His daughters each had a room. The largest bedroom in the right wing of the house was occupied by Joe and Peggy Garcia, the couple who were butler and housekeeper, managed everything regarding the home for him. A second room in the right wing housed Joe and Peggy's son, Angel, who was working his way through the U. of Miami by being a handyman and doing some gardening. Tara also had a room. She liked her separate space—and certainly needed it. She'd never "lived" with him, though she'd stayed with him often enough, and even on those occasions, had wanted her own space. She took up . . . space. Her bathroom was filled to the rim with different lotions, hand things, face things, body things. For a good night's sleep before a shoot, she liked to stretch out alone. But Jordan had also wanted his own space. The arrangement had worked out.

Despite the size of the main house, for the party he was planning, they were short a room.

"I can move into your room for the time," Tara said. "That will be easy enough."

"It isn't necessary."

"But I don't mind at all."

"No. My father and my daughters will be here, remember?"

"Oh, they don't know we sleep together?"

"Tara, we've always kept separate rooms."

"Jordan, you're over forty! Your daughters are grown up now, they know you have relationships— know that we have one! Under the circumstances, we should just give up the luxury of a little extra space. I don't mind."

"I do."

"You are beginning to hurt my feelings."

"I don't mean to. This is just one time when I need my space."

"So" she inquired with a sudden streak of rancor, "Do I just slip your ex-wife in with you?"

"You don't need to slip anyone anywhere, Tara. Peggy will work out who goes where."

"I'm trying to help you, Jordan."

Maybe he was being a louse.

"The main house has fourteen rooms, but," he reminded her, "you're forgetting the guest house."

"I am, as you should be!" she said, lifting her glasses again to stare at him. "The last time you all were together, the guest house burned to the ground. Who is going to want to stay where Keith died? You're not going to be able to put anyone else out there!"

"I'm not going to try to."

"Honestly, Jordan, you've become so damned weird over this whole thing! If you're not going to put a guest out there—"

He glanced her way, arching a brow, smiling slightly. "I'll be out there myself, Tara. It's exactly where I want to be."

Shelley Thompson sat in her small dressing room, staring at her reflection in the mirror. She moved closer. Good. A few little lines, that was natural. But all in all, she looked really good. The surgeon she was using now had the most deft hands in the universe. Up close, she might look thirty-five. At a distance, she could pass for a woman in her twenties. All right, late twenties. But she did look good. It wasn't going to be difficult to go back. Not on that level, at least.

Her hair had always been a dusty blond, and she kept it highlighted a few shades more to the gold. Her eyes were her best feature, large and green. Her nose had been fixed quite nicely, and she knew she had a pretty face.

The last decade had been both hard on her and good. For all of her life before, she'd had the band. She hadn't made decisions, she had gone with the flow. The money came in; she spent it. Then Blue Heron had been gone, and there she'd been. Like the others, she received a decent income. But she had expensive tastes—especially in plastic surgeons. And she did love jewelry. And clothes. On her own, she had one hell of a tendency to run into debt.

Jordan, though he had dissolved the band, would have helped her at any time. Any of the guys would have helped her. Kathy would have helped her.

But she hadn't wanted to go to them. To go back. She'd been afraid to go back. Keith was dead. Buried. Doors once closed were best left that way.

Sometimes, it seemed that the past came after her. Every once in a while, she'd get a phone call, a letter in the mail, and she'd know that the past never really let go.

But she wasn't going to confront it. Not alone.

So she'd managed on her own, and she hadn't done so badly. Most of the time, she did "oldies" in Vegas. A few times, she had gotten roles on Broadway. She went under the stage name of Shelley Adams, since she'd discovered different receptions to her past at different auditions. Some of the young kids directing now weren't very familiar with Blue Heron. Some of the directors were. Some wanted to gossip, and some didn't think rock stars belonged on Broadway, no matter what others had done in the past. As Shelley Adams, she'd done all right, though. She hadn't gotten a lead, hadn't stormed the Big Apple, but she'd worked steadily and she'd kept her five-foot-three-inch form in damned decent shape, to keep up with the twenty-year-olds.

She glanced at her watch. Fifteen minutes until showtime. Fifteen minutes. She had to call and call now.

She set her hand on the phone and plucked it up, then dialed the number she had known a very long time, but never used before.

She went through a receptionist, and was finally connected with Kathryn Connoly.

"Shelley?" came the surprised voice.

"Kath?"

"Yes. My God! How are you? What have you been up to? What have you been doing?"

Shelley smiled, twirling the wire in her fingers. It was good to hear Kathy's voice. So natural. The warmth was all there, the enthusiasm that was so *Kathy*.

"Working."

"Where?"

"All over. Mostly Vegas." She hesitated. "In New York now and then."

"Shelley! Why didn't you ever let me know? I'd have loved to have seen you!"

"Well, you know, the way you and Jordan split up, I guess we just all kind of assumed you wanted a new life with the past completely erased."

"You don't erase old friends!" Kathy admonished.

"Can you really erase old husbands?"

"Not completely," Kathy agreed.

"I . . . uh . . . have to be on in just a few minutes, lunch show out here, but I wanted to ask you— you are coming back for the reunion, right?"

"Yes. Are you?"

"Yeah, sure. I can't wait to see you!" Shelley rushed on. She meant it. The words were sincere. Kathy Treveryan— Connoly now— had been the best friend she'd ever had.

"You too, Shelley. You too. I can't wait to catch up."

"No new husbands, huh?"

"Nope. How about you?"

"I never married. You know me. Too fickle. I guess I'd better go now, the lunch crowd is the sober one, they know whether a show starts on time or not. Really, Kathy, I just can't wait."

"Me, too."

" 'Bye then. See you next week."

"Next week."

Shelley set the receiver down. She hesitated, picked it up, dialed, listened to the ringing. It was answered.

"She's coming."

"Definitely?"

"Definitely."

"Good."

"Yeah."

"Well, then, we'll all see each other next week, right?"

Shelley swallowed hard. "Right."

There was a click in her ear. With another hard swallow, she set the receiver down.

She stood, startled by the little blur in her eyes. She was afraid.

Showtime!

She worked for a living. She couldn't afford to forget that. Not for a minute. Not for anyone.

Not even for herself.

Derrick Flanaghan wheezed, gasped, and dripped more sweat—but kept going, running hard on his treadmill. He still had a week before going down to Florida, and if it halfway killed him, he was going to knock off ten more pounds before getting there.

From her armchair in their comfortable L.A. home, Judy shook her head, not looking his way. "You're going to kill yourself, Derrick. Drop dead of a heart attack."

He didn't answer her; he didn't have the breath to do so. But the timer on his machine mercifully buzzed then, and he slowed his gait. Down to a walk, he glanced at his wife.

Judy was wraith thin. She had a metabolism that moved a thousand miles an hour, or so it seemed. It might have come from sheer cussedness. Judy spoke her mind, did what she wanted, and moved mountains when she chose. What she lacked in tact she made up in energy. She hadn't wanted children; they didn't have any. Pets ruined carpets— they didn't have any of those, either. According to Judy, he couldn't really make music on his own. He'd never really tried. Actually, he was glad they'd never had children. He believed in the theory that children lived up to or down to their parents expectations. Judy was, in her terms, a realist.

His children would have been basket weavers.

But there was a lot that was good about Judy, too. She was striking. She always had been. Always would be. Her features were elegant. All of that energy of hers, which she'd never had to put into a job or family, had been given over to the perfection of her skin. She'd never needed to work out, but she loved tennis and ate only organic food. She and California had been made for one another.

And it had been the best place in the world for a man to find work writing advertising jingles.

Derrick grabbed his towel and mopped the sweat from his face, stepping from his treadmill to walk over to the bay window area of their bedroom where Judy was sitting in her chair, sipping iced tea as she leafed through magazines. She looked up at him. "You are dripping ickily upon me."

"Ickily?"

"Okay, you're gross."

"I'm no more than a few pounds overweight."

She grinned. Lifted a hand. Waved it in the air.

"You need a shower."

"I know. How about a sip of your tea first."

She sighed. Offered it to him. He swallowed it down. It was tart and strange. Bitter.

"Yuck. There's no sugar in it."

"You don't need sugar."

"No, it's fat you don't need."

"Derrick, if you've just been on a treadmill for an hour, you don't need fat or sugar. Trust me. And that tea is organic Oolong. It's delicious. Give it back if you don't like it."

"I'm too thirsty."

She shook her head, watching him. "You're like a little kid, all excited about going back."

"Darned right. I'll get to play again."

"You play the piano every day of your life."

"I write stupid lyrics and bubble-gum music. In Florida, I'll get to *play*."

Judy shook her head, looking back to her magazine. "You guys will probably stink."

"Thanks, Jude."

"I just look at things—"

"Realistically. I know."

She shrugged, then patted his hand, smiling up at him.

That was another of Judy's good qualities. She loved him. She wasn't a bowlful of optimism or encouragement, but she loved him for what she saw him to be.

He bent down and kissed her forehead despite the face she made at him. "Go take a shower!" she commanded.

"Yep," he said, turning and starting for the bath in their room. "And I am excited about going back! Aren't you?"

Judy set down her magazine. The bathroom door had already closed. He hadn't really been expecting an answer.

She looked outside and a shiver streaked down her spine. "Oh, yeah," she said softly. "I'm excited. I'm just so damned fucking excited I'm about to pee in my pants!"

Jordan stood by the window in his room, looking out at the guest house.

Eerie.

It could have been another time; the new structure was so similar to the old.

He heard her come to his room. Heard her slip through the doorway, come up behind him. Run a finger down his back. "Hey, old man!" she whispered softly. "I've got to leave soon."

"I know."

She leaned against him. He was still wearing cut-offs from the pool. The coolness of her face felt good against his skin.

She slipped a hand inside the waistband of his cut-offs. "Want to fool around?"

He wasn't sure what his answer might have been except that her touch was darned persuasive. He turned, taking her into her arms, wondering if he was getting old, or worse, if he was losing his mind, becoming obsessed with the past, with his past . . .

With a woman who had left him as if she were running from something evil, slamming an iron gate behind her.

He told himself that Tara was perfection. That she was what every man wanted. Warm, giving. Sleek, curved, slim, musky, enticing. She all but purred. Her breath was hot mint, her fingers were nimble, she moved like a cat. Her heart thundered as their lips met, as they groped one another by the window. Her excitement was instantaneous, contagious. She knew how to arouse, how to tease. She gave back all she demanded.

Her lips parted from his, her voice breathy as she spoke while he tore away the strings of her bikini.

"Jordan . . . the floor . . . the floor."

"The bed."

"The floor. Here, now."

"The bed." As passionate as she could make him feel, he felt like laughing. "My back can't take the floor."

She was agreeable. Yet as she drew him down, he seemed to suddenly withdraw into himself.

Her room. They'd always made love in her room. Or . . . elsewhere. Never in here. This had really become his private sanctuary. It held too much of the past. He could remember bringing the girls home as babies. They'd lain on the bed between him and Kathy while he and she marveled at the perfection they'd created.

Tara crawled over him. Lips and hands touching, stroking. He responded. Held her. Touched her. Heard her excited little cries . . .

She had a great body. Stomach flat, perfectly smooth. Kathy had two tiny little white lines that stretched from her pubis upward toward her belly button. They hadn't distressed her terribly. She'd acquired one with each child. She'd teased him, saying that if they ever did decide they wanted more than the two children they'd agreed upon, they'd have to procreate in even numbers since she wanted even stretch marks. He'd told her he liked the slight imperfections of those marks, they were special, they were unique . . .

They were. He'd always liked her body. A little bit heavier, a bit thinner. She was long, with just the right curves. Nice breasts, not too big, not miniscule. Nipples a dusky rose shade, darkened just a little after the kids. Her body had been a part of her. Like her face. The way the amber tints in her eyes could change. The way she could smile. The million ways she could laugh, whisper . . .

Too bad she hadn't decently decayed with time, he thought. Gained a hundred pounds, grown warts on her nose, turned to stone. Or married one of her writers, a publishing mogul . . .

Her young Muscleman. With whom she was sleeping even now?

Tara was good. Damned good.

And despite it, he felt something within— and without— withering away.

He pulled away from her suddenly, maybe just a little bit embarrassed.

"Jordan?" she asked softly.

Back to life, old man! he admonished himself. You can't bring back the past! *His wife had left him, he hadn't left his wife.*

Maybe he could bring her back here, but it remained true that he couldn't bring back the past. Their past.

He looked out the window again. Twilight was falling. Nighttime. Darkness to wash away the reminders. Ten years had gone by. He'd kept on living. Hell, he'd lived well and heartily, many a day.

And life would go on still, after the reunion, he reminded himself bleakly.

But not here, not tonight. Too many ghosts were haunting this bed.

He stood up, forgot that he would wreck his back, and swept Tara off the bed. Her brows shot up, her lips curled into a smile.

"Yeah? Where are we going?"

"I like your room better."

"You do?"

"Yeah. With the scent of your perfume all around . . ."

"Mmm . . ." she murmured, curling naked and sinuous, against him.

Yet later he'd showered industriously, trying to rid himself of her scent. And when he'd said good-bye and she had left to fly away, he'd been

glad to go back to his solitary vigil once again,
staring out at the night.

At the guest house.

The back looked just exactly the same.

Maybe, just maybe, he could bring the past
back to life.

Miles Reeves sat in the darkness of his back
porch. Just this spring Megan had convinced
him to screen it in for the coming summer. At
the time, he had thought she was crazy. Boston— all of Massachusetts and all of the North-
east, for that matter— had just endured one of
the most brutal winters on record. But Megan
had been right; summer was proving to be hot
as all blazes, and at this time of night, or morning as it might be, the porch was beautiful.

He picked up his flute, absently, lovingly, running his fingers over the instrument. Funny to
think back. Not that he didn't think about Blue
Heron often enough. They all thought about
Blue Heron because radio and video stations
played their old music regularly. But he'd gotten
used to that. He could even listen and think with
pride that they'd been good, damned good.
They would endure. Years from now, radio and
video stations would still be playing Blue Heron
music, other groups would copy them, learn
from them.

Well, once around again for Blue Heron. It
seemed a good idea. With or without Keith's
death, Miles thought, the group would have

split. Keith, dead or alive, was or would have been the cause. But now they were going back.

He broodingly looked up from his flute. Though he sat in the darkness, the street lights from his busy Boston suburb filtered in enough light to create some vision, some shadow. The hutch at the far wall of the porch held a large mirror, and he could see himself as he sat in his wicker rocker, next to the wicker table on which he had rested his flute, where his fingers still played idly over his favorite instrument. He hadn't changed. In the darkness, he might have been the same man. Medium height, medium build. Freckled face, hazel eyes, headful of red hair. By the light of day, there was some gray interwoven with the red, but now, in this sweet, dim shadow, he looked just the same as he had the day he had met Jordan, Keith, and Kathy; the day they had graduated from Juilliard, the day they had finally hit the charts with their first Blue Heron single.

He smiled suddenly. He didn't miss the notoriety of the band. He and Kathy had always been the shyest, okay on stage, moving to the background when fans came too close or the media converged. What a strange group they'd been. He and Kathy the peacemakers, Jordan the undisputed leader, Keith the undisputed genius. Shelley always ready to tear into anyone over Keith, Judy the one with the complaints. Derrick obedient to his wife, Larry impatient with them all.

And all of them with their secrets. Strange

little secrets. Like dominos, one secret bared and the whole row begins to topple.

He didn't miss the wild applause in a concert hall. He liked what he did now, loved it, in fact. He was with a small group of players calling themselves The Molly Maguires, and they worked well and frequently in Boston and the surrounding areas. They had a set gig at Tim O'Malley's Fine Dining and Pub from Thursdays to Sundays, but they were also able to play special performances elsewhere because O'Malley—who really did own his "fine dining and pub"—was willing to give newcomers a chance to fill in for The Molly Maguires.

Miles was also going to be able to leave for Florida because The Molly Maguires was a group of six and they could all fill in for one another when the occasion arose.

And oddly enough, as much as he dreaded it, he was anxious to go back. He wanted to play with Jordan again. Miles's mother being Brenda O'Casey of the O'Caseys of Cork, he did love his Irish music. But with Jordan, he could play anything. They were the two who had always loved the flute and guitar above all else, the two who had most enjoyed adding elements of Gaelic, classical, folk, and other musical forms to their rock. He did miss playing with Jordan. Missed talking with him and Kathy. Missed . . . Shelley.

How strange. He had been in love with Shelley all of his life. She hadn't been in love with him. Or maybe she had, just a little bit, at the end. It hadn't mattered. She had always been his best friend. Strange, though, once they'd left Blue Heron for the last time, they'd never seen one another again. Never called.

Because there were just too many damned secrets among those who had been in Blue Heron. And one knew just who knew whose secrets . . .

He looked out into the shadows of his tree-lined yard and closed his eyes. He should go in to bed. If Megan woke, she would worry. He didn't want that. Megan played with The Molly Maguires as well. She was a flutist, and had a beautiful, soft, pure soprano. Perfect for their work. He'd lived with her for a little more than five years now. He cared for her a great deal; she was one of the nicest, sweetest, most compassionate women he had ever known. She had just turned forty last May, and though she never said a word to him, he knew that she wanted marriage and a chance at a family before it became too late even with today's reproductive capabilities. He wanted to fall in love with her, wanted to marry her, wanted to make her happy.

But always held back.

Because of the secrets that still haunted Blue Heron? Because of Shelley?

He didn't know. Life could seem so insane. People lost people, people went on. As they all had. He loved Megan.

Jordan had acquired a succession of lovers.

Shelley had always had a succession of lovers.

He had Megan, and Kathy, well . . . Kathy

had always been quiet and discreet, the best keeper of secrets.

Was Jordan pulling Blue Heron back together again to attempt to retrieve his lost wife? If rumor had it right, he was involved with a glamorous young model/actress, more model than actress, but then Clint Eastwood hadn't started off an Olivier.

Jordan was an unusual man. His thoughts—feelings, ideas, emotions, music—were passionate and deep. Maybe he was still in love with Kathy. Just as Miles had been in love with a distant ghost, Shelley Thompson, all these years.

What did it matter? They were going back. Miles, too. He couldn't have refused if he'd wanted to. He felt like a lead slug being pulled by a magnet.

Maybe he wanted a life when it was over. Maybe he wanted to exorcise Shelley, marry Megan.

Yet . . .

What if *all* the secrets were to come out?

One thing was certain.

Once again there would be an explosion.

And they would, each man and woman, survive.

Or they would burn.

Eight

Packing to go to Star Island was strange.

Even getting on the plane Friday night was a bit rough. Though she wasn't afraid of flying, Kathy found herself gripping her seat from the second she sat down.

Her mother wasn't coming down until Sunday or Monday, the girls had gone ahead to Florida on Wednesday night. Alex, though still in college, made her summer income by independent means. She'd never hesitated in attempting to sell her photographs to newspapers and magazines, and she already had a few major credits behind her. She was a lot like her father in that. Jordan had always known what he wanted and had gone straight for it. Bren wasn't quite as assertive or as certain about her future, but she had talked about taking a summer job. Kathy assumed that meant the others had known about this reunion a long time ago.

"You are tense!" Jeremy told her. He seemed as happy as could be. He loved the size of the seat, and the fact that he'd been plied with champagne since they'd boarded the plane. Jor-

dan had sent them two first-class round-trip tick-
ets despite her assurance that she'd come on her
own. It was a business expense, he had told her,
all wrapped up in the benefit performance.

Though Jeremy was relaxed, as the flight came
closer to Miami, Kathy's apprehension grew. This
was a mistake. She had flown away nearly a decade ago. She had lived with her decision, hadn't
ever tried to come back, because she hadn't dared
take a closer look at what she had done.

She was flying straight into ten days of torture
which would be sure to leave her miserable for
the rest of her life.

Dinner came and went. She felt fingers curl
over hers on the plush chair and she turned to
Jeremy. His eyes were warm, concerned. "It's going to be okay."

"Is it?"

"I promise."

"I'm crazy. No woman in her right mind
would do this."

"In my opinion, no woman in her right mind
would work the hours you do, so we're certainly
agreed you're halfway crazy at least."

She tried to smile. The champagne should
have helped, but she still felt frozen. As if she
couldn't talk or smile, move her head to the
right or the left.

The plane landed. She had forgotten how
much she hated Miami International Airport.
And it had gotten worse. On a Friday night, the
place was a mad pool of people speaking various
languages, bustling about, rudely brushing by

one another, all in a hurry. Still, she had barely stepped from the plane and into the Friday-night melee when a handsome young man stepped up to her. "Kathy? Er . . . Ms Connoly?"

She knew him . . . and didn't know him. She paused, half-smiling, staring at him. "Angel!" she gasped suddenly. She dropped her overnight case on the floor with surprise, hugging the man who smiled broadly, hugging her back with enthusiasm. Finally she pulled back, studying the boy. He had been twelve years old when she had seen him last. All dark eyes and floppy black hair. Now he was tall, lean, trim, and exceedingly handsome, with a very Latin flair despite his mother's English background.

"Ms Connoly, it's great to have you back," Angel said.

"Thank you. It's wonderful to see you. My God, you've grown!"

"Well, I should hope so, Ms Connoly," he said, flushing slightly.

"Angel, you always called me Kathy. Please don't stop now. And, of course, you've grown. I'm sorry, I— Jeremy, Angel Garcia. His folks run the Star Island estate. Angel, Jeremy Hunt, a very good friend."

The two shook hands. Angel reached for Kathy's overnight bag. "Jordan had planned on coming to the airport himself, but there's been a sudden surge in the press interest in all of this, and he's trying to keep a low profile until the benefit. You know, he wants to keep his daughter's birthday party as private as possible, and naturally he doesn't want the media around while you all practice for the performance."

"Ummm. He didn't leave much practice time, did he?" Kathy queried. "Think the media should hear us even when they're supposed to?"

Angel laughed. "I think you'll all be great. It will be like riding a bicycle. One jam session together and you'll be in perfect harmony."

"You really think so?"

"Well, if not, I do think you'll be ready by Saturday night!" he grinned.

"Let's hope."

"People will come out of curiosity and because it's a benefit performance for a good cause."

Kathy smiled wryly. "Yes, but we were *good!* We have our pride to maintain, you know."

Angel shrugged. "You'll be good," he said with assurance. "Jordan has never stopped playing. He'll whip everyone together."

"He always did," Kathy said lightly.

Angel grinned. "Let me get you both out of this madhouse. Mom and Dad can't wait to see you, Kathy."

"I've missed them," she said, but once again she thought she was insane to do this. It was going to be too painful. She should never have agreed to come.

But the drive from the airport to Star Island was somehow good. She had loved the city of Miami at night. Night hid the blemishes, the homeless sleeping beneath the bridges downtown, the graffiti that marred most major cities, and the inevitable trash of such a large metropolis. Night brought out the beauty of light on water, the balmy breezes. Starlight made the Miami River shimmer; the moonglow on the bay let each tiny whitecap glitter as if a spray of diamonds rested over the seas. Bridges arched and rose, the skyscrapers of downtown created their own glow in the night. It was the right time for the city. And oddly enough, as much as she dreaded arriving at the house, she was comfortable in the night in the city, back where she loved to be.

They left downtown behind, heading on the expressway across to the bridge toward the beach, turning off onto the bridge to the island. She was vaguely aware when they passed through the guard gate and moved onto Star Island. She loved the island as well. Granted, it could have a brash quality to it. It was often a haven for the rich— and nouveaux riches. But it was a haven for intriguing and interesting nouveaux riches. Gangsters had made their homes here in the thirties; an Arabian prince had sent real estate skyrocketing here when he had borrowed millions to redo his mansion . . . before defaulting on all the loans. Actors, actresses, rock stars had often come here, along with bankers, newspaper moguls, old-time money, Jews, Gentiles, Canadians, the Irish, founding fathers, Middle Easterners.

A deep U-shaped driveway ran from the front of the house to the street, heavy iron gates breaking the barrier of the coral rock wall. Parts of the house itself were built of coral rock, along with thick concrete, cement block, and stucco. The front was flanked by a glassed-in patio surrounded by high archways decorated with gargoyles. The driveway led to seven tile steps and the canopied archway before the front door.

When they'd bought the place, it had needed paint badly. The little gargoyles had been sad indeed.

Now, everything was pristine, Kathy noted. And when she stepped out of the car to start up the steps, a trembling began inside her, attacking her limbs, fingers, and feet. She clutched her purse and overnight bag more tightly, felt Jeremy's fingers wind supportively around her arm.

She had been insane. This was her house. She should never have come back to it. She wouldn't be able to nod and be dignified when Tara Hughes smiled good night, clutched Jordan's arm, and walked up to Kathy's bedroom. She couldn't be a guest here, she couldn't be polite, unchurlish. No one could expect her to. She had to go back. She had—

"Kathy!"

The door had opened, and Jordan was coming down down the steps, the girls behind him. He was genuinely pleased, taking her hand, turning to Jeremy as the girls hugged her, both talking away a mile a minute.

Maybe they had been afraid that she couldn't do it, couldn't come.

But she was here. And now, with a child on either side of her and Jordan asking Jeremy about their flight, she could not run. She was being led up the steps.

"Kathryn, Kathryn, oh, it is so good to see you!" Peggy Garcia said, greeting her as she stepped through the arched entry doors and into the foyer. Peggy looped her arms around Kathy, holding her tight, then backing away. "My Lord, you haven't changed, you don't look a day older than when you left here. Thin . . . you're thinner. What have you been doing? Too much organic food?"

Kathy laughed, looking Peggy over at the same time. She was skinny as a rail herself and always had been. She had a touch of an English accent remaining, which sometimes sounded a bit odd, because after all her years of marriage to Joe, she interspersed her English now and then with Spanish words and Cuban expressions.

"Peggy, leave her be! Calling her skinny! That's the pot calling the kettle black, eh, *chica*?" Garcia said to Kathy. Tall and lean himself, with distinguishedly graying hair and coal dark eyes; he stepped up next to his wife, offering Kathy a warm hug. Again, it was sweet. Again, it was painful. She had left so much behind.

"Joe, you are as devilishly handsome as ever," she assured him, touching his cheek and looking back to Peggy who was still smiling, still warm, and still watching her with something like grave concern. "Peggy, I have missed you so much. And your son is all grown up, I didn't even recognize him!"

"The kids have gotten big, eh?" Peggy Garcia smiled.

"Big kids, big trouble," Jordan said, stepping into the foyer with Jeremy and Joe at his side, the three of them bringing in luggage.

"We've been waiting for you to head out to South Beach," Alex said, slipping an arm around her mother.

"South Beach? Tonight?" Kathy asked, dismayed. She'd gotten up at five to finish packing and she'd put in a whole day of work. She'd clenched her chair arm for the entire flight. She couldn't go out. Not tonight.

"Mom, you have been gone a long time," Bren moaned, her amber eyes wide. "It's the most happening place in the world. The clubs are great."

"Is she old enough for those clubs?" Kathy asked Jordan. He'd changed again since she'd seen him last. Shaved. The beard and mustache were gone. He looked younger. She felt more haggard.

"I let her go with her sister and Angel and a friend of his— don't worry, it's a guy I've checked out."

"This can be a dangerous city."

"Right. That's why we've been waiting for you to come out with us. So you can look after us," Alex said cheerfully. "Ask Dad, there's some great music out there. We know what to avoid and what's okay."

"And how to manage ourselves," Bren murmured dryly. "But, Mom, we want to go out with you."

"Kathy, I've been dying to see South Beach," Jeremy urged. She was certain that Bren had just stomped on his foot, "hinting" for help.

She looked to Peggy for help herself. "You've all just got to forgive me. Jordan, honest, I know they'll be happy with you—"

"Not on your life," Jordan said. "I've been staying in for the last week. I've been tripping over paparazzi out there lately.

"Dad is acting old and weary. We had high hopes for you," Alex said. She stood as her father did, leaning back slightly, her arms crossed over her chest as she smiled at Kathy, still certain of a good response, now that she'd been challenged.

But Kathy shook her head. "I can't. Honest to God."

"Jeremy is dying to see South Beach," Bren reminded her.

"And Jeremy should see it," Kathy said. "He won't mind going with you."

"But Mom—" Bren began again.

"Hey!" Alex said suddenly to her sister. "You know, if she's worn out, she's worn out. And if Jeremy wants to come, he's welcome. Right?"

"Well, I don't know. If Kathy is tired—" Jeremy began.

"Mom wouldn't dream of holding you back," Bren said. Both of Kathy's daughters stared at her innocently.

"Excuse me!" Joe Garcia interrupted. "Angel and me, we will take the bags on up to the rooms, eh? He'll be right back down and take anyone who decides to go down to the beach. Eh, Jordan?"

Jordan, slightly on the outside of the group, arms crossed over his chest and his stance similar to that of his oldest daughter, smiled and nodded. "Sounds good to me. Girls, you haven't let your mother and Mr. Hunt out of the doorway. Want to give them a little breathing space?"

"Sure," Alex said, edging toward the two tiled steps that led down to the massive, high-ceilinged living room of the house. Toward the back wall a broad, curving stairway led up to the second floor. To the right, another few steps led out to the rear glassed-in patios, and to the far left, a coral rock fireplace stretched across half the wall. "Jeremy, you're not too tired, are you? You don't need to change, you look great."

And he did—as always. He had a flair for clothes. He wore jeans, but they were jet black unfaded, well pressed. His shirt was a cool blue silk. He could pass for well dressed or casual.

"No, I . . . uh . . . don't need to change," he said, but he looked quickly to Kathy. "I don't feel that I should go—"

"It's all right, really," she insisted.

"Great!" Alex said. She kissed her mother's cheek, then her father's, and grabbed Jeremy's hand. "Tell Angel we headed out to the car. Love you both. Don't wait up. We won't be too late."

She was out the door in a flash, dragging Jeremy behind her. Bren, looking a bit guilty, kissed her mother, then her father, then her mother again, and hurried after the other two.

"What can I get for you?" Peggy asked Kathy. "Are you hungry? Airplane food is so awful—"

"The plane food was just fine," Kathy said. "I'm not hungry in the least."

Joe and Angel came back down the stairs then. Angel arched a brow to Jordan and looked at Kathy.

"The Wild Bunch is in the car," Jordan said. "Kathy, we haven't convinced you to come?"

She shook her head. "No, thank you. Have a nice night. And keep a good eye on my daughters, will you?"

He grinned. "I always do."

He turned, kissed his mother, nodded to his father and Jordan, and started on out. "Don't wait up, they'll be in good hands, I promise."

When the door had closed, Joe cleared his throat. "I, for one, cannot wait up for the young ones. If you will all excuse me . . . Jordan, if there is nothing else you need?"

"All set, Joe. Thanks . . . and good night."

"Peggy?" her husband queried.

"I think Kathy needs something to eat," Peggy said stubbornly.

"Peggy, I'm fine, honest. And if I weren't—"

"If she weren't, and if I intended to starve her, she'd still remember where the kitchen was," Jordan said firmly.

Peggy grimaced. "Mock me if you will!" she said good-naturedly. "Good night then." Impulsively she hugged Kathy again. "It is just so good to see you back, *mia amiga!*" she whispered affectionately. But she quickly joined her husband then, bidding them both good night.

When they were gone, Kathy found herself still in the foyer, alone with Jordan. A sudden, sharp, knifing sweep of nostalgia swept over her. Nothing had changed here. Nothing. She could see the huge Chesterfield she had bought— in dreadful condition and refurbished herself— sitting across from the fireplace, right where it had always been. Her handsome Cavalier paintings still hung on the walls. The wicker furnishings were out on the glassed-in patio.

"Well, welcome back," Jordan said lightly.

She grinned ruefully. "The girls were really anxious to see me."

"They've only been away from you for two days," he reminded her.

"I really hope you didn't stay here to be polite."

"I stayed here because I haven't the stamina to go out."

She nodded, felt her heart take a damning plunge, and inquired, "Where's Miss Hughes?"

"Bimini."

"Oh?"

"She had a shoot. I imagine she'll arrive for the party by Monday."

"Oh," Kathy murmured.

"Come on in. I can't believe your daughters didn't get you all the way into the house before disappearing. With your friend."

Kathy kept quiet, hurrying ahead when she felt

his hand on the small of her back, urging her toward the patio. She took the steps down, sank gratefully onto the well-padded armchair near the sliding door to the pool and outside area.

Jordan came after, stepping behind the bar. For a second she winced as she heard a blender whir. She arched a brow as he approached her with a something that looked like a chocolate Slurpee.

"Mudslide. Alex's invention."

"She isn't twenty-one yet," Kathy murmured, accepting the drink.

"They were in honor of you."

"Weren't they all supposed to share in it then?" Kathy queried, watching as he walked back across the bar, taking one of the tall rattan seats. She suddenly smiled. "I mean, this is an awkward situation, isn't it? The ex-wife coming back to her old house?"

"I don't feel awkward."

"I sure as hell do."

He shrugged, a glitter of amusement in his eyes. "Drink the damned mudslide then. Relax."

"Just another night around the house, right?" Kathy queried. She sipped the drink. It *tasted* like a chocolate Slurpee. A little sweet, but smooth and easy. She sipped it again. What the hell! She presumed she could sleep all morning if she chose.

"Is it really that hard for you to go out now?" she asked him, a touch of sympathy in her voice.

He nodded. Waved a hand in the air. "Most of the time I do what I please. I might be asked for a few autographs if I go out to dinner. But there's been a surge of renewed interest since the movie business started up. A few of the weekly tabloids have hit on the fact that Keith will have been dead for exactly ten years on the night of the benefit. It's made things a little uncomfortable. How about you? How's your job? Do you get hounded about the past?"

She shook her head. "Not often. My young authors usually don't associate me with any kind of fame. Some people are aware of my connection with Blue Heron, but most of them are through with asking questions about that by now."

"What about your older authors? Do they ever wonder why a rock star turned into an editor?"

She shrugged. "I always tell them rock stars like to have backup careers, that they wear out and want to get out somewhere along the line."

"So which was it with you? Did you get old or worn out?"

"Both."

"You're a liar," he said suddenly.

"Damn you, Jordan, I like my work, I *love* my work!"

"I'm not disputing that! Yes, you love books, writing, words, you always have!" She sensed tension in him again, the same tension she had felt when he had gripped her arms so tightly that night in New York. "But you didn't change your life because you were old or because you were tired or because you were afraid you would be.

What you did was drop out. You just dropped out."

"All right," she said smoothly after a moment. "Maybe I wasn't old or tired. Maybe I got hurt."

"You left me," he shot back swiftly.

"You divorced me," she reminded him, as quickly.

"You left me and took my children to a hotel room in New York."

"I booked two hotel rooms in New York. If you had wanted to talk with me, I was waiting."

"I don't remember an invitation. I didn't know I was supposed to come, that it was a command performance. You walked out on me. Left me."

"Damn it, Jordan, I might have moved out of the house. But you'd left me long before I walked out." She was silent a second, then told him, "It seemed you actually left me the night Keith died."

He was dead silent then, staring at her. He stood, walking to the patio doors.

After a moment he spoke, his voice deep and husky with a startling emotion. "You *lied* to me."

"I lied? About what?"

"About being with Keith."

She stood herself, both surprised, dismayed, and amazingly hurt all over again. "I didn't lie to you. I wasn't over there."

"I *saw* you."

"I don't know who or what you saw, but it wasn't me! Damn you, Jordan, it wasn't me!"

She realized suddenly that *nothing* had changed. Nothing at all. They'd had this same argument before.

The very night she had left.

She set her drink down on the coffee table before the chair. "We've had this fight before!" she reminded him angrily. "I will not get into it again!"

He was silent, staring at her. Then, "I'm sorry."

Sorry? Did he mean it.

"Really, I'm sorry."

"Sorry because you caused a fight tonight, within thirty minutes of my arrival? Sorry that you still believe I'm a liar? Or sorry that you thought I was one to begin with?" she demanded.

"Kathy, I—"

"Fine."

"I was about to say I believe you. I just don't know what the hell happened back then."

"I don't know either," she murmured. "But I really am exhausted, and I don't want to revive old fights. I'm going to bed. Thank you for the drink, for the hospitality."

She spun around and started for the stairs with great dignity. Halfway there, she realized that she was wrong, that something had changed. She had changed. She wasn't his wife anymore, and it wasn't her house anymore.

She might be going to bed, but she didn't know *where*.

She turned back to him, clearing her throat, trying to maintain the precious dignity that was so damned important to her. "Excuse me. Which room is mine for my stay?"

"Your old one."

"What?" She didn't mean to snap it out; she did.

"Don't worry; I won't be in it."

"Oh." She hesitated, then curiosity got the better of her. "You moved out of the master bedroom?"

He shrugged. "Just for the time being. I needed the rooms. Jeremy has my office. I didn't know what kind of arrangements you wanted. With the whole crew coming in along with your mom and my dad, I needed all the rooms in the main house. I'm out in the guest house for this time."

"I don't like putting you out of your own house."

"The guest house is mine as well."

"I would have been fine out there."

He arched a brow at her. "I didn't know if anyone would be comfortable there."

"Oh!" she gasped, remembering Keith and the fire. "I . . . I wouldn't have been afraid." Now she was lying. The guest house, rebuilt, might be just a bit eerie.

"Kathy, I want to be out in the guest house."

"Yes, but what about . . . Tara?"

He didn't blink. "Tara has her own room here, the one we called the Blue Room. She likes lots of space for her things. We . . . both like space."

"Oh. Still . . ."

"If you'll be too uncomfortable, I can have Peggy rearrange the room assignments."

"No, it's all right. Good night."

"Good night."

She turned away from him and hurried up the stairs, knowing then exactly where she was going. Third door down the hallway to the left, the huge room with the wonderfully decadent bath that looked out over the patio and pool area, to the bay— to the guest house.

The light was on when she came into the bedroom. She saw it and its contents instantly and it was like being hit by bricks. It was the same. The huge bed with the old brass fittings, customized to the new size. The sheer curtains beneath the heavier brocade, the early American dressers, washstand and wardrobe. The black and peach patterned Oriental rug on the floor over the polished hard wood. She swallowed. She almost felt as if she had been physically punched, a right-hander from Rocky, straight into the gut. She closed her eyes. Oh, God, it hadn't changed.

She forced herself to step into the room. Her suitcase had been set on the floor. She grunted as she threw it up on the bed, opened it blindly, dug out her things. She started for the bathroom, hesitated, biting her lip as she wondered what she would find within it that belonged to Tara Hughes. But Miss April kept her own room— she needed lots of space. Still, mightn't she have a few things in Jordan's bath?

To Kathy's relief, she did not. The bathroom was as masculine as Jordan himself. It was tiled in black and beige, the fixtures were gold-plated. The tub was a huge Jacuzzi, the one they had ordered as one of their first expenses for the place. There was a separate shower, double sinks. She laid out her toiletries, stared at her reflection as she brushed her hair. This was torture. She was nuts.

That had already been established.

He was still convinced he had seen her running to Keith the night of the fire.

God, why? How could he?

She turned away from the mirror, startled that tears were stinging her eyes. It was why she had left. And damn, she had been right. He still didn't believe her, no matter what he said. And if he didn't believe her, wasn't it possible that he thought even worse of her. Not just that she had been cheating on him in some strange way, but that she might have been responsible for the drugs Keith had taken, for the fire that had started?

Mechanically, she turned on the water in the shower. She'd been so exhausted. Now she felt restless.

She showered, the past and present a frightening blur in her mind. She stepped from the shower and wrapped herself in a towel. Found her nightgown, slipped it on. Brushed her teeth. Mechanically. Things to do for bed. Like breathing.

She wished she'd finished the mudslide. Had more champagne on the plane. Kept a bottle of Valium in her suitcase.

She left the bath and returned to the bedroom. Gazing around it before switching off the light, she lay down on the bed, and cursed herself for remembering the feel of it. Memories flooded back to her. Good memories. So many good memories. They'd talked in bed, argued in bed, made love in bed. She laid her suitcase on this bed when she was packing to leave. She could remember it with painful clarity. She had packed because they had quit talking. Because there had been something in the way he looked at her. *Because he hadn't believed in her anymore, hadn't believed what she was saying. He didn't persist in calling her a liar, he just looked at her with eyes that accused her, the warmth had left his touch. She was desperate to talk, but he wouldn't talk. She could remember the night before she left, lying here, lying beside him.*

"Say it, Jordan, damn you, say what's on your mind!"

But he was silent, staring up at the ceiling, his fingers laced behind his head.

"There's nothing more to say."

"I wasn't with Keith the night he died."

"I know, you told me."

"But you don't believe me."

"It's over."

"Damn you, Jordan, you don't believe it is!"

"Keith is dead; for God's sake, leave it alone."

"We need to talk—"

"Go to sleep, Kathy. Keith is dead."

Keith was dead. The fire that had consumed him now a bitter, haunting scent wrapped around their lives. She slammed a fist against Jordan's chest. "You bastard, you stinking, self-righteous bastard. Yes! Keith is dead. And so are we! I hate you for what you think and feel. I hate you, I hate you—''

She kept slamming her knotted fists against him. Suddenly he was swearing, shouting back. Suddenly she was in his arms and they were saying hateful things, and in their fury, they were making love, cursing one another still. Even as he lay atop her spent, she whispered out the lie that seemed the only way to salvage something of her pride and soul.

"I hate you for this, Jordan, damn you!"

She didn't hate him. She wanted to touch him somehow, really reach him. Striking him, loving him, none of it seemed to matter anymore. She couldn't really get into his heart, his soul or his mind. She had lost something special that had been hers for so very much of her life.

He turned his back on her. The distance gaped between them on the bed. She wanted to touch him so badly, to shake him, make him believe her. But she had tried. Something was in his mind, and he wouldn't believe her. The next day when they'd gone to the studio, she'd come out to find him laughing with the receptionist. He hadn't laughed with her since Keith had died. She'd walked past him, and out of the place. She'd thought he would follow her. She had still thought he would follow when she'd packed that night. Rashly, angrily. It hadn't been the receptionist. It had been the look in his eyes.

He hadn't followed her home, and he certainly hadn't followed her to New York. He'd filed divorce papers instead.

There was no way she could sleep.

She stood. She walked around the room. Prowled it.

At last came to a halt.

She stood by the window in what used to be her room, looking out at the night on what used to be her patio. Oh, God. She shouldn't have left. She should have forced every issue. Fought him harder. She'd been hurt; he'd been hurt. She'd run.

She shouldn't have left.

But, dear God, for the sake of her heart and soul, she shouldn't have come back.

The moon was a crescent, high in the night sky. Its glow was picked up in the azure pool water below her. Beyond the pool and the columns and the trellis, the night lights set crystal prisms down upon the darkness of the bay water.

And to her left, was the guest house.

At the upstairs bedroom window, there was a silhouette.

As she was silhouetted, she realized. The bedroom light was not on in the guest house and she did not have her light on. Her room was illuminated by a soft glow from the bathroom, as was the bedroom of the guest house.

A man stood by the window. She couldn't make out his face, much less his eyes, yet she knew it was Jordan, knew he was watching her as she watched him. A tall, silent, dark sentinel, watching her.

Even as she stared out across the space between them, he lifted a hand to her. She lifted hers without thinking in response.

Minutes ticked by. He did not turn away. Neither did she. Then he lifted his hand again, and moved away from the window at last.

And her heart began to thunder.

He was leaving the room. Coming to her.

Because the fight wasn't done. And they were going to fight it again.

Nine

Kathy turned from the window herself, cursing softly beneath her breath.

Why was she so sure he was coming here?

Because once again, she had no makeup on, and her choice of nightwear was simple, cotton, tailored. She was clean—that was the best she could say for herself.

What difference does it make? she taunted herself. If he was coming, he was coming just to talk.

It was human nature. She wanted to look good. Sexy. She was competing with Tara Hughes, for God's sake. No, she wasn't . . . She had left the ring.

She heard him tapping on her door. God, he could move fast when he wanted to!

She bit into her lower lip. Tired, she was really tired, she'd just tell him that; she couldn't keep on talking.

The door opened a crack. "Kathy?" It was Jordan's room, Jordan's house, and he was . . . Jordan.

"Kathy, damn it, are you all right?"

She inhaled and exhaled, alarmed by the hot tremors that seemed to be streaking through her.

She found strength and life and hurried across to the door, opening it the rest of the way. "Jordan, I'm fine. Just tired, really tired . . ."

She broke off, staring at him. He looked wonderful. Face so smooth now, hair a little shaggy and silvered. He was wearing a black terry robe, open at the throat and chest, falling just to his knees. His gaze was intense as he looked down at her. "Kathy . . ."

Her name was a strange, pained whisper. She felt as if something caught in her throat, as if her breath were being subtly sucked away.

"Kathy . . ."

Then suddenly his eyes lifted from hers. He was staring past her and through the window. "What the hell is that? What is going on?" he demanded, striding past her to stare hard outside.

"What?" she said, hurrying after him.

Looking out, she saw what he had seen. Light in the guest house. A small vein of light, like that from a flashlight. Moving.

Jordan turned from the window, starting back across the room.

"Wait!" Kathy exclaimed.

He paused, annoyed as he looked at her.

"Jordan, it could be dangerous, a prowler. Can't you just call the police? This place has an alarm, right? Call security!"

"No, I want to see who it is *myself.*"

He started out of the room again. She followed closely behind him. He stopped.

"What are you doing?"

"Going with you."

"Kathy, it may be— "

"Dangerous. Right. You shouldn't be going."

"Kathy, stay here!"

He started out again. She waited until he was halfway down to the first floor, then she charged after him, silent in her bare feet.

He swung on her. "Kathy— "

"Go! I'm behind you."

"Stay behind me!"

"I will!"

He strode through the living room and into and out of the large kitchen, thereby following a path that skirted around the grounds rather than traversing the lighted patio area. They moved quickly along the brush to the side door of the guest house, slipping inside that way. Jordan hesitated, picking up an old baseball bat from the pantry, then coming into the living-room area. The guest house was silent. He started up the stairs with her behind him. She kept peering into the dimly lit darkness, making certain no one was coming upon them from behind, while he kept his eyes glued in the direction they followed.

They reached the second floor. She watched his fingers curl tightly around the bat as they came up into the bedroom, the only room of the second floor. Kathy saw the light, moving . . .

Close up behind Jordan, she instinctively

clutched his hips, trying to look around him. Then she saw his shoulders slump as the tension suddenly eased from them.

"What is it?"

"Nothing!" he muttered in self-disgust, moving aside to allow her a view of the room. To the far side, she saw that a light in the closet had been left on. The flow of an air-conditioning vent was causing a sleeve to flutter backward and forward over the light, creating the illusion that someone was moving about the darkened room.

"Oh, God!" Kathy breathed; then she laughed uneasily. "It was nothing!" Her gaze swept around the guest house bedroom. Nice. It had been furnished in Mission style with bold, square-cut furniture with no-nonsense lines. The drapes were crimson over white, the upholstery was done in complementing shades of crimson and deep royal blue. A clean-lined marble mantel stretched across the wall opposite the closet, along it an entertainment center with television, stereo, and disc player. All state of the art. Near the stairs that led straight into the room was a small refrigerator/bar combination.

This room was different, but then, the original guest house had been part of the old property, built in the nineteen twenties. He might have had the outside built to the exact specifications of the original, but inside he had modernized. Nicely.

She glanced at Jordan. He was barely aware of her it seemed, staring outside, into the night, again.

"Jordan, who did you think was in here? Why didn't you want to call the police?"

"What? Oh, it's a damned good thing I didn't call the police, isn't it? I would have looked like an idiot."

"Please tell me, what the hell is going on with you?"

He shook his head, then lifted his hands. "Nothing." He shook his head again as if disgusted with himself. "Nothing," he repeated.

She didn't know exactly why— Jordan was not the type to elicit sympathy— but she was struck with the sudden urge to go to him, touch his face, reach out, understand. But he was standing tall and hard as brick, his features taut, and he wasn't welcoming her into his thoughts. He didn't want her.

It was why she had left.

She bit into her lip, swiftly lowering her eyes as she felt the sting of tears behind them. She had to get out, away from him. She started quickly from the room, passing him at a brisk stride to escape the guest house.

"Kathy!"

She ignored him, hurrying down the stairs. He caught up with her just as she had left the place, his fingers wrapping around her arm to swing her back around to face him. "Kathy, what the hell— "

"Let go."

"But what— ?"

"Listen, you don't have any answers for me, I don't have any for you. Let me go."

She jerked her arm back. He was still then, letting her walk away.

Was that what had happened before? she wondered bitterly. She had left, so he had watched her go?

She returned to the main house, entering it the way she had left it, through the kitchen, through the living room, up the stairs, and back to the bedroom. She strode to the window, certain that she would see Jordan out there, looking up now, standing straight and stiff, angry but enigmatic.

Yet even as she stared out the window, she heard a shuddering of wood and she spun around again. Jordan hadn't remained where she had left him. He had followed her back. He stood in the doorway, staring at her for a second, then he stepped into the room, closing the door behind him.

"Damn it, Kathryn, what the hell do you want me to say to you? Something was wrong ten years ago—"

"Yes! Keith died!" she cried out.

He shook his head, looking pained again. "It was more, damn it. He didn't just become careless or suicidal. Something happened that night."

"And you've dragged me back here because you blame me?" she demanded, surprised to discover that she was shaking. She pushed away from the window, fists clenched at her sides as she approached him, defiance and challenge glistening along with the pain in her eyes. "Do you, is that it? Do you blame me?"

169

"No!" He shouted at her. His hands were suddenly upon her shoulders, their fingers like vises, "No, damn it, that isn't it!"

"Then what?" she cried, amazed at the force of emotion rushing through her. This was a nightmare, standing here. Oh, God, it was so much the same as it had been before . . .

Too much the same.

One of his hands moved. Caught and lifted her chin, tenderness defying the tension as his eyes locked with hers. Calloused fingers, made rough and rugged from constant play upon guitar strings, brushed, feather-light and shaking, over her flesh. He was going to speak—but he didn't. His mouth lowered to hers. She could have moved. She didn't. She waited for the touch, for the contact. It came within milliseconds, yet by then she felt like a puppet, jerked within and without by strings of searing mercury. His mouth melded to hers. Time again eclipsed. She knew his lips, the feel of his kiss, the intoxication and hunger it could fuel. She could have broken away. No bonds held her. No force coerced her. Intelligence dictated she run.

Simple yearning kept her there, feeling evermore the pressure of his mouth, the power of his hands. His touch . . . Oh, God, she was touching him as well, she had wanted so badly to feel his face, smooth-shaven now, to stroke his hair, explore, remember . . .

She was unaware of exactly when the buttons seemed to slip free from her tailored nightgown, fully conscious only of the feel of his hands on her nakedness, of the absolute *need* to touch in turn.

This was Jordan. Jordan, whom she had known all her life, so it seemed. When he had been young and lanky and all bones. When he had matured, when his chest had broadened, when his muscles had formed. She was so familiar with the slight clefts at the small of his back; she knew the tiny scar, caused by a fishing hook, at the top of his right thigh. She knew the feel of his flesh, the way that he moved. Knew his warmth and his scent, the way he could touch and tease her in return, tantalize . . .

It was insane, she told herself. If she just paused to think about this . . .

But she couldn't convince herself to do that. Her flesh— her blood— didn't want her to think, no part of her wanted thought to intrude. Just as she wasn't quite sure when her buttons started to slip open, she didn't quite remember moving, walking, reaching the bed, finding herself sinking down within it. But she was there. And he was with her. And the sweetly burning heat of his body was pressing into hers with a wild, urgent, fantastic energy that seemed to sweep any possible threat of thought from her mind. His mouth was upon hers . . . gone from hers. Her breath was ragged. Her heartbeat seemed constant, but that was because it combined with the thunder of his. Within, without, she throbbed with that beat; hungry, wanting. The frantic trail of his kiss against her. She did take a second to be grateful for the darkness, for the kind glow of the moon outside and the pale gleam that filtered in from the bath. Darkness was sweet, so sweet. She didn't have to think in the darkness, she didn't have to be afraid . . .

Of what?

He couldn't see her clearly.

Couldn't see *time*.

Couldn't see the things in her eyes she was so afraid she might betray . . .

Oh, God, it was *good* . . .

She'd known, all of her life, that he was a good lover. So giving. Creating a spiral. Aroused by his partner's arousal, excited anew, re-creating excitement. She realized these things, soft cries escaping her as he unerringly *remembered* . . . a whisper against her earlobe, a stroke down her back. The soft brush of his tongue between her breasts, upon them . . . the stroke of a finger, lower, higher, lower again. Liquid fire, the trail of his kiss, following where the flurry of touch had come before. She writhed and twisted in his arms, lips pressed to his shoulders, his throat, his chest, fingers entwined in his hair, nails scraping delicately over his flesh. The sensations became blinding. Oh, God, it had never been this good, this sweet, this wonderful, this delicious before.

It had. It was . . .

His hand moved over her buttocks. His stroke— oh, Lord— was inside her. Touching, deeper, finding, evoking . . .

His name. Whispered on her lips. Cried out, whispered again. The pleasure so long denied almost an agony. She could find no words. Only his name again. A plea, a demand, a whisper once more. She was suddenly aware of his eyes in the darkness. Then his kiss. Upon her lips. Her throat. Her breast, his tongue raggedly caressing her nipples. Once more, his kiss on her naked flesh, more intimate. He knelt between her parted thighs. Touched, stroked. Dared. More. More and more intimacy. His touch, his kiss, incredible intimacy. A stroke of his finger. Parting her. Liquid warmth. His. Hers. His name on her lips again, a whisper, a hoarse cry, something very near a shriek. A sob.

Then he was with her. Arms around her, sex within her. The thunder that had been their heartbeats was part of the throbbing that filled her like the heady pulse of a drum, harder, faster, still harder, still faster. Sweat slicked her body, his. Her fingers played into the dampness of his hair while she sought and strained, writhing, closer to him, ever closer, wanting more of him, feeling that she would burst with him, needing, reaching.

And when the climax burst upon her, it was fantastic. Rising so sweetly, cresting with a burst of liquid magic, shuddering through her with a startling, frightening violence, yet still so unbearably sweet. Wracking the length of her again and again, sweeping her even as she felt him find his own release, his form from head to toe going steel hard, sinking within her in wild, tight thrust, groaning, holding, sinking gently down upon her again, then rolling with her that they might remain as one, yet without her having to take the fullness of his weight upon her.

Seconds ticked by, then minutes. She hadn't allowed herself to think, and she didn't regret that. Yet now thoughts rushed in upon her. What now? A taste of paradise again, memories for the cold, lonely days ahead. A reminder, just in case she had forgotten how much she had once loved her husband, how she'd loved making love with him, lying with him, waking up beside him, laughing, arguing, fighting over the blankets, stealing one another's pillows.

In this room.

She'd walked out because she'd had to. Because she'd lost him already. Because something had lain between them that she hadn't been able to combat. She'd thought he'd come for her; he'd filed papers against her. Maybe he'd loved her then as she had loved him, despite what lay between them. Despite the bitterness that had inevitably come.

But now . . .

Now he was involved with a thirty-year-old woman. One considered by many to be one of her generation's great beauties. And that woman would be here. Soon.

Kathy swallowed hard. She'd told herself she was insane— and she was. She gently tried to extricate herself from him.

"Please, don't," he said. The darkness still blanketed them. His voice was rich and husky and filled with something of the poignancy that seemed to rip at her own heart.

"What were we thinking?" she asked a little desperately.

"We weren't thinking," he said.

"My God, what were we doing—"

"Kathy, we both know what we were doing."

"But here, tonight . . ." Desperation still edged her voice. He was silent for a second, then he sighed.

"I really don't want to ruin your life. But I don't want to give this up. Not for a few minutes, at least. But I guess I do owe it to you to go away. The kids will probably keep Jeremy out fairly late. But will he come here when he returns? He has his own room. Next door. The girls will take him there. If you're afraid he'll come here—"

"He won't."

"Why not?"

"Because he'll— he'll respect the fact that I told him I was exhausted."

"Oh," Jordan said after a moment. It was clear that he thought any lover worth his salt should be checking on her when he returned from a night out.

"He's very courteous that way."

"A courteous relationship. Great."

"It is!" she said defensively, then added, "People do need their own space, remember? Miss Hughes does keep her own room, right?"

"Ummm," he murmured, growing serious. "Kathy?"

"Yes?"

"Thanks."

"Thanks?"

"For tonight. Whatever happens . . . we had this. You didn't jump up and tell me it was an awful mistake. We had something we used to have. If only for a few moments."

"It . . . wasn't a mistake," she whispered. "I did what I did on purpose."

Oh, dear Lord, that was true. What a tragic admission. Some things suddenly seemed clear. Among them that she should have had more sex over the years. No matter what she had taught her daughters about the importance of absolutely responsible behavior, she should have had more sex herself.

If so, she might not have felt so powerless when he had barely touched her.

"How the hell did we mess it all up so badly?" he asked her softly.

"Rumors, lies, mistrust."

"Why did you leave me?"

"Because, honest to God, you had left me."

"It was a long time ago, wasn't it?"

"A lifetime, it seems."

"A decade is all. But look at us. You've got your Mr. Muscleman."

"And you have Miss April."

He hesitated just briefly. "Yeah, but do you know what?"

"What?"

"I have never . . . been with anyone in this room."

She leaned up on an elbow, studying him curiously. "Really?"

He grinned, delightfully sheepish. Nodded.

She smiled. "That's kind of nice."

"I'm not saying I haven't been with a number of women, I have."

"I know. If I don't read the papers, I can always count on a few good friends to fill me in on the details of your life."

"Jealous?"

"Maybe. Just a little bit."

"And now tonight—"

"Was nice," Kathy said.

He sat halfway up. "Nice? *Nice?* Well, my dear, you have just managed to make me feel absolutely ancient. It was supposed to be unbearably exciting. Hot, wild. Not *nice.* My God, I must be decaying big time!"

She laughed softly. "I don't think you need fear anything of the sort. You are dating a sweet young thing who apparently finds you just as hot as a furnace."

"And how do you find me?"

"I find you to be . . . Jordan," she said huskily after a moment. She had to be careful! she warned herself. She was starting to sound like something from *True Confessions.* In fact, despite the darkness, she was beginning to feel uncomfortable.

Afraid.

Don't look at me too closely. Don't let the magic go, she thought, and tried again to untangle herself from his limbs, his one leg cast over hers, the other caught beneath.

"Jordan . . ."

"Yeah, I guess we should move. What if one

of the girls were to check on you? We wouldn't want to disappoint either of the children, ummm?"

"Ummm . . . right," she murmured. The sting of tears now seemed to be slamming against her eyelids. She was tired. She could still breathe in the scent of him. She had disentangled— she didn't want the warm feel of his flesh to go away.

He started away, then paused. His knuckle touched her chin; his lips brushed hers, melded softly, evocatively to them. Briefly. Too briefly. "It doesn't seem right to walk away," he said.

"It would be damned easy just to fall asleep," she admitted on a breath.

His mouth touched hers again.

But even as her bones began to melt, a strident screeching jangled her nerves and she nearly jumped sky-high.

"Phone," he muttered with a curse, starting to reach across her body to pick it up.

"I'll get it," she offered, and slipped the receiver from the sleek telephone on the bedside table.

"Hello?"

Silence greeted her at first. She thought perhaps it was Tara Hughes, that she might not appreciate Kathy answering the phone in the house, in Jordan's room.

But then she heard the strangest inhalation of breath. Like someone choking, barely able to breathe.

"Ka . . . thy!" A chilling voice. "Sweet Kathy, back home again."

Jordan snatched the phone from her. "Who the hell is this?" he demanded.

As Kathy watched, his face hardened and aged. She heard the grinding of his teeth.

"You son-of-a-bitch— " he began; then he cursed and slammed the receiver down. He made a nimble leap over her, staring at the phone base.

"Jordan, what the hell is going on?"

He ignored her and jerked open the drawer beneath the phone, pulled out a pen and pad, and jotted down the number displayed in a small box on the phone.

"Jordan?" Kathy repeated.

He shook his head, standing, walking around to the foot of the bed to find his robe. Aware that he was about to turn the light on, Kathy made a mad dive for her tailored nightgown, slipping into it even as he reached the wall and hit the switch, flooding them with light.

"Don't you worry about this. And excuse me, but I . . . I've got something to take care of," he told her. "Important."

"Jordan, damn it, don't do this to me, don't close me out, tell me what's going on!" she demanded.

But he was already out the door, closing it behind him.

Her turn, she determined. She threw the door back open, and followed him. He was already down the stairs. In the living room.

He was on the phone there, despite the fact that it had to be nearly two A.M.

"I've got a number this time," he was telling

someone tersely. He looked up, saw her. His eyes narrowed angrily. He read out the figures he had written down. "Yes. Fine. Thanks. Let me know."

He hung up.

"Kathy, will you please go up to— "

"Not on your life," she said, shaking her head. She crossed her arms over her chest and approached him determinedly. "We gave up Blue Heron. We gave up our marriage. We've got new lives. But I'll be damned if I'll have any ghosts following me this time when the reunion is over. Jordan, I swear, if you don't start talking to me, I'll walk out of this house tonight. What is it?"

He sank down onto the refurbished Chesterfield sofa. "You can't do that."

"Why?"

"Because I'm afraid."

"Of what?"

"Of what might happen."

"To whom?"

He hesitated, then shook his head. "To you."

She sank down onto the sofa beside him. "Jordan— "

"Damn it, Kathryn, you said I didn't believe you. Well, you didn't believe me. Believe now. Keith didn't just die. He wasn't a tragic rock-suicide; his death *was not an accident.*"

"Jordan, damn you, I'm telling you again that I didn't run to the guest house to see him that night!"

"I believe you."

"Then— "

"Kathryn, it wasn't you. It *was* someone."

"But—"

"That someone killed Keith, Kathryn. And I'm damned afraid that someone may be ready to kill again."

Ten

Kathy stared at Jordan blankly, aware that he was serious. She shook her head, trying to grasp the reason he could be so certain Keith had been murdered.

"I don't understand . . ."

"Kathy—"

"I'm trying to."

"Think back. You know as well as I do that Keith wasn't in the least suicidal."

"But he did do drugs," Kathy reminded him painfully. "Jordan, that was the main reason we fought over him all the time."

"Yeah, I used to say he'd have to quit or he was out. And you used to tell me that was no way to help someone with a serious problem."

"In retrospect, you were probably right. He'd have become a shoe salesman or the like and be alive now."

Jordan shook his head, smiling slightly. "Not Keith. He wouldn't have lived without music."

"He might have shaped up. But it doesn't matter who was right and who was wrong Jordan, the drugs killed him."

"The smoke killed him."

"He wouldn't have been out flat while he burned to a cinder if it hadn't been for the drugs."

Jordan nodded, running his fingers through his hair. "Yeah, he took drugs. He came late to practice, he screwed up like crazy. But he never overdosed, he had a talent for getting high, for being out of it without causing serious injury to himself."

"Usually. That night he took too much. And he'd been smoking that ridiculous Oriental pipe of his at the same time, the bed caught fire, and he died."

"I don't believe it. I didn't believe it then, and I don't believe it now. And," he added quietly, "someone out there *knows* Keith was murdered. Someone who's afraid of Blue Heron getting back together, someone who's afraid of the truth."

"You're saying this because of that phone call?" Kathy queried, more concerned about Jordan at the moment than the possibility that he might be right. This was very strange and frightening. He had closed off from her after Keith's death. Immediately after the funeral, when everyone had been in shock, they couldn't have been closer. Perhaps because they'd clung to life. But then they had begun to fight. And she knew he had been suspicious of her; she had really hated him for it, and she still did.

Amazing, she taunted herself. That hadn't stopped her from leaping into bed with him just now. She really should have gotten around more over the past decade.

It would have been no help now, she admitted to herself.

She'd never before realized just how serious the issue of Keith's death was with him, that there had been more than the suspicion she might have been closer to Keith than she had ever let Jordan know.

"I've had a number of phone calls," he told her.

"Threatening phone calls?"

"Some. It's strange. There are two callers. One threatens that someone else might die if Blue Heron comes together. Another says I'm the only one who can make things right."

"Pranksters make phone calls. People make phone calls for kicks. Nine hundred numbers are making small fortunes for entrepreneurs aware of the fact that some people get off on things they can say and hear on the phone!"

He shook his head with exasperation. "Kathy, I don't know what to do with you, how to knock sense into you!"

"Jordan, let's look at this clearly. Ten years ago we had really achieved success. We weren't a flash in the pan. We had proven ourselves as talented musicians with staying power. We were recognized, we were making money. Too much money, too much fame, maybe. Enough money for Keith to buy whatever drugs he wanted. And we'd been together so long we were like a family, a family of growing children. We had been together too long perhaps; we fought, we squabbled, we grew apart. We wanted different things. We were too close. You and I argued, our friends who wanted different things often used that, used us. Judy and Derrick argued, Miles lusted after Shelley. Shelley, I think, lusted after Keith. Judy wanted to see us all beaten with burning sticks for veering from career and money at any time." She inhaled and exhaled on a deep breath. "Keith finally took it all a step too far. He lived recklessly, he was a genius, he loved you, he used you, and he did the same with me. Then he died, and we fell apart. It was as if Humpty Dumpty had fallen off his wall. Groups split for lesser reasons. People are involved— personalities, egos. The Beatles split over artistic differences—"

"And other problems," Jordan added.

"Exactly my point. Think about this. We were kids, not even playing ourselves, when Hendrix died. We were discovering how deeply we wanted to be working musicians when Woodstock happened, and remember, Jordan, just about anything went back then. Think about the world since. Vietnam and the peace movement, Afros, and bell-bottoms. The tragedy of Kennedy's death, the fights that finally gave us the beginnings of desegregation. Free sex, free love— those hideous neon guru jackets we wore at one time. What I'm trying to say is, we were a product of our time. Drugs were in before drugs were out. We fought for good things sometimes while doing bad."

"Kathryn, I'm actually enjoying this. You've always been so passionate in your beliefs and ideas, and you haven't changed a bit, but I admit I am completely lost."

She shook her head. "Jordan, my point is that the hippies of years gone by became the yuppies of today. Men and women who slept in parks extolling the virtues of the stars became the ones who drove the BMWs to work in their three-piece designer suits. Keith got lost in the transition. Everyone learned that drugs were dangerous, that life was precious. Keith just didn't give a damn."

"You're still defending him."

"Jordan, he's dead! I can't help but defend him. Look how many bands have existed, and how many bands exist today, how many artists have been a part of how many different bands! Remember the ones who started out before us. Look at the drug deaths— Janice Joplin, Jimmy Hendrix, Jim Morrison. Fame and fortune could be had, but there were traps to fall into. Keith fell into one. In a way, the rest of us did exactly the same thing."

Jordan shook his head. "I don't know."

"Damn it, the rest of us were not perfect!"

"No, but we had some sense of responsibility."

"He was your best friend."

"Yeah, oh, yeah. And I dug him out of trouble time and time again."

"You sound so bitter!"

"I am. He taunted me about everything; yet

when he really needed help, he didn't come to me."

"Jordan, he was always asking me to pave the way for him to come to you—"

"Yeah, he liked to use you, all right. I never really knew the truth of what was going on between the two of you."

Again, that very bitter edge was in his voice. Kathy gritted her teeth, angered, but she determined to remain calm and cool. "You didn't want to talk about it ten years ago. What the hell kind of an accusation is that now."

"It's not an accusation," he said quietly, his eyes lowering. He looked at her again, lifted a hand awkwardly. Shrugged. "I wonder why, Kath. I was confident, even as a kid. Assured. I knew where I wanted to go, knew I wanted to go with you. Keith had the ability to make me strangely insecure."

"And you're still wondering if I slept with him?" she demanded flatly.

"Kathy—"

"I'm telling you now, Jordan, with nothing to gain and nothing to lose. There was never anything between us."

"That might be true—"

"*Might?* You idiot, you're dating Shirley Temple and my life has been my own for a decade, so why the hell would I be lying to you? And you have your nerve! You were the one who practically wore women as if they were scarves dangling off your shoulders!"

"The hell I did!"

"The hell you didn't. And you dare say something to me like that 'might be true.' I—"

Kathy broke off abruptly, hearing a car coming around the curving driveway.

"They're home!" she gasped, forgetting the argument as a strange sensation of panic seized her. There stood Jordan, his robe barely tied, and here she was, hair a tangled mane and the oddest sensation of guilt descending on her. Thank God she had bought tailored-type nightshirts. But the little buttons at the top of this one were half-open, and it wasn't exactly the outfit one would sit around in with an ex-husband, especially when the ex-husband was wearing nothing but a terry. Not only that, she felt as she might have when they had been teenagers, madly in love, dating for two years already, and fooling around but still doing so very secretly since their parents would have been shocked at that point. At first she'd feared that someone could just look at her and *know* she'd been having sex. Wild, wanton, undeniable sex, of sex, because they'd been young, discovering, and certain then that they were as destined for one another as Scarlett O'Hara and Rhett Butler, Anthony and Cleopatra— which mightn't have been such a misconception since those pairings had ended badly.

She leapt up, staring at Jordan.

"What do we do?" she gasped.

"About what?"

"About what . . . we did?"

He arched a brow to her and replied with an

edge. "Worried about Jeremy? Kathy, he won't know if you don't choose to tell him."

She wasn't sure why she felt so hostile. "You won't tell my sweet young thing if I don't tell yours?"

His eyes narrowed. "Something like that."

"I wasn't worried about Jeremy, I was thinking about my daughters."

"Do you mean *our* daughters?"

She ignored that. "I don't want them to think— I don't want them to begin to hope . . ."

"Kathy," he said, and now there was a strange, almost gentle twist to his voice, "they will not know. Just sit. I'll make coffee— "

"Yes, coffee. I'll make coffee. Oh, sorry, it is your house now— "

"Kathy, please, by all means. You do make better coffee. Let's get to the kitchen. That will be better than them seeing you flying up the stairs like the cat who ate the canary."

She made a face at him, dashing for the kitchen behind him just as she heard a key twisting in the lock.

A second later, the foyer was filled with soft laughter as the foursome who had gone out partying on the beach returned. By the time the group reached the kitchen, however, following the light and the sounds coming from it, Kathy had an almond-flavored decaf brewing and Jordan had set bread, mayo, mustard, sandwich meat, and cheese out on the table.

"Hey!" Alex said delightedly, slipping up behind Kathy to give her mother a hug. "You guys have been talking, huh?"

"Actually," Jordan said, staring at Kathy. "We'd both gone to bed." He smiled pleasantly. "We seem to have gotten the urge to raid the kitchen at the same time. Jeremy, how did you like the wild side of South Beach."

"Great, it was great," Jeremy said, leaning against the kitchen counter. "I've never seen so many different people, not even in New York. Young people, old people, girls in short-shorts, women all wrapped up in serapes, people in suits, cut-offs. They moved liked a herd down the sidewalk. And the music was great. It was like a feast for the senses."

"A feast for the senses," Jordan repeated. Kathy, leaning against the kitchen counter, felt warm. She realized he was staring at her again, but she didn't know whether he mocked her or meant the words in a nostalgic way.

Miss April wasn't here tonight. But she was coming. And things were even more disturbing now. Kathy still couldn't believe that Keith had been murdered. She could have argued Jordan on the point all night.

But if she paused to remember how her name had sounded, whispered over the phone . . .

She jumped as she suddenly heard a ringing.

"Just the phone," Angel said lightly.

"At this time of night?" Bren murmured.

"Tara might be calling in," Alex said, staring at her father.

"I'll take it," Jordan said, returning his

daughter's stare as he crossed the kitchen to answer the phone. "One way or the other," he told her firmly, "it is probably for me."

Alex made a face and moved out of the way. "Coffee's done, Mom."

"So it is. Who's having some?"

"Decaf?" Jeremy asked.

Kathy nodded and began to pour. Angel and Bren passed cups around, Alex dug into the refrigerator, determined on milk instead. Kathy was dying to walk over to Jordan herself with a cup to find out who was on the phone and what he was saying.

Probably Miss April. If she listened in, she'd just be hurting herself. No denying that Miss April was coming and coming soon, still Kathy didn't think she was on the phone right now. Whoever it was had something to do with the crank phone calls Jordan had been receiving.

She managed to casually bring a cup of coffee over to him, but even as she did so, he handed the phone to Bren. "I'll take it in the living room. I can't hear in here."

"Sorry, Dad," Bren said. "We can be quieter."

"Don't be silly. Just hang up after I pick up; will you?"

"Thanks," he told Kathy, taking the cup from her and walking on out to the living room. A second later, Bren must have heard her father's instructions to hang up because she did so.

She smiled at her mother, slipped an arm around her. "It's so good to have you here,

Mom,'' she whispered to her. ''Thanks for coming!''

Kathy nodded, hugging her daughter back, wondering what Bren would think if she were to snatch up the phone and listen in on Jordan's conversation.

But Alex suddenly breezed by to give her a kiss and a whisper, ''Thanks, Mom. See, you two can get along like old friends. This is so good.''

Ummm. Good. The night was wonderful so far. She'd just discovered that sex with her ex-husband was as natural and life-sustaining as breathing, the stunningly beautiful and very young woman he usually slept with was due back momentarily, and Jordan was convinced that Keith had expired because of a murderer's calculated acts. At the very least, Jordan was receiving crank phone calls.

Kathy leaned against the counter, sipping her coffee, realizing that it was around three in the morning and that more had happened in her life since midnight than usually went on in a year these days.

She discovered suddenly that Jeremy had come to stand next to her, shoulder to shoulder, against the counter. Concern etched his handsome face, but he smiled as he asked softly, ''Everything okay?''

Kathy nodded. ''Fine.''

''It's a great vacation for me,'' he told her. ''Honest to God, Kathy, that is the wildest place I've ever seen. And I speak as a born and bred New Yorker!''

Jordan returned to the kitchen as Jeremy spoke intimately against her ear. Kathy met his gaze, but nothing in his cool green eyes or hard countenance gave away his thoughts.

"Who was it at this hour, Dad?" Alex asked. She was seated at the table with Angel, and the two of them had been head to head, laughing over something that had happened that night.

He started to speak. He was going to say it had been Tara, Kathy was certain, but he didn't. This was one of those times when she did seem to know Jordan very well. Tara would have been the right lie, but Tara might come and blithely let everyone know she hadn't called.

"One of the musicians playing with us," Jordan said.

"At this hour?" Bren said.

"You know musicians," her father told her.

He was lying, Kathy knew. He'd called the police— or someone— about the phone call to have them check on the number from which the call had originated. The police— or someone— had called him back.

"I suppose," Bren agreed, blithely ignorant of any undercurrents. She yawned and stood. "I give up, guys. I can't stay awake any longer." She patted Angel and her sister on the head, hugged and kissed her father, her mother, and gave Jeremy a hug as well. Kathy should have been elated. Bren's weary instinct to kiss a good friend good night certainly gave credence to Kathy's relationship with Jeremy. Just as her own very close friendship with him made them look intimate now.

Somehow, though, she was just uncomfortable. She almost hated Jordan for it. If he hadn't come to New York, she wouldn't have come here. If she hadn't come, she wouldn't have gone to bed with him, if she hadn't gone to bed with him, she wouldn't be feeling now as if . . .

As if she at least wanted the magic of waking up beside him one more time.

She wouldn't be wishing she could really come back. That she'd forced the issue when she'd had the chance. Maybe that she hadn't run away. That she still had him. She had almost gift-wrapped him for the Tara Hugheses he had had over the years.

"Yeah," Alex said, rising. "I guess I'm beat, too. 'Night, guys." She, in turn, kissed everyone good night, pausing by her mother. "Last copout, Mom. You've got to vacation with us from now on, okay? You see, you're still awake. You didn't go to bed. You should have come with us tonight."

Kathy blinked. Ah, there was the irony. She did go to bed. "I should have," she agreed.

Jordan made a slightly choking sound over his coffee.

"Jeremy, your things are up in Dad's office. It's as nice as any of the bedrooms and is next to Mom. Want me to show you?"

"Yes," Jeremy said, apparently forgetting for the moment that he might want to appear to go up with Kathy.

"Shall I make sure we're all locked up?" Angel asked Jordan.

"Yep, thanks, Angel. I'll take a walk around the premises myself once I go out."

"Good night then," Angel said.

Jordan stood by the table; Kathy still leaned against the counter. They looked at one another, listening to the footsteps as the others went up the stairs, to Angel locking the front door, setting the alarm.

"Who called?" Kathy asked.

"Mickey."

"Dean?" she asked, frowning. Mickey was a good friend. They'd gone to Miami High together, graduated in the same class. Mickey had helped them through the inquest, the red tape, the pain when Keith had died.

"Mickey Dean," Jordan agreed.

"And?"

He shrugged, crossing his arms over his chest as he stared at her.

"You don't believe in my fears and concerns. So why are you questioning me now?"

"Because I happened to answer the phone!" Kathy said with aggravation. "Because I now know what you're thinking, and because someone is playing a hoax— or something— on you."

He was silent a minute, still watching her.

"Isn't Muscleman going to miss you?"

"Jordan, answer me."

"Whoever called did it from a phone booth."

"A phone booth where?"

"South Beach."

"South Beach!" she gasped. "But that's where the girls were tonight!"

"It wasn't the girls!"

She shook her head wildly. "That's not what I mean. They could have been in danger. Maybe they were being stalked. Maybe whoever called was following them and knew you weren't with them, maybe even knew that I was here and that I wasn't with— "

"Calm down! You're the one convinced that these are just crank calls, that Keith's death was a tragedy, nothing more."

"Jordan, I don't like any of this. It doesn't make any sense. But there are all kinds of lunatics in the world. We can't let the girls go out and that's that."

He arched a brow at her. "Kathryn, remember, you finally came here because your oldest daughter is about to become twenty-one. You're going to ground her now?"

"I want to talk to Mickey," she said stubbornly. "And I don't want them out anywhere tomorrow."

He shrugged. "We can take the boat out tomorrow. That will keep everyone together. For a day. And we can go out with Mickey tomorrow night alone for dinner. No, we can't."

"Why not?"

"What could you possibly tell Jeremy?"

She waved a hand in the air. "Something. I can think of something."

He arched a brow. "Interesting. You've got him that much under heel?"

"Jordan, my relationships are none of your business." She frowned.

"Just trying to keep this one afloat for you," he said.

"I can keep things afloat myself, thank you. What about the child?" she asked sweetly.

"Which child? Bren or Alex?"

Kathy sighed. "Neither. I'm talking about Tara."

"Funny, Kathy, funny. Think you might be just a little bit jealous of her age?"

"Not when I have Muscleman at my side," she replied sweetly. She wanted to bite her lip, take back her words. Too late. She had been catty. And she'd gotten what she deserved. A save-play had been all that was left to her.

She shook her head, setting her cup in the sink, moving industriously about to pick up the sandwich meats and set them back in the refrigerator.

"How do we go out with Mickey and make sure they stay safely home?"

"The girls aren't in any danger."

"Why?"

"They were little kids when Keith died."

"Not so small. He died right after Alex's eleventh birthday. Bren was nine."

"Kathy, they'll stay home if you ask them to. You haven't realized that the little sweethearts think they *can* put Humpty Dumpty back together? They'll be a pair of chattering-magpie matchmakers if they think we're going out alone together."

"We'll tell them we're going out with old friends. We can't— "

"We can't what?" he demanded.

"We can't give them false hopes," she finished softly.

Her eyes lowered. Strangely, she felt his remain upon her. She could almost feel them pierce her like a ray of heat.

"Right," Jordan said. "Well, thanks, this is all picked up. I guess I'll make a few rounds and then go to bed. Good night."

She looked up at him again. Good night. She suddenly felt chilled, miserable. Well, they were adults. Divorced. A long time ago. She'd stepped back into his house, and just like a fool, into his bed. Passion— nature— sated. They were adults. Mature adults. The little indiscretion was over. Good night. She needed to be just as cool and casual about it.

"Yeah. Good night," she told him. Good. Cool, casual. She turned and headed quickly out of the kitchen.

But she paused then, turning back. He was standing exactly as she had left him, not even looking out after her.

"There's one thing about Keith's death you haven't brought up."

"What's that?"

"Motive."

"What?"

"Motive. Think about it. Who could have possibly wanted to kill Keith? Why would anyone have murdered him?"

"Motives aren't always that easy to see."

"Right. You guys could be passionate about your music. But he wasn't killed in the heat of passion or anything like that. If he was murdered, someone thought it all out carefully. Knocked him out with his own drugs, burned the guest house to the ground. Someone was really angry with him."

Jordan shrugged. "Hell, I was furious with him half the time."

"That's right. You two were the best of friends. You loved each other, and you hated each other. You might be one person with a motive," Kathy informed him.

"Ummm. He was my best friend. And he was in love with you," Jordan said flatly.

"He wasn't in love with me."

"He was."

"Damn you, Jordan—"

"I didn't say you acted on it. Or even that you knew. But he was in love with you and he used you, and you didn't stop him from doing it."

"Jordan—"

"Kathy, truce! I swear, I'm not saying you slept with him or anything. He used your friendship, your affection."

She smiled bitterly. "This is a ridiculous conversation now. And yet . . . we should have had it ten years ago."

"Perhaps. But you left."

"You weren't talking. I kept trying to talk, and all that happened was that we fought."

"Maybe I was afraid you had responded to Keith."

"And maybe I was afraid you had responded to a number of creatures in skirts."

"Thanks. Boy, we really did have a lot of faith in one another!"

"Strange, I had trusted you."

"And I trusted you."

"Always?" she inquired with skeptical courtesy. "With Keith, right."

"Keith was always around."

"Your best friend."

"In love with you."

"I told you—"

"I know," he said quietly. "But we're funny creatures, aren't we? And when things begin to crumble—"

"Humpty Dumpty falls right off the wall," she murmured.

"Yeah. More or less."

Humpty Dumpty, shattered to bits. It suddenly seemed incredibly sad that it had all happened, that the pieces were scattered like dust in the wind.

"Well— again— good night," Jordan said after a moment. He sounded very cool. Casual. Humpty Dumpty had fallen nearly a decade ago.

"Uh-huh. Good night," she replied, just as casually. But her heart seemed to be beating a thousand miles an hour again, and she could feel a red flush creeping into her flesh. What an evening. She walked into his house, into his arms, panting, half-weeping— and now they might have shared nothing more than a hand-shake.

Fine. Dignity was the order of the day. Damn, how did she keep forgetting that?

She spun around, and left him.

After hurrying up the stairs, she closed herself into her room. His room. Once their room. The bed still an absolute tangle, subtly scented with him, his body, the very, very light musk lingering from their love-making.

Great! Now she had to sleep here!

Damn him, she was going to.

She straightened the sheets, cursing softly beneath her breath, and lay down, her hands folded over her chest, and stared up at the ceiling.

She winced, realizing she was positioned like a corpse. She turned to her side. A shower might help. Take away the lingering scent and feel of him.

A shower would help.

Somehow, she didn't quite get up to take one. She didn't sleep, she didn't move. She lay there.

Awake.

Aware of all the subtle scents and memories that lingered within the room.

Eleven

Angel Garcia was both completely competent
and entirely trustworthy, but that night, Jordan
went around checking the locks himself. He exited the main house by the kitchen as he had
done with Kathy before, then walked around to
the front of the main house. He had almost two
full acres on the island with two hundred feet on
the water in the rear. The house, pool, and guest
house used up a lot of space, making it a large,
comfortable home and yet not an ostentatious
one. He still loved the place. Even if he did feel
a touch of bitterness regarding it now and then.

In the bedroom on the second floor of the
guest house he found himself riveted to the window once again, looking across the pool and patio
to his own bedroom window. He wouldn't see her
again; he knew it. He was right. No sign of her.

He turned away, feeling the most ungodly tension streak through him.

There wasn't a damn thing he could do.

The human psyche was strange, maybe that
of the male of the species even stranger. His
urge was to walk back over to the house again,

slam open the door, and toss Muscleman out on his tight and perfect buttocks.

Maybe Muscleman was actually sleeping in his own room.

Why?

Because Kathy might want to be alone. He couldn't begin to imagine his ex-wife switching men quite so quickly.

And what would have happened if Tara had been here?

None of it made sense to question. He shouldn't have gone to the room, and he sure as hell shouldn't have made love to his ex-wife. He hurt too badly now, with a pain he couldn't quite understand. Were such things possible, he wouldn't go back and undo what had happened between them for anything in the world. It had happened too quickly, too naturally. And it seemed to reinforce something that he had never been able to shake. A commitment that went deeper than words on paper, feelings so entangled that no matter what the beauty of the word "love," it failed to describe them.

For all of their lives, there had been something there. They'd met so young. He'd known he wanted her with him from the very first time he had seen her. To touch, kiss, protect, talk with, walk with . . .

It was all insane. Perhaps he should have let the dead remain buried. Let them all go on with their lives.

Or maybe he should just walk over to the main house, wrench her out of bed, and flatten

Muscleman. Once, he would have reacted on instinct. He hadn't always controlled his temper, and he had physically plucked up his wife and taken her away upon occasion. They'd fought, they'd made love, they'd made up. But she wasn't his wife anymore, and she might be sleeping with Muscleman, who, though he obviously did have some kind of a relationship with Kathy, seemed to be a decent enough person.

He forced himself to lie down. Stared at the ceiling. Cast an arm over his eyes, creating a greater darkness. He still couldn't sleep, or even cause the restlessness in him to abate. By Sunday, the others would be coming in. His dad, Sally. Shelley, Miles, Derrick, and Judy. Mr. and Mrs. Larry Haley— Jordan hadn't met the most recent Mrs. Haley as of yet. By Monday they'd start with some intense jam sessions, see if they could bring the old magic back— just for a night. He had a strange faith that it would happen. No matter what else was going on.

And even if Keith wasn't with them.

He'd known Keith almost as long as he'd known Kathy. They'd met in their first year of high school. He could always remember the day he'd met Keith because when he'd seen him, Keith had been playing the drums. Jordan had come back into the band room for his guitar, and Keith had been there. He was playing a set of beat-up school drums, but in all of his life, Jordan had never heard anyone play with such an ease and natural feel for percussion. Keith didn't see him, and for once in his life, Jordan had been barely aware of Kathy at his side, her hand in his. He stood, watching Keith. Watching him move, watching his body, his hands, listening to the passion and perfection of rhythm. When Keith finally stopped, he looked at them, but his eyes were soon riveted on Kathy. She smiled. "You're good."

"You're great," Jordan corrected, walking to him, a hand outstretched. "I'm Jordan—"

"Treveryan, everyone knows you." Keith looked at him suspiciously for a minute. He'd been a good-looking kid with handsome, aesthetic features, gray eyes, dark hair. He was slim, and shy in those days.

"You're the football player, right?"

Jordan shook his head. "I'm not playing."

Keith frowned. "Why? I heard they wanted you—a sophomore—on varsity."

"It takes too much time to play football. I study music. My dad's a musician. He says if you love it, you give it your time."

"Yeah?" Keith regarded him, both suspicious and impressed. Then he took the outstretched hand. "I'm Keith Duncan. And my dad wishes he could make me play football. He hates my drumming."

"You can drum at my house," Jordan told him.

"And mine. I'm Kathy—"

"Connoly. I know," Keith said. He flushed, watching her, and shrugged. "Everyone knows you. They say you're the prettiest and the nicest girl in the class. You're quite a couple, aren't you?"

"Well, we went through junior high and grade

school together," Kathy said, glancing Jordan's way. "We've just been together . . . forever." She'd already had those smiles back then. Great smiles. The kind that said a hundred different things, and could be so damned special, so damned intimate. "But I'm not a great musician, and you are—"

"I'm a kid banging on drums," Keith said humbly.

"You're a kid doing a great job banging on drums," Jordan said. "We've got to see what we can do together."

"Yeah, we should."

They did.

They became the best of friends, all three of them. Hanging around together. Working together, jamming together. By their junior year, they began to get gigs doing parties. In their senior year, there were more parties. Keith wanted to move forward. He'd had some offers from a few of the places where they went, and he'd heard some of the solid groups beginning to take flight, like the Image and the Place. They imitated John Lennon, wearing granny glasses, guru jackets, and bell bottoms.

Keith met all manner of roadies around the groups. He wanted out of school; he was convinced they could pick up a few more players and go out on the road professionally. They probably could have. Jordan was insistent that they work harder on their own music first. "And we go to college."

"Where?"

"Juilliard."

"I'll never get in."

"You will."

"I don't need to."

"I do. I don't want to play for a few years and become a has-been. I want to play and write and create and do it forever. I want to know everything I can about music, old music, new music, classic music."

"He's right, you know," Kathy said.

Keith took a look at Kathy. "Is that what you think?"

She nodded. "Keith, take a look at some of the groups who are really good. Not just popular. *Good.* There's Queen. All trained musicians. Then there's Yes—"

"Then there's the Beatles, who played in pubs in Liverpool and Germany. They seemed to do all right."

"Keith, we're talking about our lives," Kathy told him seriously. "The rest of our lives. Doing what we love best for a living. Forever. We need to give it everything. Besides which, you guys have to stay in school." The week before, one of her cousins had been killed in Vietnam. Sally had gone to stay with her sister and the entire family remained in grief and shock. "You have to stay in school— or go to war."

Keith had kissed her hand then. Jordan could relive that image awake or sleep, in or out of his dreams, forever. The way Keith looked at Kathy . . . the way the argument was over.

"My folks aren't going to help me any, you

know. They think we all belong in Vietnam. If I died a hero, it would be better than having a rock 'n' roll drummer for a son."

"We'll get by without your folks. You're good enough for a scholarship, and we'll get enough gigs. First of all, we've got to get in."

They did get in. Keith was accepted by Juilliard before either Jordan or Kathy. His audition piece was so filled with passion, emotion, and control that there was no question of his talent.

Kathy, afraid that she hadn't the talent or the strength to gain entry, managed to get in too. She did an a cappella rendition of a song she had written herself. It would, eventually become Blue Heron's first hit— their first in the top ten of the music charts.

In the end, the three of them were accepted. Soon after they started college, they met up with Derrick Flanaghan, and his soon-to-be wife, Judy. The five of them started playing their way through school, and the summer after their twenty-first birthdays, Jordan and Kathy were married. Shelley Thompson, whom they had found soon after Derrick, had joined them. She was Kathy's maid of honor, while Keith was best man. Kathy's father had given her away, she'd looked elegant in a medieval-style white gown with delicate flowers and satin ribbons threaded within the bodice, sleeves, and hem. Friends from voice classes sang the Carpenters' "We've Only Just Begun," while other friends created what surely had to be one of the most fantastic musical ensembles for a wedding ever. The organist was joined by flutists, guitarists, harpists, and violinists. Kathy wore a crown of fresh daisies in her hair, and a trail of them down the length of her back. He'd never forget her walking down the aisle, never forget the promises to love and cherish for all of their lives.

While memories came to him, Jordan slept, yet the memories continued to recur. He tossed and turned, suddenly caught in a nightmare realm, seeing the years unwind.

After their marriage, it seemed that the world was theirs. They lived in newlywed bliss. She burned food one night, created fantastic culinary masterpieces another. He worried about finances, juggling their earnings, their scholarships, and the help their parents sent— as much as they could. Keith never complained about college anymore. Right and left, their friends were being sent to Vietnam.

He and Jordan shared many classes and Jordan often thought they were like a pair of sponges, Keith perhaps even more so than he, hungering for all that could be learned. It occurred to Jordan then that perhaps the greatest gift was not being able to play music, to create it, but to love it. To feel it, have it in the blood, sense it, taste it.

But college came to an end. They threw their caps into the air. Keith's parents came along with his younger sister and brother. His father was a tradesman who had knuckled down for everything he'd ever gotten. He wasn't quite the taskmaster his son had made him out to be, he simply had no dreams left in him. But there was pride in his eyes at that graduation, and something special between him and Keith when they hugged one another.

For Kathy and Jordan, it was another celebration, another goal achieved in their dream of the perfect life. The folks suggested that college was over, it was time for grandchildren. Kathy and Jordan tolerantly promised that they'd have kids in good time, but back home the jobs started coming. Weddings, anniversaries. Then club dates. They had their group together solidly working, with Judy to supervise, to tell them what was good, what was great, and what wasn't fit for mourning dogs. They cut their first single, then their first album.

They made it to the charts, Kathy's song the one to do it for them.

The dream was soaring along on golden wings. But then it was nearly crushed by their draft notices.

They had bought a home on Key Biscayne at the time. It had been built in the fifties, and nothing had been done to it since then, but they loved it. It wasn't on the water, however, the property gave them access to a private beach and provided plenty of space in which to work. Their neighbors were tolerant of the sound systems, which they kept down as much as possible. They worked hard, but the work was good. Indeed, theirs was a charmed life.

Jordan had picked up the mail en route to the beach for an early picnic dinner. It was around five, and the sun had just lost its real heat, the kind that beat down so mercilessly there. An evening breeze was just coming in off the water as he sat on the sand, feeling it sink between his toes as he saw the official insignia of the United States Army.

He'd been expecting the letter. The draft had become a lottery, and his number was high. Still, as he sat there, feeling the water against his flesh, the balmy warmth of the falling sun, the sweetness of the breeze, a shudder of denial swept through him. He didn't want to die. The war had been raging a long time, and the reports on it were shocking. The images on the nightly news were horrifying. He had a home, a wife, a career, a future. Dying in a godforsaken rice field thousands and thousands of miles from home seemed unthinkable.

But possible. He was to report immediately for a physical.

He hadn't wanted to go. Blue Heron was just testing its wings. They'd had their first taste of success. And even those who'd first thought the war protestors cowardly draft dodgers were becoming appalled by the loss of American lives with no victory, or end, in sight.

But neither did he want to run to Canada— or find himself arrested and in jail.

He stood, no longer aware of the water lapping at his toes. He watched the sun dipping into the horizon, magenta into blue, creating sweeping ripples of fire just above it. He started to walk. He heard Kathy calling him, but kept walking, then started running over the sand. She called out his name again and again. Finally she caught him. Breathless he fell to the sand with her.

"Damn you Jordan! What is it?"

He reached out. Touched her hair. Studied the amber in her eyes, the beauty of her face. Her skin was warm from the sun. He couldn't bear to leave her. Selfish, but he couldn't bear the thought of her leaving him, of finding companionship, solace . . . love . . . with anyone else.

He didn't answer her. Angrily she pushed away from him and rose. Found the discarded notice in the sand, the bills from the Southeast Mortgage Company and Florida Power and Light. She cried out, buckling down into the sand. He went to her. She was instantly adamant.

"We're going to Canada."

"We're not."

"You're not going."

"I'm not going to jail, and I'm not spending my life running."

"You are becoming famous, you can pull some strings— "

"Kathy, I'm far from famous, and even Elvis went into the service," he reminded her. "Besides, I don't want to pull strings."

"I don't want you to die!"

"I don't plan on doing that."

"Who the hell does?"

"Kathy— "

"I guarantee you I won't be killed."

"How can you guarantee me that?"

"Because I love you. Because I'll love you for

all of your life. Hell, I don't want to go, but I want a life when it's over!"

He held her both tenderly and possessively. Kissed her. She responded. Then pushed him away, jumped up, and ran home.

He watched the sun go all the way down. When he came home at last, she was sitting in the darkness. Stiff, silent. She didn't speak to him; he didn't try to speak to her. But he knelt before her and took her into his arms. She suddenly threw her arms around him in turn, sobbing softly. Still no words were exchanged. He carried her into their bedroom. They made love with a furious intensity. Eventually, they slept. Silent, wet tears still streaked her face.

Keith Duncan received his draft notice the same week. He and Jordan were to report for physicals on the same day. They did so. Jordan had suspected his friend might try the Canada route. But Keith showed up. The two were lined up together in their B.V.D.s as the doctors went by. Keith hacked and wheezed through the physical. He'd never been heavy or even large, but in the few weeks since they had received their notices, he had managed to drop enough weight to appear in sad condition. He was given a deferment.

"How the hell did you manage that?" Jordan asked him, proclaimed fit as a fiddle himself.

Keith, his black hair recently down to his shoulders but cut neatly into something close to a buzz for the physical, grinned. "Gotta know the right stuff to take for a history of asthma. I could have helped you out."

"Keith, those damned drugs are going to kill you."

"Oh, like a bullet or a bomb wouldn't? We've already lost this war."

"We haven't actually lost—"

"But we can't win. A few more boys are just going to have to die so that we can pull out with whatever grace is possible. Damn it, Jordan, you shouldn't be going. You're almost over the draft age."

"Yeah. It looks like it."

"It's stupid, and too damned bad. You're a married man."

"Lots of married men have gone."

"You know I'll look after Kathy for you. I always look out for her anyway. Can't quite help it. She's like a sister."

"Just like a sister."

"We'll all be waiting for you, Jordan, you know that. We won't do anything until you come back. Anything at all. We aren't anything without you, we never have been."

"Don't be ridiculous. I believe in myself, but no one has the natural talent you do."

"You put us together. You are Blue Heron."

"Not without you and Kathy."

"We'll wait."

Every word Keith said to him was spoken as a good friend. But Jordan was angry. He didn't know why. Keith didn't want to go, he'd known a way out. Jordan didn't want to go either, and he wondered if he wasn't a fool.

They had a huge party right before he left for boot camp. Kathy kept up a good front for it. When other friends had gone home, Blue Heron stayed behind. They seemed an incredibly tightly knit group of friends. Kathy, Keith, him. Derrick and Judy Flanaghan. Larry Haley with his present light of love— an exotic dancer at the time, if he remembered right— Shelley Thompson there with Miles Reeves, arm in arm, those two the best of friends, so critical of one another's love lives that they found fault with each other's dates.

They sat around all night with wine and Jack Black. Finally Judy made everyone leave, reminding them that Kathy and Jordan needed some time alone before the dawn broke and it was time for Jordan to go.

Something very sad by Jim Croce was playing on the stereo. When the last of them had gone, hugging Jordan one by one, Kathy still kept up a good front. They never slept. They held one another, made love, held one another again. She didn't cry until he was actually turning away, and then she shed silent tears, the kind that just swept down her cheeks.

He made friends in boot camp quickly— he soon earned something of a reputation for himself. His drill sergeant was a hard worker, a good man. Jordan had never felt more physically fit; he knew they were run ragged because that was the only way to train a man to stay alive once he hit the front lines.

And he did hit them. Right after boot camp he was given a nine-month tour of duty. He was from Florida. He should have been accustomed to mosquitoes and heat and humidity, and he'd seen enough of the war on the nightly news. But nothing had prepared him for the realities of jungle warfare in Vietnam— the rain, the humidity, the heat, the sheer brutality and carnage there. Battle itself was so terrible it was difficult to imagine that men created it. Sometimes it was impersonal, bombs falling, bursting into walls of flame, decimating earth and flesh. Sometimes it was far more intimate, one man staring at another, firing a gun, hearing the *rat-tat-tat*, knowing it tore through flesh, that blood erupted, and yet finding that so much better than feeling steel within his own flesh, crushing blood and bone.

The waiting, the endless days, could be as bad as battle. The heat by day, the chill by night. The constant dampness. Days of endless rain. Men lived recklessly, fearing death and dismemberment. Men wrote home, listened to music, popped uppers and downers, smoked hashish. They saw their comrades go by, armless, legless, completely limbless . . . blinded . . . dead. They smoked more hashish. They wrote letters home, and received letters from home.

Friends wrote, his folks wrote, Kathy wrote. Almost daily. Keith wrote, too.

Had dinner with Kathy last night. She's doing well, hanging in there.

Kathy's letters included Keith as well.

Keith stopped by for coffee, brought some flowers. He's really a sweetheart, thinking of little things to help me keep my mind off the fact that you're so far away.

Four months into his stay, Jordan watched three of his friends explode when a shell hit. They could have run in time. They didn't. He screamed their names. He didn't know what they'd been on at the time; he only knew it had slowed them down so badly they couldn't move when the attack came.

A month later, he finally received a week's R & R with his wife. He met Kathy in Hawaii. Nothing had been as brutal as the war, and nothing was as sweet— as good— as this meeting. The first days he couldn't talk, all he wanted to do was hold her, smell her, make love to her, wake up beside her, and hold her some more. The last days he talked. Talked and talked, told her what he saw, what he felt, how he hurt, how he was afraid. He'd never considered anything so necessary as her love. She listened, she refreshed him, she took all his hunger and pain, she somehow managed to give him a sense that life could be beautiful as well. He had feared it would be harder to go back once he had seen her. It was nearly impossible to draw away from her, yet it was better that he had been with her. There was only a slight strangeness about their meeting, and that was her casual reference to Keith. *Keith was always around.* Jordan had wanted to take her words at face value, to be glad his friend was watching out for his wife. He'd wanted Keith to fall off the face of the earth.

He had ninety days to go, then eighty, then sixty. Kathy wrote that she was pregnant. Fifty days, forty. He was convinced that he would not be killed—he would not allow himself to be killed.

Finally, he went home. And he received his honorable discharge from the service. He'd survived the nightmare. Life was good again. And if he had any doubts about his wife and his best friend, he wisely managed to keep them deeply hidden. He was grateful in the end that they had never surfaced, for when Alex was born, she was in his image. Her eyes were never blue; they were green. Her hair was sandy, and she was born with a full head of it. She never had the wrinkled-old-man appearance of many a newborn, but from the moment she was slipped into his arms from the doctor's own—since she was only a minute old—she had looked just like him.

Still, it wasn't long after his return and the birth of his daughter that he began to notice things had changed in his absence. He found a pipe on the porch. It was Keith's. The nickel bags of pot were Keith's. He knew damned well that a few joints hadn't led his friends in Nam to their deaths, but he was furious. Maybe irrationally so, as Kathy implied, and maybe not. He had a baby; it was his house. They burst into an explosive argument. He was even angrier because she seemed to think he had come home traumatized. It wasn't that. All his life he had seen the pitfalls, and he had been determined that they wouldn't fall into them. Drugs were prevalent, their use casual, popular. Maybe the dark experience of Vietnam had created the ambivalence in him. He'd just seen too much, and he didn't want it to happen to them. Especially not with the baby.

They got into a shouting match. Afraid of his anger at her, Jordan just stopped speaking. When he heard Alex crying, he went to the baby, picked her up and wrapped her in a soft blanket, and started from the house. Frightened, in tears, Kathy came after him. She swore she hadn't taken anything herself, she'd have never risked it, not with a baby. He knew she was telling the truth, and the argument ended with Alex sweetly sleeping again, their tempest channeled into passion. He was home; Keith needn't spend so much time at their house. They were rehearsing again, working again. And, suddenly, they were becoming a tremendous success.

Time began to pass. Good years, tragic years. Bren was born, another perfect, beautiful baby. But the year after, they lost Kathy's father to a heart attack, and three years later Jordan's mom passed away from cancer. Blue Heron grew close, drifted apart. They had megahits, achieved their first platinum album. They fought, they quarreled, but they succeeded. He and Kathy bought the house on Star Island. The perfect family home. A monument to the triumph they had fought so hard for, had planned so carefully to achieve.

And then . . .

He started to toss and turn in his sleep. Then

had come the sessions when Keith hadn't shown up—the interviews when he had walked in—obviously stoned. Jordan's arguments with Keith. Shelley subtly standing up to him. Miles claiming he didn't give a damn. Judy insisting Keith had to go, and Keith finding Kathy everywhere, pouring his heart out to her, using her friendship. He'd even found Keith with Kathy in his own bedroom once, trying to explain where he'd been when they'd had an important interview.

That had probably been the worst argument ever. Jordan had nearly thrown Keith out by the hair. Then Jordan and Kathy had fought, and Kathy had called up Shelley and left the house with her and the girls. Keith had come to Jordan, apologetic, desperate, telling him that he needed what the drugs gave him, that he couldn't quit. That Kathy understood him. Knew him in a way Jordan did not.

It had been a horrible day.

He flipped over, still asleep, trying to waken himself. He didn't want to live the end over again. The night he had stood at the window, staring out at the pool. Alone. Seeing the one who had been there. The woman running, moving with fleet, sure grace in the moonlight across the patio. Heading toward the guest house, where Keith was staying. Silent in the night, long hair flowing behind her . . .

Then the fire.

Again, oh, God, the fire.

Burning. Searing. Flaring to heaven. Bearing them all straight down into hell . . .

Twelve

Her dream took place in a haze. Aware that she dreamed, she knew the course the dream would take, yet she seemed powerless to stop it. The haze would eventually become smoke, yet now it was like a fog settled over the people, the house, the events, almost as if some strange ground mist had slowly crept in from the water, embracing them all. She stood in the left-wing studio by the windows, as she had then, only now she could see the fog rolling in, and knew what was coming. She could see Derrick striking low, deep chords on his bass. Larry moving his fingers over the keyboards. The sounds were discordant, strange, harsh. No one spoke until Jordan exploded with a curse, throwing his hands up into the air.

"I can't keep doing this. We should just call the band quits. Everybody start over."

Judy, magazine in hand, seated in a chair across from the elevation supporting the players, the instruments and the sound system, looked up. "Damn it, Jordan, it's just Keith. Get rid of

Keith. You warned him that he's going to be out, make him be out."

"Why don't you leave this to Jordan and Keith?" Shelley suggested to her. "This is really between them."

"Why should it be?" Judy demanded. "The rest of us suffer all the time!"

"Because it's really their band. We all came after."

"Their band? Their band?" Larry snapped, incredulous. "We've all got over a decade in this now, too. This is a decision we all have to make."

"Why don't we give this just a few more minutes?" Kathy heard herself suggest. "We decided to spend the time here together, to really concentrate on the new material, and we knew if we were all under one roof and working in the studio, we couldn't possibly be *too* late."

"Kathy," Jordan said, looking at her moodily, "he's not your child; you can't keep defending him."

"He may need some real help."

Judy snorted. "He needs a kick in the ass."

"It would be nice if you just weren't so self-righteous, Judy," Shelley suggested sweetly.

"Lay off her, Shell," Derrick said, defending his wife. But Judy didn't need defending.

"The fact that you do drugs—and sleep with Keith—does not make me self-righteous," she informed Shelley.

"I'm not married. Where I sleep is my own business," Shelley returned, her eyes narrowed.

"Just what is that supposed to mean?" Judy challenged.

"It means where I sleep is my own business," Shelley repeated.

"Guys, please!" Miles said. "Listen, this is the main reason his lateness is a problem— we sit here and argue like two-year-olds while we wait. Come on. We're friends here, right? We create something beautiful together."

"Miles, that's so good and kindhearted, I think I'm going to puke!" Shelley said, but she was laughing, her eyes warm for Miles. He grinned back, happy at any time to have obliged her.

"We need Keith," Larry said. "He and Jordan are the real talents here."

"Oh, yeah, and the rest of you are just a bunch of assholes, hmmm?" Judy said sweetly.

Miles, even tempered no matter what, suddenly barked at Judy. "You just spent half the day with Keith. Maybe if you'd left him alone, he'd be here now."

Derrick Flanaghan's head shot up. He frowned. "What were you doing with Keith?"

Judy hesitated just a second. "Giving him a good lecture on the virtues of punctuality. Apparently, he wasn't listening."

" 'Cause you took too much of his time giving him the lecture," Larry said dryly.

Shelley, especially attractive that day in form-hugging jeans and a tank top, her hair whisked up in a high ponytail, set down her violin. "Jordan, maybe this is really innocent. Maybe he's fallen asleep."

"You know, that could be. He was up really late last night, working on music for that new sheet of lyrics Kathy gave him," Miles said. "Kathy, what was he doing when you left him?"

"When I left him?" Kathy said blankly. Everyone's eyes were on her. She sensed them— Jordan's the most. He had the ability to make her feel he was staring right through her. "I wasn't with him today at all."

"But I saw— " Miles began. "Never mind," he said quickly. "I must have been wrong."

"We need to split," Jordan said.

He was still staring at Kathy. Was he talking about the band or the two of them?

Judy swore. "Split! We're making a fortune. We're on the top of the charts. Jordan, I know you and Keith are at odds, but other people can play drums!"

"Not like Keith," Kathy said evenly, staring at her husband, defying him to find anything wrong in her defense of their mutual friend.

"So he's a pain in the butt. But he can play drums, we are making the big bucks, and I do kinda like this job!" Larry said, trying to be light, trying to make them smile.

But no one did. Derrick was staring at Judy, who was looking as if she'd like to slit Shelley's throat. Shelley seemed to want to strangle Larry. Kathy could still feel both Miles and her husband watching her, Miles with a worried curiosity, her husband with something more.

At that moment, the studio door opened. Keith, oblivious to the rancor displayed in his absence, walked in with a broad smile and sheafs of paper for all of them. "Jordan, I think I've got it! This song is a hit, number one on the charts, I swear it, it's all fallen in just right. I tried changing the breaks the way you said when we were working last night, and it's made all the difference. Anybody have any objections to working on this first? Kathy, these are great lyrics, wonderful!" He walked to her, took her head in his hands, and kissed her on both cheeks. "We're not ready to record, but we could introduce this piece tonight at the press party. Shall we work on it? Are they any objections?"

A strained silence greeted his words. "No objections," Jordan said. Kathy knew he was staring at Keith, relieved that he was clean and sober. Jordan didn't want his friend to leave the band. He would rather have no band. She wondered if the others realized that. It had been Jordan and Keith from the start. Jordan sometimes seemed to hate Keith, but he loved him, too.

The two were head to head then, poring over the music. Jordan glanced up at her suddenly, staring at her again. Keith started to give Larry special instructions for the keyboards, and Larry tested out what he was saying. Instruments screeched as they were tuned.

The fog kept rolling in. Darkness was falling. Because night was coming . . .

She knew she was dreaming and she commanded herself to wake up. She didn't want to live through any more of that night. She forced herself to try to open her eyes. It was nearly ten years later. She was in her old room, Jordan's, and she didn't really belong here, no matter how right or comfortable it was, and like the biggest fool in the entire world, she'd slept with her ex-husband.

Her eyes opened. The room remained in darkness, except for the shaft of light coming from the bathroom, dimmed now, as if it had grown narrower. Shadows filled the room. Shadows of different lengths and sizes. Shadows the size of . . .

A man.

"Who is it?" she gasped out, panic seizing her as she realized that yes, someone was there. Someone silently standing over her as she slept. There was something so unnerving about it that a slow terror crept into her. "Who is it?" she repeated. She wanted to shout, but she had just come forth from a dream, and as in nightmares, when it was time to scream, she was so frightened she couldn't quite dredge up the voice she wanted.

But it didn't matter. The figure turned in silence, and fled, slipping out of the bedroom door so quickly that it was only a matter of seconds before she began to wonder if she had dreamed the intruder along with the past.

For several long moments, she lay in bed, shaking.

She leapt up then and walked out to the hallway in her bare feet. No one about. She walked down the hall to Jordan's office, Jeremy's room for the night. She hesitated, then twisted the knob and went in. Jeremy's head rested on his pillow, the sheets were drawn to his shoulders. She came closer to him and listened to his deep breathing. He was definitely asleep and had been.

Jordan? What the hell was he up to? Should she go back to bed or walk over and confront him?

It suddenly seemed to her that their pasts had been a series of unspoken accusations. Whatever happened between them, she wasn't going that route again.

She left Jeremy's room and walked purposefully along the hallway to the stairs, down them and to the kitchen. Jordan had keyed in the alarm at the kitchen door. The little red light meant he had done it to protect those sleeping within the house. She hesitated a second, wondering if he might have changed things in the past decade and if she might not bring the police force down on them. She punched in the old number and the light flicked off. He hadn't changed the code. She slipped outside and over to the guest house.

The door was unlocked. She started up the stairs, then paused. She could hear movement, sounds. She hesitated, chilled, then became too warm as a strange heat swept through her. Was he alone?

She started to turn away, but one of the sounds seemed like a groan— not one denoting ecstasy. He might be in some kind of deep and private pain. She had seen him twist, heard him moan before.

What if she was wrong? If he was with someone, if Tara had arrived early, if . . .

He groaned again.

Kathy rushed up the stairs, pausing at the landing to catch her breath and stare across the room.

Jordan was alone. In bed. His body was sleekly bathed in sweat, he had been tossing and turning so that he had kicked off his sheets. He was dreaming, in a nightmare. She had seen him this way before, but it had been very long ago, right after he had come back from Vietnam.

She wasn't his wife anymore, she shouldn't be here. If they hadn't already had the strange experience of sudden sex after a decade apart she would have felt very awkward indeed.

But he was in pain. And she had already seen his sweat-sheened body tonight. To walk away would be—

Churlish.

She could not do it.

"Jordan!" She knelt at the side of the bed, softly touching his face, his cheek, trying to wake him gently. "Jordan, you're dreaming. Jordan . . ."

He bolted up suddenly, eyes wild. They landed on her. For a moment Kathy thought he was lost in time. Then he blinked. His broadshouldered frame shuddered, and he shook his head, shaking away the dream.

"Kathy," he murmured. "Kathy . . ." Then, "What happened? Hmmm. Maybe I'm *nicer* than I thought. You left Muscleman to come back to me?"

"Damn you, Jordan, you were in the middle of a nightmare and I was trying to help you."

"Thank you. But why are you here?"

She stood, irritated by her previous desire to ease him from the dark grips of his dream. The kindness was backfiring on her now. "There was a man in my room."

"I thought you invited him."

"Jeremy was not the man in my room."

"You invited another man?"

"Jordan, I'm going to slap you in a minute." It was quite obvious that he didn't believe her.

"There was a man in your room, uninvited. In the middle of the night, in a house with an alarm. Well, did Jeremy catch him?"

"Jeremy is sleeping. I was sleeping. I looked up, and someone was in my room. I thought it was you."

His eyes lowered suddenly. "I've been right here," he said, his tone somewhat bitter.

"I can see that," Kathy told him. Irritably, she clutched the tousled sheets and threw them over his body.

"Tempted?" he asked her pleasantly.

"Jordan, damn you—"

"I am," he said very softly, suddenly smiling in a way that caught her entirely off guard.

Leave it to Jordan. Even when he was somewhat embarrassed at being caught in the middle of such a wretched dream. What had the nightmare been? He wasn't going to share it with her, so it seemed, and was determined to taunt her instead.

"Don't you think we've been foolish enough for one night?" she asked him.

"Then what are you doing here?"

"I'm going to slap you at any instant Jordan, I saw someone."

"You're sure?"

She started to say that she was, then paused. She wasn't. She'd been dreaming herself. Haunted by the past. By a houseful of people. By a night that had exploded on them all.

"I thought I was sure."

He shifted over to one side of the bed, drawing the sheet tightly over him so that he looked decent. He patted the bed beside him. "Sit, tell me what you think you saw."

She looked at the bed. "Sit?"

"Lie, then. Want me to make coffee?"

"I'm probably up because of the coffee."

"It was decaf. The company is probably over-stimulating."

"Jordan—"

"Kathy, please come here. Lie down, relax. I just—"

"Just what?"

He shrugged. A slow smile curved his mouth. "Lie next to me. Talk to me. Let me hold you. Auld lang syne. I always wanted to protect you, you know. Be the great provider, make the shadows in the night go away."

She hesitated, then slipped down beside him. Resting her head on the pillow, she gave in to sheer longing and turned against him, her head and face nuzzling his chest, her body close to his, his arms around her, his long fingers moving through her hair.

"Jordan, this is insane. What are we doing?"

"Does it matter? We are adults."

"And we have separate lives. There are . . . there are others to worry about now."

"He shouldn't have left you."

"What?"

"Muscleman. He shouldn't have left you to the shadows of the night."

"And what about Miss April?"

He hesitated. "She isn't here."

"Jordan, does it make this right?"

"Does it make it wrong?"

"Well, actually . . . yes."

He didn't say anything right away. Didn't agree with her, didn't disagree.

"Kathy," he said huskily at last, "it's good to hold you. I always loved you so very much."

The burning of tears stung her eyelids. She tightened her jaw. "When you didn't think I was sleeping with Keith."

"Kathy—"

"I don't think I realized until now that you really went farther than suspicion. You had condemned me."

"I hadn't."

"I believe you did."

"I don't know what I thought back then."

"Which would have been worse— that I'd somehow killed him or that I'd slept with him?"

"Kathy . . ." He groaned.

She suddenly pushed up and straddled him, staring down at him, demanding an answer. For a moment, there might not have been a Miss April or a borrowed Muscleman. It was amazing how the closeness, the intimacy between them returned.

"Which?" she snapped down to him.

He looked up at her, one brow arched high. "All right, I wasn't made of stone, I was afraid. I hated you both sometimes when I was gone and in hell and I knew you two were together. I had visions of the two of you, head to head, commiserating with one another, laughing perhaps, getting high, talking music . . . needing comfort."

"It never happened. Jordan, we fought over Keith when you came back from Vietnam. It was just over his drugs then, the stuff he'd left all over the house."

"Yes, I know."

"But you were already suspicious."

"I think Keith wanted me to be. Maybe he even wanted to split us up. It didn't happen then, but he liked to keep that wedge in there."

"Nothing happened between us."

"I believed you."

"Most of the time."

"Then . . . well, then . . . ' He hesitated, then stared at her. "I thought I saw you the night he died, going to him. And Miles said he saw you with him before. It just seemed that people always saw you with him."

She shook her head, suddenly more confused

than angry. Yet it was true, if she thought about it. Miles had thought she'd been with Keith the afternoon he had died, and she hadn't been. It was strange. And a little chilling. "Jordan, it wasn't me. I mean, I was with Keith many times, not *with* Keith. As a friend, talking to him. I never lied to you. I wouldn't have, I had no reason to. I did talk to him a while that day after the practice— "

"In our bedroom," Jordan reminded her icily.

"Talked, Jordan. He'd been in that room before. Miles, Larry, Derrick— and Shelley and Judy— had been in our room at one time or another to talk to us. I'd been in Judy and Derrick's room. If that implies— "

"It implies that I didn't like him in our room, and that's all," Jordan said firmly.

"He was so excited about that last piece of music. It was as if he was about to turn around on his own. Clean up his act."

Jordan stared at her, shaking his head. "Kathy, you always want to see the good in everyone. You'd argue like hell with me, but defend Keith or anyone else like a pit bull."

"You never meant to throw him out of the band."

"No, but I did mean to end it," he said softly.

"You were a perfectionist. You wanted that from others."

"Maybe I was too hard."

"But . . ."

"But what?"

She shook her head. "Jordan, I still can't believe someone killed him. It was just us here—Blue Heron. And the Garcias." She shivered suddenly. "Then he died. And now you're getting phone calls."

"Cranks. Hoaxes. That's what you told me."

"But now I could swear someone was standing over my bed."

He hesitated just a second. "Do you think it might have been Jeremy, just making sure you were sleeping where you were supposed to be—and alone?"

"It wasn't him."

"Kathy, how can you be so certain that he isn't the least bit afraid there might still be a spark between us?"

"Impossible," she said flatly.

"That would be incredibly insulting, murder on my ego, if there weren't a spark remaining between us," he said innocently. "I think it was Jeremy."

"It wasn't."

"How can you be so damned sure?"

"Because . . ." she began and broke off.

"Yes?"

"He was just . . . sleeping so soundly."

"Tara would be damned suspicious, were she here. But she isn't, thank God."

"Jordan! You have a relationship with that woman—"

"I have one with you at the moment."

"You don't."

"Damn! I do!" he told her. She started to speak, choked up, felt as if lava straight from

Vesuvius poured though her. Color touched her cheeks. She had chosen her position, straddling his hips, nothing but the thin sheet between them. And now . . .

She could feel him. Fully aroused. Very warm. No, hot. Swollen. Stimulating. Intriguing. Exciting . . .

Where was her willpower?

Not where he touched her, that was for damned sure.

He made a sudden shift, arms upon her shoulders. Sweeping her down beneath him, he kissed her lips with both slow-burning passion and sweet coercion. She barely felt his fingertips on the buttons of her nightgown . . . against her flesh. The touch slow. Hypnotic. His hands were calloused, but so gentle. Rough, soft. Caressing. Almost like a breath of air. Fingertips against her belly . . . a palm erotically rubbing against her nipple, his hand lower again, the whisper of a touch against her thighs, then suddenly a stroke into the dampness of her sex while all the while his tongue bathed her other . . .

"Jordan!" she managed his name when his mouth broke from hers.

"You still smell like me," he whispered huskily. "Like you and me. Like sex. Musky. Erotic. Enticing."

"Jordan, we shouldn't— "

His eyes were on hers then. But he hadn't withdrawn his touch. She trembled, feeling as if he were completely within her, in her soul, her mind, filling her with his essence.

"Kathy, can you really leave?" he demanded. There was the oddest hint of anguish to the words.

She nodded.

She was lying.

He knew it.

"Do you really want to leave?"

She inhaled. Choked. Caught his head, her fingers threading in his hair, and pulled his mouth back to hers. She kissed him. Tasting the dreams she'd lost for a decade. Warning herself that she played recklessly with a fire that could scorch and burn and hurt her again, ripping open scars that had never really healed . . .

But it didn't matter. Not tonight. Tomorrow the world would change again. They could go their separate ways. Keep their distance. Right now . . .

Right now his touch was upon her. Within her. Her fingers relished the feel of him. His open-mouthed kiss ground down upon her lips, tongue sweeping deep into her mouth as the thrust of his fingers moved and stroked between her thighs. So much was sweetly familiar, so much had so long been denied. She touched him. Hands upon him. Fingers stroking down his chest. He was hers to touch again for this moment. Briefly, perhaps. But the ghosts of the past faded in the hungers of the present, as did the knowledge that he was no longer hers; for in these sweet moments, he was hers again. To touch, brush, pet. Stroke. Her palms upon his heated flesh. Fingers and kisses, liquid caresses, as intimate as any he might offer her. She'd missed the feel of him. Missed the length of his back, the muscles of his torso, his arms. The silvering, crisp sandy curls that grew in abundance on his chest. The tautness that remained at his waistline, the intoxicating fullness of his sex, the sheer sensual pleasure of closing her fingers around it . . .

They touched everywhere, kissed; aroused. He brought her down upon him. They moved like rabbits, wild, erratic, seeking more and more of one another, remembering, learning anew. He swept her beneath him, impatient with his own deepening desire, giving, demanding. She could no longer touch, kiss, caress . . . just hunger, seek, desire, demand, crave in turn. Waiting, feeling the sizzle of pure erotic pleasure build within her, crying out when it burst violently upon her, within her, throughout her. She was barely aware of him, then keenly aware of him, the fullness of him, the hardness of him, moving once more against her, as if he could become a part of her. Then he remained there.

She became aware of the air-conditioning again. Cool now that they were glittering with sweat touched by the moonglow and night lights streaking in upon them. He had shifted from her, but remained locked with her. So it had been during most of their married life.

She was tempted to ask him wistfully if it was the same way he made love to Tara Hughes. She didn't speak. She lay still, trying not to think, trying to savor the minutes that were still hers.

"We did so much so wrong," she said after a moment.

He moved his hands in her hair, remaining quiet, pensive. So be it. They had to be careful what they said. They lived separate lives now.

"Well, the girls would be happy that we've managed to get along," she murmured, pushing up. She could still rest her face against his slick shoulder. Feel him breathe, enjoy the warmth of his body.

He set an arm around her, pulling her back beside him, bringing her head to rest against his shoulder again. "Yeah, the girls would be glad."

She closed her eyes, thinking there was so much more to be said, then realizing that she didn't want to talk. She didn't want to move, didn't want to plan ahead, worry, regret what they had done.

Twice now.

She just wanted to lie beside him. Not too long. Soon enough, she'd have to rise. Slip back across the patio to the main house. To her own room.

Once upon a time, her room.

His fingers moved in her hair. The feel was absolutely lulling. She closed her eyes. A mistake. When she opened them again, the sky was bright outside the guest-house windows. She was tangled partially in the sheet, and partially with his body. One of her legs lay beneath him. One of his was draped over her hip. His hand was set just beneath her breast. His chest was against her side. His breath just touched her cheek, coming slowly, evenly, smoothly.

She stared at him a moment, felt wonderful for a second, then pained and alarmed. She'd touched him. It was morning. Morning's light was pouring in on her. Darkness had surely been far kinder.

Tara Hughes was one of the most perfectly formed females.

She was insane! Worrying, fearing her looks. It was daylight. People could be up and about.

She propped herself up, trying to stare over Jordan's still prone body and out to the patio beyond. What time was it? Early enough still? How the hell was she going to sneak back to the house?

"Seven-thirty," she heard suddenly. "Too early for the party crowd to be up and around."

She looked down. Jordan had sensed her movement and awakened. His eyes were cool upon her, narrowed, assessing. "Don't worry. You can salvage an image of innocence for Muscleman."

She frowned. "Jordan, that's horrible. I told you, Jeremy is smart and kind."

"I see. You mean 'Miss April' as a kind term."

She smiled ruefully. "She is a lovely child."

"So is he. And if he means a lot to you, I'll help you sneak back to the house."

She shook her head. "I'm worried about the girls. A very honest concern, don't you think? Since you are heavily involved with Miss April—"

"And you are surely all but engaged to Muscleman?"

"Jordan . . ." She broke off. Cold seemed to be racing through her. A sense of pure panic.

Because Miss April had arrived. She was stepping out of the Florida room doors, Peggy at her side, pointing to the guest house. Tara smiled, listened, nodded. Peggy stepped back into the Florida room, and Tara looked over to the guest house, pausing for a moment.

She was bone slim, casual, her white blond hair feathered around her oval face, a form-hugging short blue sheath emphasizing the beauty of her form, even her sandals displaying feet that were perfect.

And young.

"Oh, God!" Kathy gasped.

"What?"

She stared at Jordan, wild. "It's her!"

"Her?"

"Tara."

"She isn't due yet."

"Well, she's here!" Kathy started to leap up. She was amazed when he came to his knees, grasping her arm. "Kathy, damn it—!"

"Jordan, don't you understand me? Your lover— your mistress— is coming across the patio as we speak."

"Kathy, it's all right! Don't panic so, I—"

"Oh, God!" Kathy said desperately, wrenching away from him, finding her nightgown. "Jordan, the buttons are ripped, they're here on the floor. But I've got them. Oh, what am I going to do? I can't walk out like this. I—"

"It's all right!"

"It's not."

He gritted his teeth, staring at her hard, opened his mouth as if about to speak, then changed his mind. He swore softly.

"Fine. You don't want to be caught here." He leapt up, still stark naked, and amazingly unaffected and totally unself-conscious.

Yet totally appealing still. Even more so by the light of day.

He strode across the room to one of the drawers, bent down, opened it. He tossed something to Kathy, drawing out a pair of trunks for himself.

"Well, put it on."

"But Jordan—"

"It's a bathing suit, Kathy. We can have been going for an early swim when I suggested coffee."

"Jordan—"

"It's the best I can do, Kath. Since you are so determined to pretend nothing has happened."

"Things have happened. But things haven't changed!" she whispered miserably.

He stepped into the trunks. "Let's go swimming then," he said harshly.

Downstairs someone was trying the front door.

Kathy stumbled into the bathing suit in a flash. Jordan was already heading down the stairs.

And a soft tapping now fell upon the front door to the guest house . . .

Thirteen

"Jordan!"

Kathy came down the stairs just in time to see
Jordan open the door to Tara Hughes.

The young woman entered the guest house
with a great deal of enthusiasm, throwing her
arms around Jordan and placing a wet, passionate kiss on his lips with almost frantic fervor.
Kathy thought Jordan was rather stiff beneath
the onslaught, but then maybe she wanted him
to be not quite as receptive to his beloved as he
usually was.

"Jordan, I thought I'd be working through
Sunday at the earliest, but they finished up early
and one of the photographers has his own little
seaplane and was willing to deliver me right to
a dock on the beach! I'm so glad to be here; I
know how important this week is to you. Did the
gorgon arrive? Is she behaving? Is . . . is . . . ?"

Tara broke off, having seen Kathy standing at
the foot of the stairs.

Kathy would have happily strangled Jordan at
that moment. He had crawled into a nice, nor-
mal, conservative man's bathing suit, but he had

handed her a contraption with no back and a front so low it might as well have been next to nonexistent. She felt nearly naked, and even if she had half-killed herself with Jeremy at the gym, even if her most intimate, continual relationship of late had been with a Stairmaster, Tara's startled scrutiny made her incredibly uncomfortable.

But the younger woman appeared stunned and humiliated herself. After all, she had just referred to Kathy as a gorgon.

"I . . . I . . ." the blonde stuttered, sounding very much like a version of Ricky Ricardo. "I— "

Kathy couldn't bear to let her discomfort go on any longer. She stepped up to introduce herself, amazed to feel a certain sympathy, though why one of the most gorgeous young women in the world would want or need it, she didn't know.

"Tara— " she began, but Jordan was already stepping in as well.

"Tara, this is— "

"Yes, it's Kathy Treveryan, I, er, know. My God, you haven't changed. You are Kathy, right? Of course. I'm babbling. I've seen your pictures. I'm sorry. I'm very sorry. I didn't mean— "

"To call me a gorgon?" Kathy inquired, smiling.

"Oh, Lord." Tara moaned.

"Kathy, Tara Hughes. Tara, the gorgon," Jordan muttered wryly.

"I am sorry!" Tara repeated.

"It's quite all right." Kathy glanced at Jordan. "He has called me much worse over time."

"He never called you a gorgon," Tara said, then blushed furiously. She seemed to gather her poise then. "I am so sorry. I just didn't expect to see you— here. I mean, so soon. I mean— "

"It's quite all right. Really," Kathy said. "And my name is Connoly. Jordan and I are divorced. Let me say that it really is a pleasure to meet you. You're as gorgeous in person as you are in pictures."

"Thank you," Tara murmured. Her huge blue eyes wide, she looked from Kathy to Jordan. "I . . . didn't mean to interrupt anything," she said.

That was a lie. She'd be damned happy to interrupt anything brewing, Kathy thought. But Kathy was the one treading on Tara's territory.

"How sweet, but don't be ridiculous. Of course, you're not interrupting anything," Kathy told her quickly. "We'd been about to go for a swim— obviously, right?— but then we thought coffee sounded good first. Jordan was about to make some. I wonder if that's really necessary now. I'm sure Peggy has some brewing in the main house. I think I'll hurry on over and have some."

She started to make a swift retreat, trying to sail past both of them and out of the wretched situation.

"Kathy!"

She was so amazed that she nearly gasped out when Jordan reached out to stop her. He'd meant to grab her shoulder; he caught her hair, tangled the class ring he wore on his right hand in it. He tried to disentangle himself. Meanwhile Kathy stood still while Tara stared at the two of them and Jordan cursed.

"I was just going to say we'd all go over for coffee," he muttered. "I really need some. I'm sure you do too, Tara, eh?"

"You know I don't drink coffee," Tara said, frowning.

"Well, Peggy will have boiled water for tea!" he all but snapped.

Kathy was so eager to escape that she didn't care if she ripped out half of her hair, but at that moment she suddenly became free. It didn't matter. Jordan didn't intend to let her escape. He set his left hand upon the small of Kathy's back, the right upon Tara's, and nearly thrust them both from the guest house. "Let's go see what's going on over there, shall we?"

"But Jordan—" Tara began.

"It's a really perfect day," he broke in, propelling both women across the patio. "I'd thought to take the *Sand Shark* out. We should get started as soon as possible. I promised the girls we'd go diving today."

"I don't dive, Jordan," Tara reminded him a little coolly.

"Yes, but you enjoy the boat, right? You can snorkel."

"I hate snorkels, they smash your face," Tara declared testily.

"You're welcome to stay at the house," he told her.

"I wouldn't do that! I was so excited to get this time!" she said, then lowered her voice to a whisper not intended to be heard by Kathy. "To be here when you might need moral support!"

Kathy wanted to die—to jump into the pool and dive to the bottom.

"Do you know, it might be too scorching today to take the boat out," Kathy suggested.

"I promised the girls," Jordan said.

"We wouldn't want to disappoint them," Tara muttered.

When Kathy narrowed her eyes, Tara smiled sweetly.

"Then I think I'll just grab coffee and run upstairs with it and get a few things together," Kathy said.

This time, she escaped before Jordan could restrain her and raced ahead of them into the main house, annoyed with herself for desperately wishing the Stairmaster had at least hidden half the cellulite in her thighs when she could be concentrating on far more important, more adult, things—like world peace.

Either way, her wishing was farfetched.

It didn't matter.

Peggy had opened up the house, and Kathy was able to fly swiftly into it through the porch entrance. She hurried through the living room, smelled the coffee upon entering the dining room, and knew that she couldn't resist. She made a beeline for it, intending to do as she had said, snag a cup and race up the stairs. But Peggy was there, setting a cover over a chafing dish, and she smiled with such warmth and sincerity that Kathy knew she couldn't run right out.

"Kathy, excuse me, but you do look like a million bucks!" Peggy told her. "That's a beautiful suit. Where did you get it? Is that a New York style?"

Kathy opened her mouth to answer. "I . . . er . . . just picked it up somewhere along the line."

"You look much better than that one!" Peggy whispered, inclining her head toward the rear of the house, from which Jordan's and Tara's voices came to them.

Kathy poured a cup of coffee.

"She seems very sweet."

Peggy made a face. "Like saccharine."

"She's stunning."

"She's after him, big time."

"Peggy, he's a free agent. If she wants him happy—"

"He hasn't been happy since you left."

"Really? Why, she's gorgeous. She's young. She's perfect."

"You underestimate Jordan."

"Right. What man wouldn't be swayed by a woman like that?"

"Kathy—"

"Oh, Peggy!" Kathy set her cup down, swiftly hugging the wonderful woman who had once been her housekeeper. "Jordan and I are over. Have been over. You make me feel as badly as my daughters do. I can't fix things now. And apparently he's been intimate with Tara for quite some time."

Peggy shrugged. "A while."

"And I have a great life. Honestly, I do."

Peggy nodded, adjusting silver on the buffet table. "I guess so. You're dating a very nice young man." She eyed Kathy. "Young man, I repeat."

"Women are supposed to date younger men—because we outlive them. My mother told me so."

Peggy grinned. "Oh, by the way, Sally is on her way to the house."

"What?" Kathy had been picking up her coffee again, anxious to flee up the stairs before Tara and Jordan reached them. She was so startled she nearly spilled it. "She told me she wasn't coming until tomorrow or Monday."

"Seems everyone is anxious to arrive." Peggy sniffed toward the rear of the house. Jordan and Tara had obviously paused to talk outside.

What were they saying to one another? Kathy couldn't help but wonder.

"Anyway, Sally says she decided there just wasn't any reason for her not to come earlier. She called the airlines and had no problem changing her ticket. She called here about fifteen minutes ago to make sure it was all right to come on along. I assured her Jordan will be delighted to see her whenever she can get here.

I knocked on your door to see if you wanted a word with her, but I didn't get an answer. I thought you might still be sleeping."

"I must have been out by the pool," Kathy said, staring into her coffee.

Peggy didn't say anything, but Kathy could feel the question in her gaze.

"Hmmm. Didn't see you there."

"Well, I think I have to . . . brush my hair. Or something," Kathy murmured. She must get upstairs. She wanted some time to herself.

She needed a shower. Before her mother got here. And she needed to recoup some poise, some composure.

"Kathy, there's all kinds of breakfast here," Peggy offered.

"I won't be fifteen minutes!" Kathy said cheerfully. "Catch Mom when she comes in, will you? She's always in dire need of coffee this early in the morning."

"It isn't early. It's just past ten."

"She'll have been up a while. She'll need more coffee."

With that, Kathy managed to flee back up the stairs.

To her room. *Her room.*

She swallowed the coffee as if it were a shot of liquor she could gulp. It scorched her throat. She started to sit at the foot of the bed and changed her mind. She really needed that shower. She hurried into the bathroom and caught a glimpse of herself in the mirror.

What had Tara Hughes seen when she had looked at her? A gorgon?

Her hair was wild, a tangled auburn mane. Her eyes were wide, still dilated, very amber. Panic seemed to be good for her. And the bathing suit, brief though it was, was a very attractive one, designed, oddly enough, to minimize any anatomical failings with its clean cut. She looked good. Not like a thirty-year-old model, but good. Attractive. Panic even seemed to make her look sexy.

Or was it . . .

. . . Jordan?

Being with Jordan again. Almost being caught being with Jordan again.

Well, Tara was here now.

Auld lang syne was not in the past. But . . .

She didn't want to think about Jordan, Tara, herself. Or herself and Jordan, or Tara and Jordan. She wanted to curl up somewhere, pretend that the night might have gone on forever.

That nothing had ever gone wrong between them. That she was really home.

She wasn't, she told herself firmly. She was a big girl. She'd wanted sex with her ex-husband. She'd had it. Time to shower and get on.

She stripped off the bathing suit and stepped into the shower stall, turning the water on. It was so cold she jumped. That was good. She should have taken a very cold shower quite a while ago.

Such thoughts didn't help. And somewhere in the middle of her shower, she realized that warm tears were colliding with the wet spray on her cheeks. She shouldn't have come back. It hurt more than she had ever imagined. Even more now that she had touched the past.

The shower kept running. Washing away the foolish tears that should have all been shed long ago. Despite the pain, she was glad to be here. She couldn't bring back the past. She did have something back of Jordan, though, and it mattered, it counted, because he had been a part of so very much of her life. He thought someone had caused Keith's death all those years ago, and strange things were happening. It was time to exorcise some ghosts. She would do so.

With dignity.

"Mom!"

The water was still spraying down on her when Kathy heard the door burst open and herself being called. She turned off the shower and grabbed a towel, leaping from the tub. It was Alex who had come in.

Her daughter was standing by the bed, hands on her hips, staring at Kathryn. She wore her sandy blond hair to her shoulders, with a sweep that half covered one green eye. In her teal bikini, she stood barefoot, her flesh a golden tan, her slim young figure stunning.

"*She's* here!" Alex announced.

"She?" Kathy inquired, though she knew perfectly well who *she* was.

"Tara."

"I know. I've seen her."

"She was supposed to be modeling on some sandspit island," Alex said.

"Let me get dressed. I'll be right with you."

Kathy closed the bathroom door and slipped back into the bathing suit she had discovered she rather liked. She opened the bathroom door and came out, sitting beside Alex on the bed and placing an arm around her. "I wish I hadn't come here," Kathy said.

"Mom, it's been the best thing in the world—"

"Alex, I'm glad for me, and even for your father, that I did. We may finally be friends. But I'm sorry because of you and Bren. Your dad has apparently been seeing Tara fairly regularly. It makes no difference that she arrived here a day or so early."

"We were supposed to have today alone. As a family."

"You forget. Jeremy is here."

"Mom. There's nothing between you and Jeremy."

"Your dad doesn't know that—does he?"

"Of course not." Alex waved a hand in the air. "Mother, don't be so naive. Everyone knows men want what other men have. That's a fact of life."

Kathy smiled. "Oh, really? Well, what happens when one particular man has what scores of others pant over daily?"

"Mom—"

"She seems nice enough."

Alex sighed. "She's all right, I guess. Not too bright, but not dumb-blond stupid. And I'll tell you one thing, she isn't going to keep Dad long one way or the other."

"Why?" Kathy asked curiously.

Alex shrugged. "She hangs. He likes his freedom. His place and her place. She's always had her own room here. I don't think he ever sleeps through the night with her, and he didn't really want her this week."

"How do you know? Did he tell you that for a fact?"

Alex hesitated. "No. But something has been bothering him for a while. And I *know* him. He wanted this week for Blue Heron." She hesitated again. "He did tell Tara that if she was unhappy about the time he needed to spend with others this week he would understand if she wanted to go her own way."

"He said this to her in front of you?" Kathy inquired skeptically.

"Well . . ." Alex murmured. "All right, I was eavesdropping. It was the weekend I came down after classes let out for summer."

"You knew then that he was planning this, and you didn't say a word to me? Oh, that's right, you wouldn't have had time to warn me, your mother, you were busy talking to the newspapers!"

Alex flushed. "Dad asked me not to warn you. He said he wanted to speak to you, that he wanted your decision to be reached by discussion between the two of you. You mean you're not going to yell at me for eavesdropping?"

"Alex, you're almost twenty-one. I can't really

yell at you for anything. However, it was incredibly rude of you to spy on your father and Tara. Don't do it anymore."

Alex grinned, then grew somber again. "I just wish she'd stayed away a while longer."

"Well, she's here, and we're all going to be polite and make the best of it, right?"

"Thank God for Jeremy. He is so wickedly good-looking."

"Alex—"

"He has to make Dad jealous."

"A man doesn't always covet what another man has, and jealousy isn't necessarily a good thing. Trust is the most important ingredient in any relationship. Love and trust. If you have those two—"

"Did you guys have them?"

Kathy smiled. "Once. But we lost them. So don't go through life thinking it's good to torture someone you love with jealousy."

"You did invite Jeremy down."

Kathy opened her mouth to speak, then closed it. "That's not quite the same."

"You were chicken about coming alone?"

"That doesn't sound great either, but it's closer." She inhaled, started to speak again, then broke off as she heard her name called by someone down below.

"Kathy? You up there?"

Wincing, she told Alex, "Gram."

"That's super. Isn't it? I mean, I love Gram. Don't you?"

"Of course. I just wasn't ready to have *her* here yet."

Alex grinned, shaking her head. "Poor Mom! Well, I guess we'd better get back down. You know Dad. When he moves, he goes like lightning. He'll be ready to head out soon, and I'm starving."

"Kathy? Alex?"

Alex jumped up, hurrying to the door. "Hi, Gram! We'll be right down." She looked at her mother. "Come on."

"I need to get a cover-up— and dig out my deck shoes."

"There's plenty of stuff on the *Sand Shark.*"

"You'd better bring a cover-up," she told her daughter sternly. "That bathing suit is . . ."

"Indecent?" Alex queried, arching a brow.

"Almost."

"Well"— she pointed at her mother— "that one is most certainly decadent."

"Really? Should I find something else?"

"No! It's great-decadent. Come on, Mom, give Tara a run for it."

"I'm not after your father."

"Okay, then save the family honor. You look great. You used to just walk on the boat in your bathing suit and throw on one of Dad's shirts when the sun got to be too much. Be daring. Be natural. Besides, we're going diving and he has a storage room full of wet suits and skins. You'll be covered up soon enough."

"I still need deck shoes," Kathy insisted.

In the end, she slipped into deck shoes and

an old shirt, which, beneath Alex's challenging gaze, she wore open. They came down the stairs arm in arm, found out that Sally had given up waiting for them and gone in to breakfast, and walked on into the huge dining room with its wide windows. Sally was sipping coffee and chatting with her ex-son-in-law, Bren was picking apart a bagel, and Jeremy and Tara were engaged in a conversation at the far end of the table, their heads lowered. Neither of the pair noticed the newcomers.

"Darlings!" Sally said cheerfully, offering her daughter an arched-brow perusal as she hugged her granddaughter. "You both look lovely. You do take your time, though. I'm glad you can join me for a minute's worth of breakfast before taking off."

"You're not coming on the boat, Mom?" Kathy asked her. "Jordan won't mind waiting for you to get settled and changed, I'm sure."

"Not in the least," Jordan said politely. His gaze was impassive when his eyes met Kathy's.

"I know, and thanks," Sally said. "But I'm going to settle into my room and take a good book out to the pool. Maybe do some catching up with Peggy. Angel and Joe are going— you know Joe, he's always been the dive-master for all of you."

"Gram, even if you don't want to dive, it will be a nice trip out," Alex said. "Tara and Jeremy are coming." She managed to keep her distaste from her voice and smile. Her father's eyes were on her.

"I'll be fine on my own. You young people just have a nice day. Besides, Rye is due in, Jeremy tells me. And I haven't seen him in years. We can discuss really old music together."

Kathy arched a brow at Jordan. He hadn't mentioned to her that his father was coming. She would be glad to see Rye, too. He was a fine gentleman, he'd been the best father-in-law in the world, always seeing if she needed something when the girls were young, when Jordan had been in the service. "How nice," she said, and she meant it most sincerely.

"Dad wouldn't have missed Alex's birthday," he reminded her.

"Of course not," Kathy said. A knife twisted within her. How would she really know? The girls had led split lives. Most of their time had been spent with her. But they had always had a home with their father as well, and mostly due to Kathy's insistence, their time with him had been kept entirely separate.

"Want a muffin or something, Mom?" Alex suggested.

"A muffin?" Sally said indignantly. "You may all diet later. Peggy whipped up omelettes and her delicious potatoes and all sorts of wonderful things. Eat breakfast! That's exactly what I intend on doing." She started for the buffet table. The others followed her.

"Peggy cooks with low-fat everything," Jordan said, looking at his ex-wife. "You haven't given up eating, have you?" As if in challenge, he handed her a plate.

She shook her head. "An omelette sounds wonderful."

It was while she was at the buffet that she felt an arm slip around her. She nearly jumped. Luckily, she didn't. It was Jeremy.

" 'Morning," he said huskily.

" 'Morning," she returned, smiling. Bless him. He was just right. He had that devilishly wicked smile in place. He didn't do anything overt, he just touched her with an affection that truly might have been that of a lover quite comfortable in this relationship. Jordan was scooping up potatoes at her side. She thought his face tensed.

"Want some coffee?" Jeremy asked.

"Love some."

Kathy ate breakfast seated between him and Jordan while Tara was to Jordan's right.

Tara had changed into a swimsuit. It was one piece, simple and black.

Black had never looked so good.

As she engaged in light conversation, Kathy noted that there seemed to be just a slight tension between Jordan and Tara. She wondered what they were discussing. They were careful not to raise their voices.

Thirty minutes later *Sand Shark* was already out of the channel and heading south for the Keys. She was large, a beautiful vessel of fifty feet, with old wood and chrome incorporated in her design. Though she had three sails, she was running on the motor today since Jordan was anxious to get down to the reefs. He was at the wheel most of the way, while Tara sat up front on the sleek bow, bathed in lotion. She kept checking her watch.

Bren told Kathy that she did so because she wanted to get a golden color, but was careful to avoid injury from the sun.

"The sun ages you terribly, you know," Bren said, waving a hand dramatically in the air.

"She's right about that. You and your sister had better watch out for it," Kathy said sweetly.

"I won't be a hot-house flower for anyone," Bren said with a sniff.

"Honey, in this she's quite intelligent. If you're not careful you can get skin cancer. Especially when you spend so much time in this sun."

"Sure, Mom, whatever you say."

Bren left Kathy where she'd been sitting across from Jeremy, just a few feet from the helm where Jordan kept them on course.

Kathy leaned back and felt the sun on her face. It was good. Tara was right. The sun was an ager. But it felt so damned nice.

A second later, a golden skinned Tara, now wearing a white cotton cover-up, came up from the galley with a cold Bud in her hand. She slipped into the chair beside the helm, offering the Bud to Jordan.

He shook his head. Tara seemed unhappy, but popped the metal flip-top herself, took a long swallow of the beer. Jordan cast her a glance. "Thanks, but after!" he called to her over the roar of the motor. "I never drink and dive."

"Right!" Tara called. She set a hand upon his neck. Kathy leaned her head back down again, then looked across at Jeremy.

She might be suffering, but Jeremy was truly in seventh heaven. Slicked down with sun spray, he leaned back and smiled up at the blue sky. As if he sensed that Kathy was watching him, he lowered his head, then moved across to join her.

"Everything okay so far?"

She squeezed his hand. "Great. You've been a lifesaver."

"You look great, you know," he told her.

She smiled. "Thanks. You don't mind being out here, right? We won't stay down that long. Maybe thirty, forty-five minutes at a couple of sites."

"Kathy, there's a pitcher of piña colada down in the galley. The sky is blue, the sea is blue-green, I'm on holiday, and you want to know if I'm all right?"

She stroked his cheek affectionately. "Thanks," she said with a smile.

She was startled to realize that Jordan was suddenly standing over her. "Want to start suiting up? We're nearly at Molasses Reef."

Kathy looked from Jordan to the helm. Joe Garcia, muscled and brown in his swim trunks and dockers, had taken over at the helm. The girls were near him over on the starboard side, slipping into their skins with Angel's help. Their regulators and buoyancy control vests were already attached to the air cylinders. As they'd all been taught in the classes they'd taken years before, they checked the air pressure in each other's cylinders. Jordan was a stickler about diving. It was a sport, and they went about it by the rules. No one on his boat ever dove without a buddy, and no one ever went down without proper equipment.

She gazed back to Jordan. He was wearing sunglasses; she couldn't begin to read the expression in his eyes.

"Don't mind if I borrow her for a diving buddy, do you, old boy?" he asked Jeremy.

"Be my guest, sir," Jeremy responded with a smile.

"Kathy?"

"Yeah, sure," she said. She rose, following him over to the equipment. He found her a skin, a nice thin one since the day was so hot, and she crawled into it. They checked one another's regulators. It was as natural as breathing. They had done this hundreds of times.

The anchor was thrown. Kathy and Jordan were suited, masks in hand. The girls had on their skins.

"Shall we go?" Jordan asked Kathy.

She nodded, grinning. They looked like alien space creatures in their skins, vests, regulators, boots, flippers, gloves, and cylinders, their masks on backward.

"Do you really need all that stuff?" Tara inquired suddenly. "It looks so uncomfortable."

"It isn't really. You should take a class," Kathy suggested.

Tara wrinkled her nose. "I just don't have the time," she said. "Of course, it doesn't look like it can be that hard."

"It's not just a matter of knowing what to do," Jordan said. "It can be the most beautiful experience in the world, really quite simple— yet deadly if approached stupidly. Kath, let's go, shall we?"

"Have a good time, buddies!" Tara called. Too cheerfully.

"We'll be up soon," Jordan said. "Kids, you coming?"

"Yep!" Angel called to him.

"Who is whose buddy there?" Tara asked sweetly.

"When the number of divers isn't even," Alex explained gravely, "one group goes as a threesome."

Jordan was on his way to the drop-off at the stern. Kathy followed him. He stepped into the water, sank a few feet, surfaced, waited for her. She slipped her mask on, held it in place, and took her step in.

The water felt deliciously cool after the beating-down sun, and since the reef wasn't a deep one, the temperature wouldn't fall much more. It would have been delightful without the skin, but once on one of their earlier dives with the girls, they had eschewed skins and Alex had been caught by the tentacles of a jellyfish. Kathy enjoyed the protection of the skin.

Jordan let air out of his vest, sinking down toward the reef, and she followed suit.

It had been a long time since she dove. She had forgotten how much she loved it. Elegant sea fans in startling colors waved as she drifted by them, and Jordan tapped her arm, pointing out a huge grouper. When a ray swam up from the sand, she pointed the graceful creature out to him.

Time stood still; the world was eerily quiet, seductively beautiful. Kathy could hear the rhythmic sound of her own regulator and nothing more. The coolness of the sea was magical. She could have stayed beneath the surface forever.

Yet forever would not be long, not that day. Within minutes something splashed about heavily in the water, close enough to draw their attention. Frowning, Jordan motioned to Kathy. She followed at first, not understanding what had happened.

Tara was in the water. Clad in a bathing suit, buoyancy control vest and regulator, and flippers, she was thrashing about madly, trying to surface, trying to rid herself of the paraphernalia.

Jordan thrust swiftly through the water, Kathy at his side. When he tried to reach Tara, she kicked him, the blow sending him from her. Kathy realized that Tara couldn't breathe out of her regulator. She thrust her own safe-second into Tara's mouth even as Jordan regained control and shot back toward them again, grasping Tara and rising with her while she desperately sucked on air from Kathy's safe-second.

By then, the girls and Angel were aboard, though it had all happened so fast—and in shallow enough water to keep them from rising as quickly as possible. They got Tara to the surface, got the equipment off her, and handed her over to Joe and Jeremy who were anxiously waiting at the stern to hoist her up.

"You monsters!" Tara shrieked.

Kathy, pulling off her fins and hurrying up the ladder, came dripping up on deck in plenty of time to see that Tara was fine—but raging mad and shouting at Bren and Alex. "Vicious little *monsters!*" she shouted.

"Wait!" Kathy called out, stepping forward.

But Jordan was at her side, pushing past her with Joe right behind him, helping him off with his equipment. "I want to know what the hell happened here!" Jordan snapped.

Tara burst into tears, covering her face. "I'm so sorry, but I was terrified! I thought I'd drown."

Jordan, down to his skin and boots, knelt beside her, and she threw her arms around him, sobbing. "I shouldn't have done it, I wanted you to be proud of me. I know how much you love diving."

Kathy felt Joe at her back, helping her doff her equipment.

She stared at Angel, Bren, and Alex, soaked as well, helping one another with their equipment, their faces white.

"What happened?" she inquired softly.

"Tara asked us all sorts of questions," Alex said with a shrug.

"We answered them," Bren added innocently.

"Miss Hughes just decided to go diving on her own," Angel offered. "We didn't realize it until she dove into the water."

"You knew what I meant to do!" Tara suddenly accused.

"I swear," Alex told her, "I thought you were far too intelligent to attempt such a thing!"

"Whatever the hell happened," Jordan said angrily, staring from his daughter to Tara, "it was stupid and dangerous, and nothing like it had better ever happen again."

"She never asked how to turn the air on," Bren told her mother.

Jordan stood up, disentangling himself from Tara's arms.

"Jordan . . ." she said tearfully. "I— "

"We'll head back, Tara. I don't think anyone feels like diving anymore today."

He firmly placed her hands in her lap, then glanced at Joe. Joe nodded and he and Angel quickly set about securing the cylinders while Jordan returned to the helm.

It seemed a very long, very tense ride back to the house on Star Island.

When they docked, Tara made her way from the boat to the patio, sinking into one of the chairs there, and Jordan began to talk to her.

Kathy followed her daughters into the kitchen.

"What happened?" she demanded.

Alex said, "Mom, honest to God— "

"Listen to me, darlings, because I mean this. You can't do evil little things to Tara Hughes. If you encouraged her to go into the water—"

"We didn't! We'd never hurt her," Alex said. "Mom, I swear, we didn't do anything to her. We told her it was extremely dangerous to think she could dive when she couldn't."

"But you left her by the equipment!"

"Mom, she asked questions, we answered them, and that was it. Ask Angel. We wouldn't want to kill her!" Bren said.

"I know that. But you shouldn't have told her or shown her anything. She could have died."

"We weren't in more than thirty feet of water," Alex said with a sigh.

"People have drowned in just inches," Kathy reminded her.

"Honest, Mom, we had no part in this. She asked us questions, we answered them. We didn't know she meant to be a showoff and flop into the water until we heard her dive in."

"All right, I believe you. But in the future, remember, don't do anything at all to make a fool out of her."

"We didn't and we wouldn't. We don't need to. She doesn't need any help in that department," Bren said complacently.

Kathy frowned at her.

"Mom, please! I swear to God, we didn't think she'd do anything so foolish."

"All right. Just remember, you two can't fix things, no matter how much you'd like your father and me to be together again. Do you understand?"

Even as Kathy spoke, her mother came breezing into the kitchen. She went straight for the refrigerator to get a soda, and into the freezer for ice, humming as they all went silent.

She suddenly stopped humming and looked at the girls. Her eyes were twinkling. "Girls! Your own instructors would be appalled! You should never have encouraged Tara to attempt diving!"

"But we didn't . . ." Bren began. She seemed to give up and just sighed. "Right, Gram," she murmured.

"It was a horrible and dangerous thing to do to her."

"We didn't intend for her to dive in," Alex said.

"Ummm," Sally murmured. "Well, whatever. No more tricks. Your mother is just going to have to compete on her own."

"Against a thirty-year-old beauty queen," Alex said dolefully.

"Thanks." Kathy smiled.

"Have some faith, girls, Kathy really can compete on her own. She has a higher I.Q.—"

"But what about bust size?" Bren asked.

"Bren!"

"Your mother's chest is quite nice," Sally said. She grinned at Kathy and added with a mischievous innocence, "and it's still almost exactly where it's supposed to be!"

"Mother!" Kathy gasped.

"Excuse me," Sally said, "the poor little dear needs some ice and a nice cool drink." She obtained a glass from a cabinet and put ice and soda in it, humming once more. Then, without looking at them again, she left the kitchen. Kathy stared after her, then spun around as she heard her daughters discussing her once more.

"Mom's boobs are still in the right place," Bren assured Alex. "Well, almost. No one can totally defy gravity."

"Would you ladies please worry about your own anatomies?" Kathy demanded. "I believe you didn't mean any harm to Tara, but I'm warning you— behave! And quit talking about my boobs! There will be dire consequences if you do not!"

With that, she walked out of the kitchen herself, and headed for the pool.

Fourteen

Kathy was stretched out in the bathtub, surrounded by a mound of bubbles. Her head rested against the cool porcelain of the tub while she stretched out an arm to keep a manuscript page from the bubbles while she read. The bulk of the manuscript sat on a wicker foot stool about eighteen inches from the tub.

The story was excellent. Though by a new author and definitely in need of some cleaning up, the writing was fast paced, lucid, and exciting. The plot was based on an actual Texas murder case in which all the circumstantial evidence had pointed toward the woman's lover. He had been given the death penalty, but literally hours before his execution, a forensic scientist had proven that the dark hairs found in the woman's body bag had belonged to the corpse who had previously occupied it, rather than the lover-condemned-as-a-murderer. The case was fairly old and none of the players had been well known, so it had received little notoriety; the author had used that to her advantage.

Kathy rose enough to exchange the pages she

had been reading for the next few and settled back again.

She heard a tapping on her outer door.

"Who is it?" she asked, thinking that it might easily be one of her daughters and hoping that her voice would carry through the bedroom beyond the bath.

"Jordan. May I come in?"

She started to sit up, calling out, "No! I'm in the bath—" Then she broke off with a sigh, gritting her teeth as she leaned back again.

He'd already entered the bedroom and was striding on into the bathroom.

"I'm in the tub."

"So I see."

"You shouldn't be in here."

"I might have missed something before?" he asked politely.

"Jordan, it's one thing to . . . er, reminisce about the past when no one else is present—"

"The bathroom doesn't look crowded to me. Where is that handsome young hunk?"

"Jeremy is sleeping."

"Ah."

"Shouldn't you be with Tara?"

"Not at the moment. I'm here. I want to speak with you."

"Jordan, speaking with me is one thing, but I don't want to hurt other people—and I know you don't." There, that was mature and dignified. "Tara is here now. The poor child you're dating has already had a traumatic enough day." She could have bitten her tongue.

"Tara. Hmmm. Are we worrying about my child right now or your musclebound toddler?"

"Cute. Seriously, when I left you—"

"Tara is fine. I just came to make sure we're still on for dinner. Mickey is coming by at seven. We're going to go to a friend's steakhouse. They've got small private rooms where we can talk and be alone. You still feel all right about going?"

She nodded, frowning. "But I don't see how you—"

"Tara knew from the beginning that I had things to do this weekend."

"But—"

"Naturally, security for the benefit and our daughter's party concerns the two of us."

"But why wouldn't it concern Tara?"

"Kathy, why are you defending her?"

"Instinct. I always protect children."

His mouth curled in a rueful half-smile. She should have been getting used to him again, but the oddest sensation stirred within her, as if her heart thudded and fell within her chest. She was suddenly grateful to be a woman. The room had grown very warm. It might have been the slick feel of the bubbles, the ripple of the water. It might have been the fact that she just hadn't had enough sex in years. And then again, it might just be Jordan, but hot, sweet flashes of desire were streaking through her and had she had a portion of anatomy that might rise in a telltale salute, it would be doing so now.

At any rate she was covered with bubbles. And

her hand was falling, the bubbles encroaching on her manuscript pages.

"Just what are you doing?" Jordan demanded, still half smiling as he hunkered down beside her and the manuscript.

"Reading," she murmured, flushing. She should put down the threatened pages. She didn't want to rise from the water enough to do so, not and reveal nipples hard as little acorns. The water, of course. The coolness of the air against the heat of the water, surely.

Not to Jordan. He'd know right off.

"Reading?"

"Yes."

"Here? Now?"

"Yes! What's the problem? Jealous because I can still read small print?"

"Can you?"

"Well, fairly small."

"Good for you."

"Put these pages back for me, please?"

He obligingly took them, studying them curiously as he returned them to the manuscript. Then he stared at her, elbows resting upon his knees as he remained hunkered down and very close.

"What are you really doing with these?"

"A read-through."

"Pardon?"

"It's just a copy of a manuscript. I'm reading it to make a decision on whether we should buy it or not."

"You're working— now? You're on vacation, out of your office."

"Editors seldom get to *edit* in the office."

"I see. Ummm. I'm humbled. A week at your ex-husband's home, a reunion with your old group, threats due to a possible murder in the past— and you're reading!"

She sighed, folding her arms over her chest. The bubbles were suddenly melting too rapidly. "Editors read everywhere," she said defensively. "We keep tiny flashlights for reading in the backs of cabs and on subways. When the batteries die, we stretch our necks out every time we pass a street light. It's part of the job. Besides, this novel is quite compelling."

He arched a brow, that rueful smile still in place. "More so than this place, it seems."

"It's filled with suspense."

"And life isn't?"

"Well, my biggest suspense at the moment is to see that it doesn't fall into the tub."

"And what if it were to fall in?" He leaned closer to her. Bubbles seemed to be popping by the billions. She tightened her arms over her chest.

"Such things have happened. One of the major houses lost out on a *New York Times* bestseller because the only copy of the author's first manuscript was swept away in his Jacuzzi."

"Wonder what he was doing in the Jacuzzi."

"Losing the manuscript. And millions of dollars."

"But depending on what he was doing in that Jacuzzi, it just might have been worth it."

Her heart did that ridiculous flip-flop again. What was the matter with her? He was just so close now. Bathed, smelling of soap and after-shave, scents so familiar they seemed to speak to her blood, beckon to something within her over which she had no control. She was hot, she was shaking. Visibly, she was certain. She needed him out of here. This was really just too much. She tried to tell him so.

"Jordan, we're divorced, we're with other people. I agreed to come here, but you can't just walk in when I'm in the tub anymore and carry on a conversation. You can't just . . ."

"What?" He'd leaned even closer. His handsome features were very taut, his eyes held a hard glimmer. "Can't what?" he repeated on a husky whisper.

She shook her head, moistening very dry lips. "Can't . . . can't . . ."

She was still stuttering when he kissed her, his mouth suddenly rapacious as he caught her shoulders, drawing her up from the water, bringing both of them to their feet. His hands were on her breasts, feeling the hardness of her nipples. He knew. Damn. It didn't matter. Open-mouthed, wet, hot, he was still kissing her, his tongue sliding . . . in . . . out. She had her hands on him, his arms, his chest, wet fingers sliding over the cotton denim of his casual tailored shirt. Finding his belt, unbuckling it. Unzipping his jeans. Running her fingers along the waistband of his briefs, thrusting them down. She cupped her hands around his derriere, circled forward. Men. What a dead giveaway. She encircled his hardness, her fingers, caressing . . .

Dead giveaway. A little cry escaped her. He was lifting her so that she was out of the tub. His touch was all over her. Inside her.

"Oh-my-god," she heard herself babble, half whispering, half laughing. "We're too tall—"

"Never did make it in the tub," he agreed, his lips still a line of fire against her flesh.

"Can't—"

"Have to—"

"Have to, yes, have to . . ."

"Now . . ."

"Where, how—?"

"Here."

"Now."

"Turn around."

The fullness of his body was against her back; his hands caressed her again; skimming along her throat, her breast, down the length of her. Then his fingers were in her hair, his other hand causing her to bend and brace herself against a towel rack. His palms rounded over her buttocks and suddenly he was completely within her. The feeling was sheerly exquisite, undeniable. He began to move and she heard herself whispering again, babbling perhaps, her words entwining with his, encircling them, a part of them, as he was a part of her.

"Please . . ."

"Yes . . ."

"Oh, God . . ."

"Yes . . ."

"Now . . ."

"Sweet . . ."

"Ohgodohgod . . ."

She wanted, sought, reached. Arched, writhed, accommodated, whispered anew, and in the end, cried out. Loudly. Too loudly. She gasped almost instantly after, clapping her hand to her mouth in horror.

"It's all right!" Jordan whispered huskily against her ear. His arms were still around her. Protective and strong now. She could feel his clothing. Soaked from her.

There was a tapping on the door that connected Jordan's bedroom to his office.

Where Jeremy had been sleeping.

"Kathy? Kathy? Are you all right?"

She pressed against Jordan and started naked from the bath, thought again and grabbed a towel.

"Kathy . . ." Jordan began.

But she was gone. She didn't open the connecting door, she stood in front of it, wrapped in the towel. "Jeremy, I'm fine. I . . . I dropped my makeup bag. Sorry. Go back to sleep."

"Sure. As long as you're all right—"

"I'm fine. Honest."

" 'Kay."

She bit her lip, staring at the door. Then she turned. Jordan had followed her. He stood twenty feet away, clothes all rezipped and in place, hands on his hips; staring at her.

"You dropped your makeup bag?" he mocked softly, a brow arched high.

"Oh, do hush up!" she whispered back fiercely. She started to stride by him, holding her towel and chin high, but he caught her by the arm. She glared up at him, trembling and trying to hide it.

He probed her eyes, his very dark. She thought he was about to rip into her, and was startled when he said, "If you're that upset, then I'm very sorry."

"Don't be ridiculous. I . . . I have always taken responsibility for my own actions."

"Still, I—"

"Don't apologize! I'm older than you, for God's sake!"

He smiled, his jaw slightly crooked.

"I just feel . . . badly," she said lamely.

His eyes remained dark. "Amazing. I feel good. Incredibly good."

Her eyes fell. "We didn't break up because of sex," she murmured.

"No."

"And sex isn't everything."

"It can be damned important."

"But not everything. And you can't—"

"Can't what?" he demanded.

"Nothing."

She might be a few days older; he was definitely stronger. He held her, lifting her chin.

"Can't what?"

"You can't be having a bad sex life, not with

the platinum kitten out there! She probably has the most perfect body known to man!"

Kathy kept her chin high. She tried very hard to be flippant.

She'd thought she'd succeeded. But he was still smiling. That smile that was rueful, that mocked them both and the world, and somehow made her want to smile as well.

"She has a good body," he agreed.

"And a young one," Kathy supplied, damning herself for her stupidity in making sure that he noted all of Tara's sterling qualities.

"But I've always liked yours. And it's not just the body, you know. It's what one does with it as well."

"Oh?"

"You manage yours incredibly well."

"Thank you. I think."

He drew her close. "I do struggle to deal with mine as well, you realize."

"What?" She was confused.

"Well, I like to think I stay in decent shape, but then I don't compare to the Greek god in yon chamber."

"What? Oh . . . ah . . . Jeremy."

"Ummm."

"Well, he does have a good body. Still, I've always liked yours."

"Thanks."

"And you do quite well with it, too."

"Quite well?"

"Sure."

"Not *incredibly* well. Ummm. I may have to try harder to convince you—"

"Jordan!" she gasped, pushing away from him. She shook her head vehemently. "Jordan, we've got to stop this. It just isn't right. It . . ."

"It's dangerous," he agreed solemnly, holding her very gently again.

"Yes!" she agreed on a whisper. *Oh, yes!* It felt as if they shared a common ground, a sweet intimacy. Secrets residing in each other's souls. *Dangerous.*

"Dangerous. It's already caused serious problems."

She drew back. "My God. What?"

"Your manuscript."

"What?" She blinked.

"I tried to salvage it, but when you went tearing from the bathroom to reassure Muscleman, you sent it flying from the foot stool and into the tub."

"What?" She gasped again, but knew he was telling the truth. So much for shared intimacy!

"Millions of dollars!" he teased. "But, God, you were worth it! Was I?"

"Oh!"

She broke away from him and hurried back into the bathroom. He had tried to salvage the manuscript, but the pages, all soaked, had stuck together when he had tried to put them in a pile.

They were pulp.

Pulp fiction.

She almost laughed.

Jordan had followed her again. He leaned

against the door frame, watching her as she tried to look through the sodden sheets without ripping them.

"Help me!" she said.

He arched a brow. "Kath, you can't possibly salvage—"

"I'm not trying to. I just want the title page. I need the author's phone number and address. Oh, damn! This is all chapter seven. Here's eight."

Jordan sighed and hunkered down again, looking through the wet pages. Kathy hadn't realized her towel had come undone until he thrust it back at her. "Will you get decent, please?"

"I am decent!" she assured him.

He offered her a loud sniff.

"Damn you, Jordan!"

"Here."

"Here?"

"Title page. I found it. It's a two-one-two area code. Your author is right in the Big Apple."

"Give it to me."

She snatched the page from him, offering a hasty, thanks, and hurried out to the phone.

"Kathy, it's Saturday! Don't you have to call the agent or something? Shouldn't this be done on Monday morning?"

"She's not represented. This is a first manuscript— out of the slush pile. And I'm not losing it!"

She put through the call, and was relieved to talk to a very excited young woman on the phone. Kathy made her the same offer she would have made an author with an aggressive agent, but she carefully insisted on a two-book contract for the price. She'd probably offered too much money, but Marty would back her up. He trusted her instincts. And if she was right, on a hard/soft deal, with a film sale, they would make a fortune—and so would the author.

Jordan watched her throughout the phone conversation, until she hung up, satisfied, smiling.

He crossed his arms over his chest, grinning. "So . . . did sex just make her a fortune or screw her all to hell?"

"My publishing house and the author should do quite well, thank you very much," she replied curtly.

"Think nothing of it."

"Jordan, if I'm going to make dinner—"

"That's right. You have to salvage that dropped makeup bag, hmmm?"

"Jordan—"

"I'm going. Seven o'clock. Be ready."

"I will."

He inclined his head, indicating the door that connected with his office.

"You've already spoken with Jeremy and he has no problem with your having dinner with Mickey and me?"

She shook her head. "He's fine with it."

"How nice for you."

She shrugged.

"He's . . . very secure in this relationship."

"Well then, I don't know whether to be happy for him or to pity him."

Kathy bit into her lower lip, meeting his narrowed green eyes. If he only knew!

But at the moment he was busy condemning her. For Jeremy's sake.

She smiled sweetly. "I think I hear a child's voice calling your name."

"Do you really . . . ?" he said as he drew near.

A strange, hot trembling took root inside her. "We've— we've got to stop . . . this!" she whispered.

They had to stop it. She had to stop it. Being with him again was something she wanted too badly. But years ago, trust had been broken between them. Shutters had gone up; doors had closed.

Humpty Dumpty had fallen from the wall.

And now . . .

Now sex was great. Better than the invention of fireworks. Eroding what was left of trust.

Yet even as she decided that she had to somehow keep her distance from him, he was closing the gap between them. She knew she should step back and do so quickly, yet the urge to move came too late. His hands were on her, drawing her to him.

Her towel was gone, fallen to the floor. Naked she was crushed against him. Feeling again the things she didn't want to feel. The sweet, swift surge of fire within her blood, lapping through life and limb, settling in her heart and womb. She tried to wrench from him but too late, for his lips had fallen forcefully upon hers and she was in his arms, protesting, kissing him in return, not wanting him, wanting him with all of her heart.

No . . .

No, right. He released her. Lime eyes afire, his voice husky, deep, rich. Angry.

"Yeah. We've got to stop— this!"

He turned away from her, long strides taking him to the door.

She stared after him, her hand shaking as she touched her swollen lips, as he slammed his way out of the room.

Shelley liked South Beach. She always had. It had a flavor, even if the spruced-up Deco at that south tip hadn't always been there. In the early seventies, kids had made the beach a surfboard haven, though there hadn't been any real waves. It had just been a place to hang out. Donut and bagel shops were everywhere, psychedelic T-shirt stores, and ice stands. The ancient inhabitants of the run-down rooming houses had blended right in with the kids and young adults, walkers threading between roller-skaters, gray hair next to blue and green.

The television show "Miami Vice" came along and actually did a lot for the beaches. The rage had been to paint; beautiful pastels, soft and sharp, had begun to highlight whitewashed buildings, some of which were architectural masterpieces, drawn back to life. Clubs opened and clubs closed, but the beaches, South Beach in particular, found a new life all their own. The kids still blended with the old-timers. Clunky old surfboards were replaced by smaller, sleeker ones. Roller-bladers now vied with oldsters with walkers for sidewalk space.

The bagel shops sold gourmet coffees.

But it was still the beach, South Beach. Still with a soul all its own, unique.

She'd come here, taking a room at one of the very small redone Deco hotels, because she'd needed a night on her own before going to Jordan's. She'd needed a little breathing space, a little thinking space. Needed to look back. And in a way, she was sorry. So much of her life had been wasted. God, she'd sold herself out. She was afraid, excited.

She wanted to sing with Blue Heron again. Wanted time back, her life back, maybe even her soul back.

Sometime tomorrow, she'd go on over to Jordan's. Tonight, she just walked down the streets. Saturday night. They didn't really hop until very late, but the restaurants were already getting busy. Humanity was trooping by. A handsome young couple, the woman pretty with soft brown hair and eyes, the guy blue-eyed and blond. They were looking everywhere. Tourists.

More humanity. A girl with the shortest shorts Shelley had ever seen, and she'd worn some damned short ones herself! These were curved right up the butt! Funny. The girl was with a funky guy in a fringed leather jacket— in the heat of summer.

A pair of roller-bladers. One with neon-red hair, one with green. They reminded Shelley of Christmas.

She wasn't sure about their sexes.

A very old man, crusty looking, an old-timer, probably a fisherman.

German tourists.

Canadian tourists.

A trio of Latins.

Another trio. Two men and a woman. Coming closer. The woman tall, slim, with a rich sweep of auburn hair. Both men tall, the one with longish, sandy hair just beginning to gray . . .

Oh, God.

Her heart pounding, Shelley slipped into the nearest doorway. It was the entrance to a hotel. She carefully looked around the corner, keeping an eye on the trio.

They were very low key, they'd come from a parked Buick, and they were walking through the doorway of a small steakhouse.

Kathy, Jordan— and their friend, the cop. What was his name? Mickey something. Mickey Dean.

Kathy and Jordan. Not a surprise. Kathy and Jordan and the cop. What the hell did that mean?

She hesitated a long minute, biting into her lower lip.

She wanted her life back. The years wasted. Her life.

She was in her mid forties. Beautiful still, people told her. But she was stitched and sewn, and upon occasion felt she was fading fast. Not that life couldn't be good. If she'd only found something within it. Someone to love. Someone who loved her. Even if she'd had a child . . .

It was late for regrets.

She had herself— and her voice. She was talented, and she was again going to be given a chance to use her talent. She was no sweet young thing, but she might have years and years ahead of her.

She sighed, hesitated a few minutes longer.

But then she hurried away.

And found a phone. And dialed. That the cop was hanging around again just might be dangerous.

Damned dangerous.

Shelley listened to the phone ring. Once, twice, three times. If there was no answer, she would hang up. She never talked to machines.

But there was a response.

"Hello? Hello?"

She bit into her lower lip, then spoke quickly, listened in return, and hung up the phone.

For several seconds she kept her hand on the receiver. She inhaled deeply, exhaled on a sigh.

Turned around and gasped, seeing a startlingly familiar face.

"Oh, my God! What are you doing here?"

It was good to see Mickey again. He had always been down to earth, honest, warm— and so filled with integrity that he could be more blunt than a desert plateau. He hadn't changed since Kathy had seen him, not a bit. He hadn't even gained any gray in his hair, which seemed a miracle, considering his line of work.

Leaving the house had been interesting. That Tara wasn't pleased was rather painfully evident, that Jordan didn't care was even more so. However, Kathy was convinced that one day Tara might just make a fine actress, since she had managed to sweetly drape herself about Jeremy, announcing that the two would spend the evening discussing, and working on, fitness techniques. Jeremy had shrugged to Kathy, offering her an awkward smile, and she'd given him a kiss good-bye, whispering that she surely owed him a vacation trip to Hawaii by now.

Neither Bren nor Alex had been happy about the request—made to them by both parents— that they stay in for the night. Sally apparently hadn't understood it, but she had instinctively come to the fore when needed.

"My little darlings, you're to stay home and entertain your doting old grandma this evening. We'll have a thrilling game of Trivial Pursuit, and watch while the hours speed by!"

"Gram, you're neither old, nor have you ever needed entertaining!" Alex had protested, eyeing her parents suspiciously. "And— "

"And it's Saturday night, a pain to go out," Angel Garcia had said, slipping it in like a master of diplomacy. He glanced at Alex, shrugging. "Trivial Pursuit sounds great. Bren and me against you and your gram. We'll beat the pants off you."

"I beg your pardon, young man!" Sally had teased.

They'd all laughed, and the tension had dissipated. Alex had remained suspicious, but it hadn't mattered.

Within an hour Mickey had come, and they'd left the house, heading for the restaurant. It was a great place. Small. Homey. The private rooms weren't in any way lush— they offered the same dark wood tables and comfortable chairs as the main rooms— but they were havens from the din of a Saturday night. Jordan was very happy; he'd left the house with no fanfare, slipped into the restaurant without attracting any paparazzi For the first few minutes after they'd taken their seats and ordered their drinks, he'd just leaned back, quiet, letting Kathy and Mickey catch up. When Kathy realized that he just sat and listened while Mickey talked about his life and she told Mickey about hers— her excitement over the book about the murder— she realized with a tug at her heart that his being so willing to take a back seat had been something else she had loved about him. He could always have the fanfare: the press, the media, the attention. He could command it; he had not only musical ability, but a capacity to speak clearly and concisely and compellingly. And he had charm. But he often thrust others forward.

Kathy didn't want to think about that. She did

want to know what Mickey thought about the possibility of her daughters being in danger.

When she'd been served her drink— in a tall glass with a lot of ginger ale and a little Jack Black— she leaned toward Mickey. "What do you think about the phone calls?"

Mickey instantly looked to Jordan. "Well—"

"Me, Mickey, over here. Don't you dare look at him. I want some honesty here. What do you think about the phone calls?"

He threw up his hands. "Kathy, I still don't know what to make of them. Jordan was convinced ten years ago that something wasn't right."

"I know," she murmured, her voice just a little testy.

Jordan made a sound of impatience. "Kathy, I've already said—"

"Guys!" Mickey pleaded.

"Sorry," Jordan muttered.

"All right. Let's go back. Jordan is convinced that he saw someone going to the guest house minutes before it burst into flames. He thinks it might be you."

"Right," Kathy said coolly, sipping her drink and suddenly wishing she'd asked for more Jack and less ginger ale. "He thinks I must have had something to do with Keith's death."

"I never said that," Jordan interrupted tersely.

"Not in so many words."

"Guys!" Mickey said again with a sigh. He tried to smile. "Honest, if you two won't behave, I'm leaving!"

"Kathy wants to hear your opinion on the situation. I'll be good," Jordan said irritably.

"I'll be a damned angel," Kathy purred sweetly.

"Fine. Then let's go back. The group had been together a long time. There were all kinds of tensions operative. Keith had a thing for Kathy."

"Are you sure?" Kathy demanded.

"Damned sure," Mickey assured her firmly.

Her cheeks reddened, and she couldn't quite look at Jordan.

"Meantime, Shelley had a thing for Keith," he went on, "and Miles had a thing for Shelley. Larry was completely impatient with the three of them, Derrick didn't seem to give a damn about any of it, and Judy was out-and-out hostile to everyone. While Jordan, head of the clan, was furious with Keith and about to throw him out of the band."

"So it seems, if anyone wanted him dead it was me," Jordan said. "Except that I know I didn't do anything."

"And I know I was completely innocent as well," Kathy put in.

"There remains the possibility that Keith destroyed himself— along with Jordan's property," Mickey reminded them.

"But then why would we get the phone calls?" Kathy asked.

"Right," Mickey agreed with a soft sigh.

She started to speak again, but Jordan motioned to her. Their waitress had come for their order. She was an attractive young woman, dark-haired, nicely built, thirtyish. She knew both Mickey and Jordan, but seemed to have a special, deeply dimpled smile for Jordan.

Kathy wanted to kick herself. Was she going to wonder if he'd slept with every woman they ran into? Create scenarios within her mind? She didn't have the right.

"And what will you have, Mrs. Treveryan?" the waitress asked, offering her the same, warm smile. Kathy felt like a bug that should be squashed. She started automatically to correct the waitress on her name.

"The house special— a seared sirloin— is great," Jordan suggested.

Kathy smiled at the waitress. "The special, please."

The waitress thanked them for their orders, and left.

"So what about the phone calls?" Kathy demanded.

Mickey started to look at Jordan.

"Mickey!"

Dean sighed, lifting his hands. "Kathy, I swear I don't know. They could just be hoaxes. You know. Sick fans maybe. Someone wanting the group to get together, someone not wanting it."

"Someone who knows us."

"Kathy, there was a time when the world knew Blue Heron. You have to bear that in mind."

"Mickey, I'm worried about my daughters."

Dean glanced at Jordan. "Kath, I'm going to come. And I'll be at the house. As of Monday night."

Kathy glanced at Jordan. "You're out of rooms, aren't you? Of course you and—"

"I'll be on the prowl around the place," Mickey said.

"The prowl."

"Keeping an eye on things."

"Officially?"

"Taking vacation time."

"Oh."

"And Jordan will have private security at the gates."

Kathy nodded. "There's really only one problem left then." She stared from one to the other and settled her gaze on Jordan.

"What?" he asked her sharply.

"That the danger will be coming from within, and not from without!"

"If there is any danger," Mickey reminded her. She nodded, started to speak, and fell silent again. Their salads were being brought. They turned their conversation to casual topics.

But later, over café au lait, Kathy leaned toward Mickey and asked, "Should we have done this? Held this reunion exactly ten years after Keith's death?"

"It's going to be a great benefit—"

"Mickey!"

She was startled when Jordan's fingers suddenly curved around hers. His eyes were dark with tension. "I was ready to kick myself at first, I was so worried. For the girls—the others. You. But we have to find out the truth. I don't want to wonder for the rest of my life, or be afraid for all of us either. All right?"

He was asking her. Really asking. If she said the word, he'd pull the plug on the whole thing.

But he was right. She didn't want to go on wondering just what had happened, why their lives had been destroyed. If there was danger, it was time to see its face.

She nodded slowly. Maybe it was time they got to trust one another again.

"All right," she said.

His fingers squeezed around hers.

"Well!" Mickey beamed. "Maybe we should head back. Kathy, I'll show you where we're stationing security for your daughter's party."

They started from the restaurant, Kathy between the two men.

"Hey!" Mickey shouted suddenly.

Kathy stared toward Dean's nondescript Buick. A young man was bent low, slashing the tires even as Mickey called out.

"¡Como . . . !" the man shouted, leaping to his feet, starting to turn.

"Halt. *Police!*" Mickey shouted furiously.

But the tire slasher was running, weaving his way through the startled crowd that gave way in fright.

"Son of a bitch!" Mickey roared.

"I'll take the beach side, you go for the road," Jordan told him briefly.

In a split second, they were both gone, racing after the culprit. People walking along the sidewalks stopped to gawk after them. Kathy stood on her toes, staring after them as well.

She was stunned, and was taken completely off guard when a powerful arm wound around her waist and viselike fingers covered her mouth and nose, cutting off air and any sound she might have made. Lifted off her feet, she was dragged back into the dark, narrow alleyway between the steakhouse and the old hotel at its side.

No one heard a thing.

No one saw that she was taken because all eyes were on the men chasing the tire slasher.

Kathy struggled, terrified; twisting, trying to kick. She couldn't breathe, she desperately needed air, and she could barely move. The arm about her waist moved; she thought for a moment of fighting anew.

But went dead still.

The arm that had restrained her was now raised. The hand attached to it held a knife to her neck.

A wicked-looking blade. A good six inches long. Perhaps two wide. Very silvery. Gleaming. The edge was serrated and sharp, flecked here and there with either rust . . . or blood.

The fingers that had clamped over her mouth now eased from it, sliding down the length of her torso slowly. She could scream . . . but the blade threatening her jugular kept her from doing so.

"Shhh, that's right. Quiet. I don't want to hurt you. Not yet."

"What do you want? If it's money—"

"If it's money, you're worth a lot of it, eh? No, lady. I've been paid. I want to warn you."

There was an accent to the voice. Hispanic? She wasn't certain. It remained soft and chilling, barely a whisper. Husky, yet curiously sexless.

She remained absolutely still.

"Warn me? About what?" Oh, God, she couldn't believe this. Just beyond the alleyway, there were people everywhere. Still staring after Mickey and Jordan and the tire slasher. She might have been in another world. Beyond the alley, street lamps gently bathed the night. The shadows where she stood were encompassing and ominous. She couldn't see her attacker at all. Just glimpses of the hand that held the blade against her.

"Warn you, yes. Listen to me. Pay heed . . ." Soft laughter. "Feel . . ."

She did. Oh, yes. The increased pressure on the knife pressed to her flesh. She felt the sharp edge of the blade. Surely it would break through flesh in a matter of seconds. "Make him stop it, eh, Kathy? No reunion. No Blue Heron. You can make him do anything. Make him stop it now!"

The flat of the blade was drawn even more tightly against her flesh. She couldn't breathe. God, what should she do? Fight and die in a pool of blood— or suffocate?

Suddenly, forcefully, she was thrust forward. She stumbled, falling onto the sidewalk in the glowing illumination lent by a street light.

She leapt to her feet and spun around, staring into the alley, a scream rising in her throat.

Fifteen

Jordan caught up with Mickey about two blocks down from the restaurant. They had made a perfect V in pursuit of the tire slasher, but due to the crowds in the streets and the heavy flow of traffic, he had managed to elude them.

Mickey swore. "Damned vandals!"

"Ummm," Jordan murmured, bending over to catch his breath. He was in decent shape, but the kid who had eluded them was in much better condition. "You think it was just a vandal?"

"Maybe not . . ." Mickey looked thoughtful.

Jordan suddenly felt a surge of unease. "Kathy," he muttered. He turned. He was walking at first, then sprinting, then running pell-mell again, suddenly stirred by panic. Mickey was close behind him.

When he reached the outside of the restaurant again, he slowed, his sense of panic fading. Kathy was standing right where he had left her.

He started to say her name; then he began to run again, half leaping over the Buick to come to her side.

Her face was ashen. The sleek white halter dress she'd been wearing was smudged and dirtied. People were moving about her, but didn't seem to notice her.

"Kathy . . . ?"

Her fingers entwined in the material of his shirt as she gripped his arms. Her touch was painful, and shaking convulsed the length of her.

"Kathy, damn it, what happened?"

Her eyes focused on his as she struggled for control, blinking hard, forcing back tears. She managed to form words. "There was a man—I think—someone . . . in the alley. You ran and he grabbed me and—"

"And what, Kathy, what?" he demanded anxiously. "Are you all right? Are you hurt? Are you—"

"Kathy, take it slowly," Mickey said gently from behind Jordan.

She swallowed. Her fingers still had a death grip upon his arms.

"As soon as you two were gone—when everyone was staring after you—he . . . he dragged me back into the alley. He had a knife at my throat, but he said he didn't want to hurt me. Yet. He wants me to stop you from having the reunion."

"He said that?" Mickey demanded.

Jordan was trying to extract her fingers from his shirt. "Kathy, you've got to let go. We've got to try to to find him."

"Jordan, I never saw him. You can't find him. You don't know who you're looking for!"

"Someone else must have seen—"

"No one did. People were staring after the two of you. It seemed like forever, but it all happened in a matter of seconds. He threw me out and disappeared. The alley goes to the other street. He could be anywhere now, ten feet from us or ten miles, we'd never know. I haven't the faintest idea of what he looks like!"

Jordan went still. She was right. In this throng, how could they possibly look for a *suspicious* character. By now, South Beach was wickedly alive. The punks were out, the rockers were out, tourists in all shapes, colors, and sizes were out. New age music was spilling from a nearby club, vying with the sounds of a fifties revival from down the street. People were beginning to stop. A girl pointed toward them, then shouted, "It's *him!* Blue Heron! What's the guy's name, *Jordan Treveryan.*" Her voice fell slightly. "That must be his wife."

"Ex-wife," someone supplied.

Jordan could feel the crush coming toward them. A flashbulb flared with sudden brilliance, blinding them.

"What's happened here?" Someone else cried out.

"We've got to get out of here," Jordan muttered.

"Let's go," Mickey agreed.

"The tires—"

"Will get us out of here. Let's go."

Kathy seemed all but frozen. Jordan dragged her toward the car, thrusting her into the middle of the front seat, sliding in beside her. People, like a cloud of bees, started to home in on them. Mickey blared the horn, while Jordan forced a smile to his face and waved out the window, causing the crowd that had gathered to break apart for them.

They made it down the street, the rim under the slashed tire clunking and trembling all the way.

"We're wrecking your car," Kathy said suddenly.

"That's all right. I'll bill you both," Mickey said.

She was still shaking. Jordan took her hand in both of his, trying to give her warmth, wishing he could give her strength.

This was all his doing. He'd been so damned determined.

"We'll drop it," he said.

"What?" she looked at him, still pale.

"No reunion. I won't take chances with our lives."

She half smiled, her amber eyes near golden, luminous. "No."

"Kathy— "

"We can't let thugs threaten us in back alleys. Jordan, we agreed. Didn't we just discuss this? If we don't find out what's happening, we just might be in danger all our lives. And susceptible. But we can be on guard now. We're not dealing with phone calls, vague threats. We know someone is playing a dangerous game."

His fingers tightened around hers. "The girls, Kathy—"

"We'll tell them I was threatened this evening. We don't need to tell everyone the whole truth— all our suspicions. We'll just say I was mugged, that Mickey thinks we all might be in danger. The girls will understand. They're not stupid or foolish."

"They don't leave the house. Not for a minute. And neither do you, understand?" he said.

He thought she shivered again, but her chin was held high, her eyes were determined as she looked straight ahead.

"Do we report this?" Jordan asked Mickey. "Can you write up what happened? I want to get to the house and stay there. I don't want Kathy coming out again until it's all over."

"Jordan—" she began.

"I'm City of Miami, you were on Miami Beach," Mickey said unhappily. "But I can get a pal to come out to the house to talk to Kathy. Maybe we can get some kind of fix on the guy. It was a guy, right?"

"The voice . . ." Kathy shrugged, looking puzzled. "It had to be a guy. He was strong. Really strong. But there was something about his hands . . ."

"What about them?" Jordan demanded sharply.

"He was young, perhaps. I only saw one hand—because he wanted to make sure I saw the blade. I think . . . I think his flesh was very smooth." She sighed, shaking her head. "Whatever that's worth!"

"Hmmm," Mickey murmured noncommittally.

"What's the 'hmmm' for?" Kathy asked.

Jordan was looking at Mickey. He said, "I think, those guys were *hired* by someone for this mischief. They're just petty crooks, hired off the street."

"Oh!" Kathy said with dismay.

"Don't be so discouraged," Jordan told her.

"But— "

"Find these guys," Mickey supplied, "and we have a chance of finding out who hired them."

It was well into the morning hours before Kathy had a chance to lie down and try to get some sleep.

Everything in her hurt. She wasn't sure why— except that she'd been a ball of tension while that razor-sharp knife lay against her throat . . . and because the bastard had knocked her to the ground so hard. She'd been careful not to let anyone know just how badly she'd been hurting, and she'd let Jordan make her a drink that was much more Jack Black than it was ginger ale, and that had blurred a little of the pain. She'd tried to downplay everything as much as possible while trying to emphasize just how careful her daughters had to be. Jordan stayed with her while Mickey's friend from South Beach took a statement from her, but guilt pricked at her all the while. Jeremy, naturally, was deeply concerned, anxious, as good as gold to her. And her mother was wonderful, caring and solicitous without being at all hysterical. Sally could be great.

Even Tara Hughes came to the fore. She showed marked concern for Kathy's welfare, was the first to suggest a good stiff drink, and put an arm around Kathy's shoulders at any time both Jordan and Jeremy were absent.

By midnight, the Miami Beach officer left them. Within the next hour, Mickey Dean was gone as well. Jeremy, Joe, Angel, and Jordan locked all the doors to the house and set the alarm. Mickey had contacted a private agency and had hired two men to watch the house for the following week. While all this was going on, Kathy met Jordan's eyes. The danger wouldn't come from outside tonight; they both knew it. But they had to go through all the right steps anyway.

Right before going up to bed, Tara sat beside Kathy on the couch on the porch. "I— I've got some Valium, if you think you could use one. Hell, any doctor in the country would suggest you take a pill tonight."

"I'm all right, really. The drink was great. I'll sleep like a rock."

Tara shook her head. "You're something. If someone had held a knife to my throat a few hours ago, I'd still be screaming. You're brave."

Kathy shook her head, smiling. "No, I'm not. I was in terror while that guy threatened me.

But he was probably just some hired punk. If I'd been brave, I would have decked him."

Tara laughed. "If you'd tried, you might be dead now."

"Actually, I don't think I could have done it. He was so damned strong! But it's over and I'm all right, and we'll all be really careful until we know just what's going on."

Tara nodded, and shivered. "I think I'll have another drink. Hell, maybe I'll have that Valium. If I don't I'll lie awake all night. But I'm just down the hall from you. If you get scared, come down and cuddle. We'll slumber-party it." She stopped speaking suddenly, as if embarrassed to realize that she had just admitted she would not be sleeping with Jordan. She shrugged, eyeing Kathy with sudden suspicion. "But then, you have Jeremy, don't you?"

The way she looked at her then made Kathy uneasy. "I'm sure I'll curl up in a little ball all by myself tonight," Kathy told her lightly.

Tara stood looking down at her. "Yeah. I'll bet." She leaned down over Kathy. "You know, when I put my mind to it, I can usually raise the damned dead."

"And what does that mean?"

Tara smiled. "It just means . . . I wonder."

"About what."

"Your love life with Adonis."

Kathy offered her a very deep smile. "Jeremy?"

"Mmm."

"He's a completely loyal man, Tara."

"If you say so." Tara smiled, then added more seriously, "If you get frightened, come see me, though I'm certainly no heroine!"

"Thanks," Kathy called after her.

Tara went over to Jordan, and Kathy noted that he instinctively slipped an arm around her, even as he replied to something that Angel was saying. A knife seemed to turn in Kathy's stomach. There was a relationship there. Deeper than she'd wanted to believe.

And Tara wasn't really so bad.

She made a point of slipping up to bed herself as quickly as she could after Tara said good night, disengaging herself from Jordan when his concern for her had come forth all over again.

The girls followed her upstairs, hugging her, clucking over her.

"I'm all right, I swear it. This wasn't really so big a deal, guys!"

"Right. You were almost murdered."

"I was threatened."

"With a knife. You might have been killed."

"Not tonight," Kathy murmured.

"Still . . ."

They were right. She was very happy to be alive. She hugged them both fiercely, forgetting her pain, and they lay together for a while, the three of them, close in body and spirit.

"Dad would have killed him," Alex supplied.

"If he'd gotten his hands on him," Bren added.

"If Dad had killed him, Dad would be in jail, so let's be glad it didn't happen, huh?"

"Dad was good though, huh?" Alex asked her.

"A perfect gentleman."

" 'Cause he loves you," Bren supplied softly.

"Oh, guys, don't start, please!" she begged softly. "You know your dad; he's the most protective guy in the world. It's his nature."

"He does love you," Bren insisted.

"I'm your mother, a very old part of his life," Kathy said. She hesitated. "Yes, he probably still loves me. A little, maybe. Don't go making things out of it."

"We won't," Alex said.

"Go to bed, huh?" Kathy suggested.

"Yeah, sure." They both kissed her again, rising, and started from the room.

"I'm still sure he loves her," Bren said, speaking to Alex again as if Kathy couldn't possibly hear her.

"Sparks. There are absolutely sparks around them," Alex agreed.

"If we could just get rid of Tara—"

"And Jeremy."

"Jeremy's no problem!" Bren reminded her sister.

"Oh, yeah. Right. Tara then."

"Girls!" Kathy wailed.

"Good night Mom. Call if you need anything," Alex said. The two left, closing her door behind them.

Kathy closed her eyes. She tried to sleep. The drink hadn't helped enough. She rose, thinking about venturing down the hall to ask Tara for a

Valium, but walked to the window instead and stared out.

She could see Jordan, silhouetted in the frame of the guest house window. She was suddenly glad to know that he was alone.

Watching over her.

It was wrong. He was more involved with Tara than he cared to admit, and he assumed Kathy was cheating on a lover who trusted her implicitly. Not good, since the trust factor had been such an important issue between them. So what did it all mean?

That sex was good.

So for the next week occasionally, they'd have sex.

She almost groaned aloud. Surely, she had more will power than what she was displaying!

But she was locked into this now. They both were. They all were. Blue Heron was getting back together. And come what may, they were taking the roller-coaster ride.

Just what the hell had occurred ten years ago?

She didn't know, but they had to find out. Maybe it wouldn't even matter how they felt about it. Maybe the truth was going to come out one way or the other and each day was taking them inexorably closer to the past . . .

Jordan raised a hand to her in acknowledgment. She raised a hand in return.

After a minute, she left the window. Oddly enough, she was now able to sleep.

* * *

Despite the late hour when she'd retired, Kathy rose early. It was Sunday. She showered and donned a cool sundress, amazed that the fear she had known during the night had already largely faded.

She wanted to go to church.

She loved the beautiful old Episcopal Cathedral just over on the mainland on the outskirts of downtown Miami. The organ was spectacular, and they sometimes had extraordinary flutists and even bagpipe players at services.

She didn't want to behave foolishly, but neither did she want to be a prisoner. If she took the right precautions, surely no one would be looking for her in church.

When she came downstairs, things were quiet. Peggy must have been up and about because chafing dishes filled with breakfast goodies had appeared in the dining room. A large silver samovar offered coffee, and Kathy helped herself to a cup, then wandered out to the porch. She was curious when she noted that someone was already lying on one of the lounges by the pool, so she let herself out of the house through the porch door and circled around.

She cried out with delight when she saw the man stretched out in the lounge. "Dad! I mean— Gerrit!"

He was up in a matter of seconds, a tall, very straight, handsome man with thinning, snow white hair, an aging but wonderfully sculpted face, and one of the world's best smiles. Jordan's father had always been extraordinary. Kathy had kept up with him a bit over the years, Christmas cards and pictures, anything that concerned the girls.

"Kathy!" he exclaimed with pleasure. She thought he was going to take her hand, but he gave her a tremendous bear hug instead, from which she barely salvaged her coffee.

He pulled away from her a second later, rescuing the teetering coffee cup and setting it upon the ground, then holding both her hands and eyeing her somberly and carefully. "You look wonderful, Kathryn, absolutely wonderful. A sight for sore old eyes."

"You look wonderful, too. And those eyes don't look sore or old. You're the picture of health. What have you been up to?"

"Diving in Mexico," he told her. "I just became certified in cave diving."

Kathy laughed. "Good for you. Was it fun?"

"Oh, yes. I've been telling your mother all about it, trying to get her interested."

Kathy smiled. "Mom's living in New York, you know. The opportunities for cave diving are limited there."

"Ah, but in the world are many opportunities."

"Maybe," Kathy agreed politely.

He swept out a hand to her. "Have a seat."

She joined him, sitting on the lounge next to his as he sat, still watching her. "How are the books going?"

"Great. I really do love my work."

"There's not much more than that you can

ask of life. A good job, health, happiness. How about the last, Kathy? You happy?"

She grinned. "Sir, subtlety does not seem to be one of your virtues."

"It's sir, now? What happened to 'Dad'?"

"I . . ."

"You didn't divorce *me*, did you?"

A lot of Jordan came straight from his father. Gerrit liked to tease, even torment, but he'd give a stranger in need the shirt off his back. He had his ideals and beliefs, and he stuck to them like glue; he also had the most infectious grin Kathy had ever seen. He seemed truly pleased to make her smile with him as he dug into her just enough to bring both pain and laughter.

"I didn't divorce your son."

"Hmmm. Good point. So why won't you call me Dad?"

"I don't mean to be presumptuous."

"To whom?"

"Well . . . to anyone, I suppose."

"I'm the one it should matter to, and it's hurting my feelings deeply that you don't greet me with the same old affection. So?"

"So . . ." Kathy returned, gazing at him, still unable not to smile. "So, Dad, how's the world treating you."

"Fine. Now that I'm learning how to live without Mom."

"Everyone still misses her terribly."

"Thanks. I wish she was around to go cave diving with me. I just tell her about it in my dreams."

"My father used to say those who went before us became angels on our shoulders. I always think of him that way, kind of seeing after me—and the girls, of course."

"And you need him in New York City!"

"It's not a den of iniquity."

"No more so than Miami, eh?"

"No more so." She laughed.

"Glad to be back to singing?" he asked, a twinkle in his eye.

"Sure. I think. I don't know. I haven't really done anything in so long . . ."

"It will come back to you."

"I was never the main talent in the group."

He wagged a finger at her. "You never saw your own talent. There's a difference."

"First practice is tomorrow."

"Ummm. I hear there was some trouble last night."

"Minor. It's over. In fact . . ."

"In fact, what?" he asked.

"I know I promised Jordan to stay close, and I don't want to do anything foolish, but I was dying to head over—"

"Ah! To the cathedral. The pipers are playing today."

"Are they?"

"Want to slip over?"

"Think you can arrange it?"

"Sure. You just sit tight."

With an arched brow, she watched as Gerrit stood and headed for the guest house. A few minutes later he came walking back, crooking a finger her way. She stood, intrigued, and followed him. He took her arm and escorted her through the house to the front.

"You talked to your son?"

"I did."

"And?"

Angel pulled up at to the front of the house, having driven from the garage. He was behind the wheel of an old, well-kept but nondescript Lincoln. His father was in the front seat beside him.

"Our chariot awaits," Gerrit said, propelling her toward the car.

Not until she had been ushered into the middle of the back seat did Kathy realize there was a man seated behind the driver. His hair was queued back, and he was wearing large sunglasses. In a tailored suit, he was the picture of a nineties executive.

"Jordan?"

"Dad said you wanted to go to church." He sounded irritated.

"I didn't mean to cause a problem."

"Well, you did."

"Gerrit, really—" Kathy began.

"Kathy," the older man said, patting her knee, "you wanted to go to church for God's sake, no pun intended."

"I didn't mean to make you come," she told Jordan.

"Great, make me sound like an agnostic in front of my father."

"You're a grown man, Jordan; you've every right to be an agnostic if you choose."

"Oh, God," Kathy groaned, sinking farther into the seat.

The drive across the causeway to the church took only a few minutes. All four men waited patiently for Kathy to get out of the car.

"I feel as if I'm surrounded by the Mafia!" she hissed to Jordan as she alit.

"If you're not careful, you're going to need the damned Mafia," he snapped back. "You had to hear bagpipers; let's go hear them!"

The music was beautiful. They walked into the service completely unnoticed, taking seats in the back and to the side. Jordan was to Kathy's left, Gerrit to her right.

Jordan wasn't talkative. Gerrit was— despite the service going on. But he could be very soft spoken and discreet. "Lots of things happened here."

"Yes."

"The girls were baptized."

"Ummm."

"We buried your father. And my wife."

"I remember."

"You and Jordan were married."

"Another lifetime."

"How's your friend?"

"Pardon?"

"Jeremy. Nice fellow."

"Oh, yes."

"Damned good looking."

"Very."

"Hot and heavy between you two?"

"Dad!"

"Well?"

"He's a great person. And it's a good relationship."

"Must be a damned interesting one."

"Oh?"

"Considering the fellow is *not* heterosexual."

Her jaw nearly dropped to the floor. Thankfully, it was time for the sermon, and the reverend's voice suddenly boomed out, saving her for a matter of seconds.

It was a beautiful speech, all about love and trust and honoring the vows that men and women make in life.

At last Kathy had a chance to lean over and whisper to Gerrit. "Does Jordan know?"

"Don't think so."

"But you're certain."

"Oh, yes."

"How can that be?"

He smiled at her, patting her on the knee. "I'm not jealous of the poor boy, and I've been around a while longer. I know a scam when I see one."

"Well, Dad, I will thank you to keep quiet."

Jordan suddenly leaned in. "Father McGloughlin is going to scold the two of you at any moment now. Please shut up!"

They both smiled sweetly at him.

The pipers played again during communion; the melodies were beautiful.

Jordan's mood seemed somewhat better when

they left. As they slipped out he talked to his father, and they reached the car without incident.

"Never could master the pipes," he said.

"Ah, son, you never really tried!" Gerrit assured him. He winked at Kathy. "He really could master just about anything, once he set his mind to it." He crawled on into the car.

"Ummm. And anyone!" Kathy agreed beneath her breath.

But Jordan was right behind her, holding the door for her to enter before doing so himself. She felt his breath as he whispered, "Amazing. I don't seem to remember ever being able to master you."

"What a shame. Me and the bagpipes."

"Maybe I'll get to the bagpipes one day."

"Maybe."

"There's time yet to take care of you, too," he said ominously, causing her to arch a brow. But his meaning was indiscernible since his glasses were so very dark.

"Maybe, maybe not—"

"Kathy, get in the car!"

She decided to comply, scooting as close to Gerrit as she could manage.

When they reached the house, there was a great deal of activity. Two taxis and a limo were pulling out of the driveway. Inside, just in the foyer, Derrick and Judy Flanaghan were greeting Peggy and the girls. Larry Haley and his wide-eyed, attractive young wife were being welcomed by Sally, while Tara and Jeremy were chatting with Shelley.

"OhmyGod!" Larry Haley exclaimed, seeing Jordan come in. "He must be going into politics. Jordan, God, but you look good!"

Larry strode across the floor, encompassing Jordan in a bear hug.

"Manly hug!" Jeremy whispered to Kathy, coming up behind her and setting his hands easily upon her shoulders. She got the feeling that he might not have known Larry long, but it was long enough to know he wasn't crazy about him.

Now Larry had turned his attention on Kathy, while Jordan was being engulfed by the Flanaghans and his dad and the Garcias slipped unobtrusively by them to reach Sally and the girls.

"Kath! *Kath!*" Larry exploded. "Back in the fold. Sweetie, you look hot as ever. It's great to see you!"

The enthusiasm in his voice seemed honest enough; his hug for her was warm. He assured her that he'd met Jeremy while he drew the pretty blonde with him forward. "My wife, Vicky Sue."

Vicky Sue rather solemnly greeted them, shaking hands and finally managing to smile shyly. "It's such a pleasure to meet y'all. I've heard such great things from Larry, and of course, I've seen Blue Heron videos, y'all weren't just great, you were legendary."

"Ummm, yes, that's it!" Shelley Thompson suddenly chimed in, slipping on over to them. "Kathy!" She hugged her fiercely, almost like a lost child hugs her mother when found, then stood back, smiling for Vicky Sue, glancing back to Kathy. "That's it, all right. There are days when I do feel just like a legend!"

"Ignore her!" Kathy warned Vicky Sue, her knit brow warning Shelley to be gentle with Larry's new young bride. "It's a pleasure to meet you, too. We're delighted that you could be here."

Vicky Sue beamed. She was a cut above Larry's usual bimbo. Pretty, yes. Young, yes. But Kathy decided to hold neither of these things against her. She seemed warm as well, very *real*, if such an expression could hold merit.

"I'm not so sure Larry wanted me to come," Vicky Sue admitted. "I mean, I think this reunion thing is so special, and so very unique to y'all— "

"But not so private," Jeremy cut in politely. He offered her his best smile. "I'm here. So is Tara. Neither of us was part of Blue Heron."

"Yeah. Yeah, thanks," Vicky Sue agreed, pleased with his reasoning. Kathy could have kissed Jeremy. Bless him, he had a way with a smile and a few simple words. And he was being an absolute charmer now. He must have been out by the pool when people had started arriving. He was in black boxer-style trunks and a polo shirt, standing tall and straight, every muscle on him gleaming and tan. Because of the relationship he and Kathy did share, he was able to create a naturalness between them that was very convincing.

To anyone other than her ex-father-in-law.

And maybe Tara.

"Kathy!"

Judy Flanaghan reached her, hugging her, talking a mile a minute.

"Kathy, your daughters are beauties, absolutely. And so smart, I hear. Well, leave it to you and Jordan. Together or apart. But, honey, you look fab yourself. Who's your surgeon?"

"I haven't tried one yet."

"Oh, sorry!"

"Well, I haven't nixed the idea for the future," Kathy assured her.

"Ignore her!" Derrick warned, slipping by his wife to kiss Kathy's cheek. "Hey, kid. Good to see you."

"You, too."

"The girls are beauties."

"Thanks."

"Who could possibly believe that Alex is about to be twenty-one!" Shelley said with a sigh.

"Just think how old that makes all of us!" Judy murmured.

"Oh, you look like a million bucks, and you know it," Jordan told her gallantly.

"Thank you, Mr. Treveryan. That was most kind, but I warn you, I intend to remain your toughest critic over the next week so that Blue Heron is *not* a laughing stock when you little darlings get back up on stage."

Shelley groaned. "My God, it's going to be the week from hell."

"You betcha, sweetie," Judy teased.

"It's going to be fun," Derrick said.

"Before all this fun and torture can begin,"

Jordan suggested, "why don't you all get settled in your rooms; then we can barbecue out by the pool. Angel, Bren, and Alex are acting as host and hostesses. They'll show you all to your rooms and—"

"I'll bet we're in the same rooms we were in ten years ago," Shelley said.

There was silence for a minute. "Maybe," Jordan said. He turned to Peggy. "Are they?"

She shrugged. "Could be. I don't remember where everyone was ten years ago."

"Really," Shelley murmured. "Well, we'll see, won't we?" She arched a brow pleasantly, walking over to the pile of baggage to take up an overnight bag. Still beautiful, petite, and graceful, she offered them all her catlike smile again. "Follow me, Bren, and see if I don't know exactly where I'm going!"

"We can try to do the same," Derrick told his wife.

"I'll help you with your things, Mr. Flanaghan," Angel told him, reaching for one of his bags.

Derrick winced. "Eh? I'm not that old, son. Call me Derrick. You called me by my first name when you were a boy. Don't make me feel like an aging politician now, okay?"

"Okay," Angel agreed, setting the bag down.

"Angel, I'm not old, but I'm not that young. Go ahead and take up that suitcase," Derrick told him.

Angel laughed, and did as he was told. Judy

was already halfway up the staircase, following on Shelley's heels. The two were talking away.

Jeremy left Kathy's side to help Vicky Sue with a bag as Larry hefted up the others, helped by Jordan with whom he was still talking.

Tara slipped around in back of Kathy.

"Too bad you missed the arrival."

Kathy turned around. "I guess."

"Over your fright from last night?"

Kathy nodded. "I haven't been to the cathedral in a long time. I wanted to go over there much more than I feared going out."

"How nice."

Kathy wasn't sure what the elegant blond beauty queen was getting at. But then Tara grinned at her with saccharine sweetness.

"Praying to get your husband back?"

Kathy didn't reply. Tara had spoken softly enough so that no one remaining in the foyer had heard her.

"Miss Hughes, if this is your customary mode of behavior, I may not have to pray," Kathy said pleasantly. She started to turn away just as the doorbell began ringing.

Joe Garcia strode to answer it.

A tall man stood within the frame, a dark form against the sunlight. He moved in.

Shelley suddenly shrieked from the top of the stairway.

"Miles! Miles!"

She came tearing back down, racing by them. Miles Reeves stepped on into the house. Lean, appealing with his craggy face, smiling just a little bit awkwardly.

"Hello, all. It's good to see everyone."

Shelley flew into his arms, and he caught her, grinning down at her after she planted a sloppy kiss right on his lips.

"My, my!" Judy drawled from the stairway. "The gang's all here. Hell yes, the gang's all here!"

"Well, except for one," Jordan said, speaking softly, but his rich voice seeming to ring out and encompass them all.

"Who?" Tara said blankly.

"Keith," Jordan said softly. "Keith isn't here."

A pin could have dropped, and its landing been heard by all.

"But then, of course," Jordan added pleasantly, "I'm sure he's with us in spirit. In fact, I'm certain he'll be with every single one of us all week."

He smiled, picked up one of Larry's bags, and started for the stairway himself.

Sixteen

To Kathy's surprise, Sunday turned out to be a nice day.

The weather was perfect and they spent the afternoon and evening out by the pool. Bit by bit, they settled into little groups, catching up on one another's lives. Kathy was delighted to realize that Miles loved what he did, enjoyed his Irish music tremendously, and had even been considering marriage. "This is good for me, maybe what I needed to really change my life," he told her as they sat alone. He was sipping a beer. "So how about you?" He lifted his beer bottle toward where Jeremy was involved in a volleyball game with Bren, Alex, and Angel Garcia. "Is marriage in the cards? You'd certainly have beautiful children with him!"

"I have beautiful children now."

"Oh, yeah, of course. Jeez, Kathy, I didn't mean—"

"I know."

"Bren and Alex aren't just beautiful you know. They're polite, charming, warm, and caring. You and Jordan made beautiful people."

"Thanks, Miles. That's nice."

He grinned. "We always tried, didn't we? You and I were usually the peacemakers."

"I guess."

He took another swig of his beer, then leaned back, letting the sun beat down on him. He grinned at her again. "I don't think I quite rated with you. Thank God you were married. We all might have canonized you otherwise." He looked straight ahead. "I know Keith thought you could solve any problem. He idolized the ground you walked on."

Kathy sighed. "Miles—"

"God, I keep putting my foot into it, don't I? I didn't mean anything by that. We all knew you were his friend, nothing more. But what a group, eh? You madly in love with our fearless leader Jordan, Keith trailing after you like a puppy dog, then Shelley trailing after him, and there was me, ready for any little handout she was ready to give."

"You two were always together."

"Sure. I was her buddy. I loved her, she patted me on the head now and then."

"But she really did care about you. Still does."

"Yeah, maybe. Isn't it funny? What a bunch of loners we were. Like spoiled children. If we couldn't have the one we wanted, we just didn't want anyone at all."

"Larry is remarried—for the . . . I'm not sure how many times," Kathy pointed out.

"Yeah, well, Larry is different. He doesn't know how to be alone. Some people don't."

"His wife is very sweet."

"Too sweet for him."

"Miles—"

"Yeah, I know. Not nice. Larry's all right. He'd just screw his own mother to get ahead."

"Derrick and Judy are still together."

"She probably hasn't given him permission to leave."

"He dotes on her."

"She gives him no choice."

Kathy laughed. "Whoa! You are carrying around some venom there, my friend!"

"Am I?" Miles flushed, offering her a rueful smile. "Maybe. Maybe that's why I was so glad to come back. I want to shake a little of it off my shoulders. And then, of course, I'm anxious to play with your husband again. Ex-husband," he amended quickly, and looked at her curiously. "Must have been murder for you to come back."

"Er . . . murder," she agreed.

He was silent a minute. "Jordan still thinks there was more to Keith's death than just an accidental fire."

"He is my ex-husband. We haven't kept in touch," Kathy told him evasively.

Miles smiled at her, then leaned back again, slipping dark sunglasses over his eyes. "You've been divorced nearly ten years. Neither of you has remarried. He's dating Miss America, and you're here with Mr. America. Amazing, if you'll take a look. Mr. America is off playing with the younger generation, and Miss America is rather discontentedly floating in the swimming pool."

Kathy took a look. Jeremy was still engaged in a game with her daughters and Angel. Tara was lying on a pool float, stomach down, trailing her fingers in the water as the float moved about. Kathy looked around for Jordan. She wasn't surprised to see him manning the large, built-in barbecue, but she was surprised to realize that Mickey Dean had arrived. He'd come as a guest in swimming trunks and a tank top. He saw her looking his way and lifted a hand bearing a potato chip to wave in acknowledgment. He smiled. She instinctively started to rise, but he shook his head in warning that it wasn't the time or place to talk. She sank back into her chair.

"Know what I think?" Miles asked her.

"What?"

"That some of us are just hopeless. Like you and Jordan."

"We're not. We're divorced."

"By accident, I imagine."

"Miles—"

"Don't protest with me," he said, inclining his head in Tara's direction. "I don't care if she stepped out live from the centerfold of *Playboy*. Looks count, sure. And for some men, like Derrick, a younger woman makes them feel younger themselves. But that's not Jordan. You fall in love with people because of the way they think, feel, laugh, smile. Because of the things on the outside as well as on the inside. Take me. I live with a nice girl, talented, kind, great. And very pretty.

But half of my nights, I've still slept with Shelley in my dreams. Sick, huh? But I really loved her, you see." He gazed across the pool to where Shelley was stretched out on a lounge by Judy Flanaghan. "I really loved her." His voice grew passionate. "I loved her so much I would have done anything in the world for her, to have her."

Chills suddenly ripped into Kathy. Anything?

Did that include murdering Keith, eliminating the competition?

"There's still time," she suggested.

"Maybe," he mused. "I came here partially to convince myself that I loved someone else and was ready to settle down with her. Then I saw Shelley."

"And?"

"Now I don't know anything anymore." He frowned, looking across the pool. Larry Haley had settled down on the lounge next to Shelley. With determined effort Miles turned purposefully from Shelley and looked at Kathy again, changing the conversation. "I hear there was some trouble here last night."

She shrugged.

"You're all right?"

"Fine?"

"What happened?"

"A thug in an alley attacked me, then threw me back on the sidewalk."

"Crazies!"

She hadn't realized that Derrick Flanaghan had been close enough to hear their conversation until he stepped right into it, wandering around from behind their lounges to perch on the end of Kathy's. He grimaced. "The world is full of them. My company did a jingle to support a new brand of peanut butter a few years ago. Next thing we knew, we had a bomb threat from some fellow who thought we were trying to undermine Annette Funicello." He shook his head, stirring some kind of purple concoction, complete with a little Oriental umbrella, that he'd mixed up for himself behind the bar.

"So what is this crazy after?" Miles asked.

Derrick shrugged. "Someone who hates music?" he suggested.

"Or . . ." Judy drawled, striding around to join them as well, "someone who loves music and can't bear to let Blue Heron get back together again."

"Judy!" Derrick said with annoyance.

"Oh, I'm just kidding!" she murmured, settling down across from her husband at the end of Miles's lounge. She, too, was enjoying a purple concoction— complete with Oriental umbrella.

"There are a lot of crazies in the world. Maybe some guy couldn't get his own music on the air. Maybe some band lost their big publicity break when the radio stations got wind of this concert. Who knows? The point is, screw 'em— and be careful."

"Good advice," Kathy agreed. She glanced toward the barbecue. Jordan was watching them. He was probably close enough to hear what was being said, but he was listening to Mickey as well. He nodded to something Mickey said, then handed him the barbecue fork and wandered over to the lounges where Kathy sat with the others.

"Food's done. Grab plates. We've got the picnic tables set up at the end by the guest house. Help yourselves."

"How chummy," Judy remarked.

"Everyone can talk to everyone else that way," Jordan said.

"And hear everything said by everyone." Derrick laughed. "As we comment on the changes in us."

"We haven't changed," Miles said.

"I have," Derrick told them woefully. "There's more of me."

Everyone laughed. As they rose one by one, Jordan beckoned across the pool to where the others sat. Everyone made up a plate of food, gathering at the picnic tables. Kathy found herself sandwiched between Jeremy and Miles, across from Jordan, Tara, and Mickey. The Flanaghans were to her left while Larry Haley and his new wife were across to the right. Shelley wound up on the other side of Mickey. The girls and Angel had decided to eat a little later, and Sally and Gerrit were still stretched out at the far end of the pool, beneath the shade of two giant palms.

Between "Pass the ketchup, please," and "May I have the salt," the conversation ranged from new groups to old uncertainties, then wandered back to the evening before.

"Kathy is probably lucky she was with Mickey

and Jordan," Vicky Sue said gravely. "Why she could have been . . . killed."

"Poor, dear Kathy!" Tara murmured.

"I imagine I was lucky," Kathy told Vicky Sue.

"Ummm. And so were the rest of you, I imagine," Mickey said. He glanced at Kathy with a shrug, then looked down the length of the table. "All of you were here last night as well, weren't you?"

Dead silence greeted his words; then Derrick said sheepishly, "Yeah. Well, at least Judy and I were. I wanted to get my bearings in South Florida before showing up on Jordan's doorstep. Take a deep breath, you know?"

"I was here," Miles admitted. "Same reason, I guess."

"You were!" Shelley exclaimed. Then she started to giggle. "I came in early, too. I wanted a head start on a tan. And a look around as well."

Mickey looked at Larry Haley, arching a brow. Larry shrugged his shoulders.

" 'Fess up down there!" Miles called.

"Only to Kathy! She's the one we always gave our deep dark secrets. At least Keith always did, right Kathy?"

She could almost feel the silence settling over them, like a blanket of cool air.

"He needed a lot of advice," she said quietly. She looked across the table to Jordan. "I guess he didn't take very much of it."

"Well, were any of you bothered by anyone?" Mickey demanded, drawing everyone's attention back to the original question.

"Er . . . no!" Shelley said.

Larry was shaking his head, still staring at Kathy. "We weren't bothered. But then, I think Jordan and Kathy have always been more visible than the rest of us. I mean, think about it. Think of all the groups out there. Ardent fans can recognize lead singers, but half the time the other band members are all but invisible, right?"

"Most people recognize all the surviving Beatles," Mickey said with a laugh.

"These guys weren't exactly the Beatles," Judy assured him.

"They were almost as well known here at home, in the old U.S. of A.," Mickey insisted.

"I'm telling you, the world is full of crazies," Derrick said with a shake of his head.

"Crazies who apparently don't want us getting back together again," Jordan said, staring at Larry. He then looked up and down the table. "But you all should be aware that we might be in danger from getting back together."

"Maybe y'all shouldn't get back together!" Vicky Sue said with a shiver.

"Honey, I don't let varmints ruin my life!" Shelley told her. "Jordan, may I have the salt again, please."

Jordan passed it to her. "Anyone want out?" he asked.

There was silence around the table. Derrick cleared his throat. "You've got some security planned, I take it?"

"I do," Jordan said.

"I think we're all in," Miles told him.

"Good, I'm glad."

"Yeah," Mickey said, sitting back. "And I'm sure glad none of you was bothered last night like Kathy," he said blandly.

"So are we," Miles said with a laugh. He tussled Kathy's hair, then gave her a quick hug. "We can't lose our queen. We're all going to have to take special care of her."

"Yes, we'll just have to do that," Tara murmured.

"I'll be watching out for her," Jeremy said, slipping an arm around Kathy and staring at Tara.

"Excuse me," Jordan said, rising. "My throat is dry." He strode away from the table, heading for the bar. Mickey stared at Kathy with a shrug.

She longed to race after Jordan. Despite Jeremy's gallant and comforting presence, and the fact that Mickey would certainly be a wonderful defender, she suddenly felt adrift on an alien sea.

They had all been there! They had all been on South Beach last night. Any one of them could have hired thugs, paid them cash, and given them instructions on how to terrorize her.

The various conversations seemed to blend into a buzz. She smiled, she passed things, she poured more soda for someone, and she even ate a few mouthfuls of barbecued chicken. Finally, the meal ended.

Dusk was falling.

Peggy brought out coffee and after dinner liqueurs. Joe played bartender, mixing up different concoctions.

Jordan returned, and they all wound up sitting around one edge of the pool.

Kathy noted that her mother and Gerrit had disappeared. Hmmm. Curious.

The kids were eating by now, alone at the picnic table, laughing together.

Kids. They were grown up. Angel seemed to be a responsible and handsome young man. Alex and Bren were both incredibly fond of him.

People were laughing. Shelley was telling a story about a bawdy comedian who worked in Vegas. She was a good storyteller. She always had been.

Tara excused herself, asking Jordan if he could spare her a minute; she wanted to ask him a few questions in private. They disappeared. Jeremy yawned at Kathy's side. She whispered to him that he was free to go inside and shower and sleep whenever he chose.

They began to split up then, Judy going to her room, Shelley wandering in to see Miles's flute, Larry deciding to walk his wife up to their room.

Finally, alone by the water, Kathy decided that plunging in, now that she'd have the aqua expanse all to herself, seemed a wonderful idea. She thought she'd pick up a few of the coffee cups left around the pool first, though. Peggy had additional help while there were so many people at the place, but Kathy knew she would still be working well into the night.

She brought the dishes into the kitchen, not passing anyone, and eventually she had the pool area picked up. When she came back out through the porch, she saw that the downstairs bathroom light was on. She was about to open the door and flick it off when it went off of its own accord. She stared at the bathroom, then heard whispering from within.

"What the hell do you think you're doing? Trying to announce to the world just what's going on?"

"You're causing this—"

"You should have come to my room."

"Right. She would have really enjoyed that."

"Is it her you're worried about?"

"Well, what are you worried about?"

"You!"

"You said you wanted to talk—"

"Pulling me into the bathroom with a light on isn't exactly the way to accomplish it!"

"Neither was last night!"

"What?"

"Shh! Someone is out there."

"Oh, that's just great! What are we going to do now, stay in the bathroom all night and pray that someone isn't waiting to use the john?"

"Shh!"

"Ouch!"

Kathy hesitated, unsure as to whether to confront the pair or hide and then watch what they did. She was suddenly chilled, the steel of the blade as real, as if it were against her flesh again.

A shriek from outside the house made her swing around and race toward the sound. Her daughters were out there. Her heart in her throat, Kathy burst into the pool area again.

Her hand flew to her throat and she gritted her teeth, praying for her heart to cease its desperate beating.

It was Alex shrieking. She was doing so because Angel was about to toss her into the pool.

He saw Kathy and, flushing, instantly set Alex down.

"Mom!" Alex cried. "Come in the water now— it's beautiful."

"I'm— I'm sure it is," Kathy breathed out. She was blind. No, not really. She hadn't had the opportunity to see. Her daughter and Angel were a pair. How much of a pair she didn't know. She had no objection. She loved both Peggy and Joe, who were fine people. She wondered if Angel was afraid she wouldn't feel that way. And she wondered if she had missed her chance to discover what was going on when she had run from the hall by the bathroom.

Worse.

Perhaps the pair in the bathroom now knew she had been the one standing outside, listening.

"Mom, come in!" Alex insisted.

"Yeah, Mom!" Bren entreated from the water.

Kathy shrieked out herself when she was suddenly swept up from behind. Fear knifed into her, until she realized she had been plucked up by Jordan.

Their daughters cheered as he ran, carrying her, to the very edge of the deep water, then, still holding her, plunged into the pool. She jackknifed free from him, surfacing, ready to

yell at him but falling silent as she met his eyes.
He shouldn't have frightened her. He knew it.

He didn't want the girls to know that she had
been frightened. Here. In what had once been
her home.

Treading water, Kathy thrust her hands forward, sending a wave of the crystal water over
his head. As he shook it from his eyes, she dove
beneath him. The pool was nine feet at its deep-
est, so it was easy for her to come up, grab his
ankles, and drag him downward.

Escaping wasn't so easy.

She had just surfaced when her own ankle
was caught. She drew in air, then went under.
He released her instantly and she surfaced
again, gasping. Bren, Alex, and Angel were
laughing.

"She got you, Dad," Alex told Jordan.

"Ah, but I got her in return," Jordan replied.
"She can strike, but she can't do so and walk
away cleanly." He was swimming just a few feet
from her then. Kathy grinned. "It's that mastery
thing. Still working on me and the bagpipes, eh?"

"Maybe Alex is right, maybe you've been gotten— and mastered."

"Is that a macho thing?" she teased.

He shook his head, swimming closer. "After
last night you need a master. Leaving the house
this morning might have been damned stupid."

She shook her head passionately in return.
"Jordan, they were all here last night. Blue
Heron. Except Keith, of course, and you're
damned right, he is haunting everyone. If any-

one is trying to hurt me, you, us, or Blue Heron, that person is probably right here. And, Jordan, someone was whispering in the bathroom."

He arched a brow. "Whispering in the bathroom? Dangerously?"

She made a face. "No, I mean two people were in the bathroom whispering to one another. They didn't really say anything significant, but one of them was mad because the other might be letting everyone know what was going on."

"Could be somebody's just having an affair."

"They mentioned last night."

"Who the hell was it?"

She shook her head. "One of the girls shrieked out here then—just playing—but I was afraid . . ." Her voice trailed away.

"So someone in the house is dangerous."

"We don't really know that."

"I should be sleeping with you."

Her heart thundered. "Jordan, I'm serious. And you have slept with me," she reminded him in confusion.

"No, no. I mean, you shouldn't be alone. Sorry. Of course, you've got Muscleman."

"And you've got that sweet child to worry about. Has Mickey found out anything? Or should I say, have the 'Beach' police found out anything?"

He shook his head. "Not yet. They have a few leads on the tire slasher, but no one saw the guy who attacked you, so it's going to be damned hard to go after him."

"Jordan, I don't want the girls to be alone."

"They can bunk in together."

"I want Angel with them."

He arched a brow.

"On a couch!" she said with a sigh.

"You're right," he agreed. "Want me to arrange it?"

"I think I'd like to handle it," she replied, just as a wave sluiced over her. She kicked the water hard, shooting out of it. Alex was now paddling near them, grinning with pleasure almost as if she were a small child again.

"Chicken fights!" she said.

"What?" Kathy echoed.

"Chicken fights!" Bren called. She was an incredibly graceful swimmer. She barely seemed to move to stay afloat, her amber eyes nearly gold as they reflected the house lights that now fell on the water as darkness approached. "Angel and Alex against you and Dad. I take on the winner by the shoulders of the loser."

"Bren, Alex, we're far too old for such—"

"A challenge?" Jordan interrupted her. "The hell we are. You're on. Kathy, get over here. We used to be good at this."

"Yeah! A million years ago!" Bren teased.

"You're right. You guys are on!" Kathy laughed.

She was still laughing when, balanced upon Jordan's shoulders, she was ready to face her eldest daughter, who was balanced atop Angel. Angel took a step forward. "Alex! You're strangling me. No hands on my throat!" Angel begged.

"Don't worry. She'll be in the water in a split

second. Her mother has always been tough as nails," Jordan advised. "Ouch! Kathy, you're sitting on my hair."

"That will teach you to get a respectable haircut!" Kathy advised. She reached out to Alex in a taunting gesture. "Come on, come on! Chicken? Get over here. Let me take you on. I'm just a regular iron maiden."

A second later, she and Alex clashed. Jordan and Angel, face to face, nearly tripping over one another, were laughing. Bren was calling out advice to all four of them, and Kathy was laughing so hard she could scarcely grapple with her daughter, but in the end, she called out to Jordan to take a step back at just the right time for Alex to be dislodged from Angel's shoulders by her own weight. The two struggled to regain their balance, teetered precariously for a minute, then fell, splashing into the water together, only to rise again in a fit of giggling.

"Next!" Kathy demanded.

"Yeah, and hurry. These are old shoulders she's sitting upon. The back may go at any minute."

"Are you insinuating I'm heavy?" Kathy demanded.

"Would I do such a thing?" he demanded. He stared at Bren. "Get a move on. Your mother's heavy— for a light little thing. I admitted they were old shoulders, right?"

Bren, giggling, crawled up on Angel's shoulders. It was Alex's turn to call out advice, which she did with gusto. Bren nearly dragged her mother down. But, her pride at stake, Kathy refused to fall, tightening her legs around Jordan's shoulders and torso.

"Ouch!" he cried.

"Oh, hush, be a man!" Kathy taunted, tapping him on the head. "Are we going to let these children beat us?"

"If we don't beat them soon we are!" Jordan assured her.

"To your left!" Kathy cried, drawing Bren in the opposite direction as she gave the command. She toppled her younger daughter in the same manner in which she had disposed of Alex, but at the end, Bren went down with Kathy's wrist locked tenaciously within her fingers. So Kathy fell as well, dragging Jordan with her. They all surfaced, laughing, disentangling.

Alex sobered suddenly, staring at the end of the pool. Everyone's gaze followed hers.

Tara stood at the end of the pool, clad in a short cotton dress with a flare skirt and white sandals. She looked very young, and very hurt. She offered them a smile. "Family fun time, huh?"

Then she burst into tears, and turned and ran away.

Jordan groaned.

"Dad, she's just trying to get a rise out of you!" Alex said impatiently.

"You should go after her," Kathy told him.

"I told her when this week began—"

"That you were going to exclude her while you played with your kids and your ex-wife?" Kathy asked softly. "Jordan, it really isn't fair."

"But she knows—"

"Maybe you're not exactly ready for the kind of relationship she wants, but you really need to say something to her."

"— I don't—"

"Please, at least talk to her. I'd feel better," Kathy said.

He stared at her as if he'd like to throttle her.

"Mom, you don't have to be Mary Poppins or Glinda the Good Witch of the South!" Alex snapped.

She stared at the girls. "This doesn't concern you."

"Actually, Mom, it doesn't concern *you*," Bren said. "If Dad doesn't want to talk to— "

"Don't talk to your mother that way!" Jordan snapped.

Angel cleared his throat, looking mortified.

"Sorry, Mom," Bren said sullenly.

"Please . . ." Kathy said to Jordan.

He sighed, lifted himself from the pool with a hitch of his arms, and padded, wet and dripping, toward the house.

"Mom, we were having such a great evening," Alex said.

"You can't manipulate the two of us back together," Kathy told her. "Right, Angel?"

"Oh, I, er . . ."

Kathy laughed. "Didn't mean to put you on the spot. Bren, Alex, listen to me. Dad has to resolve his relationship with Tara, one way or the other, understand?"

Neither answered her.

"Understand."

She got two sullen ummms in return.

Leaving them behind, Kathy swam down to the deep end of the pool and lifted herself from the water to perch on the tile rim. A second later, they followed her, quietly pulling themselves out one by one to join her.

"Well," Kathy said, "now that Dad and Tara are settled, Angel, I want you to sleep with my daughters."

Despite his dark tan, Angel managed to turn crimson while his jaw worked.

"What?" Alex gasped.

"Angel, don't look at me like that!" Kathy told him. "Obviously something is going on between you and Alex, and if you were to ask my blessing, which you certainly don't need, you'd have it. But what I'm saying is I don't want the girls alone. You don't need to tell anyone else in the house, but, Bren, I want you in with Alex— her room is bigger. And Angel, please, I want you keeping guard on the daybed."

Alex and Bren gaped at her. Angel looked from Alex to Kathy. "I . . . I—" he began.

"Mom, what's wrong?" Alex asked, concerned.

Kathy shook her head. "I don't really know. But I was attacked last night, and Dad has never been happy about what happened here ten years ago. Will you all do what I asked? Angel?"

"Of course, Mrs. Treveryan."

"Kathy. Connoly," she said softly. "Thanks, Angel. And nothing kinky, huh?"

"Mom!" Bren said with horror.

But Alex was grinning. "She trusts us, Bren. She's just teasing."

"Oh, yeah, of course," Bren said, relieved. She giggled. "But what are we afraid of?"

"It's who," Kathy said. "And I don't know."

They all nodded. "I'm going to shower and *subtly* bring a few things to Alex's room," Bren said, starting from the pool area.

"I'll go make room," Alex said, rising to follow her sister.

"I'll keep watch," Angel said with a grin, rising. He started away, then turned back to where Kathy remained perched on the tile at the deep end of the pool.

"I love Alex very much. Bren, too, of course," he said. "We've kind of grown up together. I mean, I only love Alex in . . . in a romantic way, but we're all the best of friends. I mean . . . oh, God, I mean . . . nothing kinky."

Kathy smiled. "I know, Angel."

"You really don't mind?"

She shook her head, hugging her knees to her chest. "You seem to be a very fine man. I'm glad for Alex."

He smiled. "Thanks. Thank you very much."

"I imagine Jordan knows all about this."

He shrugged. "We've never really said anything, but he's always known how much we're together."

"He knows," Kathy said. "And trust me, if he didn't think the world of you, he'd have said something by now."

Angel nodded, pleased.

"Keep them safe."

"By my life!" he swore with all the conviction and passion of youth. Then he gave her a wave and started after the girls. Kathy leaned back on the edge of the pool, closing her eyes. The night breeze was soft and beautiful. She could hear the subtle movement of the water. The night touched her with gentle, balmy fingers.

Why the hell had she sent Jordan after Tara?

"Ah, Kathy! All alone? I've been looking for you." The voice was husky. Like a whisper.

Belonging to *the* whisperer— or one of them, at least?

She jerked up, seeing that Larry Haley had come to stand by her. He grinned, then took a seat next to her, dangling his feet in the water. She looked quickly around. She couldn't see or hear anyone else, the patio was deserted. There might not have been another soul within miles of them.

"You know, Kathy, I think we really all missed you most," Larry told her, sighing.

"Really? How . . . nice," she said.

"I was anxious to see if you would come. But then I thought you would. Actually I was pretty damned sure we'd all show up."

"Why?"

He shrugged. "Why not? None of us have been quite the same since Blue Heron ended. We had such glory days back then! Maybe we all had to recapture them. The good— and the bad."

"Maybe." She stared at him, drawn by curiosity, yet somewhat unnerved. "Didn't you want to get back together just for the fun of doing it?"

"I did want to get back together, and I didn't."

"Why not?" she asked.

He moved closer to her again.

"Ah, indeed, why not?" He hesitated, then looked at her, narrowing his eyes. "Should I confess? Like our dear departed friend Keith was always prone to do? He always said nobody could listen the way you did. That you could make people see things in a new light. That you had heart and compassion. Of course, he did think you had much more. So much time has passed, but if I were to tell you the truth, how could I know you would keep my secrets as you kept his?"

Kathy was acutely uncomfortable. She was with Larry. Alone. At the pool. The deep end. Just across the water and a spit of grass from the place where Keith had died, perishing in flames . . .

Someone in the house had been whispering . . .

And Larry was talking about confessions.

Keith might have been murdered. She had been attacked by a man with a knife.

She could swim, of course, if Larry meant to push her into the water.

But what if he didn't just mean to do that. He was in his swim trunks as well, and he was in good shape. Not a huge man, but a wiry one, strong, nicely muscled. If he wanted to, he could force her in, and then under . . .

She'd never thought she'd be *afraid* of Larry

Haley. He could be offensive, but was usually so blunt she had always taken him with a grain of salt. He was just Larry. A little rough around the edges. Afraid of aging. A man who needed to be in some business where people flocked around him, where he could be the center of the attention.

He'd been in town last night. When the attacker had brought the knife to her throat.

"Larry, don't feel that because we're back together again you're compelled to talk to me," she told him. She smiled. She inched away.

He inched closer again.

His features had become tense. The look in his eyes was serious. He moved even closer. Her heart beat a thousand miles an hour. She wanted to jump up and run.

She wanted to hear what he had to say.

Her throat was clogging, and it might well be that she needed to scream. After all, he'd been looking for her. So very soon after she'd had that knife pressed against her throat, her jugular.

"Larry— "

"I did it."

She nearly choked on dry air. Then she inhaled, desperate for air.

He reached for her shoulders. "Oh, God, Kathy, I'm the one. I did it! I did it, I did it, I did it!"

His fingers dug into her shoulders. Terror filled her. She opened her mouth to scream as his face kept coming closer to her own . . .

Seventeen

Tara hadn't headed for her own room— she'd apparently known that he'd follow her, eventually— but had made a beeline for the guest house. She must really want privacy, he thought, closing the door quietly behind him as he entered through the kitchen.

She was in the downstairs living room, looking out the window, frowning. She must have seen him leave, and she'd probably assumed he was coming after her, but then she'd lost sight of him somehow and she seemed worried.

He must have made a sound because she turned around and stared at him. To his surprise, her cheeks were really damp, which made him feel like a heel.

"You don't need to do this," she said accusingly. She inhaled on a sob, sounding dramatic.

"Do what?" he inquired carefully. Come after her?

"Play Mr. Dad with your ex. She's a big girl, she's got a new beau. Except the way you're flirting with her, it's as if you're trying to tell her something— or me."

He didn't reply for a very long time. She stared at him, growing indignant. "Jordan!"

He shook his head. "Tara, I did warn you that this might not be a great weekend for you to be around."

"You wanted a vacation from me so you could sleep with your ex-wife?" she inquired incredulously.

He folded his arms over his chest. "Tara, we— you and I— enjoy one another's company. We've had a nice relationship. A great relationship. But I don't remember making any commitment in which I'd have to ask for a *vacation* to sleep with someone else. *If* that was what I wanted."

"So you haven't slept with her?" Tara said, striding toward him like a cat about to pounce.

"I've had two children with her. They were not by immaculate conception."

"Jordan, damn you!" she cried, throwing herself against him. Instinctively, he caught her. She sighed, leaning against his shoulder.

"I love you," she said.

He held her, stroking her hair. "You know I care for you . . ."

She let out a wretched sob again. "But you don't love me."

"Tara—"

"I really love you, Jordan!" she said, pulling away slightly to stare up into his eyes. "What is going on here?" she whispered.

He felt awful. He shook his head. "Tara—"

"You can't possibly prefer her to me! She's— she's nearly fifteen years older. She isn't . . ."

"You?" he queried, the edge softening on his guilt. He wasn't sure whether Tara was really so desperately in love with him or whether she simply couldn't bear the possibility that she wasn't more alluring than a woman a decade older.

"I'm only thirty," she reminded him, "and I work my tail to the bone for you. There isn't an ounce of cellulite on me."

"No, there isn't. But, darling, you don't work your tail to the bone for me, you do so for your career, which is a far better thing."

"You're not making any sense, Jordan."

"Yes, I am, Tara," he said wearily. "You should always want to be what you want to be for yourself and no one else. It's good to share achievements, desires, dreams— and tragedies— but love shouldn't make you want to be anything you don't want to be for yourself. You're missing just what that emotion is all about. It isn't about absolute perfection or beauty. It's in a smile, the sound of laughter. Shared memories. Beliefs. Passions, concerns— "

"You *are* in love with her still, you bastard!" Tara charged him, slamming a fist against his chest.

"I never said that."

"How could you be in love with her, you idiot? I try to give to give you everything!"

He circled his fingers around her wrists, holding her still. A cavalcade of emotions swept through him, one after the other. In her way, she was in love with him. In his way, he cared for her. She'd been with him, she'd been fun, she'd made him laugh. In good times. When threatened, she was selfish, conceited, and petulant. He hadn't been much better himself. He'd let jealousy turn him into someone harsh and cold.

What would he be thinking and feeling if he thought Kathy was sharing his bedroom with her friend? He'd probably be clinging to Tara like a drowning man grasping a raft.

Why was he so convinced Kathy had cooled things since she'd come here?

And did it matter? He did want to sleep with his ex-wife. He was still in love with her. He had never fallen out of love with her.

Maybe that didn't matter either. In another seven days, Kathy would most probably walk away again.

He'd better pray that she was able to do it! If he thought about the threat to her, it was chilling.

"Tara, if you're hurt, I'm very sorry. If you're miserable here, you can leave—"

"Oh, my God! You're throwing me out."

"Of course not," he said impatiently, "I'd never do that."

"Maybe you do love me," she whispered suddenly. "You did until you started feeling responsible again. And those wretched children of yours—"

"Watch it!"

"Oh, God, I'm sorry. The girls aren't wretched—just to me," she muttered bitterly.

"Tara . . ."

"Don't worry. I don't know what she's done

to you, but no matter what, I'm going to stand by your side. I'll be here. I won't give you up— or give up on you. You need me. Much more than you know!"

She encircled his neck with her arms, pressing her body sinuously against his. Her fingers moved through his hair, massaging the back of his skull.

He was about to pull away, but she suddenly spoke so softly that something tugged at his heart.

"I love you, Jordan."

"Tara, you're very beautiful, you've the entire the world in your hands and—"

She kissed him, swallowing his words. She was, and always had been, a practiced lover. She could seduce and sway. He had loved her in his way; he didn't want to hurt her. Her kiss was coercive, evocative.

For a moment, the bitterness of the past settled over his shoulders. Kathy had left him. Called it quits. He had told himself then as he told himself now that he wasn't going to spend his days pining after a woman who didn't want him anymore. Life went on. And there was solace. Solace such as he held now.

Yet in the midst of both bitterness and seduction, he opened his eyes, and looked out the window. Kathy was alone— except for Larry Haley. Larry's hands were on her shoulders.

He clasped Tara, lifting her out of his way in a single, swift motion. "Excuse me," he told her distractedly.

"Excuse me?" she whispered indignantly. "Jordan Treveryan, there is no damned excuse!"

But he had already started across the room to the front door, the closest route to the pool.

"Tara, Kathy was threatened at knife point. I have to keep an eye on her."

"Oh!" Tara sighed. "Of course you do!" she added sweetly, a change in her attitude. Real? Feigned? She only followed him halfway out. "I'll be here, Jordan. I love you. I'll be patient—and understanding."

Oh, God.

But it didn't matter. As long as he reached Kathy.

If they couldn't both stay alive, none of the rest of it mattered!

"The drugs!" Larry said.

"Drugs?" Kathy squeaked out in lieu of a scream. Oh, Lord. He wasn't admitting to murder. At least, she didn't think so.

"I don't believe I'm doing this, saying this. It's almost as if I've been dying to confess to someone. I wish I would have done so back then. I was the one with the drugs, Kathy. God, I didn't want anyone to know when we were caught with them. I was terrified that Jordan would find out. I let Keith take the heat for it because, hell, he had talent. I didn't. I was hanging on."

"What?"

Miserably, Larry nodded.

"Don't you remember? The last real big blow-out when Keith was still alive was over the drugs found with the group's equipment when we were just coming back into the United States. Jordan all but went for Keith's throat. Keith denied it all. Remember?"

Kathy nodded painfully. "Yes, of course, I do."

"I had to tell you. But"— he paused— "I don't think I'm ready to tell Jordan yet. Give me time, huh?"

She frowned, wondering why he had suddenly started speaking so hastily. Then she glanced up to see that Jordan was headed back around the pool in their direction.

"Kathy, please, be my champion, like you were Keith's."

"I wasn't anyone's champion, I tried to be a peacekeeper, that's all. We were good when we were together. We fell apart because we all had a habit of acting like children."

"Keep my secret for now?"

"Why did you feel compelled to tell me this now?" Kathy demanded with exasperation. Did he have other little "secrets" that he wasn't sharing with her? And how could she not tell Jordan, with everything else that was going on.

Jordan had almost reached them. If Larry had been about to attempt a drowning, at least Jordan had made it before paramedics. But then, she had been foolish to be so afraid. If Larry Haley had been about to confess murder and then kill her, he'd probably not have done so here. She'd felt alone at the pool, but she was visible from both the main and guest houses. She stared at Larry hard. "Tell me," she demanded quickly. "Does anyone else know your secret?"

He frowned. "What?"

"I said—"

"Kathy, shh!"

He either hadn't understood her question, or had pretended he didn't. He was rising, smiling as Jordan reached them. "You know, this is great. I haven't had so much fun since I filmed mating chimps in the wilds of Africa. Seriously, thanks for having us. I hope this get-together accomplishes all that you wanted it to."

"Yeah, I hope so too," Jordan said dryly.

"Which is?" Larry asked bluntly.

Jordan arched a brow to him, then shrugged. "With the movie and all the interest, I thought it was time we all got back together."

"We need to give the movie a good ending, huh?"

"We're going to benefit the burn center," Kathy reminded him.

He smiled ruefully, then stared straight at her. "He died from the smoke, you know. He never knew what hit him. There were probably benefits to being a druggie for Keith."

"How can you say that?" Kathy demanded. "He'd have put out the fire or run away from it if he hadn't been wasted!"

"Well, that's true, too," Larry admitted. He shivered. "But at least he didn't feel it. God, I can't think of a worse way to die. You know what? I think I'm going to call it quits for tonight. You did say you wanted to start practicing early tomorrow morning, right?"

"Ten o'clock," Jordan agreed.

" 'Night, then. Let's hope we don't all stink. Well, you won't. And Miles won't. Shelley will probably be okay. I'll be as rusty as an old door handle, and Derrick will surely squeak a little. How about you, Kathy?"

"I'll be an old door handle, too."

"No recent performances?"

"Only in my shower."

Larry grinned. "Who's taking the drums?"

"Miles."

"Ah!" Larry said thoughtfully. "Well, we'll see, huh?"

"We'll see."

He grinned, waved, and left the two of them at the pool. Kathy was still sitting. Jordan came down beside her, staring at her anxiously. "What the hell was going on?"

She returned his stare, lifting a brow, fighting an inward battle. She should tell him what Larry had said to her. But Larry had said he wanted to tell Jordan in his own time. Didn't she owe him that much?

Or did she?

She hadn't asked for any confessions from him! Hadn't wanted any.

And far too recently she'd been brutally held in an alley, a knife at her throat.

"Kathy?"

She lowered her eyes. Larry might be a murderer. Then again, he might not.

She had to give him a little time.

"I think he's nervous," she said.

"What?"

Kathy shrugged and offered him a rueful half-smile. "Well, you kept working on your own after the band split up. I found work I liked better. Larry—"

"Larry has become a very successful film maker," Jordan said somewhat gruffly.

Kathy looked at him curiously. He was staring out over the water of the pool.

"He might be a successful film maker, but he loved being a rock musician more," she said softly, then realized that Jordan knew it. And deep inside, he might be feeling just a little bit guilty because his decision to end the group had influenced the lives of those who had been in it with him.

"Maybe," he agreed huskily. Then he turned his sharp green stare on her again. "But the way he was looking at you scared the hell out of me for a minute there. And he had his hands on your shoulders . . ."

"He's excitable, you know that."

Jordan cocked his head. "Think you know who was whispering in the bathroom yet?"

She shrugged, shaking her head.

"Kathy," he told her sternly, "don't forget what happened last night! This is a serious situation."

"I'm not forgetting anything. I just . . ."

"What?"

She hesitated, forming her words haltingly. "I don't know if this makes any sense or not, but, well . . . Larry has been a sleazeball upon occasion— maybe even the sleazeball of the Western world— but that's just about it."

"Being sleazy exonerates him?" Jordan demanded skeptically.

She shook her head impatiently. "I don't know. Maybe."

"You're just a soft touch," he told her.

She shrugged uncomfortably. Was she? Falling for both Larry's confession and his plea?

But then, wasn't her falling for Jordan just the same?

She leapt to her feet, suddenly yawning. "I guess I'm a little tired, too. Considering that I'm probably the rustiest one of all, I'd best get some sleep since we start practicing tomorrow."

She was afraid for a minute that he'd stand up beside her, try to waylay her. He didn't. He continued to stare broodingly at the aqua water of the pool.

"Good night," she told him.

He nodded, not looking up.

Kathy turned around and walked from the patio to the house. She turned back. He was still staring at the water. She walked on up to her room without seeing anyone else, closed the door behind her, locking it, and then sighed and went in to shower, still thinking about what Larry had said to her. Did the fact that he was such a sleazeball mean he wasn't a murderer.

Larry could be slick, sly— he had let Keith take the blame for his illegal activities.

She dried herself vigorously when she stepped from the shower, her mind a jumble of nerve-racking thoughts. She slipped into a cool satin nightgown, pacing the room, remembering the whispered conversation she had overheard. If she hadn't been distracted by her daughter . . .

But she had— she'd nearly jumped out of her skin at hearing that cry. Was she a fool for not telling Jordan what Larry had said to her?

Idiot! she chastised herself. After all, with no effort, she could recall exactly what it had felt like to have the sharp blade of a knife against her throat.

She groaned out loud, turned out her light, and slipped into bed, determined to sleep. But she tossed and turned.

So much for determination.

Exhaustion finally began to creep over her. She wasn't really sleeping, but she dozed.

Then she . . . woke.

Prickles seemed to dance upon her skin, and her blood ran hot, then cold throughout her body. She didn't know how she sensed that some-one was in her room, she just did.

Had she heard . . . a click?

She bolted up, looking around, certain she was about to face a murderer, ready to shout.

Her shout died. There was no one there.

Shakily, she lay back down. Fool! She was be-coming paranoid. Well, she had the right.

But she had to sleep. She must will herself to sleep.

She must have done so, because again she awoke. Aware. Feeling with every pore and cell in her body.

A scream rose in her throat. Someone was with her, watching her. Someone . . .

A hand fell over her mouth, stifling her scream just when it was about to rip fervently and harshly from her throat.

"It's me!"

Jordan!

Damn him!

Shaking like a leaf, she sat up, thrusting his hand away from her face.

"What the hell's the matter with you?" she demanded furiously

"Shhh! Dammit. I didn't mean to startle— "

"Scare the hell out of me!"

"Damn, Kath, I just now stepped in here. I couldn't bang on the door and announce my presence!"

It was dark in the room. She could barely make out his form at first. He was wearing a knee-length terry robe. She looked at his face. His features were hard and taut in the night. Unnerved, she leapt out of bed, staring at him. Not that she could see much.

Shadows.

"Jordan you can't keep doing this to me."

"I was worried. I couldn't leave you alone."

"My door was locked."

"It wasn't."

"It certainly was! I locked it!"

"Kathy, it wasn't."

"Jordan— "

"My God, what do you want me to do? Swear on the lives of my daughters? Well, I do. And that's exactly why I was so worried about you. You're a trusting little fool— "

"Don't you dare call me a fool!"

"Shhh!"

She fell silent, aware that she was still shaking. She was losing her mind in this house. She suddenly remembered the *click* she had heard. Someone opening her door? Or closing it? Had someone other than Jordan come into her room, and stood there staring at her? She had thought it had happened before, on the night she had first come. But none of the others had been in the house then, only Jordan.

That was it. He was trying to convince her that she was insane. Jordan had hated Keith, he had tried to get Keith to take more drugs, he had killed Keith . . .

God. She was losing her mind.

"Jordan, I swear to you, I locked my door." Had she? Or had she only thought so?

"The point is, you didn't."

She opened her mouth to argue with him, then didn't. She swung around, pacing to the window, parting the drapes, staring down to the patio, hoping the tranquil aqua water of the pool would ease the tumult that had claimed her. "The point is," she said in a firm, angry whisper, "you shouldn't be here!"

He was silent. His belated reply was a stark and angry whisper. "I was worried. I had a right to be."

She looked at him. "Worried?"

"You don't want the girls alone; I'm worried about you being alone." He indicated the connecting door to Jeremy's room with an inclination of his head. "Even if Muscleman is sleeping yonder."

"Jordan, damn you, he could come in—"

"Will he? I thought he didn't enter without knocking."

"Which is more than I can say for you!" she muttered, looking back absently to the patio.

"He has no reason to worry about your well-being."

"You're not helping it any."

"I just came to stand sentinel."

"But—" Kathy broke off, stunned, as she suddenly saw a figure move fleetly across the patio.

A woman's figure. Slim, wraithlike in the night, running from the main house to the guest house.

Long, dark red hair trailing behind her. White nightgown flowing in the moonlight.

"Jordan." She tried to give sound to his name. She had no air in her lungs. She had to inhale before gasping out his name again.

"Jordan!" She motioned furiously for him to come to the window.

He arrived just in time to see the figure disappearing around the side of the guest house. Maybe she was seeing things. No! She could tell, staring at him, at the tension in his features, *he had seen the woman, too!*

The woman . . .

Her. That long-ago night.

He pushed away from the window, striding quickly for the door to her room. She raced after him, frantically grabbing his arm. "Jordan, wait!"

"Kathy, let go of me! I have to find out who it is!"

"No! You could get hurt."

"By a woman in a nightgown?" he demanded.

"Jordan . . . it's . . . me!"

"Right. But it's not you."

"It may not even be a woman. It may be a man. An armed man. An armed woman. Someone who hopes you will follow, someone—"

"Kathy, I *have* to go!"

He wrenched free of her. "Lock your door. This time really do it, and don't open the damned thing until you hear my voice, got it?"

"Jordan—"

"Lock it! Dammit, I'm armed as well. I'll be all right. Don't make me worry about you! It could be my downfall, Kathy. For the love of God, do as I say!"

"Jordan—"

But he was gone. As if he were a wraith himself, he had disappeared from the room.

She wanted to follow him.

But he had told her he was armed. Would he really be better off without having to worry about her? She bit into her lower lip, closed and locked the door. Carefully. Certainly. Then she raced back to the window, just in time to see Jordan streaking across the patio area.

Then around the side of the guest house . . .

Eons passed. An ungodly time. She aged a thousand years. She kept staring at the guest house. Watching, waiting, afraid to blink. She felt like screaming, like dialing 911, bursting into Jeremy's room and waking him up.

Just when she thought she could bear it no longer, she heard a tapping at her door. She nearly leapt a mile, right out of her skin.

But then she heard his whisper.

"Kathy!"

She flung open the door. He stood alone, a small pistol shoved into his pants. He quickly stepped into her room, quietly closing the door behind him.

"Well?" she demanded breathlessly.

But he shook his head in disgust. "No one."

"But— "

"I looked all over. Inside the guest house, outside the guest house. I walked around the halls, the bushes, the dock— everywhere."

"But we both saw— "

"Yeah, we both saw," he agreed quietly. He walked back to the window himself, arms crossed over his chest as he leaned against the wall, staring down at the patio. "We saw what I must have seen ten years ago," he said softly.

"But who . . . what?"

He shook his head. "I don't know."

"It's like my book," Kathy said, walking over to look out at the now still night once again.

"What?"

She looked at him. "You know, the manuscript I just bought. What we see with our own eyes isn't really the truth—circumstantial evidence means nothing. And sometimes things are just so damned evident that we can't see them."

He arched a brow, a slow, crooked smile curving his lip in the shadows of night.

"Nothing is evident to me. I admit to being more baffled than ever, so if anything seems evident to you—"

"Not really," Kathy said. "It's just that . . . I think, what we saw, *wasn't.*"

"We're really making sense now."

"It will make sense, at some time, I think."

He shrugged, then glanced toward the door. "Lock it again."

"You're staying here?" she demanded.

"Me and my trusty pistol."

She sniffed. "You're lucky you haven't shot your balls off, the way you're wearing the damned thing."

"The safety is on, but I'm delighted that you're concerned about my anatomy."

"Jordan—"

"Let's get some sleep, Kathy, huh?"

He suddenly sounded not just tired but bone weary. Beyond all tension. He set the gun on the nightstand on the left side of the bed, and lay down, casting an arm over his eyes. She stared at him a long moment. He seemed oblivious to her.

After deciding that she would sleep better with him in the room, she started across the room to her bed.

"Check the door," he said. She paused, both irritated and glad that he had heard her near silent, barefoot step.

She did as he asked and then crawled in beside him.

He lay on his side. She lay on hers. Silent.

At length she whispered. "Jordan, *who* was it?"

"I don't know. And I don't know *why* she—"

"Or *he!*"

"Right. Was running across the patio. And yet . . ."

"Yet?"

"I think we're somehow closer."

"Sure," Kathy agreed dubiously.

"Let's get some sleep. We can't afford to be exhausted."

"Right."

"Good night."

"Yeah. Good night." She lay down. Sat back up. "Jordan?"

"Yeah?"

"You're not going to shoot me with that thing by mistake?"

"Or on purpose," he said dryly.

"Not amusing."

"Not meant to be. Kathy—"

"I know. I know. I'm going to sleep."

Once again, she lay back down. She stared at the ceiling. She felt him, not touching her, beside her.

After a while, she was amazed to realize that her eyes were closing, the tension was easing from her body. It was better with him here. She did feel secure. There might be a maniacal killer in the house, but she felt more secure. She slept. Deeply.

Very deeply. And dreamed.

She was somewhere cool, a place where soft, sweet breezes caressed her body. She lay in comfort, deep within the down of clouds. Delicate wings brushed her flesh, smoothed her hair, slowly, sensuously . . .

Hmmm. Wings. Like hell.

Hands . . .

Great hands. Masculine, seductive, long fingered. Gentle one second, more demanding the next. Atop the satin of her nightgown, beneath it. Her flesh felt like fire.

She wasn't going to move, wasn't going to fall for this. Wasn't going to allow him . . .

Oh, God. That touch. Against her naked flesh. Insistent. A touch again, a thrust. His hands, his body, in her, on her. Her breasts. His body. Seeking . . . finding. Moving . . .

Ummm, she was going to fall . . .

Oh, God, she was a damned rock; she'd fallen in a plummeting whirl, incredibly awake and aware, on fire with sensation, hungry for him, startled, awed. *Glad* to have him spooned around her, hands holding her taut to his tempo, his breath against her nape, his lips, his whisper, his movement, harder and harder against her, inside of her . . .

She bit into her knuckles rather than shriek out when the drenching sweetness of climax suddenly burst upon her. For seconds she felt nothing but the bliss of stars exploding within her, then she became aware of him, one last frantic movement, a surge of heat . . .

He kissed her neck. Without a word, eased himself onto his back.

She stared into the night.

Hmmm. Go to sleep, Kathy. Right. Great. He'd seduced her in that sleep, taken her swiftly from behind . . .

And gone back to sleep.

Hell.

What did he think?

That they were married or something?

She should have thrown him right out of the bed— if one could throw Jordan. She should have shouted, protested.

Instead, she smiled slightly. Fool. Well, she was glad to have him and his bedside pistol.

And other things.

She slept again. Like a baby. And for the moment, it just didn't matter if she was a fool or not.

Eighteen

"Boy, oh, boy. We were really into hair in those days, weren't we?" Larry said. He idly tapped his chin as the group stared at one of their old videos. They were up in Jordan's soundproof studio, their instruments awaiting them on the dais. Jordan had suggested they take a minute to look back before getting started.

It was so strange, like watching a time capsule that had come of age.

They *had* been into hair, Kathy thought dryly. There was Keith on the drum, his head swinging with every beat, his hair flying right along with every strike upon the drums. Her own hair had been down her back, past her waist. She was tossing it as well. In fact, the lot of them were rather heavily into hair tossing.

"Seems like some of us are still into hair!" Shelley teased, tugging on Larry's ponytail.

"Careful," he growled teasingly. "It's harder to keep the hair on the head these days."

"The hair doesn't matter, the sound does," Jordan advised. "Listen, this is what we've got to try to achieve again— Kathy, Shelley, you've a perfect harmony going there. The breaks and bridges are just right. Our harmonies were a large part of what made us special, along with the fact that we wrote almost all of our music. That's what we need to achieve again— the harmony, the balance. Okay?"

"Rusty harmony!" Larry said ruefully.

"We're going to be all right," Miles assured him, confident.

"Yeah. So let's get to it," Jordan said.

And again it was strange. Damned strange.

Everyone took his or her place. Jordan had said he didn't want anyone but the group in on the first jam sessions, which excluded Larry's sweet, young Vicky Sue, Jeremy, and Tara.

Judy, however, was in place in front of them, critically watching, just as she had always been.

"Let's go with 'Shadows'," Jordan said.

"Shadows!" Kathy gasped.

The others were silent. *Dead* silent, she thought, feeling a little bubble of hysterical laughter forming in her throat. It was her song— not that that meant anything special. She had written— or helped write— the lyrics to most of their songs.

This was the last song she had written. The last song they had really rehearsed.

The last song for which Keith had written the music. They had worked on it the day he died, had introduced it at the party that night.

"Yeah. 'Shadows'," Jordan repeated, looking around at the lot of them. "If we can get it together, we can use it for the benefit opener, do a recording, and make some money for charity. Does anyone have a problem with that?"

Silently, one by one, they shook their heads at him. Jordan stared at Kathy last.

"It's a great song. The music and the lyrics are perfect together. Right?"

She found herself nodding. Oh, yeah. Perfect. It brought back to mind Keith's last smile, his enthusiasm. The anger that had been boiling over in all of them.

Was that what Jordan had in mind?

"Let's get it right, guys, shall we?" he said lightly.

No one argued with him.

He slipped his guitar strap over his shoulder, looked at Miles behind the drum set, then tapped out the beat with his foot, nodding to the others.

Amazingly, they all started off right on the beat. The music, then the lyrics, Shelley's sweet soprano blending with Kathy's throatier alto.

"Shadows here and shadows there,
Shadows haunting everywhere . . .
Shadows rise and shadows fall;
Shadows twist and rise and call;
Shadows dart along the hall, and
Shadows dance upon the wall . . .
Shadows . . .
Shadows . . .
Dark . . .
Dim . . .
Haunting . . .

> Falling . . .
> Shadows . . ."

One after the other, their voices fell upon the chorus, the harmony amazingly like that of waves upon the ocean, lulling, soft, hauntingly beautiful, fading away, the two women picking up the verse once again.

Unbelievably in sinc.

> "I can feel them reach for me,
> Shadows will not set me free,
> Shadows harsh and shadows kind,
> Shadows play upon my mind.
> Shadows of the days gone by,
> Hear them laugh, and hear them cry,
> Shadows . . ."

Once again, the voices of the men falling upon each other as they picked up the chorus. Then their voices fading away, the sounds of the instruments blended, fading away, and in the end just the beat of drums and the soft, magical whisper of a flute.

And when they finished, silence. They stared at one another. Something suddenly electric, exciting, filling the air. A magic.

"Well, I'll be damned!" Judy stated flatly. "I wouldn't have believed it."

"Shit! We were good," Larry said, startled himself. "We were—"

"We were *wicked* good," Miles said, incredulous.

"And we've got to keep it up," Jordan said firmly. "That was one song. We've got lots to go. Let's not go patting ourselves on the back too hard yet, huh?"

"Sure, right." Miles responded, but he winked at Kathy. She saw that he was delighted.

And despite Jordan's skepticism, the session continued to proceed as if charmed. They had created such excitement amongst themselves that the rehearsal seemed effortless. They went from song to song. Switched instruments upon occasion, switched positions, harmonies. No one suggested a break. No one noticed the passing of time.

Eventually, when they finished with a soft ballad, they heard a knocking on the door. Judy dutifully rose and went to it. Through the glass, they could see Tara and Jeremy.

Judy looked at Jordan who shrugged. She opened the door.

"Sorry to interrupt," Jeremy said cheerfully, "but Peggy suggested that, despite her best efforts, her dinner will not be edible if you don't all come and eat very shortly."

"Dinner?" Shelley said.

"It's six o'clock," Tara informed them, a slight edge to her voice despite her smile. She looked strained, Kathy thought.

"Wow! Wow!" Larry said excitedly. He turned to Miles. "Eight hours! Eight hours and we've been great—"

"So damned good we didn't even notice the time!" Derrick said happily.

"You were so good I didn't even notice the time," Judy said with a grin.

"Really?" Shelley asked her. "All of them? It felt good. Wonderful. Tight and right and great even though Keith—" She broke off, then stared at Jordan. She seemed confused. "Jordan, we were good. Even without him. Right?"

Jordan nodded solemnly to her, then smiled slightly. "Keith was good. Maybe the best. But we were all good, Shelley. Part of a whole. And yeah, we can be great—even without Keith."

"Well, I don't like to break up this mutual admiration society," Tara said sweetly, "but Peggy is waiting."

"And it has been a productive enough day." Jordan looked happy. "Let's call it quits and eat."

Tara slipped into the studio, going to him, slipping an arm around him. "You must be exhausted."

"I feel great," he told her. He studied her, seemingly oblivious to all else.

A coldness slipped over Kathy. She wanted to kick herself. This was crazy. And maybe her own fault. He was enjoying entertaining himself with her. A week with the ex-wife, with his girlfriend in residence. With Jeremy very nearby—and Jordan completely unaware that Jeremy had no sexual interest in her.

Well, she was a fool. Clinging to the crumbs that fell her way, convincing herself that she was glad of his protection.

"Dinner," she murmured, her own triumph and exultation over the incredible session ebbing away. She hurried out of the studio, not wanting to watch Jordan with Tara.

She wasn't even aware of the man following closely behind her until she heard Jeremy whisper, "Hey, wait up, will you? I'm trying to be the perfect lover and you don't even notice when I'm about to put a loverly arm around you!"

She slowed her pace, glancing up at him, offering him rueful smile. "Put that loverly arm around me, huh? I could use a good hug from a friend."

He hugged her. The feeling was warm and fierce. She closed her eyes, grateful that she had such a good friend. She opened her eyes just in time to see Jordan passing her in the hallway.

She felt a little queasy.

Then she caught herself. *Good!*

Downstairs, she discovered that Peggy had set out a beautiful buffet. The girls and Angel had started getting their plates, but Sally and Gerrit were nowhere to be seen.

"Where's your grandmother?" Kathy asked Bren.

"Ummm, out by the pool, I think. Want me to look?" Bren asked.

Kathy shook her head. "I'll go."

She hurried out to the patio, glancing to the guest house as she did so and wondering again who in God's name could have dressed up to look like her and run around the estate. So much was confusing.

And scary.

She shook the thought, determined to ask Jordan about getting a gun herself so he wouldn't feel obliged to *protect* her at night.

She walked around the pool, startled to see her mother and Gerrit's father sitting in lounges so close to one another that Kathy was surprised they weren't toppling over. Their heads were bowed together, extremely close. So close that they appeared to be . . .

Kissing.

Startled, she stopped.

"Mom?"

Sally looked up. She smiled.

"Dinner's ready."

"Oh, how lovely," Gerrit said.

Kathy finally realized that she was staring at them, open-mouthed. In fact, her jaw was almost on the ground.

"I . . . I . . . uh . . . I didn't mean to interrupt you. I— My God, were you . . . necking?" she heard herself blurt out. She winced.

"Necking?" Sally said. She looked at Gerrit.

He grinned. "Do old people *neck?*" he asked Sally.

"Do they?" Sally laughed.

He shook his head sadly. "Ummm, I don't think so. Sometimes they *look* like they're necking, but they've actually just fallen asleep upon one another."

"Ah!" Sally said. She grinned at Kathy. "Guess we weren't necking, just *napping*. Do you mind?"

"I . . . Of course not!" Kathy gasped. Her cheeks reddened, then she started to laugh. "I'm just—"

"Shocked?" Gerrit teased.

"No! Yes, come to think of it, I guess so. But happy. I don't think you're too old to neck!" She smiled sweetly at her mother. "Even if you are past your prime!" she told Sally.

"Past my prime!" Sally protested, then she remembered.

"What was that?" Gerrit asked.

"Nothing. Ignore her. Wretched child. You know how they can be."

"Do I!" Gerrit said sadly.

Kathy grinned, then spun quickly on a heel, ready to burst into laughter. Her mother. And Gerrit's father. How sweet, how wonderful . . .

What torture! If the two of them were together, her ex-husband would be even more ingrained in her life.

If she had a life when this was over!

Dinner was a boisterous affair that evening, everyone in the group excited that their first practice session after nearly ten years had gone so well. When dessert was being served, Jordan excused himself, saying he had phone calls to make concerning the performance. Because the night was so balmy and beautiful, they naturally seemed to ebb outside toward the patio, finding chairs and lounges near to one another.

"It's all very well and good that you're so industriously congratulating one another," Tara said, "but when do we plebian partners get to judge?"

Miles, smiling, glanced at Kathy, then Derrick. Derrick grinned and looked to Shelley, who stared over at Larry. "As far as I'm concerned," Larry said generously, "anyone can listen in at any time."

"You couldn't have been that good! Not after all those years," Gerrit warned gruffly. Kathy noted that Jordan's father and her mother weren't as closely knit as they had been before, but their chairs were still drawn companionably close. And they both seemed so happy. They're special people, she thought. Both of them. They had loved and lost, but both had known a special beauty in their loves, something many people never know, no matter how long they live. Both had always been good and generous to those around them, and they'd probably missed having a very special person in theirs lives for a long time. It was just . . . rather a surprise. But a good one.

"But they were," Judy said, a strange tone in her voice, as if she still couldn't believe just how good. "It was as if they'd never stopped playing together. As if they were just the same. Just as if—"

"As if Keith were still with us?" Shelley suggested.

Judy shrugged, swinging her feet over her lounge. "Actually the group sounded better to me than it ever had. There was no hint of tension in the room. Don't you remember some of the last few sessions before Keith's— before the band broke up?"

"Yeah, I guess we all do," Miles said huskily.

Kathy closed her eyes. Larry answered Miles, and the discussion continued, then altered, then changed. Conversations around her seemed to fade.

She could remember one practice session all too well. This morning she remembered it with a great deal of discomfort.

They'd been in the house, not long back from Europe. Kathy had been certain that the humiliation of the arrest bothered Jordan more than anything. Half of the group had been late to practice, and he had been pacing like a caged bull. Keith had shown up, not quite wasted but certainly under the influence. They'd started a number, just one, and it had been painfully off. They'd never finished it. Jordan had pulled his guitar off his shoulder and had all but thrown it down, uncharacteristic behavior for him. Unlike some of the showmen of that rock age, Jordan couldn't destroy a musical instrument for anyone's entertainment.

"Forget it, Jesus Christ, forget it! We may as well toss the whole damned thing in. Keith, you're loaded."

"The hell I am!"

"And you've got your bloody nerve to be doped up after what you did to us all."

"I told you, I didn't try to smuggle any damned drugs anywhere!" Keith lashed back.

And there Jordan had stood, hands on his hips, fury in his eyes. "I can't— I won't— work like this."

"All right, I'm sorry. I'm wrong today. Wrong. But I won't do it again."

"Three strikes. You're out, Keith. And I don't care how damned long we've been friends."

"Damn you, Mr. Self-Righteous! I didn't get us all arrested, can't you understand that?"

He'd sounded hurt, desperate.

Jordan hadn't supported him. "I can't work like this. Kathy, you coming?" He hadn't glanced her way. He'd reached out a hand, waiting for her. But there had been something so desperate in Keith's denial that she'd waited.

"I'll be along," she'd said.

Then he'd looked at her. He hadn't said a word, he hadn't forced the issue. He'd thought she'd chosen Keith instead of him. He'd stared at her a moment longer, then had walked away. Jordan, the strong one, the leader. It hadn't seemed that he'd needed anyone then. Not even her.

And once he'd been out of the soundproof room— cacophony.

"Keith, you stinking lousy bastard!" Judy had hissed. "To the rest of us, this is a livelihood! Can't you keep yourself straight for a few damned hours a day?"

"Not when you're always sharpening the edge on that tongue of yours, baby," Keith said nonchalantly.

"God dammit—" Derrick had said.

"Leave him alone!" Shelley had snapped, whirling on Judy. "Who the hell are you to criticize any of us?"

"If you knew just how many people he'd slept with other than you, pumpkin, you wouldn't defend him quite so hotly," Judy said.

Shelley gasped. "You shrew! Leave me the hell alone, and leave Keith alone."

"Shelley, I don't need help here," Keith interrupted coldly, staring at Judy. "Not anyone's."

Miles had leapt into it then. "There's no damned reason to hurt her, Keith. She's been there for you every damned time, and you treat her like dirt."

It had gone far enough. Kathy picked up Jordan's guitar and struck a discordant note, silencing them all. They stared at her.

"You're all going to get your personal problems out of these sessions, or there won't be anything left for any of us to worry about, got it?" She stared at them firmly, one after another. She wondered if she wasn't an incredible fool, risking her marriage to hold onto something that was slipping away from them all. "It all stops!" she snapped. They all stared back at her, finally shamed and quiet. Larry lowered his eyes first. Now she knew why.

She opened her eyes. How different it was tonight! Judy's words had sobered them all somewhat, but they hadn't changed them back into a pack of snarling harpies. Judy was talking quietly to Vicky Sue, Miles was smiling over something Shelley was saying. Tara was offering Derrick her sweetest smile as he explained the mechanics of writing music. Larry and Jeremy had turned to a discussion on sports; the kids, who had gone swimming soon after the main meal, were just crawling out the pool and heading inside to change.

The older generation— not Kathy's own, her mother's— were still just cuddly close in their lounge chairs.

"Well, I'm going up. Good night, all," Judy said.

"Yeah. You know, I'm exhausted," Miles said. "I was so exuberant— and I still am— but I must be too old to be that exuberant for long."

Kathy grinned. "Hey, think of it this way. Lots of us older guys are out there working now— just taking carrot juice on tour instead of champagne and the like."

"Right." Shelley groaned. "I'm off. See you all in the morning. Tara, tell our host thanks for us all again, huh?"

"Yeah, sure," Tara said casually.

People began to drift away, toward the house, moving slowly, chatting with each other. The kids were coming out of the pool, drying off. Kathy noticed that Sally and Gerrit were moving on into the house as well— they had both forgotten to say good night to her.

Jeremy gave her a kiss on the forehead and went on in, and Kathy found herself alone by the pool with Tara, who was giving her what she considered a definitely evil look.

"Nice night," Kathy said.

"It could be," Tara agreed somewhat sullenly.

"Well, nice as it is, I think I'll call it quits myself."

"Ummm, the older one gets, the more sleep one needs," Tara told her innocently.

Kathy settled back. "Actually, I've heard we all sleep a little less as we get older."

"Because we move so much slower, the older we get?"

"Maybe. But then, we're not in such a hurry to prove things once we get a little older," Kathy said.

"You should just go home." Tara lashed out suddenly, the kid gloves off, pretense of friendship vanished.

"Actually, I don't think that I could do that right now."

"You know he feels responsible for you, though after what you did to him—"

"I don't think that our past concerns you," Kathy said calmly. She was amazed to realize that her heart seemed to be beating a thousand slams a second.

"God knows why he's so concerned about you."

"He's always been considerate of others."

"That's right," Tara said, rising. Tonight she was dressed in an ankle-length, black concoction that was truly exotic and was becoming on her. Her hair was swept up, her eyes sparkled like diamonds. She was undeniably beautiful. And of course, very young.

Kathy experienced a wavering of confidence. She fought it, trying to tell herself that she wasn't competing with Tara Hughes.

But in a way she was.

"You just mustn't go getting the wrong ideas. We have a strong relationship, Jordan and I."

"Do you?" Kathy said pleasantly. She rose herself. "Well then, good for you. I'm very tired myself. Good night, Tara."

She started walking away from the blonde.

"Kathy!" Tara said, her voice sharp.

Kathy turned back. "Yes?"

"I really do love him. I'm not giving up. So don't go thinking there can be something between the two of you now."

"If you do love him, you shouldn't give up."

Tara stamped a foot on the poolside decking. "Would you stop it? You know you're after him again!"

Kathy arched a brow. "Well then, if I really love him, I shouldn't give up either, right? Good night, Tara, I am exhausted."

She turned again.

"Just because you can sing—" Tara began.

"Good night!" Kathy repeated.

"And because you had his children— He can have more children you know. I can have boys. All men want boys."

"Maybe!" Kathy called back. Then she paused, smiling, shaking her head. "A word of wisdom, Tara— from someone of my age-old experience. All men are not the same. They do not want the same things. Good night!" This time, she walked away very swiftly, determined not to be stopped again. She reached the house— thank God— and hurried through the porch and the living room, pounding up the stairs.

She almost ran into her room, closing the door behind her, leaning against it and staring about. It hadn't changed much. She could stand there and go back ten years, could stand here and wish the time had never been, that she could be close to thirty again.

No, no! She didn't want that. The years had been painful at times, rich at others. She had met wonderful people, learned to stand on her own two feet. She'd discovered just how much she loved not just the written word, but books, writing, novels, fact, fiction . . . The years had been worthwhile. They didn't keep the present from being scary, nor did being on her own all that time give her the confidence she needed now. People aged, people toughened. But the heart and soul didn't quite keep up with it all. One could still be vulnerable, feel pain, know such uncertainty.

Tara was afraid that, for all her youth and beauty, she was losing Jordan. Maybe she was. Maybe she wasn't. If she was right and Jordan was just being responsible, then perhaps he didn't feel committed to either one of them.

Tara was afraid, Kathy was afraid. Tara might love Jordan, but Kathy knew she did . . . and more deeply. More richly. She had for all of her life.

But not even that could guarantee her a successful relationship. They had let mistrust chip away at them once. Had let outside forces become stronger than the love they shared. Perhaps trust could never be regained.

She started to walk toward the bed, tired, ready just to stretch out and rest for a minute.

Then she remembered that she had more to fear in the next few days than the possibility that Tara would win out and have Jordan.

Someone might well be in mortal danger . . .

She turned, threw open her door, and hurried out into the hallway, racing down it until she came to Alex's room. She twisted the door handle, thrust her way in, then felt like a fool. Bren, Alex, Peggy, and Angel were arranged around a Monopoly board. The four of them looked up at her expectantly, and not without surprise. "Ah, hi, guys. Sorry. I was . . . making sure you were all in for the night."

"We are, Mom. Want to play?" Alex offered.

"You're already into your game."

"We could start over."

"No, thanks. Your dad worked us all long and hard today. I think I'll get some sleep."

"Can I get you anything?" Peggy asked her anxiously.

Kathy shook her head. "Thanks. Go back to playing!"

She backed out of the room, walking slowly back to her own. The hallway was in shadow. She turned on a light, almost expecting some demon to jump out of the shadows after her.

The glow dispelled the shadows, and she walked on into her room, stretched out on the bed.

She stared at the ceiling. It was all so strange. She shivered slightly, but a second later, she smiled, still amazed.

They had been good that afternoon. Really

good. *She* had been good. It was a nice feeling. Even a lulling feeling. She allowed her eyes to close, and she drifted into a light sleep.

Caterers, roadies, organizers, rich men, poor men, philanthropic women. Jordan felt he had talked with half the population of the southern tip of the state. He rubbed his face wearily, rising to glance out at the patio from the bedroom of the guest house, where he had been working on his calls.

He rubbed his neck, frowning. It seemed like a few minutes ago the patio had been full. He had seen every one of his guests, his daughters, Angel . . . All had been safe, present, and accounted for. Now the patio was empty. The pool, lit from above and within, sparkled beautifully and presented a most lovely and innocent of scenes. But Jordan's neck prickled. He felt uncomfortable.

The phone by the bed started to ring. Instinctively, he picked up the receiver.

"Hello?"

"I know who's been dressing up as your wife!" came from an excited voice.

Jordan began to form the word "who," but it remained unspoken.

Before sound could leave his lips, the stillness of the night was pierced by an earth-shattering scream.

Nineteen

It came from below, from where the bushes partially obscured the side entrance to the guest house.

Jordan was sure it took him only a matter of seconds to tear down the stairs and reach the area from which he was certain the scream had come. Still, by the time he burst out of the side guest-house door, Mickey Dean was nearly at the spot as well. It had been Mickey on the phone, telling him he knew who had been masquerading as Kathy.

"What the hell . . . ?" Mickey demanded, staring at Jordan. Dean had been on the property, discreetly watching the house, since the attack on Kathy. Now he was both alarmed and baffled.

Jordan shook his head. "Let's split."

"I'll go left, you'll go right."

They turned in synch, but Jordan had barely taken a step before he heard a groaning. He dropped down by the bushes, his heart hammering. A woman's form lay beside a colorful hibiscus, red hair streaming down her back against the soft gauzelike material of a nightgown. His breath seemed to stop. Kathy. Alive. She had to be groaning to be alive. And there was no blood. No blood around her . . .

Just the shattered pieces of one of the heavy S-shaped tiles from the roof.

A tile? Fallen suddenly in the night?

He dropped to his knees in a split second, carefully lifting her, and even as he did so, he knew instantly that he'd nearly been duped by an impostor again. It wasn't Kathy. As he carefully turned the woman in his arms, the red wig fell from her head.

Tara.

He gasped out the name, then looked up as he suddenly realized that her scream hadn't just alarmed him and Mickey but everyone in the house. A sea of faces stared at him as he blinked against the hazy glare of the pool lights. Who was there? Larry, Judy, Miles, Jeremy, Bren, Alex, Vicky Sue. Peggy and Joe holding one another. Angel off to the side a little, ready to assist if needed. Derrick, Shelley, his dad with an arm around Sally. Hmmm. It seemed his father and Sally had come down together. Those who should have been together— like maybe Derrick and Judy and Larry and Vicky Sue— were not.

Kathy. She stood a little bit apart as well, wearing one of those tailored things which should have been concealing and somehow managed to be sexy. Odd the things that popped into a man's head at such moments. He'd always liked

the way Kathy got ready for bed. No long ordeal
with ointments or the like, just a good face
scrub, shower, and body lotion. A light scent.
She was always good to smell, soft to touch . . .

Tara groaned again. Guilt filled him and he
looked down. What in God's name was going
on? Why was she dressed up like his ex-wife?
And who would want to harm Tara?

And just how badly was she hurt?

Her eyes fluttered open and she stared up at
him, smiling, then wincing.

"Hurts!" she whispered.

He felt a tug at his heart.

"What hurts, Tara? What happened?"

"My head."

"Don't try to move, just help me a little if you
can. Does anything else hurt?"

"My elbow. I fell."

"What happened?"

"I was coming to the house and something . . . hit me. In the head. I— I heard it.
Like a whooshing sound, a whispering. Maybe
something falling from a tree, the roof, I don't
know. I tried to scream, tried to run . . ."

Her voice trailed away. She winced again.

He knelt closer to her, whispering softly.
"Tara, why were you running around in a red
wig?"

Her eyes remained closed. She grimaced, before wincing again.

"You seem to like redheads better than
blondes," she whispered back, so softly he barely
heard the words.

He sat back slightly on his haunches and realized that Kathy had come to kneel down on the other side of Tara. She watched the younger woman's pale face as she said, "Mickey's called for an ambulance. She's got to be checked out, Jordan."

Tara must have heard Kathy, for her eyes opened again and she offered her a half-smile. "Hurts," she said again.

"It must," Kathy said, taking one of her hands. "Don't move too much."

"I think . . . I'm okay. But I don't like being a redhead. Maybe the guest house thought I was you." She tried to grin. "Maybe it's on my side."

"Could be," Kathy agreed. "Tara, you're hurt. Don't try to talk much right now. We'll get you to the hospital, and everything will be all right."

"Thanks," Tara murmured, closing her eyes. Her fingers squeezed around Kathy's for a moment.

They could already hear the screeching of the ambulance; in a few minutes, paramedics were coming through the yard. Kathy stepped back; Jordan helped Tara answer their questions as competently as possible. As they lifted her onto the stretcher, she clung wildly to his hand. "Jordan, don't leave me, please. I'm . . . afraid!" she whispered.

He didn't want to take the ambulance off the island to the mainland. He didn't understand why, and he silently chastised himself for being the biggest cad in the world. "Cad." Old-fashioned word. He wondered if Tara knew it.

He had to go with her. She was hurt.

"I'm here, with you," he said quietly.

He looked up. Kathy was watching him with clear, grave, unfathomable eyes. He could almost feel the distance inching between them again, almost hear the tearing apart of whatever closeness they had achieved.

But he realized there was a question in her eyes as well.

Just how the hell had one tile managed to fall from the guest-house roof at precisely the time Tara— dressed as Kathy— was passing beneath it?

The ambulance attendants were lifting the stretcher; Tara was clinging to his hand.

And Jeremy appeared suddenly. Handsome, young, in perfect tone. The man who never lost his temper, never made a scene . . . and he seemed to trust Kathy blindly. What the hell kind of a relationship was it? Jordan wondered bitterly. Right now, the mature young muscleman was looking at him gravely.

"Things will be fine here." He said with assurance, as if he sensed he should be watching over Kathy carefully. Perhaps that wasn't so strange. Kathy had been attacked with a knife.

Now Tara, in a red wig, was headed for the hospital.

Jordan addressed the group, looking from Kathy to Jeremy to Mickey. "I'll be back as soon as I can— "

"We're just fine, Jordan. See to Tara!" Judy Flanaghan urged with a grim smile, her arms crossed over her chest. "Stay with her as long as you need to." She winked. "I'll make them practice without you."

"Yeah, Jordan," Miles said. "We'll be fine. Tara honey, you're going to be all right, too."

The others called out encouraging words as well. Only Kathy was silent. He saw her, standing slightly behind as the others surged forward with him, heading around the house for the ambulance. He wound up thrust into the back of the vehicle, seated beside Tara. The rear door slammed; he looked out. Damn. He didn't want to leave the house.

Tara's fingers tightened convulsively around his own. He had no choice.

Mickey was at the house. He wouldn't leave Kathy. She would be all right. Mickey would never let anything happen to Kathy.

Still, he couldn't wait to reach the hospital and escape Tara's clinging fingers for just a few minutes. Just long enough to call Mickey and make damned sure.

Peggy was the ultimate housekeeper, creating a calming effect on those around her with her suggestion of some stiff tea with whiskey or hot coffee with a liqueur. Sympathetically clucking over poor Tara's injury and shaking their heads, the bulk of the guests began to move into the house, following Peggy's lead.

Kathy stood pat.

"I have to stay with you," Jeremy said firmly to her.

"Go have a drink and watch over my daughters with that handsome young flirt Angel. Mickey is a cop, I'll be fine with him, okay?"

Jeremy shook his head, and turned away.

"Mom?" Alex said, hanging back worriedly.

"I'll be right along, dear. I just want a word with Mickey."

"You'll stay with her, right?" Alex demanded of Dean.

"Sure, Alex. I'll be here."

Though Alex still didn't look happy, she headed for the house, glancing back over her shoulder several times.

When she was gone, Kathy spun to Mickey. "A tile fell like hell! She could have been killed!"

Mickey was staring up at the roof. "I can get someone out in the morning to try to figure out what happened."

Kathy shook her head, her lips tight. "Damn! They were all here in split seconds! No one away from the group. How are we ever going to know just what in God's name is going on?"

"Everyone makes a mistake somewhere along the line, Kathy. Drops a clue. Rushes. Forgets some minute detail."

She lifted her hands dejectedly. "I keep trying to put it in order. Ten years ago, Keith died, and even to me, it looked like a drug overdose. Back then, Jordan was convinced Keith was murdered. It's not flattering, but he considered me one of the suspects. The group splits, we all go our own ways. Jordan plans a reunion and starts getting phone calls; then I'm attacked in an alley. Now this. And still we haven't the faintest idea of what was going on! Tara was knocked out— she didn't see anyone. The accident was planned— for Tara or for me, it's hard to tell. But no one saw anything. We all reached the front at about the same time. But it would have been very easy for anyone halfway agile to toss down a tile, slip down from the roof and mix with the group, then look as innocent and concerned as the rest of the gang."

"Kathy—"

"Mickey, I'm just so damned frustrated!"

Dean sighed, looking at her unhappily. "You can't think of anything anyone has said or done that might provide some clue to the past?"

"No, I . . ." she broke off momentarily. She was lying.

There was Larry. Scaring her half to death at the pool and then admitting he'd been the drug smuggler. He'd had good reason to kill Keith. To silence him. Then Larry wouldn't be exposed.

She was a fool. She had to tell someone.

If she did, Larry would become a suspect in the murder . . .

He was a suspect already in her mind!

What if he was the wrong one? Did she have the right to halfway hang him when he'd come to her for help?

She'd gotten in trouble before for trying to be helpful!

"Dammit, I just wish our murderer would make one mistake!"

"Kathy, don't hope that mistake is made too soon."

"Why?"

"Because someone who has already committed murder won't hesitate to it do again if he or she is in danger—from having made a mistake."

Kathy shook her head. "We've got to know, Mickey. If we don't find out soon, we won't find out at all!"

As Kathy spoke, her mother poked her head out the back door. "Jordan just called."

"For me?" Kathy asked, starting to walk toward the house. "Is Tara going to be all right?"

"She's going to be fine, and Jordan called for Mickey!" Sally said. "Mick, he wants you to call him back on your cellular phone." Sally rattled off the number and Mickey thanked her, flipping out his pocket phone and putting through the call. Kathy ambled a few feet away, her arms crossed over her chest, wanting to hear his conversation and yet not wishing to intrude. She stared at the broken tiles. She didn't wish Tara ill, and was truly sorry the young woman had been hurt, but she was disturbed because Tara had been hurt while wearing a red wig.

Kathy sighed, studying the guest house, wishing it didn't look so much now like it did back then. She shivered, experiencing a strange sense of déjà vu, suddenly smelling smoke again, seeing flames skyrocketing into the air.

She turned away from the guest house, trying to shake off the feeling that someone was watching her as she walked away from it. Mickey was beckoning to her.

"Yeah, you take care there. Glad Tara's going to be just fine. I'll put Kathy on for you now."

He handed Kathy the phone, grinned, and walked away; heading back toward the guest house himself. Out of hearing range, he stooped by the trampled hibiscus and broken tile.

"Hi, everything okay?" Kathy asked lightly.

"Everything sucks," Jordan said.

"Tara is going to be all right?"

"They're still doing tests, but the doctor thinks she's got a mild concussion, nothing more."

"I'm sure she's going to be fine."

"So am I, but it would be difficult for me to leave here now."

"Jordan, Tara is hurt. I'm not."

"She's in the hospital. Safe. You're there—"

"With Mickey, my mother, your father, our children—"

"And whoever threw that tile at Tara, thinking she was you."

"We've no proof—"

"Right. The tile must have jumped off rather than fallen to have cleared the bushes so well! I don't like this. We've gotten nowhere at all."

"Sure we have. We found out you saw Tara

dressed up in a red wig last night." She hesitated. "Why?"

He hesitated in return. "She thinks I like redheads."

"What?"

She heard his long sigh over the phone. "She dressed up last night and tried to find me. She said she found the wig in the costume storage vault at the back of the studio. But I wasn't in the guest house; I'd come to your room. I ran after her; but she'd slipped out and walked down to the dock. She came back the long way, which is why you didn't see her. Mickey noticed her, though, while he was watching the place. He hadn't been able get me all day because we were rehearsing. He'd just called to tell me when she screamed."

"So we know who played dress-up," Kathy said softly.

"Right. We know that, but we're getting nowhere regarding the murder. Tara wasn't even here when Keith died."

"Tara wasn't out of diapers when Keith died," Kathy said morosely. But then she added thoughtfully, "Tara wasn't here, but . . ."

"But what?"

"I think we still have the answer."

"To what?" he asked wearily.

"Okay, think back to that night. You were absolutely convinced that you saw me running to Keith. But I wasn't. I wasn't anywhere near Keith. I'd been in Bren's room, pacing around.

That's how I saw you when you ran across the patio."

He arched a brow. "Go on?"

"Well, the point is, we know that it was Tara who dressed up recently, but we were both right about what happened the night Keith died. I wasn't out there and you didn't see me, but you did think you had. For some reason, someone was masquerading as me back then as well. Tara said she found the wig with some of the costume stuff in the studio storeroom, right?"

"Right," he said softly.

"So someone was else *was* dressing up ten years ago. We need to know who did it the night Keith died— and why."

"It could be a man or a woman," Jordan said flatly.

Tara frowned. "A woman, I imagine."

"Why?" he queried. "I was in the house, at a distance. Hell, I was right on top of Tara tonight before I was certain it wasn't you."

"Well, that's complimentary," Kathy said dryly. "Better than your thinking I was a man!"

"My point is, I was at a distance. You— or the fake you— was moving fluidly in a white flowing thing, and had long flowing hair. Anyone could have pulled it off. But again, why?"

She shook her head, forgetting that he couldn't see her over the phone.

"I don't know," she said at last.

"Kathy, sleep with Jeremy tonight."

"What?" She pulled the phone from her ear, staring at it, stunned. What was he telling her?

With Tara's accident, he'd realized how much he cared for his blond bombshell? It was time for them to quit playing back to memory lane?

"I don't want you alone," he said.

She bit her lower lip, startled at the rush of tears that filled her eyes.

"I'm a big girl. I don't need to sleep with anyone."

"Kathy—"

"Jordan."

"What?"

"Do you really want me to sleep with him?"

He hesitated. "I want you safe."

"But do you—"

"No, dammit, I just don't want you hurt."

She smiled. "I'll be all right. I'm going to hang out with Mickey for a while, and when I'm not actually with him, I'll make sure to be with others. I'll sleep with my mother. Unless she's sleeping with your father. Wow, Jordan, do you think the two of them might really be involved with one another?"

"You think they're too old for sex?" he queried teasingly.

"I—"

"I'd like to imagine I'm going to want sex in another twenty to thirty years."

"You're already past your prime. My mother said so."

"She did?"

"It's all right. I defended you."

"Oh?"

"It was before— Never mind. Anyway, she said I was past my prime as well."

"It's kind of what we make it, don't you think? Anyway, I guess I'd better get back and be a hand to hold. I do feel awful about what happened."

"So do I. Go take care of Tara. I'll be safe, I swear it."

"I'm still not happy— "

"Neither am I. But I'm all right. Good night, Jordan. Don't worry about anything here, please."

"Yeah, well— "

"Good night," she said, smiling and feeling curiously light under the circumstances. She pressed the button on the phone, cutting their connection.

Mickey walked back to her. "I'm your watch-dog, you know."

She smiled. "Want some coffee or tea with the others?"

"Sure."

Bren, Alex, and Angel apparently preferred their own company to that of the others after the incident, as did Gerrit and Sally, since the five of them were nowhere to be seen. Peggy had made the coffee and tea with Joe at her side helping, and Larry was playing bartender, adding generous servings of various liqueurs to each serving. Kathy chose Tía Maria, intrigued to realize that the rest of the group seemed to believe the tile's falling had been a bizarre accident.

"He'd better be good to that child! He'll have

a lawsuit on his hands from her," Larry said dolefully.

"She's not like that, Mr. Skeptical!" Vicky Sue remonstrated. "She's a sweet girl, especially for one as beautiful as she is! Don't you think so, Kathy?"

The question, coming from Vicky Sue, was completely guileless and innocent.

"A sweet, charming child." Compelled to agree, Kathy wasn't sure which of the words she spoke were completely truthful, other than "a" and "child."

"Ummm," Larry murmured, studying Kathy as he took a generous sip of whatever "coffee" he was drinking. "Interesting that she was wearing that red wig. Wouldn't you say?"

Kathy shrugged. "It's not really my place to judge."

"If not you, who?" Shelley laughed. She lowered her voice. "She was trying to look like you."

"It's amazing that she'd try to look like anyone else," Larry said admiringly.

Vicky Sue kicked him.

"You're the one who says she's so sweet!" Larry reminded her with a scowl.

"Yes, well. Never mind," Vicky Sue told him.

"Jordan still has a thing for you, huh, Kath?" Miles said, smiling benignly. "More so than I imagined." He turned and smiled at Shelley. "It's really amazing how the years just don't change some things."

"They do change things," Shelley said somewhat tensely.

"What's different?"

"Keith has been dead a long time now," Shelley stated.

"Dead is dead," Derrick supplied dryly.

Shelley shook her head in the negative, watching Miles. "No. With death, time makes a difference."

"It 'healeth all wounds,' right?" Judy laughed.

"Is that right, 'healeth'?" Miles asked. "Hey, Kath, you're the editor, you're supposed to know."

"When you want it to be 'healeth,' 'healeth' is just fine," she told him. They were in the back, on the glassed-in porch by the French doors overlooking the pool. Shelley was sitting on the floor, leaning slightly back against Miles's legs. Vicky Sue was perched on a bar stool while Larry was behind the bar itself. Jeremy was perched near Vicky Sue at the bar, gravely chewing a swizzle stick, while Derrick and Judy Flanaghan were seated in the wicker swing seat that backed up to the glass window.

They all seemed so damned relaxed. How could any one of these people have been responsible for the attack on Tara?

And why would any of them have attacked her, unless Kathy was to be the target. Because she was coming close . . . .

But she wasn't. She was getting nowhere, though she kept asking herself who would have killed Keith and why.

Jordan . . . because of her, because he and Keith fought constantly.

She herself . . . because he was ruining her marriage and destroying the group.

Shelley . . . because Keith played with her and never really loved her.

Miles . . . because he had loved Shelley and hated the way that Keith played with her.

Larry . . . ummm. Because he wanted Keith to take the blame for his drugging into eternity.

Derrick . . . because Keith was a better musician.

Judy . . . because Keith was a better musician than Derrick.

And Joe and Peggy had been there as well. Maybe they had planned the killing together, to save the band— and their jobs. Oh, God, she was getting ridiculous. She was tired. She rose, glancing down at Mickey. How were they going to manage this?

"You staying the night?" Peggy asked him. "I can put clean sheets in Tara's room, or the guest house is empty—"

"I'm going to snooze, dressed, on Tara's bed, right on the comforter, you don't have to do a thing for me, Peggy. Get yourself a good night's rest," Mickey told her.

"Well, I don't know about the rest of you, but I think I need a snooze," Kathy said.

Jeremy rose as well. "I guess I'll call it a night."

His movement brought them all up. Kathy picked up her cup, the others did the same, taking their glasses and demitasses into the kitchen while thanking Peggy and Joe for suggesting coffee and a relaxing drink. They then climbed the stairs together, all saying good night on the second-floor landing and walking down the hall to their rooms. Mickey hovered, pretending to chat lightly with Kathy and Jeremy until the last door in the hallway had closed.

"I'll check your room for you, Kath," he said. He strode down the hall, and disappeared into it.

"We can bunk together," Jeremy told her, grinning. "I'm harmless, you know."

She smiled. "Yeah, but I'm okay. I know you're right next to me."

Mickey came back down the hall. "Get in there and lock that door," he told her.

"I will."

She gave him a quick kiss on the cheek, did the same with Jeremy, and scooted into her room, bolting the door. Having decided to wait until the morning for a shower, she was starting to slip out of her clothing when there was a light tapping on her door.

She walked to it. "Mrs. Treveryan?"

She bit her lip. Angel. Angel would still call her that.

She opened the door, suddenly anxious because she knew the girls had been worried about her.

"Is everything all right?" she asked him quickly. She heard her voice rising and quickly lowered it. She didn't want Jeremy to hear her and become worried as well. She stepped out into the hall with Angel, motioning that they should move down it toward's Alex's room. "Angel, what is it?"

"Nothing, nothing is wrong!" he told her quickly. "I just needed to talk to you."

She arched a brow, saw that he was serious and concerned, and motioned him on down the hallway. "Bren is in with Alex as she's supposed to be?"

"Yes."

"In here."

She didn't switch on a light. Bren's drapes were open and the illumination streaming in from the pool and patio area enabled them to see one another.

"Tell me, Angel, what is it?"

"With all that's occurring, I just wanted to, er, let you know what happened when you first came here."

"What do you mean?"

Even in the very dim light, she could see that he was flushed and uncomfortable. He lowered his voice and spoke hastily, "Everything seems so confusing, and I know you and Jordan are desperately trying to figure out who was where, and when. So I wanted you to know . . ."

"Know what?" Kathy demanded.

"Well, the first night you were here, I was in your room."

Shadows were dancing all around them. She stared at Angel, at his handsome young face. Was there something sinister in it?

"Why?" she demanded on a quick breath.

"Because Alex asked me to check on you."

"Why did she do that?"

"To make sure you were safe. But you woke up, I panicked and ran. I came back, ready to apologize then, but you were . . . Well, I didn't come in again because you were . . ."

She'd been with Jordan. But Angel had supposedly been out with her daughters.

"I saw you drive away that night, taking the girls and Jeremy to South Beach— "

"I left them at a friend's club and doubled back. Alex had a hunch you might be in danger. She insisted. I was only here about fifteen minutes. And then I knew, of course, that you were safe, so— "

"Tell Alex she's grounded."

"You've already asked us to stay in."

"Tell her she's grounded until the wedding."

"Whose— "

"Yours. Whenever you two get around to it."

"I feel just awful. I didn't mean to spy."

"It's all right, Angel. It's important to know why and how each and every thing has happened. Get back to my daughters and make sure they know I'm fine, okay?"

"I'll walk you back to your room first."

She didn't argue, and he escorted her down the hallway. She pushed open the door to her room and turned on the light, then turned it off quickly. She didn't want to call attention to her conversation in the hall. "All's quiet. Thanks, Angel."

He nodded, still flushing, and left her.

Kathy closed the door thoughtfully, then

blinked against the darkness. There was a figure in front of her. A shadow against the wall, a form— someone who had been there when she had opened the door *but hiding behind it.*

She inhaled, ready to cry out.

But then . . .

Twenty

Jordan glanced at his watch. Three-thirty A.M. Tara was going through another scan to make sure no slivers of bone had been chipped off. From the time they had entered the emergency room, doctors had assured him that she was going to be all right, that the skull was really tough since its job was to protect the brain. Still, with a head injury, it was advisable to take every precaution, and poor Tara definitely had a concussion.

She was, strangely enough, enjoying herself in the hospital, being charming to every doctor and nurse in the place, nobly giving out autographs and modeling advice despite her weakened condition. She looked as frail as a hot-house rose, but Jordan thought, with some amusement, that she was tough as steel beneath that facade. She exuded strength when there was someone to charm; then she clung to Jordan's hand each time they were alone, each time the doctor explained some procedure.

"I'm so afraid, Jordan," she said once, speaking very softly but making sure the nurse on duty could hear her as well. "You won't leave me tonight, will you? Please don't."

If he'd ever doubted her abilities as an actress, he had no more reason to do so after that night. Her last words carried just a hint of a sob. Doctors, nurses, and technicians all looked at him curiously, assuming, of course, that he'd never think of deserting such a gorgeous woman—his lover—in this kind of distress. Well, if there was the least hint of anything wrong back at the house, they'd just have to think what they wanted about him. He didn't know exactly why he was so unnerved.

Why? He was mocking himself.

How about threatening phone calls, a knife to Kathy's throat, and now a tile on Tara's head?

But everyone from the original group had been there right after the tile had fallen. All of them. Derrick and Judy, Larry and Vicky Sue, Miles and Shelley, Peggy and Joe, the kids, Kathy. He'd been there, Mickey too. Everyone who had been present ten years ago.

He stopped pacing Tara's room and sat down by the bed. Picking up the phone, he started to dial the house, then ran his fingers through his hair, hanging up and dialing Mickey's cellular line.

Mickey picked up promptly.

"Yo, Jordan?"

"Yeah, Mick, it's me. What's going on?"

"Quiet as a church here."

"Everyone in bed?"

"Yeah."

"Kathy?"

"I checked out her room and made her lock herself in it."

"You're sure she's there and okay."

"Jordan—"

"Yeah, yeah, Mickey, I know. You're thorough, you're good. I'm sorry."

"How's Tara?"

"Reigning well."

"What?"

"Never mind. I know you're trying to get some sleep, but I may check in now and then. You can sleep once I make it back tomorrow, huh?"

"Yeah, sure. Hey, Jordan, I'm here."

"I know, Mickey, thanks."

"Get some rest—if you can."

"I will, and you call me here if anything happens." He gave Mickey Tara's phone number, then hung up.

Mickey was a cop. His best friend. A guy who had known Kathy forever, too. He would protect her with his life. That still didn't seem like enough.

He stood up. They were wheeling Tara back into the room. A nurse and an orderly chatted softly as they slipped her back into bed. She was hooked up to an I.V. and a monitor. The nurse and orderly left.

Tara looked young, wan, and pretty with her very blond hair splayed out on the pillow. She reached for his hand. He gave it to her. The audience was gone.

"You will stay with me, Jordan?" she asked. "Please."

"Yeah."

She closed her eyes. He thought she was sleeping. "You're still in love with her, aren't you?"

He thought about lying.

"Jordan?"

"Yeah, maybe."

"I just don't understand. You've got me. I could stay with you forever."

"Tara, love is an emotion. We can't control it, we just feel it. It has much more power over us than we ever have over it."

"I do love you."

"I love you, too."

"You just love her more."

He squeezed her hand. "Tara— "

"It's all right. Just don't leave me tonight, please. I'm afraid."

"You're afraid? Why?"

She shivered, her eyes closing. "I don't know. It just seemed there were shadows everywhere tonight. Eyes. People watching me. And then the tile . . ."

She was drifting off. He let her. She was afraid, but so was he. And he couldn't define it any more clearly himself.

"Kathy, don't scream, please don't scream! It's me, just me, Shelley!"

Shelley! Kathy was so relieved she felt she might fall. Her knees seemed weak.

She backed over to the bed and sank down on it. "Why in God's name are you lurking in the shadows in my room?"

"Because I've got to talk to you."

Kathy groaned, burying her face into her hands. "You're going to confess something."

"Kathy, yes, I—"

"Why me? Shelley, I—"

"Kathy!"

To Kathy's amazement, Shelley ran to the bed and sat beside her, hugging her. She was shaking. "I don't know what's going on!" Shelley whispered.

Kathy eased herself from the frantic hug and set an arm around Shelley's shoulders, steadying her.

"Let me get this straight— you don't know what's going on, but you're going to confess to me."

Shelley managed a half-smile in the darkness of the room. "That tile tonight . . . the attack on you Saturday. It's terrifying, Kathy."

"But you don't know anything about it?"

Shelley shook her head. "I only know . . ."

"Know what?"

Shelley bit her lower lip. "You heard the other day in the bathroom, right?"

Kathy arched a brow. So this was it. Shelley was one of the whisperers in the bathroom. And she thought she'd been caught.

"Go on," Kathy said simply.

"Larry didn't want the group to get back together. He was making calls to Jordan."

"Larry."

"Right."

"And you knew?"

She lowered her head. "He'd helped me out a few times. I—I had a drug habit of my own. I shook it—eight years ago now. But I owed Larry. He got me a few jobs when I was desperate. I was supposed to find out about you because Larry was certain the group wouldn't get back together if you didn't come. And he was afraid—"

"Afraid of what?"

"Well, that maybe you knew things about him. About his drug habit."

"That he was the one smuggling drugs when Keith took the rap for it?"

"You knew!"

"No, I didn't. But Larry confessed to me the other night."

"He's finally gone straight."

"Yeah. But he still hasn't done the right thing and told Jordan."

"And you haven't spilled the beans?"

Kathy shook her head. "I'm still trying to give him the opportunity to do so."

"This is going to be hard for you to believe, but he has changed. Vicky Sue is making a big difference in his life. And I know that . . ."

"That what?"

Shelley shivered. "Larry made phone calls, Larry lied, Larry would have let Keith take the rap for him, but he wouldn't have threatened your life, Kathy."

"Someone did just that. On the phone. Friday night."

Shelley shook her head. "Larry didn't make the call Friday night. He was with Vicky Sue the entire evening."

"You're sure."

"Yes. Vicky Sue told me. She's not half as naïve as she acts at times. She made him stay by her side—like glue—on Friday, reminding him he was going to have to stick to the straight and narrow if he wanted to be with the group again. Besides, Larry would never have hired a thug to hold a knife to your throat. And he wouldn't have tried to kill you himself—tonight."

Kathy leaned back slightly, trying to study Shelley's face in the darkness. "So what do you think happened to Keith? And what do you think is happening now?"

Shelley suddenly drew her hands up to her face. When she lowered them, Kathy realized she had been silently crying. "I don't know!" she said huskily. "I loved him, I adored him. I was ready to take anything he had to give. But you—"

"I what?"

"He was in love with you, and you were seeing him, too!"

Kathy inhaled and exhaled, fighting a wave of trembling and of anger. "But I wasn't."

"Then someone who looked exactly like you was!"

No wonder Jordan had been so damned sure

she'd been cheating on him. Everyone, including Shelley, was certain that had been the case.

"Shelley, I'm telling you, I never slept with Keith. Ever. Not at any time during my friendship with him. He was a friend, one who was on a very wrong course, one I tried to help, but I failed. And that's it. I swear it."

Shelley looked away from her. "I thought you'd been with him the night he died."

"Because you thought you saw him with me?" Shelley nodded gravely.

"You never said that at the inquest."

"I loved you, too. You were my best friend. I didn't think you killed him, I just thought you'd been sleeping with him. You didn't deserve jail or the electric chair for that."

"Thanks," Kathy said wryly.

"I had to come talk to you. I had to let you know what was going on with Larry and me"— she hesitated, shrugging— "explain it. I wanted to come back. So badly. And so did Larry. But he was afraid. He said once that you always managed to find out everything. And, well, Derrick and Judy were always pretty brutal. They'd be pointing fingers at him and shrieking away that he had to go. Maybe not Derrick. But our critic extraordinaire, Judy. He really wants to talk to Jordan, but now he's got even more to confess! Kathy, we've all been afraid of the sins of the past, I imagine."

"What was your sin?" Kathy demanded. "Larry did drugs, not you."

Shelley hesitated. "Miles. He was my sin. I

used him like Keith used me. I didn't love him, but he adored me. He protected me, he picked up the pieces after me all the time. He would have done anything for me, anything at all. And, in return, I just used him." She stood up, staring at Kathy. "Forgive me? You've always meant a lot to me."

Kathy stood up and hugged her again. "Shelley, I forgive you. But we've got to get all this out in the open, okay? Talk to Larry, let him know that Jordan won't judge him for the past, we've just got to sort out the truth."

"I think he already knows it," Shelley said huskily. "Kathy, thanks for listening, thanks for being you."

"Get back to your room, and lock your door, huh?"

Shelley nodded, and Kathy walked her to the door, watched her slip silently out into the hallway. She locked her door securely then, and lay down on the bed.

As she pressed her palm to her temple, she decided Larry was a schmuck. So what else was new? He was sly and cunning, but according to Shelley, he was a schmuck with his own brand of integrity.

Larry had been with his wife during one of the phone calls, *if* Vicky Sue had told Shelley the truth.

Shelley had been desperately in love with Keith. Miles had been desperately in love with Shelley. He would have done anything for her.

Shelley's own words. Did that include killing the man who'd so often made Shelley so miserable?

Kathy rolled over, realizing she was coming down with a splitting headache. She closed her eyes, then opened them again, lay on her back and stared at the ceiling. She tossed, she turned. Finally, she slept.

At ten A.M., even without Jordan, they began practicing again. The session went well, though they stumbled some that day. They were tired, tense. They went over things several times, working mainly on the numbers in which Kathy and Shelley were the lead singers, avoiding those with long guitar solos. They still sounded like practiced musicians, but something was slightly off.

They now sounded more like they had the night Keith had died.

At three o'clock, Jordan appeared. He looked haggard. He'd showered and changed, but his eyes were red. He had such wonderful features he was always striking, but on this day he looked like a man in his forties. The group worked another few hours with Jordan, and it was amazing how things fell into place; Miles did exceptionally well with the drums, taking Keith's place. They did old numbers, and "Shadows," the song with which they would open and close the benefit performance. Jordan made a major difference in the way things were going.

When they at last broke up the session, they

were more somber than they had been the night before. Jordan explained Tara's condition— a full-blown concussion— and he said he was going back to the hospital after supper.

As Kathy listened to him, she wondered if the accident hadn't perhaps strengthened Tara's hold on Jordan. She made a point of sitting between Jeremy and Mickey at dinner, determined to make Jordan realize that she was independent, that she didn't need pity, didn't need someone to take care of her.

After dinner, Jordan disappeared into the guest house. Kathy was sitting by the pool with Mickey and Jeremy when she heard shouting coming from the downstairs floor. She glanced at the two men, then leapt up, hurrying toward the door.

Jeremy started to follow her.

"Let her go alone," Mickey advised.

When Kathy reached the guest house, Larry was just bursting out of it.

"He's the same self-righteous bastard he always was! No one is allowed a mistake!" he said.

"Wait— "

"Dammit, Kathy, what the hell is the matter with you!" Jordan suddenly thundered.

The door slammed, Larry was gone. Jordan had been packing a small bag. It stood open on the kitchen counter. He threw a razor into it and zipped it shut. "In case you didn't know, Larry was smuggling drugs."

"Ten years ago— "

He swung on her. "You did know."

"Just recently—"

"But you didn't tell me." He turned coldly back to his bag.

"I wanted to let him tell you."

"Yeah, and you wanted Keith to talk to me. You know so damned much all the time, while I'm tearing my hair out, yet you don't choose to share a damned thing with me. Tell me, did you know Larry was making the phone calls as well?"

"I hadn't—"

"Until recently," he snapped dryly. "But you didn't share that with me, either."

"Damn you, Jordan—"

"He threatened lives, Kathy. He played games, he nearly destroyed all of us, and—damn him to eternity—he made a mockery of my friendship with Keith and destroyed our marriage."

"We destroyed our marriage, Jordan. If we'd trusted one another—"

"He's out."

"What?"

"He's out. I want him out of here tomorrow. There won't be a Blue Heron with him in it."

"Jordan, that's wrong! He never had to come forward with the truth—"

"He was afraid it would be discovered!"

"But he didn't have to come clean. He deserves a chance. Shelley says he's clean—"

"She's another bleeding heart!" Jordan said impatiently. He was tired, she saw. Angry. Unreasonable. Once before, he had put up this shield, and hadn't let her through. He was doing it again.

"You've got to give him a chance."

"I want him out of my house."

"Well, I don't!"

He swung on her, the Jordan she knew and had always loved. Tall, imposing, as striking in his forties as he had ever been. But suddenly a stranger. "You know what, Kathy? This isn't your house anymore. You left it. Remember? You left me."

"And I had a right to do it!" she cried out. "You don't listen, you—"

"He threatened your life, Kathy. There was a knife held against your throat—"

"But you don't know that Larry was responsible—"

"Will you excuse me, please?"

"What?"

"I've got to get back to the hospital."

"Oh."

"Mickey will be keeping an eye on Mr. Lawrence Haley, so you'll be safe."

"Right. You won't need to sleep with me in order to save my life."

He grabbed his overnight bag, starting to walk by her, then paused. "How convenient. You've already tortured young Jeremy enough, eh? You won't have to sleep with me to titillate your young Lothario."

He was near enough to be slapped. She did it— with everything she had in her. He remained dead still, staring at her. She wanted to undo it, she wanted to undo all the words they had exchanged. He was just wrong! Unless she was wrong, perhaps, taking everyone's side but his. Still, he had judged Larry too harshly. He was exhausted, he'd been under too much tension . . .

And she'd played right into that.

"Lock yourself in your room," he said curtly.

"Damn you— "

"Lock yourself in your room. Do you hear me?"

"I do. But remember, I walked out. I don't have any say about how this house is run, and you don't have any say over me."

He grasped her arm. "You little fool! Don't go getting yourself killed!"

He was hurting her. She wrenched herself free of his grasp. "I'll lock my door, but you can just go to hell. Larry's got you down pat. You are a self-righteous bastard." She turned and ran from the guest house.

Jordan watched her go, his whole body shaking. As she ran past the pool, Jeremy leapt up, alarm and concern etched deeply into his young, handsome features.

Sweet Jesus, Jordan thought, he was letting everything slip away again. What the hell was the matter with him? Larry's strange, hasty confession had set his blood to boiling, and all he could remember for a while was the way he had torn into Keith, the way he had fought with Kathy, condemning them both. And he'd been wrong. Now . . .

Was he wrong again?

He didn't know. He was exhausted— and worried. Tara was hurt, and he owed her his presence, even if he didn't want to be with her when he was worried about Kathy. He'd been a fool last night, doubting Mickey's ability to protect her. He was tired, he was wrong . . .

"Jordan?"

Angel tapped lightly on his door. "Are you ready, sir?" he asked quietly. "I've brought the car around."

"All set. But you know what? I'm going to drive myself. I'm not going to stay. I'm just going to explain to Tara that things are so tense here I'm afraid to be away from home."

Angel nodded. "I'm sure she'll understand," he said without conviction.

"Oh, yeah," Jordan agreed. "Women. They're so understanding, aren't they?"

Angel grinned suddenly. "Actually, sir, I've discovered they're usually much better when you choose to deal with only one at a time."

"Oh, great." Jordan groaned, "I'm receiving worldly advice from my future son-in-law!"

Angel shrugged. "Well, sir, it's just that I'm not quite as tired as you are at the moment."

"Is that it, hmmm? Stay awake, then, and hold down the fort. I'm going to be back as soon as possible."

Jeremy followed Kathy up to her room, tapping softly and calling out her name when she closed the door, not even realizing that he was there.

She let him in, hugging him, crying softly on his shoulder. "I thought I could manage this, that I could even sleep with him. It's a disaster. I was a fool. He does care about her, she's gorgeous—"

"Shhh, Kath, shhh!" Jeremy soothed. "People fight; it doesn't mean they don't love one another."

"It's the same, this is the way things began to fall apart before."

"So don't let it happen this time. Change things."

"What?"

"Change the pattern. Don't fight—or do fight—but make him listen. He will. Although I suggest you let the man get some sleep first!"

She eased back from his arms, quickly drying her cheeks, trying to tell herself that she was too old, too mature, to feel so hurt, lost, and confused. She abandoned the effort. She would never be too old for that—or for feeling ecstatic, elated. If anything, she had acquired some wisdom, enough to realize that Jeremy might be right.

"I think he really loves you, Kathy."

"Yeah?"

"Sure sounds like it at night."

Color rushed to her cheeks.

"You can hear—"

"I'm not deaf."

"Oh, God."

"But that's not why I think he loves you. I believe he does because I've watched him talk to you, look at you. Kathy, face it: you came back here because you weren't ready to give him up."

"I had to have been! He was with Tara—"

Jeremy shook his head. "Not good enough. We can all be 'with' different people. If you want him, don't run this time. Make it different. Are you listening to me?"

She nodded. "Yeah."

"Want to go down and have a bedtime drink?"

"Are you suggesting Ovaltine?"

He laughed. "Naw, an Amaretto on the rocks. My days in a life of luxury are numbered. I want to take full advantage."

"Sure. Let's get a drink."

It was quiet when they ventured downstairs. The girls were out by the pool, with Angel, and Derrick was on a lounge, watching them. Jeremy made their drinks, and then they went out and settled on lounge chairs next to Derrick, until Jeremy excused himself to toss a ball back into the water to the kids.

"You okay?" Derrick asked her softly.

She arched a brow to him.

"Well, news travels fast. We've all heard that Larry and Jordan had a blowup and that . . . You always did defend everyone Kathy. But you know what? We loved you for it."

"Thanks. But was I right?"

"Right and wrong aren't always that easy to determine. Still, it's strange. I'd never imagined you and Jordan divorced. This week, with both

of you here— and your daughters, your folks—
it's like it never happened."

"Ah, but it did."

"One day you'll get back together."

"We've made too many mistakes. But you
haven't. You and Judy have managed to stay
married, together, through everything. No big
blowups. You talk like human beings."

Derrick laughed. "I'm glad you can say that.
But, Kathy, most of us only see the outside of
other people's lives. I guess we have an okay
marriage. Unexciting, uneventful. But it hasn't
been perfect. Years ago I had an affair. It wasn't
long before it broke up, but then Judy pretended she was having one, for revenge I think.
We nearly split up. What saved us was that we
became suburban. I started writing jingles, she
became the perfect corporate wife. We mellowed
into one another. You and Jordan are different.
But it's obvious that you still love one another."

"Obvious?" Kathy asked doubtfully.

"Yeah." He patted her on the knee. "Poor
Tara. Hell, maybe not 'poor.' She's the most
beautiful creature I've ever seen."

"That she is." Kathy was silent for a minute.
"It's not that I don't value myself, but then . . .
why would he want me?"

" 'Cause you're beautiful all way through!"
Derrick told her cheerfully.

"That's sweet. Really sweet. Thank you."

"My pleasure."

Jeremy was coming back toward her. She knew

he had promised Mickey he'd see that her room was clear and that she'd locked herself into it.

"When you are going to let that pleasant young Mr. Buns of yours off the hook?" Derrick asked her.

She winked. "He never was on it," she said simply. Jeremy had reached her by then.

"Shall we go up, Kath?"

"Just a minute." She walked to the pool, leaning down to kiss both her daughters and warning them to remain with Angel and to stay in Alex's room throughout the night.

She gave Angel's wet cheek a kiss as well.

"He's coming back," Angel whispered softly. "Jordan's coming back. He's really worried now. He just felt he owed it to Tara to explain that he really couldn't stay with her."

"Thanks, Angel."

The young man nodded and then slipped back into the water.

"Jeremy, let's go on up. 'Night, girls, Angel!" Kathy called. After they waved to her, she stooped and gave Derrick a kiss on the forehead. " 'Night. See you at breakfast," she said.

Arm in arm, she went up the steps with Jeremy. He dutifully went through her room. She locked the door to the hallway, then he went through the connecting door to his own room, telling her good night.

Kathy changed into a white tailored nightgown, lay down, and pounded her pillow.

She stared up at the ceiling.

Then she began to run over every snatch of

conversation she'd heard since she'd come to Star Island.

. . . he'd do anything for me . . . anything . . .

. . . being a sleazeball exonerates him?

. . . it was me . . .

I had to tell you . . .

She tossed and turned. She stared up at the ceiling. She narrowed her eyes. The room was dappled with light and shadow, moonglow and illumination seeping in from the patio, since she hadn't fully closed the drapes. She rose restlessly, walked to the window and pulled the drapes back farther. Then she inhaled sharply.

He was back. Jordan was standing by the window. The guest house was bathed in very soft light within, perhaps from a downstairs lamp, while Jordan was a dark form in the bedroom window. His was a compelling silhouette.

He was watching Kathy.

He raised a hand, beckoning to her.

She bit into her lower lip, furious with him.

She had to change things, if she wanted them to be different. She didn't want to be proud or stubborn, to make him come to her. She just wanted to make things work.

She turned quickly, unlocking her door, silently running through the hallway, her white nightgown and red hair streaming behind her. She raced across the patio, around the bushes, to the side guest-house door.

She burst in.

And only then did she realize that it hadn't been Jordan beckoning to her.

Only then did she recognize the murderer. For even as she entered the shadowed realm, a hand with a drug-soaked rag was slapped over her face.

And too late it all began to fall into place, even as she fell to the floor . . .

Twenty-one

"Tara, you know you're going to be all right. They're releasing you in the morning, and I'll pick you up. I'm afraid to stay away from the house right now."

"You don't want to stay away from her," Tara told him petulantly.

She really looked stunning. Despite her concussion, she'd had the nurses bathe her, wash her hair, and dress her in something frothy and pink. She was glorious. And once again, reigning. Reporters had dropped by to interview her. God knew what they were going to write when all hell finally broke loose.

Actually, he didn't care. Just as long as Kathy came out of it safely. And the others, of course. Why did he feel that Kathy was in the greatest danger? Because they all confessed to her, brought her their secrets? Because she was warm, caring, a champion . . .

His fear for her suddenly and irrationally began to grow. He stood.

"Tara, I'm sorry. I've got to go back. I'll come for you tomorrow morning."

He turned to leave. She caught his hand. "You've got to come back for me, Jordan. I have my career, you know; I can't be humiliated."

"God, no. We won't let that happen," he promised her. He kissed her forehead, extricated his hand, and escaped her hospital room. Impatiently he waited for the elevator to carry him to the ground floor.

He was running as he headed for his car.

Kathy had come around groggily, feeling as though she weighed a million pounds. She couldn't move her limbs. It took all her strength just to open her eyes. When she managed to do so, the room was swaying. Nothing was clear.

She was staring at herself. At a very watery reflection of herself. Amazing. It was like a distorted mirror. Her reflection smiled. It wasn't her. She wasn't smiling.

She tried to form words. Could barely move her mouth. She knew she ought to scream, but she even couldn't even whisper.

"You!" She managed to form the word at last. "You were sleeping with Keith."

"You were bound to figure it out in time. Frankly, Keith was so devoted to you, I thought he might have talked about our affair to you before he died. I guess he didn't. He wanted to be Lancelot, you know, adoring you from afar, except that he liked women too much and that silly little Shelley would have slept with him anywhere, any time . . . Still, he liked my game better. Because I pretended to be you. I could talk like you, laugh like you. Maybe he even imagined I made love like you, who knows? The wig was an inspiration. The rest all came from it."

Judy Flanaghan pushed away from the guest-house bed, smiling. The light before Kathy's eyes was still wavering. She tried to move her hands. She couldn't. She concentrated on rolling from the bed. She couldn't do that either.

"What .... ?" she managed to whisper.

"I got you with chloroform at the door, then slipped a few too many muscle relaxants down your throat. The drugs won't kill you. They didn't kill Keith, though he took them much more willingly. He was such an ass! Always trying to ruin everything."

Kathy could barely speak. She had to make each word count. "Why . . . kill him?"

"He was threatening to go to Derrick and to Jordan with the whole thing. Derrick needed the group. I needed the group. You see, you're the wonderful, miraculous Kathy! Put her with Jordan, and she's a singer, popular from day one. Take Jordan away, and she's still an important person, moving into the world of publishing. You've never doubted yourself, never faltered, never been anything but perfect, marvelous, wonderful Kathy. Even Keith saw you as perfection; he laughed at me. I tried to help him when Jordan was so furious, but he laughed and told me I didn't mean anything to him, that he didn't need me. He didn't care if the group fell apart. If Jordan said it was over, it was going to be over.

And if he felt like it, he'd tell Derrick exactly what I was doing."

Yes . . .

She might have seen it, but she hadn't. Because other people had motives that were more obvious. Larry, the sleazebag, could have murdered Keith to keep his secret. Shelley could have killed him in a jealous rage; Miles could have killed him on Shelley's behalf.

But Judy . . .

She had resented them all. She had wanted the limelight, had wanted to pay her husband back for his infidelities. She hadn't loved Keith, but he had been unique, talented.

"It hurt you when I dressed up as you. I let other people see me. I let Jordan think his precious, perfect wife was sleeping with his best friend. That night it was so strange. I hadn't really planned to kill him. But he was so cocky. So damned self-assured. Insulting. Threatening. And laughing all the while. He kept playing with his lighter. I played his game. I was so mad I wanted to beat him. Just beat him until he was nothing but blood and gore. I wanted to wrench his heart out of his chest. God, I hated him at that moment. Then I saw all the stuff he had around him. He was drugged and laughing when I started spraying the place— with simple things. Hair spray. Imagine. But I'd always liked fire. I knew how to make it work. He had lots of aerosols up here. They made it easy to make this place just burn and burn and burn . . ."

Kathy could move her eyes more easily now, her lips. She could swallow.

"I don't do drugs. They know it. Someone will suspect. You can't get away with this a second time."

Judy, her wig waving over Kathy's face, laughed softly. "Everyone knows you and Jordan had another blowup today. Jordan would make the perfect murder suspect if it were ever determined that Keith had been killed. He was jealous, we all know he has a horrendous temper, and he hated Keith. He thought Keith was sleeping with his wife."

"Jordan's at the hospital."

"I stole the muscle relaxants from Miles. He has a bad back, poor baby. Perhaps you came here desolate. You tried to win your husband back. Same old story. You lost him to a younger woman. What a shame. Sad. So sad. Things like that happen. You're older now. Aging well, but aging. You can't bear it; there's just nothing left to live for anymore. Why not hurt Jordan with your suicide, the way he's hurt you? Burn yourself to the ground, just the way his best friend did, the best friend with whom you'd been cuckolding him all those years ago."

"Judy, you'll be caught this time."

"Maybe. But this is my only chance. People tell you things, Kathy. Derrick probably said something somewhere along the line that gave me away. Of course, he thought I was only pretending to have an affair. He's always liked games. You know, sex games, dress-up, fantasies.

That's where I got the idea of dressing up as you for Keith. If you didn't figure it out, Derrick would say something to you that would click. You would know if we stayed together much longer. I tried to keep Jordan from allowing this to happen. I paid a cutthroat from one of Castro's prisons to put the fear of God into him and you. It didn't work. Jordan just had to have the truth; he couldn't just allow a guilty man to burn. Because Keith was guilty. He was a druggie, even if he wasn't guilty the time it was pinned on him. He was a user. And he used people up, too. He deserved what he got. Then last night . . . that silly twit. Tara. Who would have imagined that the little fool was running around playing dress-up, too? If I'd been a little more on target, she'd be dead now. Instead, she'll live to help Jordan grieve for you. Charming picture, eh?"

Kathy tried to twist her head to watch Judy as she moved across the room, pulling the wig off at the dresser, picking up a large can of hairspray and playing with her natural cut. The air was becoming heavy with the smell of the aerosol spray.

Judy turned back to her, smiling, beginning to spray the bedcover, spraying Kathy's clothes. Kathy twisted her head again, once more willing her limbs to motion. She saw the bedside table. Judy had placed a few household cleaners on it. All highly flammable. Smiling, she now sprayed the rug, the drapes.

"You'd be amazed at how gullible people

are—and just how impossible it would be to prove something like this *beyond the shadow of a doubt*. That's the only way to convict a person in our court system. Beyond the shadow of a doubt."

"Judy, don't do this to me. I never hurt you!"

"But you did."

"How?"

"You'd never know. Never. You've never been on the outside, looking in. Taking the crumbs. Standing outside the limelight while the audience went wild. Never mind, it doesn't matter now. After the inquest, we'll all get to go home again."

Smiling, she reached into her pocket for something.

A book of matches.

"Tell Keith hi for me, and say that one day I'll see you both in hell."

She struck a match. The flame jumped up, a brilliant red, yellow, and blue.

She dropped the match . . . and smiled as she watched fire spread like a flaming sea over the bedcover.

There was no traffic. He drove at a breakneck speed, unable to understand the sudden panic that had seized him. He left the mainland, ripped onto the causeway, and burst onto the bridge to the island, ignoring everyone and everything in his path.

He drove up to his house, amazed to see that

everything was quiet, the usual lights were on, and there seemed to be no activity.

Yet even as he jerked the car to a screeching halt and leapt from the driver's seat, he saw the sudden arrow of fire, bursting out above the roof . . .

From the guest house out in back.

Mickey awoke, puzzled at first as to what had disturbed him. He heard nothing.

Then he realized there was something strange about the air. The smell of smoke. . . .

He bolted up. Raced to the window. Dialed 911. Raced out into the hallway.

"Fire!"

Instinctively, he headed for Kathy's room. Banged on the door. Screamed her name.

The sheets caught fire in a sudden, small inferno. Kathy managed to scream, and willed herself to roll. God! She shrieked silently, trying desperately to move! The fall to the floor was an impact for which she couldn't really brace herself. Stunned, she lay where she'd landed, terrifyingly aware of how quickly the flames were spreading, how smoke was already beginning to fill the room.

She heard Judy's laughter, a chilling sound. The woman was psychotic. An absurd realization. And one made too late . . .

She was aware that Judy was starting to move,

ready to escape the blaze before it could devour her. Again, Kathy managed an aching, dragging movement, half rolling, half twisting her body toward the foot of the bed. Just in time to trip Judy as she ran.

Judy shrieked, falling herself, her head striking the footboard as she went down. Momentarily dazed, she stared at Kathy with glazed eyes.

Kathy lifted an arm, forced her fingers to grasp Judy, inched herself across the floor.

With every aching, grasping movement, her limbs fought the drugs that froze them.

Yet as she slowly struggled, the fire flickered, then spread. With a violent whoosh, the drapes went up in flames. The bed was now an inferno.

Someone had to come. God, she had survived the bed! Someone must come . . .

But smoke was blackening the place, and she was spasmodically coughing, choking— moving inch by inch.

The stairs. She pulled herself along Judy's body, moving like a snake, slithering, desperate to reach the stairs. She came to them. She pushed herself— slid, tumbled, moved downward . . .

"No!" Judy was up, after her. Falling, crashing, coming down the stairs herself. She fell upon Kathy at the landing. Kathy fought her hold, until she realized that Judy wasn't fighting her. Judy had knocked herself out again; it was just her weight that was holding Kathy down.

She could hear the fire. Within seconds, it

had swirled into a wild, raging thing. The drapes were ablaze on the ground floor. Tongues of flame were dancing down the stairs. A sofa shot up into an orange inferno.

She crawled. Elbows on the floor, toes trying to find a hold. The door was so very near. So very far. The smoke, oh, God, the smoke was blackening the room, it was filling her lungs, she couldn't see, couldn't think, couldn't fight.

She had to, had to . . .

Her eyes teared, her mind worked in an hysterical fashion, warning her to keep close to the floor when she could do nothing less. She kept crawling, no *slithering*, for what seemed like eons but was only seconds. She prayed . . .

Then hands were on her. She discovered that she had a voice again. She shrieked out, thinking it was Judy holding her back, trying to take her into the flames. She wouldn't be like Keith, unconscious. Nearly paralyzed, she would be unable to move quickly enough to escape a searing agony. She would . . .

Die.

Oh, God, she would die.

She had to keep moving, had to fight the smoke, the coughing, the heat, the flames, licking closer and closer to her, oh, God, oh, God . . .

Somebody was trying to grab her, hold her. Oh, sweet Lord, maybe help.

She twisted around. Judy. Judy, her face blackened and shadowed, her eyes wild. She had something in her hands. A broken piece of two by four, charred by the fire, still smoking. She

shrieked out in fury, and started to swing it
downward with all her strength.

Kathy discovered that she again had the power
to scream.

"Sweet Lord!" Vicky Sue gasped, bolting up
in bed. "Larry, dammit, wake up!"

Haley bolted up, dazed, dragged from a deep
sleep. Vicky Sue punched him in the arm, pointing to the window.

The guest house was ablaze.

"Wow!" he exclaimed. "I don't believe it.
Thank God Jordan's at the hospital. It's un-
canny. The damned thing is burning to the
ground again."

Derrick Flanaghan woke. "Judy?" He ran his
hands over his wife's side of the bed.

He could hear shouting. "Judy?" he repeated,
his voice trembling.

Ten years ago, he had awakened to cries of
"Fire!" while alone in his bed. Now, he was doing so again.

He put his hands to his face and a shuddering
sob escaped him.

God, no.

Yes . . .

They began to gather on the patio.

Just as they had gathered once before.

Miles, Shelley. Larry, Vicky Sue. Miles had told them to stand back when he'd tried to enter the burning house. The heat had thrown him back at first, but Larry had gotten him the hose so that he could soak himself and go in.

Then suddenly, Alex Treveryan came racing pell-mell out of the main house, shrieking. "My mother! My mother isn't in her room. Oh, God, my mother!" Tears streaming down her face, she raced toward the guest house.

"Stop her!" Shelley shrieked. "For the love of God, stop her! It's an inferno!"

Miles flew into action, struggling with Alex, who hit him in her frenzy to escape. Yet even as she broke Miles's hold, she was suddenly caught up again.

"Get back!"

Startled, Alex went still, focusing on the man in front of her, gripping her arms. Her father.

"Mom!" Alex cried hysterically.

"Get back! I'll get her. I'll get her."

"Jordan!" Miles cried. "Jordan, you can't—"

But he could. He pushed past Mickey, letting Larry soak him with water as he did so, and went into the house.

Sally, Gerrit, Bren, and Jeremy hurried out of the house, Sally sobbing. Jeremy caught hold of Bren when she would have followed her father. Gerrit held Sally.

"He'll get her. Believe me. He'll bring her out alive. Have faith."

* * *

He heard Kathy's scream, leaped over a burning piece of cypress fallen from the roof, tore through the kitchen. Kathy was close to the door, rolling in just the nick of time to escape a blow from the smoke-blackened figure standing over her. The figure screamed in rage, raising its club of charred wood again. Jordan let out a roar, racing forward, plummeting into the figure, knocking it away from Kathy, ready to take on any foe.

Judy. He landed atop her. Judy Flanaghan. He was so stunned that he merely stared at her for precious milliseconds. "Good God!" he breathed out.

She shrieked something, trying to strike him then. He hadn't the time. He leapt up. When she charged him, he sidestepped her. She screamed in anguish, falling onto the burning sofa.

Mickey burst into the blazing house, a drenched housecoat over his head and shoulders.

"It's Judy, get her," Jordan yelled. "But watch out!"

He knelt down by Kathy. She was still. Oh, God, the smoke. So much smoke.

He started to whisper her name, like a chant, over and over as he swept her up, praying. Don't let her be dead, God. Please don't let her be dead. Please, please, don't let her be dead. Please . . .

He burst out of the house, carrying her, stumbling onto the grass. There was an explosion from within; windows shattered and spray shards of glass, flames shot high into the night. He covered Kathy with his body, heard the scream and shriek of sirens.

He lifted his weight from her body and looked down, still praying, half-aloud, half in silence . . .

Her eyes were open. "Hi."

Her voice was husky, rasped by smoke inhalation. And her cheeks were smudged, her eyes a startlingly rich amber, like a good whiskey.

She was beautiful. Never more beautiful.

"Thank God you know when to come home," she managed to whisper.

He smiled down at her, shaking. Thank you, God, thank you, God, thank you . . .

"Think you know when to come home?"

She smiled. "Yeah. Maybe. I don't know. Is that an invitation?"

"Maybe. No— that's exactly what it is."

She smiled, then winced. Her throat was burning and raw. Her lungs ached, her head ached. "Oh, Lord!" she gasped out. "Judy . . . was in the fire."

"Mickey got her."

Kathy nodded. There were suddenly firemen everywhere. Nothing else that could be said between them because Alex and Bren were crying, half sobbing, half laughing, falling on the grass beside their mother, hugging her. And Sally was there, with Gerrit. Shelley, Miles.

The hugs, Kathy thought vaguely, were so tight they were almost painful. Wonderful. And, dear Lord, by some sweet miracle, she was able to hug back.

But for a precious little time. The paramedics came, putting her on a stretcher. Jordan managed to make her understand that she had to be treated for smoke inhalation, and she realized, looking at him, that he appeared somewhat strange— parts of his eyebrows had been singed away. He didn't seem to notice. He rode with her in the ambulance, holding her hand.

"It was Judy," she said incredulously.

"I know."

"So strange. We just didn't see it."

He folded both his hands around her fingers. "Well, life is kind of like that great manuscript of yours. The one you just bought for your company. So much seems so obvious. We tend to believe what we think we see without looking beyond it. Not trusting other instincts. I should have trusted you."

"Yeah. You should."

"And you shouldn't have run away."

"Maybe not. But you were a miserable wretch."

"Agreed. I'm still a miserable wretch— sometimes. Want to marry me anyway?"

She smiled. "Sure."

"There won't be any problem with Muscleman."

She smiled very slowly, looking directly at him. "Not if we make sure to ask his boy friend to the wedding. He's a wonderful person, too. You're really going to like him."

He stared at her, shocked. Then he started to laugh. "Oh, I deserved that. Hell! I'm telling you, the husband is always the last to know."

"Ex-husband."

"Soon to change."

"What about Tara?"

"Oh, I think she'll be all right. I've promised her a discreet breakup. Her career, you know."

"Ah!"

"So you will marry me, have my baby, all that stuff?"

"I've had your baby— twice. Remember those beautiful little creatures following behind us?"

"Ah, yes, how could I forget?"

They reached the hospital. One of the E.R. nurses had been on duty the night he'd come in with Tara.

"Mr. Treveryan, I have to say, sir, it seems you are just hell on women!"

"Oh, he is. He's hell on women," Kathy agreed. She was sooty, singed— a mess. So was he. And strange with those burnt eyebrows.

It didn't matter. She willed herself to find strength. With him, it seemed easy. She stood on tiptoe, threw her arms around him, and kissed him.

Their prime, she decided, was just beginning.

Epilogue

Naturally, due to the circumstances, the benefit performance by Blue Heron was postponed. Judy came out of the fire alive, but Derrick was devastated.

Kathy was somewhat surprised to realize that she didn't hate Judy for what had happened, but her own life was so full that she could pity a woman so jealous of those around her that she would resort to murder.

The papers had a heyday with everything that had gone on, and Blue Heron music had never been more popular.

Alex's twenty-first birthday was celebrated in a far more quiet manner than had been intended, but that was all right with Alex. She was surrounded by her family and very close friends. And Angel gave her an elegant diamond, one he had saved long and hard to purchase. She assured her parents it was the best twenty-first birthday a girl could possibly have.

Tony Grant, Jeremy's just-as-nicely-muscled roommate, arrived Thursday morning, anxious because of the shocking news stories. Kathy noted with humor that Jordan was delighted to welcome him, and that he and Jeremy quickly became good friends with Jordan, just as they had earlier with Kathy and the girls.

As for Tara, she became engaged to a well-known doctor before she left the hospital.

Kathy didn't leave the publishing field. She wasn't going back to a full-time job; she was never leaving Jordan again. But she would work freelance, editing certain manuscripts at home. She also made Marty very happy by promising him that she would try to write that book on Blue Heron as soon as she had a little distance from the events that had just occurred.

In September, while under psychiatric observation, Judy expired of congestive heart failure. Jordan, Kathy, Miles, Shelley, Larry, and Vicky Sue attended the funeral with Derrick. He seemed broken and lost. He wasn't ready to work with them yet, but he was grateful for their presence.

In October, Jordan and Kathy were remarried in the beautiful cathedral where they had first exchanged their vows. Gerrit was best man, while Sally was matron of honor. Those two had recently been married themselves.

And Sally had changed her tune. She now claimed that any time of life could be prime time. It depended on what one made of it.

Kathy and Jordan didn't go on a honeymoon right away because the postponed performance by Blue Heron had been rescheduled for the end of the month. By the time they played, Derrick had rejoined them. He was a different man. He'd developed an inner strength. Though still sad, he was glad to be playing with them again. They had their ghosts— Keith and Judy— but they had a new lease on life as well. Gerrit was going to join them for a few numbers; and on three songs, the girls were singing. Life had its cycles, but as Kathy knew, all of them could be good. For one number at the performance, three generations of Treveryans were on stage. That was very special. The audience went wild.

Tara was a guest that evening. She found Kathy backstage after the show, hugged her fiercely. Kathy hugged her in return.

"I had to tell you . . . the director called me— well, I think Jordan had something to do with it. I'm going to play you in the movie! That is . . . if you don't mind."

Kathy started to laugh. "I think it's great. I would have suggested it myself. I'm delighted."

Late that night— very late— after the press had disappeared and the party was over, as was everything else that went with the performance, Kathy and Jordan finally left for their honeymoon.

He'd suggested Paris; she'd asked for something very quiet. They'd decided on a private French island in the Caribbean. And near noon on the following day, they were lying together beneath an umbrella on an absolutely secluded beach, lazily watching the endless waves and the white sand that surrounded them.

"So, did you suggest Tara for the movie?" Kathy asked.

Jordan lifted his sunglasses, but couldn't quite see Kathy's eyes beneath the darkness of hers. "Yes, I did. I admit to some guilt on her behalf. She's a good little actress. Do you mind?"

Kathy smiled, shaking her head. "Not at all. She'll get an actor as Jordan Treveryan. I get the real thing."

He grinned, tossing aside his sunglasses, tossing aside hers. Then he poised above her in the sand, balancing his weight over her. "I do love you, Kathy. So much."

"And I love you. Have loved you. For all of my life."

He bent his head down and kissed her.

And kissed her . . .

And indeed . . .

. . . it was the prime of life.

Don't miss TEMPESTUOUS EDEN,
Heather Graham's next novel of romantic suspense,
coming soon from Zebra!

Tempted

It should have been an easy mission: employ any
means to get the American woman out of the
war-torn Central American country—
and tell her nothing.
But Blair Morgan was beautiful, and for all his
professionalism, special agent Craig Taylor
found himself falling for her.

Torrid

Since the assassination of her beloved husband,
Blair had been afraid to risk her heart again.
Then she met Craig. Brave, generous, physically
compelling, he was everything she wanted in a man,
and their passionate nights together melted her
defenses. Until the order arrived
and Blair became Craig's hostage.

Tormented

Suddenly a pawn in a terrorist's political game,
Blair struggled to forgive her abductor,
the man to whom she had given her soul.
Their journey through a jungle filled with
dangerous rebels became a battle of wills
between a man of honor and a woman of pride,
as they fought to find the shattered remains
of a love that left them both longing for more.